# Candle in the Dark

*Also by Helen Cannam*

A KIND OF PARADISE
A THREAD OF GOLD
A HIGH AND LONELY ROAD
THE LAST BALLAD
STRANGER IN THE LAND

# CANDLE IN THE DARK

*Helen Cannam*

LITTLE, BROWN AND COMPANY

A *Little, Brown* Book

First published in Great Britain in 1993
by Little, Brown and Company

Copyright © Helen Cannam 1993

The moral right of the author has been asserted.

A CIP catalogue record for this book is
available from the British Library.

ISBN 0 316 90409 0

Typeset in Times by Leaper & Gard Ltd, Bristol
Printed and bound in Great Britain by
BPCC Hazell Books Ltd
Member of BPCC Ltd

Little, Brown and Company (UK) Limited
165 Great Dover Street
London SE1 4YA

*For my sister Liz, with love.*

# AUTHOR'S NOTE

I could not begin to list here all the historians whose talks and writings have fed and nurtured my fascination with the French Revolution since my student days. Suffice it to say that in this novel the inevitable oversimplifications of an immensely complicated period are all my own, as are any errors of fact.

As far as the English part of the book goes, I should like to express particular thanks to the staff of the Northumberland County Record Office for their enthusiastic help with my researches.

Finally, while various people on the fringes of this story clearly had an existence in history, the central characters are all imaginary and are not based on any other individuals, alive or dead.

# Chapter One

It all started in a very ordinary way. There she was in the candlelit salon, where her cousins sat languidly at cards, gathered close about the battered table before a fire that did little to dispel the autumnal chill of the room. The draughts from the long shuttered windows stirred curtains and tapestries, so that they seemed living things; the candle flames shivered and bent, the incessant movement of the light strengthening the illusion that only the human beings were lifeless, caught and held for ever in the immobility of supreme boredom. Watching from the shadows, she could almost imagine herself at home, for it was all so familiar in its uncomfortable grandeur. Not that Blackheugh was quite as grand as this.

Thinking of home reminded her how little time she had. In two days she would be going back to England, and might never come here again. Her schooling was at an end now and a new phase of her life about to begin, which would certainly include the constraints of marriage and the management of a house and servants and, in time, children. It showed how much of a child she still was that she wanted to satisfy her curiosity before she left; she even smiled at the thought, mocking herself. But she did not care much for cards and it had rained all day and she longed for distraction. And there it was, waiting for her, a whole tower unexplored, with the door that led into it opening from the end of the passage outside her room. It was not expressly forbidden to her, but no one went there, and for that reason it drew her. Perhaps it was haunted, a thought that gave her a delightful shiver of excitement. She was too used to tales of hauntings to be seriously frightened at the prospect. She had never heard of a ghost in France to match Blackheugh's redcap, and even he was only an old tale.

She went through the lengthy ritual of saying goodnight and left the room, closing the door behind her. The dim light of the single hall candle showed her someone emerging from the darkness near the front door, on his way to the salon. She could not quite make him out, but she thought it was her elder cousin. She said goodnight, but he gave no reply, and she wondered if she had been mistaken. Perhaps it was just a trick of the light and there had been no one there at all.

At the foot of the stairs she began to run, driven by a sense of relief – or was it panic? If so, there was no reason for it. In her room she lit her own candle and set out again, along the passage towards that tempting closed door.

It was not locked – she knew that, because she had already tried it once, only Catherine had found her and laughed and said, 'There's nothing in there!' Opening it now she realised that Catherine was probably quite right. She walked about the room, holding her candle high, and saw tapestries on the walls, so dingy and old that she could not make out their designs, and a worn sofa; and that seemed to be it. She crossed to a further door and pushed it open. It gave onto a spiral stair, which she climbed, finding herself in a room much like the one below.

She thought, then, that she heard a movement of some kind in the lower room. Quickly, with a rather irrational sense of guilt (after all, no one had told her she had no right to be here), she closed the door behind her and then, sure of concealment, set out to explore the room more fully. At its far side a chest of drawers looked inviting.

She heard the step on the stair only a moment before the door was opened. She glanced sharply round, and saw who was there. She searched her mind for some suitable explanation – she wished it had been his brother rather than him, for he had always seemed cold and aloof, given to looking her over in silence with eyes that expressed clear contempt for her youthful high spirits.

Before she could find suitable words, he opened his mouth, and she thought he was going to be the first to speak. All she heard was an odd noise, which might have been a muttered word or phrase, or might simply have been an exclamation, or even just a clearing of his throat.

It was then that a series of events, normal, ordinary, mundane, was suddenly twisted abruptly into nightmare.

For an instant she saw his face, distorted and strange in the flickering candlelight. The next moment, the candle went out, and there was only darkness, and the sound of his breathing. A small sound – his feet . . . She felt him move towards her, and the first warning wave of fear set her heart thudding. She stepped back and back, but there was the wall, the harsh feel of damp tapestry beneath her groping hands. Then he was against her, pinning her to the wall with arms of surprising strength, and an angular body pressing on hers, and there was no escape. She heard a hissing whisper: 'Be silent!'

There were no more words between them, no sound at all but his breathing, which grew more and more laboured, until its harsh wrenching noise filled the room. His hands dragged at her clothes, scratching, tearing, bruising. Somehow then she was on the floor, paralysed by terror. A part of her mind said, 'This is a dream, I'm imagining it all, it's not real.' She did not know what was happening, understood nothing, except that there was fear and pain and powerlessness, an agonising feeling of being ripped open and taken over by some horrible thing that was not quite human, a monstrous animal making animal sounds. She did not scream, yet all of her was a scream.

She struggled, once, twice, but he only hurt her the more. Nothing for it but to endure, the pain, the animal grunts; longing, longing for it to end . . . It must be over soon, it must, nothing lasted for ever . . .

A jolt, the sound of rain. Daylight. A voice singing, distantly, a familiar tune, whose words, indistinguishable at this distance, echoed in her head:

3

*My love he built a bonny bower,*
*And covered it o'er wi' lily flower;*
*A brawer bower ye ne'er did see,*
*Than my true love he built for me.*

*There came a man by middle day;*
*He spied his sport and went away.*
*He came again that very night*
*And slew my man within my sight...*

Oh, the relief! It was not real, it was a dream after all, a nightmare, ended now. She had woken in her own familiar bed in the simply furnished room with its small window open to the wind from the Cheviots. She was Isabella Milburn, sixteen, at home and safe.

She turned on her side, drowsy with relief, relaxing again into sleep. And then, sickeningly, she remembered.

It had been a dream, oh yes; a nightmare from which she had woken. But the stuff of the nightmare was also the stuff of memory, a thing that had happened to her, as horribly, as truly, as in her dream. And a thing whose consequences were with her still. The nightmare had ended with her sleep; but the other thing would be with her as long as she lived.

# Chapter Two

A narrow back stair led down to the working quarters of the house. Isabella, hastily dressed in what clothes lay nearest to hand, slipped down the stair and along the passage that ran past the kitchen into the stable yard. A girl was just coming in from outside, with a newly killed chicken dangling by its neck in her bloodied hand. She looked curiously at Isabella, but said nothing. The servants knew, of course, where Miss Milburn was going, and that she would not be here to eat the meal for which the chicken's neck had been wrung. She would never eat dinner at Blackheugh again, yet life would go on all the same, as if her absence was of little account.

The stable yard was deserted, to her relief. She could hear the singing still, coming from one of the further stalls on the north side, but that was not where she was going. She turned left, to the westerly wing of the stables, and the stall where Bonny, hearing her coming, was already making soft welcoming snorting noises. She slipped in beside him and put her arms about his broad shaggy neck and laid her head against his coarse mane, and then simply stood there, trying to find some sort of comfort in his accepting presence. He would never betray a trust, never let her down; never judge her. From the moment she had first sat on his back at ten years old he had carried her faithfully, with sure feet and unflagging energy. He would do the same still, if it were asked of him. Of all she was leaving behind she thought she would miss him most.

5

He tossed his head, reaching round in search of a titbit; for once she had not brought one with her. He would be expecting a ride, she supposed. He would have one, a little later, as far as the carriage road, where they would part for ever. Unless—

She had a sudden clear picture in her mind ... *She had Bonny saddled, now, here, in the next few minutes, before anyone knew what she was doing. She had mounted, gathered the reins in her hand, urged him out of the yard and then up onto the moor behind the house. Then they were galloping over the wastes of heather and grass, on and on, over the Tarset burn, past Kielder and Deadwater and across the border, into the wild debatable lands where no one would ever find them; and where they could seek a hidden refuge, safe from capture, as so many of her lawless ancestors had done before her.*

She knew it was a dream. It could only ever be a dream. She could leave Blackheugh behind, and her family, all of them. But one thing she could not leave behind, for it had been a part of her for five months now and would stay with her all her life, like a scar or a stain that nothing could wipe clean; like an evil wraith clinging to her shoulder, marking her guilt. No flight could wipe it away, for it was in her very flesh and blood, in her soul. There was only one way that offered hope of cleansing, and it was that way she was to take today. She knew that, accepted it; yet the ache of parting was almost more than she could bear.

'Bella!'

She turned sharply, not having heard him come. He stood just outside the half door of the stall, his hair shining like a flame in the greyness of the early light. He grinned, but kindly; she had never known him anything but kind. 'You going to do a flit then? Hey, how would it be if we eloped?' Then before she could draw breath and recover from her astonishment, colour flooded his fair skin and he said, suddenly very correct, 'Forget I said that, Miss Milburn. I don't know what got into me.'

She stared at him. A moment before she had seen Jamie the stable lad, who was more of a brother to her than John Milburn had ever been. Now it was not Jamie she saw, but a man, two years older than herself, and with feelings she could not trust. In the instant before he made that embarrassed retraction, she had felt a tremor of fear. This, too, that thing had done to her; to make her afraid of Jamie, if only in passing.

'It's time I got to work in here, if I'm to be ready,' Jamie said. He moved to open the door and then halted again, studying her face. 'What's up, Bella? They said it was what you wanted – you know, to go away.'

'Yes,' she said. 'It is.' But of course he did not know what had made it seem the right, the only, choice she could make. Only her immediate family knew that, and Father Duncan.

There was a little silence, while still he watched her. Then he said, 'You used to tell me everything.' He was no longer looking at her, but at one of his fingers, which was rubbing its way along the rim of the stall with great concentration, braving splinters.

She knew it was an appeal; or, rather, an offer of sympathy. He must have seen clearly enough how changed she had been on her return home last November. He could not have failed to notice too how she had avoided him, avoided everyone. Now, part of her longed to tell him everything. But she knew she could not do it. There was too much, things she could not begin to put into words, even to Jamie, who had been her friend and companion since he first came to work in the stables at Blackheugh ten years ago, things she supposed she would never tell to anyone; not even to her confessor. Besides, there was no time, not any more. The sun was already up.

'I must go to Mass,' she said, and pushed her way past him.

She went back to her room and dressed more carefully and then made her way across the landing to the wide main staircase of the house.

The painted eyes of her ancestors watched as she descended. Some of them had been evil and wayward individuals whose fine clothes and languid poses belied a life of violence and savagery, common enough to any border family, though the details she had only learned piecemeal, from Jamie or her

7

grandmother. Others, whose censorious gaze she felt like darts, had been held up to her all her life as examples for her to follow: Mary Milburn who had been tortured to death under Elizabeth for harbouring a priest; Charles Milburn the Jesuit, martyred during the Civil War; her namesake Isabella, a devout matron who had devoted her last years to holiness and good works; her great uncle Cuthbert, who had lost his life in the service of Bonnie Prince Charlie; and generations of more ordinary Milburns who had refused to conform to the established Church of England and had consequently suffered the fines and humiliations, the occasional imprisonment and the constant battle against destitution that went with the Recusant life. What must they think, these heroes of her faith, of this errant child of their line?

Near the foot of the stairs hung one of the more recent portraits – a family group, mother and father, surrounded by children and dogs; and among them all an upright little girl with fair hair and blue eyes. Her aunt Anna Milburn, who had grown up to marry an impoverished French aristocrat . . .

Isabella looked quickly away, feeling her heart turn over and her stomach give a sickening lurch. The portrait had been quickly obscured by a more sombre vision, of the great granite château with its dark passages, the room in the west tower where the candle had blown out . . . Terror and pain and the nightmare without end that had followed them.

As she reached the hall the terror faded a little, and her more usual mood took its place. For most of the time she felt little, of any kind, beyond a heavy weight of unhappiness that turned the world grey and cut her off from all those around her. 'It is the weight of sin, burdening your soul,' Father Duncan had told her, when she had spoken of it to him. 'Repent and humble yourself, offer your life to God, and you may hope to find joy again in another world, by his mercy.' And so she would do. It was easy enough to decide to renounce the world, when it seemed to offer her neither hope nor happiness.

Yet a faint fleeting recollection of happiness once known did still come to her, now and then, as it had this morning in the stable, like something glimpsed from the corner of the eye that disappeared when the head was turned to look at it. Then she would feel herself riding again with Jamie over the hills; playing boisterous games in draughty rooms in winter, by the river or up the Tarset burn or on the moors in summer; sitting on a stool at her grandmother's knee, hearing the old tales; sharing girlish giggles with her bosom friends in her convent school in Paris, that city to which now she was returning, in such very different circumstances.

Her father was waiting at the foot of the stairs. 'You are ready I see. Good.'

There was no warmth in his expression, nothing to match the faint suggestion of approval in the words. But then she knew it was not approval, only satisfaction that she had not added waste of his time to all the other errors she had already committed against him. Approval was something she had long ceased to expect from him. There were two things she thought she had always known: that the one great love of her father's life, his one earthly joy, had been her mother; and that it was her fault that he had lost her, for she had died at the moment of giving birth to Isabella, her second child. She knew that every time her father looked at her, he saw the reason why his wife was no longer with him. She knew too that her mother's dying wish had been that her daughter should be given to God, by entering a convent as soon as she reached the age of responsibility. It was only the persuasion of the nuns at her school in Paris that had convinced her father that she had not the least hint of a vocation and that to force one upon her would be wrong. Doubtless, like most people, they had found her too rebellious and wilful to fit comfortably into a life of obedience. Edward Milburn, regretfully accepting their advice, had resigned himself to second best and begun instead to make the necessary arrangements to find her a good Catholic husband.

He turned away from her now, not waiting for her to reach him, and led the way towards the small room behind the library that was used as a chapel. Outside its door her brother stood talking to Francesca, his wife of three months. Perhaps in the dim light he had not seen his sister coming, for he was quite evidently talking about her. 'It is my belief the fault lay in her upbringing. She should never have been allowed to run wild as she did, with servants for her playfellows. You can't expect someone reared like that to grow up with a proper sense of decorum.'

'It is not a question of decorum, but of sin,' said her father, as if he had no idea that Isabella was just behind him. 'Even servants are not beyond a knowledge of sin.'

'I would doubt how much that's true of our servants,' said her brother.

Francesca was nodding her agreement, with pursed disapproving lips. Isabella had not known her at all before her marriage, but was aware by now of a mutual dislike. It had not helped that her brother's wedding – simple and devoutly Catholic – had been darkened for her by the dreadful, disbelieving realisation of what must have happened to her as a consequence of last autumn's moment of curiosity. Of course, at that time, she had told no one about those events, though they never left her thoughts for a moment, waking or sleeping. It was in the aftermath of the wedding, when her father was at his most self satisfied, that, mentioning no names, giving no details, she had told him she was pregnant.

Edward Milburn might have done what other parents faced with such a problem had been known to do: hush the whole matter up, arrange for the child to be born in secret and disposed of to some suitable family, and then proceed with the girl's marriage arrangements as if nothing had happened, secure in the knowledge that he had done all he could to prevent discovery. But his conscience would not allow him to stoop to such deceit. Certainly, he had ensured the utmost secrecy for the child's birth, but the Bridegroom for whom Isabella was afterwards destined could not be deceived – for He knew, more even than Isabella herself, what she had done; and if He would take her still, then it was because, in spite of everything, it was His will. It almost seemed to Edward Milburn as if, in His own curious way, God had after all laid

10

special claim to the life of the girl whom her father, not able to see into the heart of things, had decided was not for Him. Why else had he so easily been able to find a convent willing to accept his erring child?

The man who had made the arrangements, his younger brother, Doctor Henry Milburn, was waiting outside the chapel too, for he had come over from Newcastle yesterday so as to accompany his niece to France – a country he knew well – there to supervise the arrangements for her lying in and the disposal of the child, and to convey her, when the time came, to the small enclosed convent where she was to pass the remainder of her life in penitence and prayer.

Isabella, gravely acquiescent in all these arrangements, had been brought to that state by the counsel of the family chaplain, Father Duncan, to whom alone she had made a full confession of her condition and the manner in which she had arrived at it. It was he who, earnestly probing, had shown her that her sense of guilt was not an unreasoning thing, but a natural consequence of her deep sinfulness. She saw that she had put temptation in the path of her cousin, for women had been endowed by the Devil with an overpowering allure for men, an allure against which they must be constantly on their guard, if it was not to bring about their downfall. A chaste woman, a woman of true purity, would never, ever, have allowed herself to be alone in a room with a man; indeed, Isabella's lively and immodest manner, bordering on the masculine, had very likely already led the young man into sinful imaginings, long before she lured him to the tower room. Seeing it all clearly at last, Isabella had acknowledged the depth of her sin, her responsibility for what had happened, her urgent need for forgiveness; and then she had been prompted to offer what remained of her life in expiation. She had at least been relieved that Father Duncan had not required her to tell her father the name of the man in the case. 'Marriage is out of the question, of course. He is your first cousin, and, besides, the family circumstances being what they are . . .' She had shuddered at the very thought that such a marriage might have been required of her. What she

11

had chosen was infinitely preferable to that.

A little bell rang inside the chapel and the family took their places, those few servants who shared their faith among them; and then Father Duncan offered up Mass, with a special intention for the new life upon which God's erring child Isabella was to set forth today.

Isabella felt a chill of fear at the words. So much of what lay ahead was unknown to her. Her experience of convents was limited to the one in which, like generations of Milburn girls before her, she had passed the four years of her schooling, an undemanding but happy enough place, where intellectual hunger (of which Isabella had little) was as neglected as physical hunger, and where even the religious instruction left something to be desired. But Isabella had enjoyed the company of the other girls, while longing sometimes for the freedom of home, the wind and the wide skies and the rides on the hills; even the masculine company she had been used to. Her greatest friend there had been her cousin Catherine, who had invited her, when their schooldays were over, to visit her family home in Brittany...

Yes, she was afraid of the convent, a little; but only a little. Burdened with guilt as she was, she knew she would find relief there, the hope of forgiveness, the possibility not only of some kind of cleansing that might restore to her in some way what she had lost, but also, in time perhaps, the achievement of holiness and peace. Once, that would have seemed to her worldly mind a small and unreal aim, not even very desirable. Now she knew that it was the very greatest gift she could hope for.

No, what she feared above all was what must precede her admittance to the convent: the birth. She wanted it to be over, longed to be rid of the monstrous thing that had taken possession of her body. She had hated it from the first, bound up as it was with the horror that had brought it into existence. Now every day she felt it flutter inside her, so that never for a moment could she forget it was there, like a leech or some other vile creature drawing its nourishment from her blood. But leeches brought healing. For her there could be no healing until this thing was expelled from her body and taken away, beyond her knowledge for ever. She hoped it would die at birth.

But she might be the one to die, in all her sin and shame. It was no rare thing after all for a woman to die in childbirth, and for that she must be ready, trying to put aside her fear and face whatever God sent with the humility and acceptance of His Holy Mother: *Fiat secundum verbum tuum – Be it unto me according to thy word.* To be the handmaid of the Lord – no woman could have a greater aspiration than that, even one as impure as she was.

Grandmother Milburn, pleading ill health, was not at Mass. The head cold was real enough, but Grandmother Milburn's piety left a good deal to be desired, so her son and her grandson and his wife certainly felt; not to mention the chaplain. Isabella suspected that her father would have preferred her to leave Blackheugh without saying goodbye to Grandmother, but in this one thing some of her old strong will reasserted itself. After Mass, refusing the light breakfast laid ready in the parlour, she made her way to the door that led to the oldest part of the house, where her grandmother insisted on living in obstinate isolation from the rest of her family. She rarely came down for meals, and when she did would often scandalise her son by eating with the servants. 'In my day the kitchen was good enough for the family. I don't see why we're too hoity toity for it all of a sudden. Besides, there's more good gossip in the kitchen, and a better fire.'

Her room was on the second floor of what had been built as a pele tower, a defence against raiders from Scotland. When more peaceful times came a new, more modern, house had been built out on its eastern side, making much of its accommodation superfluous. Jamie had told Isabella once that it was haunted, by a particularly horrible wraith called a redcap. 'They come to places where vile deeds have been done. You see, there was one of your ancestors was a wicked man, and very cruel – Randal Milburn they called him. Ever since then, the redcap's lived in the tower.' He had long nails and long

13

teeth and horrible fiery red eyes, and a red cap that he kept freshly coloured by dipping it in the blood of those he murdered. Unwary travellers spending a night in the tower were most at risk.

Isabella had carried this dreadful tale to her grandmother, who had laughed loud and long and told her not to be a goose. 'Do you think any redcap would stay long in a tower with me, Bella Milburn?' she had demanded. 'I'd soon fettle him, I can tell you.' She had then added, 'Besides, he was exorcised long since, in my father's time.' So he had been real once; Isabella had shivered with a pleasurable horror at the thought, but had never after that been afraid to go to her grandmother's room. It was large and draughty and furnished with old-fashioned solidity, its two long narrow windows allowing a good view both to the west and the south. 'Any more border raids, and I'll be the first to see them coming. I'll be up on the roof to light the warning fire before your father's stirred in his sleep.'

Isabella had seen her grandmother very little since she returned home from France. It was not that she had not wanted to see her, for Grandmother Milburn was the one of all her family whom she truly loved. But Isabella had been so ashamed, so bewildered and unhappy that – as with Jamie – she had not known how to begin to tell what had happened; and if she could not tell, then to spend time with her grandmother could only be painful in the extreme. In the end, she had told the old woman the essentials, as much as she had told her father, but no more. She had refused to answer any of the questions so gently put to her. She could not be sure what her grandmother thought about it all. There had been no word of condemnation, and she had heard rumours of a violent quarrel between her father and his mother, though what precisely it had been about she could only guess. It made no difference to anything. Grandmother Milburn was a stubborn old woman, but her son could be as strong willed, in his quieter, colder way. There was never any doubt who was master at Blackheugh.

This morning Grandmother Milburn was in her usual chair, carefully placed to allow her a clear view across the river to the graceful mansion which was the home of the Charltons, the chief family in north Tynedale, Catholics like themselves, and first among all those of that name in the valley, as the Milburns of Blackheugh were first among the Milburns. There were four Names, or 'Graynes' in Tynedale; Grandmother Milburn, a native of the valley, had been born a Robson, and there were also the Dodds. The four Names ran like a thread through all the old border tales and ballads that had enlivened Isabella's childhood.

At this moment of parting her grandmother was unusually subdued. She had no smile for Isabella as the girl came into the room. She simply sat where she was and held out her arms in silence, and Isabella, moved as she had not been for a long time, ran and flung herself at the old woman's feet and felt the arms close about her, holding her close. She did not weep, but tears were not far away.

'Now then, my hinny, I'm going to miss you,' Grandmother Milburn said. Then she took Isabella's face in her hands and looked into it with great intentness. 'Mind, I've missed you all these past months too. I've asked myself over and over, whatever became of my bright little grandbairn, the little hoyden who used to make me laugh so much? Maybe it was the sisters knocked it all out of you, but somehow I don't think so.' She waited a little while, as if hoping that Isabella would confide in her at last, but when the girl remained silent, she said sadly, 'I told your father, he's too hasty. He should bide his time, see how it goes. But he won't listen, of course. Always did think he knew best.'

'He does this time, Grandmother,' Isabella assured her. 'It is for the best.'

'I wish I thought you really meant that.'

'I do.'

'Well, there's no mending it now, I suppose. Just one thing, Bella – remember this: you've been my special grandbairn from the moment you were born, more to me than any of my own bairns, priest-ridden milk sops that they all are, God knows how! You always will be my special lass. If you have

15

to give it all up and go into a convent, at least you make sure and show them you're a true Tynedale lass, and be the very best nun they've ever had.'

Isabella laughed shakily. 'I will, Grandmother, I promise.' Then she kissed the old woman, feeling the unaccustomed tears on the wrinkled cheeks, and was folded a last time into her embrace.

Grandmother Milburn did not come to the door to see Isabella off, but the rest of them did, with Ritson the butler impassive behind them. She glimpsed the satisfaction on her brother's face, and a trace of the old enmity revived in her, pushing through the guilt and fear and misery. Always so pious, so smug, her mother's beloved, her father's pride and joy! Loving your brother was supposed to be easy, but she had never found it so. Their quarrels had often driven their father to cold anger, almost always directed exclusively against Isabella, that destroyer of all his happiness. How they must both rejoice today that they would never see her again!

She turned away from their cold and conventional parting words to find Jamie standing at her pony's head, waiting to help her mount, though he knew as well as anyone that she needed no such help. He looked at her, not smiling, but with his bright blue eyes full of sympathy. She felt a sudden rush of tears to eyes and throat.

'Goodbye, Bella,' he said, his voice low and husky. Then he put out a hand and she accepted his support as she mounted, decorously side saddle. Uncle Henry mounted his own horse and they set out at last, in silence, down the long drive, onto the eastward road, through the little grey town of Bellingham, where sprang the clear waters of Cuddy's well, sacred to St Cuthbert, from which long ago had come the water for Isabella's baptism; then, across the ford and south beside the North Tyne river, following it as far as the military road, where, at Chollerford, a carriage would be waiting for them at the end of this last ride.

Tonight they would reach Newcastle. And from there,

tomorrow, they would sail for France. Isabella would never see Northumberland again.

As they left Bellingham behind a curlew called, the first she had heard this year, its long desolate cry speaking not of spring, but of mourning for her going.

# Chapter Three

Isabella stood on the deck staring over the grey sea, the wind tugging at the plumes of her riding hat and the heavy waves of her golden brown hair beneath its brim, whipping a high colour into a face too long shut indoors. How many days had they been at sea now? She had no idea, and quickly put the question by as having neither importance nor interest. The days had passed, like all her days now, in a grey monotony – like the sea itself, a heaving greyness touched with specks of silver and white, reaching to a sky more unvaryingly grey.

She turned, and there, abruptly forcing itself on her consciousness, was the coast of France: an uneven dark shoreline, houses huddled about a harbour. Calais, she supposed, though she had not troubled to ask which port they were making for.

What happened then took her wholly unawares. All at once she saw not the crowded roofs, the grey sea and sky, the gradually increasing detail of ships and people and churches and vehicles, but a long passage, a room, a door opening; ugly distorted features in the darkness . . .

She seemed to be choking, suffocating with terror. Her heart thundered, its noise roaring in her ears, her mouth was dry, she could not breathe. She fled from the deck, taking refuge in the cramped cabin, where she crouched in a corner with her hands over her face, trying in vain to shut out the memories that were stronger, more insistent than the noise of feet on the deck, men shouting, all the sounds of a ship coming in to land.

In the end, when her uncle came to find her, she realised that the ship had docked and the moment come to disembark. Somehow she managed to bring herself under sufficient control to get up and walk at her uncle's side onto the deck and towards the gangplank that now reached down to the shore. She was aware of her uncle talking, in his quiet unflurried voice, though what he was saying she had no idea. Once, he touched her arm, and she recoiled as sharply as if he had struck her. He quickly drew away from her, though his voice murmured on, unchanged.

Then there was land beneath her feet, though it seemed to sway still with the motion of the sea.

France: the country where he lived, where the place was that the thing had happened to her. She found herself watchful at every corner, scouring every passer-by for fear one of them should be him . . .

She was being helped into a coach, and then with a sense of relief she heard the door slam shut and the vehicle jolt into movement. The sense of panic subsided a little; her heartbeat steadied again to a more comfortable rhythm, her breathing grew easier. Gradually, the old numbness was restored to her, almost comforting after that other sensation. They were, after all, a long way from the château, and no one outside her immediate family knew she was in France.

She sat staring out of the window, glad of her uncle's silence, conscious now and then of what she saw. A series of scenes passed before her eyes, sometimes scarcely registering on her consciousness, sometimes touching her briefly with a sense of the misery that they implied; sometimes stirring her memory, bringing back past scenes more substantial and real than those her eyes rested on.

. . . The suburbs of the town, old tall houses edging the street, an inn, a wine shop, a baker's from which sweet warm smells spread out into the coach, to be caught there and held, lingering . . . Beggars, loitering in church porches, clamorous at the coach doors whenever they paused to eat or change horses . . . A customs post, such as edged every town and city, to extract the dues payable on all goods coming in or out ... The great wide roads of France, made for carriages, yet largely empty of them ... The fine buildings of an abbey set among orderly woods and fertile well-tilled fields ... A château, beautiful in its formal gardens, glimpsed beyond great iron gates ...

*Another château, dark and turreted in dense woods, the thought of which made her heart thud in renewed terror. Impossible to recall now her first sight of it, so romantic, like a castle in a fairy tale.*

... Women washing at a stream, a snatch of their singing caught like the smell of the bread, held a moment, then lost ... A village, fringed with hovels whose stench made her uncle swiftly close the window of the coach ... Barefoot children playing beside a pond, a donkey and goats, geese cackling at an approaching stranger, a dog barking and barking ... A slow sleepy meandering river ... Descending from the coach in the yard of an inn at evening, with the bustle of men and horses, the smell of the stables, and something indefinable about that combination of impressions that swept her back in a moment to the stable yard at home, and her old self returning from a ride, tired and happy as she could never hope to be again ... Three laughing men in a corner of the inn parlour, exchanging obscene jokes about the Queen ...

*She had seen the Queen once, at Versailles, when she had gone there with her cousins. So much splendour in that royal palace, that she had only a chaotic recollection of gilding and candles and mirrors and the brilliant colours of silks and satins and brocades and plumed head dresses; and of her disappointment at King Louis himself, a plain ungainly young man, making little effort to hide his boredom. They said he only came to life when out hunting. But his Queen, Marie Antoinette – she was everything a Queen should be, Isabella had thought then, beautiful, extravagantly dressed, surrounded by admiring courtiers and lovely ladies, haughty with those she did not like (so they said), charming to those she favoured. Yet Isabella had heard whispers, from her cousins, from the other girls at school, of the detestation in which she was held by most of her husband's subjects. 'L'Autrichienne' they called her, 'the Austrian woman', who had never made the least attempt to love or understand her adopted country; or its King, her husband.*

... Women and girls spinning at their cottage doors, singing as the wheels turned ... A group of men working on the road, standing back, supported by their picks and shovels as the coach passed, watching it with sour resignation ('Called out for the *corvée*,' said her uncle. 'They must resent the time spent on it, when they could be working their own land – if they have any.') ... A weary-looking woman, thin and black, driving a two-horsed plough in a field ... Another, who might have been her sister, filling a cart with dung from the farmyard midden ... Game birds feeding in flocks on the new corn growing in communal strips on the edge of a village ...

*The forest near the château, and an old peasant being led away from his hovel by uniformed officials, and turning, momentarily, bleak eyes on the group on horseback of which she was one; and beyond him the little field of oats, yesterday almost ready for harvest, today destroyed by just such a flock, of which one or two lay dead by his own hand, pulled out of their hiding place by the soldiers. When he had gone, François had said, 'He knew he had no right to kill the game, birds or animals, whatever they did. He had no right even to disturb them while they fed.' She could not now remember if she had heard what became of the man – sent to the galleys, perhaps.*

... League after league of great fields, sown with flax and hemp and beans and cereals ... More abbeys and monasteries, again and again, as ubiquitous as the birds and the trees ... A town high on a hill, white walled ... Three boys in a garden, laughing as they tormented a cat ... A cottage of mud and thatch, set in a tiny field eaten down to bare earth, where a thin cow, all ribs and angular haunches, wandered seeking some remnant of food ... A wood, dense and dark. On its border, darker still against the trees, an old woman in black bending to pull grass and weeds to fill her apron – to feed the cow perhaps, or some other like it at some other hovel with too little land to give grazing to the beast that kept her from starvation ...

It was as if the whole world was suffused with misery, and all of it meeting and coagulating inside her. In the calmest scene it was there somewhere, like a crawling thing beneath a stone.

The journey merged into one, though they halted twice at night, at inns whose bleak accommodation was only too familiar from past visits. In the old days, good food had been compensation enough for the squalor of the surroundings, but she no longer had much appetite for food of any kind.

She had little idea where they were, though here and there she recognised a landmark or a signpost. She knew that they halted the second night in Amiens, for she remembered the gothic grandeur of the cathedral and the prosperous houses of the woollen merchants on whom the well-being of the town depended; and the hovels of the weavers, so many thrown out of work, especially since the recent free trade agreement with England had flooded the market with cheap English textiles.

The next morning it seemed that they had hardly started on their way when the coach came to a halt outside one of many unimpressive houses in an unimpressive street, a corner house hidden behind the high walls of a small courtyard, across which it stood at an angle. An iron gate led into the yard. Isabella was aware, as she descended from the coach, that the street opened at one end into a market place, with a church; and at the other dwindled, where the houses ended, into a country lane. She stretched cramped limbs and felt the thing inside her move too, as if relieved from constriction, as she was. Loathing it, she threw up a sort of silent half prayer that it would not survive the birth.

A large woman, presumably the owner of the house, was presented to her as Madame Bertrand. A slight weary-looking girl, none too clean in appearance or odour, turned out to be called Toinette, and was clearly the servant. Madame Bertrand was kindly enough, but more business-like than warm. Seeing how the woman's eyes ran speculatively over her, Isabella wondered what she had been told; the truth, most likely. She was, presumably, to be paid for the use made of her house, which perhaps tempered her disapproval, but Isabella thought the disapproval was there nevertheless.

The room to which she was taken was on the first floor – the house had only two floors – simply furnished, but comfortable enough, looking out at the back, with a view to one side of the clustered roofs of the town, and of a walled garden with fruit trees beyond which stretched a rather dreary expanse of fields, the earth greenish with the first shoots of various cereal crops, its monotony relieved here and there with woods, all fading under a grey evening sky.

It was easy enough to allow herself to drift along from day to day, week to week, with the routine of her new lodging, for she had no inclination to do anything else. If she could have made time pass more quickly, she would have done so; other than that she had few wishes.

She took all her meals in her room, and in fact rarely left it, except to wander about the garden, when the weather was fine enough (as it generally was), and to go on Sundays along the street and across the market place, to Mass. She hated that walk, sure that all eyes must be upon her and that everyone knew her story. She took care always to dress as inconspicuously as possible, leaving off hat and jacket for the long cloak and linen cap that most ordinary French women wore. She had no interest in clothes now, other than as a means of concealment. No one ever spoke to her at church, not even the curé, though twice he called at the house and talked to her gravely, much as Father Duncan had done at home. It was obvious even to her numbed consciousness that he had known of her circumstances in advance. She realised almost as quickly that he was known to her uncle, that indeed they were friends. She supposed, though she did not bother to ask, that his presence as curé of this small town was the reason why Uncle Henry had chosen it as a suitable refuge for her.

She had known little of her uncle before he was selected as her travelling companion. Unmarried and childless, he had always seemed a remote figure, with little to offer a lively young girl. Now, in her misery, she was surprised to find that he was exactly the companion she might have chosen, had she been in any state to choose. He seemed to know when precisely to intrude himself upon her and when to leave her alone. Calm and reflective by nature, he was able to distract her thoughts sometimes, without ever grating on her nerves. He even talked to her of political and other serious matters, more as a Frenchman might than an Englishman. She supposed that he shared the family view of her conduct – as indeed she did – but he showed no sign of reproach or disapproval. It was as if he accepted that this thing had happened, that she was suitably repentant, and that all that now remained was to take practical steps to make sure that the whole business was settled as satisfactorily as possible.

Sometimes he would join her in the garden or pass half an hour or so with her in her room. Often he went to eat at the curé's house, bringing titbits from their talk with which to try and amuse her. Now and then he left her for a few days, to visit Paris, she gathered, or to call on friends not far away.

There were no letters from home, at least not for Isabella. She thought that perhaps they did not know where precisely she was (by their own choice, of course), for the only letter her uncle received was collected by him from Paris, when he visited the capital. It was from her father, and Uncle Henry read most of it to her, including a piece of family gossip:

'... *Our sister's eldest son is to be married at last. As you would expect, she is a young woman of means. I say "woman" advisedly, for she is scarcely a lady, by the standards of that proud family. Her father made his money by some manufacturing process which they did no more than hint at, though he was recently ennobled and the girl has been respectably educated. However, they are in no position to quibble about birth – as our sister says, La Pérouse is badly in need of manure for its lands. One supposes they have enough good blood themselves to wash away the stench.*

'*Do you find there is much interest in France in the probable summoning of the Estates General? There is expectation in*

*England that its assembly will result in more considerable changes than the King and his advisors have anticipated ...'*

Uncle Henry had talked to Isabella before of the King's promise to summon the Estates General, some time within the next three years. 'I suppose they are the nearest that you will come in France to England's Houses of Parliament – except that they have not met for more than a hundred years. My good friend the curé believes very firmly that once they are assembled, then they will not disperse without some considerable changes to show for their efforts. However, as far as the King is concerned, they are to meet simply to approve new taxes and help His Majesty out of his present financial difficulties. Even that, of course, would upset the present order of things, were the nobility and clergy truly to accept their due burden of taxes ...'

But Isabella had ceased to listen to her uncle's voice. It was another voice she heard now, haughty and imperious. *'Oh, but they are parvenus!'* He had been speaking of the family of a school friend of Catherine's. *'They have no more than a hundred years of nobility at best. I do not count such mushrooms ...'* There had been a world of sneering contempt in her cousin's voice for those nobles who owed their rise to wealth and not to blood. After all, the family at La Pérouse could trace its nobility back to the days of Charlemagne, so its members insisted, their claim to illustrious birth being as ancient and as pure as that of the King himself, if not more so. The history of France was bound closely with their own history, their honour with hers. Wherever men had fought for France, whenever her Kings had called, there had always been a de La Pérouse to give his sword and his life. To marry the daughter of a parvenu must hurt his pride ... Isabella felt a small tremor of pleasure at the thought; and then she pitied the girl.

That night the nightmare returned, but this time she was no longer herself, but the despised bride, whose only eligibility lay in her father's wealth.

# Chapter Four

July that year was hot, oppressively hot, with a damp clinging heat that seemed to seep into every corner of the house, so that bedding and clothes clung to the body and tiled floors sweated beads of moisture and food went mouldy within hours. Outside, heavy mists hung over the ripening crops, or rain drenched them.

Isabella longed for relief from the heat, and from the burden that had invaded her body. She slept badly, tormented not just by the moving of the thing inside her but by horrible imaginings. She was sure it was deformed, hideously so, a monstrous thing with two heads perhaps, or lacking limbs, with features as distorted and hideous as *his* had been in the moment before the candle went out. She wished she could do something to rid herself of it, to end this horrible dependence it had on her. She hoped she would not have to see it at all, once it was born.

About the middle of the month she began to be troubled with cramps and aches and other momentary pains, short lived but sharp enough while they lasted. Her uncle questioned her calmly and examined her and then confirmed that it was nearly time. 'Though we could still have many days to wait,' he added with a smile. She could not smile back, from fear.

The next day was a Sunday. It had been stiflingly hot all night, but around dawn Isabella was woken from a final restless sleep by a sound she had not heard for a very long time: the rush of wind, setting the shutters rattling. Eagerly she slipped from the bed and hurried to the window, pushing the shutters

27

wide and leaning out. A fresh breeze lifted her hair from her forehead, brushed her face, set everything in the room rustling and stirring. She closed her eyes, breathing deeply. Then, from far off, she thought she heard a rumble of thunder. Perhaps at last this dreary heat was going to end. It seemed so long since the sun had shone.

Toinette came with breakfast, coffee and fresh white rolls. 'There's a storm brewing,' she said, putting the tray on the table. Isabella merely smiled, but stayed where she was, for it was air she wanted, not food. When Toinette had gone she leaned out once more.

In the short time since she had last looked a great cloud had appeared on the horizon, dark and heavy, contrasting sharply with the gold of the ripening corn in the fields beyond the garden, blotting out the morning light. Its upper edge was lurid, strange, sharply outlined in greenish yellow. The noise of the thunder came again, then again; and then there was a sudden brilliant flash of lightning. Fascinated in spite of herself, even excited, Isabella stayed at the window, hearing the rolls of thunder become almost continuous, watching the great jagged forks of lightning. The cloud spread and grew, filling the sky, so that it became darker and darker.

After a time the bells began to ring for Mass, their sound muffled and uneasy in the gathering storm, as if their sweetness and goodness were threatened by some evil hanging over the land. She heard voices raised in quick alarmed exchange in the adjoining house, the sound of shutters and doors being firmly closed and barred. Her uncle knocked and then came into her room, scolding her for standing at the window in her night-dress. 'You'll catch cold. You should be taking more care of yourself. I should close that window if I were you.' When he had gone, she dressed and then went back to the window, which she had no intention of closing.

It grew dark as night. The thunder merged into one endless reverberation, the lightning seared the sky incessantly, cruelly illuminating trees and fields and houses and gardens, revealing every deformity, sharpening every shadow, transforming the landscape to a ruthless delineation in black and white. The whole earth shuddered and trembled with the power of the storm. On and on it went, a clamour of noise with no apparent end, no change, no sign that it might break or subside.

One of the shutters was wrenched abruptly free of its restraining catch, and began to flap wildly. Something struck her sharply on the cheek.

She stepped back, put a hand to her face and found blood on it. There came a great roaring rattling din. The window suddenly slammed shut – open – shut, with a crash and rattle of shattered glass that flew in shards and splinters to the floor where she had been standing. Caught by the wind, the now empty frame banged wildly, on and on. Beyond it the world was roaring, not with thunder but with something that drowned all other sounds, great white stones that rumbled on the roof, bounced on the earth, crashed down in a heavy impenetrable curtain of deadly ice.

As suddenly as it had begun, it ended. A great cold silence filled the air. Just five minutes, no more, the hail had lasted, but it had taken the storm with it, and the heat. The stillness was weird, unearthly.

Shivering a little, in spite of the sunlight that now bathed the room, Isabella reached for a shawl and pulled it about her. From somewhere outside a woman began suddenly to wail, her anguished cry tearing the silence apart. Isabella went back to the shattered window and looked out; and then could not move for horror at what she saw.

A scene of utter desolation lay before her. Just a few moments ago, the landscape revealed by the lightning had been the familiar one she had gazed at every day since she came to this place: a landscape of crops, close now to harvest, the gold of corn, the blue of flax, and orchards heavy with ripening fruit among sheltering foliage, and distant dark woods, and gardens bright with flowers or neat with rows of vegetables, and tiled roofs clustering together, all safe and prosperous. Now, everywhere, beside hedges and walls, in yards and on tracks, great heaps of hailstones lay glittering in the sudden sunlight like freakish drifts of summer snow, sinister clues to the havoc that lay around them, its full extent revealed bit by bit as the hailstones melted. Every crop – barley and beans, flax and oats – had been battered beyond recognition to a dun-coloured pulp, flattened beyond any hope of harvest. Trees stood stripped like a parody of autumn, their leaves shredded and brown, branches torn off and scattered around them, their fruit tossed to the ground. House roofs gaped open to the sky, windows were shattered. In the ruined garden next door a brindled dog lay dead, its kennel reduced to a sprawl of splintered wood.

Slowly, painfully, men and women and children began to emerge into the sunlight, gathering in unnaturally silent groups in gardens and on the edges of fields, gazing at the devastation as if unable to take it in, still less to realise what it meant to them. How could so much be so utterly destroyed in so very short a time? Even Isabella, for so long numbed by her own misery, could see that those few dreadful minutes had over-turned a whole world. The line between prosperity and hunger was never very wide; this morning many of the people in the little town must have been pushed irrevocably across it. For the first time in many months her own troubles seemed just a tiny, insignificant part of a universal misery.

Her eyes on the desolation below, she leaned out to fasten the shutter back against the wall; and a great searing pain shot through her, stopping her breath, holding her bent there at the window. She heard herself moan, shut her eyes, tensed. The world shrank again to her own hateful body, the pain that possessed it. She thought it would go on for ever, but at last – thank God! – it ebbed away, releasing her to make her way trembling to the bed, where she sat down, waiting for it to return.

She knew what it was. She knew that her time had come. Her time, the end of time ... Was that what it was? There was something awful, apocalyptic about it all, that the thing that had grown inside her for so long should choose this moment of all moments, this time of devastation and disaster, to come into the world. She felt horribly afraid, not for herself, not of death (for could death be worse than what life had become?), but of what would emerge from her body. Was everything to be swallowed up in destruction on this dark Sunday, this thirteenth day of July 1788, with the thing born from her some kind of terrible beast that marked the end of the world?

Then the pains came thick and fast and she could think of nothing at all. Her uncle ran up the stairs at her cry and then sent Toinette for the midwife.

Her labour lasted all that day and into the following night. Her uncle and Toinette and the midwife took turns to watch over her, comfort her, encourage her. More than once, she heard the midwife – a large calm woman – reassuring her uncle. 'It's normal enough with the first. It could be hours yet.' Some time around midnight she persuaded him to go to bed. 'I'll wake you if you're needed.' Isabella registered, with some faint gratitude for such a mark of affection, that he was anxious about her, unnecessarily so perhaps, though she did not greatly care whether he had cause for anxiety or not.

It was not until the early hours of the following morning that the pains became focused, concentrated on the fierce urgent need of her body to expel the thing from it. She heard the midwife urging her to push, with the calm matter of factness of one who had done this many times before, and she thought how unnecessary it was, to urge her to do what she could not help but do.

One moment of fierce stupendous effort, in which pain was only a part, and she felt the thing slide out, heard the midwife's approving grunt, was conscious of a relieved bustle, a murmured exchange; and then of a thin strange wailing sound that seemed to fill the room. She dared not open her eyes. She was afraid of what she would see.

She heard the sound of someone coming up the stairs, and there was a knock on the door, and then a whispered exchange. She felt a hand on her forehead. 'I'm called away.' It was the midwife's voice. 'There's a woman gone into labour early, after the storm. It's going badly for her. I have to go. I'll wake your uncle on the way.'

*Helen Cannam*

Isabella heard the door close, and then suddenly Toinette spoke beside her. 'Here she is, bless her!'

Some instinct stronger than conscious thought opened Isabella's eyes. She saw, astonished, that the girl had a small bundle in her arms, from which a tiny crumpled red face was just visible. Not pretty perhaps, but ordinary enough, a tiny human baby. Did the swaddling cloths hide any horror, any deformity? She shrank back a little.

'Let her suck,' the girl said. 'She's hungry.'

She did not know quite how it happened, but the next moment the girl had laid the infant on the bed beside her and she was closing her arms about it, drawing it near. Toinette untied her nightdress at the neck and pulled it aside. The next moment the tiny mouth was moving towards the swollen breast, closing over the nipple, finding its way with an instinctive sureness to what it needed. A pain like an echo of the birth pangs answered the tug on the breast, and quietened again. A purposeful animal sucking filled the room, a gulping noise that seemed too loud for so tiny a creature. Isabella, dazed, afraid, looked down, and for the first time clearly saw the child.

She saw a tiny head, covered with a soft light down, eyes of a dark blue, almost closed, a tiny dimpled hand, its fingers splayed against the swell of her breast; a newborn infant, helpless and hungry. What did this thing of light and softness have to do with the horror that had haunted her for so long? This was not a thing, a monster, a parasite, but a tiny individual, separate from her yet joined to her more surely, more warmly, than ever it had been while her unwilling body fed and nurtured it unseen. This little creature was as remote as anything could be from the horrible nightmare that had happened to her. She could not even believe, looking down at it, that it could owe its existence to such ugliness. For the first time since that dreadful night, the horror receded and something new and good took its place.

Toinette went on quietly tidying the room, putting things away, though Isabella scarcely noticed her. Her whole self was

32

absorbed by the suckling child, her eyes never leaving it, gazing and gazing on its miniature perfection. Her daughter, her own child; hers alone, utterly dependent – yet she was glad of the dependence, for she had it in her to supply all that was needed.

The door opened, and her uncle came in, and Isabella looked up and smiled, from all the warm unthinking happiness that filled her.

He did not smile. What was on his face was pure horror. 'Who—? You must not! How did this happen?' He came swiftly to the bed and snatched up the child and passed it, wailing distractedly, to Toinette. 'At once – to the curé! How could you forget your instructions? Stupid girl!'

Isabella sat stilled with shock, hearing the girl run down the stairs, the wails of the infant fading away into the night. She stared at her uncle, trying to understand. 'My baby—' she began, dazed, uncomprehending.

'She'll be cared for. She's nothing to do with you any more. That's done with. Sleep now.' He mixed some concoction in a cup and brought it to her to drink. 'This will help.' There was kindness in his voice, but it did not touch Isabella. She felt only an anguish deeper than all she had suffered so far, a terrible sense of loss. Yet she could not protest, could not find words to argue. She had forfeited that right last year. It was then that her world had ended.

# Chapter Five

It was a month since the hailstorm, but all the way to Paris they saw signs of devastation wherever they looked, flattened crops, damaged houses left unrepaired because there was no money for repairs, or because the householders had lost heart. There were more beggars than ever in the streets, outside churches and abbeys, clamouring at the coach door when they halted at customs houses or inns.

'It'll be a hungry winter, this one coming,' said Uncle Henry grimly. 'Not just in the countryside, but in the cities too, especially Paris. This was France's bread basket.'

Isabella felt the tears spring to her eyes, as they did so often these days, for the least thing. Any suffering was terrible, unendurable, even in contemplation, for she felt it as a part of her own heartache. The last time they had changed horses, there had been three ragged children begging in the inn yard, and she had wept then, seeing in their pinched faces and sore, grimed feet her own child, a few years from now; if the child lived so long. She had wished it dead – would her foolish, wicked wish come true, granted even now when she no longer wanted it? Could you undo a wish? She swore she would never wish for anything ever again.

She was thankful for one thing: that they had at last left that sad house behind them, where she seemed always to hear the wailing of the child, carried up to her ears from the street, fading into the distance yet never quite silenced. Only her uncle's drugs had allowed her to have any rest at all, during the time when she was supposed to have been recovering from the birth. She had wished for something to go wrong, so that she could die, as so many women did in the aftermath of childbirth; as her own mother had done. But that passionate wish had not been granted. There was still time ... Except that she must not wish for anything any more.

Paris looked, when they reached it that evening, much as it always had: a noisy, stinking, contradictory city, half decaying, half new built (and building still), where beggars swarmed in church porches, chanting came in snatches over the walls of numberless monasteries and convents, prostitutes paraded openly among the throngs of wealthy strollers in the lamplit avenues of formal gardens and parks, under the very windows of the royal palaces. Fine new houses, splendid mansions, stood against tall decaying buildings in which each floor was crammed with ever more people, until the attics often housed several families in one cramped squalid room. It was a city whose population was swelled daily by countryfolk from every corner of France and beyond, seeking work or love, escape or forgetfulness, people who were entertained as much by the long-drawn-out cruelties of a judicial execution as by a Sunday picnic in the suburbs; who fought and hated and loved with equal violence and enthusiasm. Along streets stinking with sewage the fast one-horse cabriolets of rich young nobles sent wagons sprawling, overturned market stalls, injured children and passers-by; and men and women, painted and perfumed, in powdered wigs and brocaded coats, stepped mincingly through the dirt from a carriage to a doorway, from which candlelight spilled and music burst, pausing to go through the endless ritual of bowing and exchanging compliments before they disappeared inside; while in the wine shops men drank with the desperation of poverty, and quarrelled, and talked of the wrongs they had suffered; and sang, for everywhere there was singing.

Before, it was the glories of Paris Isabella had noticed first, and its squalor had seemed colourful and exciting to her country eyes, the whole a jumble of life in all its richness; the

36

singing had been a part of that richness. Now even the singing seemed born of desperation, for wherever she looked she saw only suffering and pain and poverty, arrogance and cruelty and a squalor without alleviation, all of a piece with the pain of her still swollen breasts and the sense of loss so great that only by sitting with hands clenched tight and teeth biting her lips until they hurt could she keep herself from screaming aloud. Fine buildings, carriages, well-clothed nobles seemed to her a kind of blasphemy set against the world around them.

They spent that night on the left bank of the Seine, at an inn that was vaguely familiar to her. She supposed she must have halted here on an earlier journey, with her family perhaps. Her cousins had a decaying mansion in the no longer fashionable Marais quarter, where she had stayed on other occasions ... There had been laughter, then, in the shabby rooms ... But she did not want to remember. Memory only brought pain, of one sort or another, and she had already borne more pain than she could endure.

She passed the night in the usual drug-induced sleep, and tried not to wonder, on waking, how she would manage when the drugs were no longer available to her. She knew that the rule of the Order for which she was bound allowed few hours of sleep; that at least would be a blessing.

Next morning, as she sipped at the coffee which was all the breakfast she wanted, her uncle said, 'As I told you, we shall meet the Superior this morning. She has of course agreed to your admission in principle, but naturally she wishes to be sure you have a true vocation. I understand she will talk to you at some length, and question you a good deal. But there is nothing to fear. She knows your story, of course.'

'Then she could refuse to take me?' Panic filled her. What would become of her, if the convent spurned her? She had nowhere else to go, no family who would accept her now, except her uncle, whose responsibility was so soon to end. The convent offered her a goal, a refuge, safe, dark, enclosed, like the tomb; with the hope of an early and holy death.

'She will take you,' he said gently, his voice warm with

reassurance. She accepted it, too weary to question it any more. The tears sprang to her eyes again, from relief.

Unlike many of the Paris religious orders, the convent was not in one of the grander quarters of the city. It was not a wealthy or fashionable order, offering the life of comfortable and undemanding piety to which the nobility would be happy to consign their daughters. Isabella and her uncle made their way to it by hired cab, lurching and swaying across the river by the Pont Neuf, and then turning east, making for the fringe of the Faubourg St Antoine, whose noisy dirty crowded streets spread out from beneath the very walls of the Bastille. The sombre fortress prison dwarfed all the crowded noisy workshops and houses around it, as if to remind the little people who strove for happiness and love in its shadow that all human happiness was fleeting, that decay and disaster and death hung over every day of their lives: a *momento mori* in stone. The convent was housed in a narrow street only a short distance from that symbol of suffering and oppression.

Isabella did not take in very much of the long interview in the Superior's office, which was furnished with the utmost austerity, and nothing like the warm and pretty room where the Abbess of her convent school used to interview recalcitrant pupils. But the severity of the woman's expression had something familiar about it, and the sharpness of her tone.

Reverend Mother explained to her first what were the rules of the Order to which she had requested admission, but as Isabella had already been told what to expect, there was nothing in that to surprise her. She knew it was an enclosed and silent Order, following a variation of the Carmelite rule. She knew what austerities would form a part of her daily life; and she was glad, for only by such means could she ever hope to be cleansed of the sin with which she was so deeply tainted.

After that the questions began, simple enough at first – was she in good health, had she ever had any serious illnesses, what schooling had she received? – but then becoming progressively more searching, more like accusations. She began to feel as if she were on trial for some crime.

'You are not able to bring to the religious life that one great gift, the greatest gift a woman can offer – the supreme treasure of her chastity. That is a loss for which there can be no recompense, and no excuse. Yet I understand that it was rather a case of culpable immodesty than outright licentiousness.'

'That is so, Mother. Except . . .' She faltered.

'Well?'

'It makes no difference. I have sinned.'

'Indeed. And now you come in all your impurity to ask to become a bride of Christ. Is that not a monstrous presumption on your part?'

'Yes, Mother. I know that I am not worthy.'

'And what then do you think you have to offer?'

'Nothing. Only repentance.'

'And you think that is enough?'

She must not weep, must not break down! She fought the tears with every ounce of her willpower, or what was left of it. 'It is not enough, but it is all I have . . . That, and what is left of my life.'

The questions seemed to go on and on, and the effort to keep control of herself became harder and harder. She felt a growing despair. What had made her think she could ever be worthy of the convent life, soiled as she was, beyond cleansing? She wanted to cry out for the interview to end. There was no point at all in going on, when the outcome was already decided. Better to finish now, and go out and throw herself in the Seine, which seemed somehow the only other choice open to her, the only means of relief. Though that way lay not salvation, but eternal torment . . . But then, without the convent, that would in any case be her inevitable fate.

She realised suddenly that the severe face across the table had softened just a little; it looked almost kindly. What was Reverend Mother saying now? '. . . in two days time you will be admitted as a postulant, to test your vocation.'

She had been accepted after all! Her relief and gratitude were so great that the tears fell at last, pouring out in an uncontrollable flood; broken words of thanks stumbled from her lips. The Superior looked reproachful. 'My child, the first lesson you must learn is to discipline your emotions. It is a lack of control that has been your greatest fault. Reserve your tears for your sins. Ask that God may help you so to do.'

She gulped. 'I will.'

She was dismissed, to wait in the parlour while her uncle made the necessary arrangements for the payment of the agreed dowry; and then, a little later, she found herself walking with him from the darkness of the convent into the hot sunlit street.

She did not go out for the two following days, even though they were to be her last in the world. The world had no interest for her now, except in the one human creature of whom she could not, dared not, allow herself to think. There was nothing else. She only wanted these days to pass, so that she could begin on her new life; her one remaining hope, that it would be brief.

On the last evening Uncle Henry had a splendid supper – the best the hotel could offer – brought up to her room. She knew why he had done it. This was to be her final meal in the world, the last chance she would have to eat fine food, before facing a lifetime of convent fare. But she had lost her appetite a long time ago, and she could do no more now than pick at the dishes he laid before her. She knew he was disappointed, but there was nothing she could do about it, except to thank him as warmly as she knew how for his thoughtfulness.

Next morning he came with her as far as the door of the convent; and there he halted and turned to face her. She realised, and was startled by it, that there were tears in his eyes. 'I wish you every true happiness in your new life,' he said, his voice husky.

She gave a tremulous smile, but could not speak. Somehow there was too much to say for her even to begin.

Then he turned and hammered on the great studded arched door. There was a pause and then the sound of steps inside, and the door swung open. In the entrance hall, stone flagged, clear of any furniture or ornament except a statue of the Virgin and Child, a priest stood, with an extern sister on either side of him.

*Candle in the Dark*

Isabella felt her uncle give her a little push from behind, and then she stepped into the hall. She heard the door close behind her.

She knelt before the priest, as she had been instructed to do, and asked for his blessing. He gave it – she felt his hand brush her head – and then he raised her to her feet and led her through what seemed innumerable doors and grilles to an inner room where the entire community was ranged, nuns and extern sisters, fifteen in all, and the Superior.

Feeling a little dazed, she heard the priest say something to the Superior, heard her reply but could not take it in, knew that more words were exchanged, that she had even responded to some of them, as she had been instructed to do. Then she was led from one to another of the nuns, knelt to each and received an embrace from each. Mingled odours of worn cloth, unwashed bodies, incense, reached her, cold dry cheeks touched her own, thin hands held her, just for a moment, with a kind of hesitant eagerness, for such human contact was a rarely permitted pleasure.

Then she was handed over to the novice mistress, a large elderly nun, and led away to a room looking over a corner of the convent's small high-walled garden, where there were three other women. Two, robed in white, were clearly novices, of which one was a middle-aged woman, the other a round-faced girl with what seemed to Isabella a vacant expression; the third, in the simple everyday clothes usual to a postulant, was a slight young woman with a gentle oval face and hair of silvery fairness. She came to greet Isabella, smiling with great sweetness.

'I am Louise de Rochefort.' She took Isabella's hands in her own. 'Welcome,' she said, and for the first time in many months Isabella felt a faint lifting of the weight of unhappiness within her.

41

# Chapter Six

'It is like spring coming after the winter,' Louise had said to Isabella on the morning of her Clothing as a novice, two months before. The phrase had startled Isabella, as had the note of joy in her voice.

Undeniably, it had been a bitter winter, even here in the shelter of the convent. Night after cold night the nuns had shivered in their cells, under the one inadequate blanket with which they were each supplied. They all remained fully dressed at night – it would have been immodest to do otherwise – but Isabella could not remember ever having been warm, not once during that interminable winter. She, who had been used to the bitter winds of the northern borders of England, chilled by a Parisian winter! It was ridiculous. But then in Northumberland it had been a simple matter of a single human body without adequate warmth. That simplicity, that individuality had gone now. On the day when her infant had ceased to be an alien parasite, feeding on her flesh, but had instead taken on a separate existence outside her body, she had lost it. It was then that the nameless creature had in truth become an intrinsic part of her, as inescapable as blood and bone. Her enclosed world had been insidiously entered and occupied, and that occupation had brought flooding in with it all the sufferings of the world outside. It did not need the prayerful concentration of the nuns on the world's needs to make her feel them. A tiny helpless scrap of humanity had already done that for her.

She knew that in the streets beyond the convent walls, the

early months of 1789 had been even worse than they had seemed inside, so bad that the Superior had brought their hardships deliberately to the community's attention. They were told that the Seine froze, that cattle died, that firewood was almost impossible to come by; that the scarcity of bread after the disaster of last year's harvest had sent prices to catastrophic levels, so that many could not afford to eat. They were asked to spare what they could for the hungry who came to the convent doors, begging for scraps. It was hard to give up anything from their two sparse meals a day, of which the most lavish, on the great feast days, consisted of eggs and bread and vegetables; but Isabella gave gladly, and so did the others. They prayed for those who were suffering and for those – many enough this year – who had died from cold or hunger. Sometimes Isabella thought she heard crying from beyond the walls, the weeping of women and children, the thin weary wail of a starving infant. The unequivocally secular singing that she used to hear often, running like a thread through the ordered sweetness of the daily Office of the convent, had ceased altogether . . . Somewhere there was a baby girl, orphaned in all but name – would she have food enough to keep her alive, would someone wrap her safe against the cold? Alone in her cell, guiltily, Isabella wept for that child, for all suffering children.

Yes, the winter had ground itself into her soul. She had felt all its pains, only too easily. They had lingered with her now that it was over; but then they had lingered in the world outside too. Spring had passed and summer was here, but the hunger was not yet at an end, for bread was scarcer than ever, and would be until after this year's harvest was gathered in. And she knew only too well how vulnerable that harvest still was to disaster, even now, in midsummer.

But the spring that Louise had spoken of, with such joy, the spring of the spirit – what did she know of that? Whatever the first months in the convent had brought her, joy had played not the remotest part in it. She could not now remember when she had last felt joy, of any kind; in childhood perhaps, riding at a canter over the border hills with the wind in her hair and the great wide Northumbrian sky above her ... Like all her memories of that distant past, it seemed not a memory, but a dream, or a scene observed from a long way off, in which she had no part.

From her very first day in the convent, she had put everything she had into her new life. When fasting was required, and often when it was not, she fasted more rigorously than anyone else; when the hours for discipline came, she scourged herself more severely; she made herself pray for longer even than the rule required, weeping over her sins. For she knew that, among them all, she was the greatest sinner, the furthest from holiness. She had further then to go before she could reach that state of perfection when God might be pleased to call her to Himself; and that she wanted above all, to reach the end of a life that had become such a burden and a misery to her. Not joy, but death . . .

Only once did the past ever intrude into her new life. In December the Superior had told her gravely of her father's death of an apoplexy. She had felt a passing sense of surprise that someone outwardly so cold could die of something so violent and so sudden. She had realised that her brother would now be master of Blackheugh, and been aware of a momentary regret; but then it was not her home any more. She had prayed for her father's soul, and then the ordered routine of the convent had wrapped her round again. It all seemed to have so little to do with her now, that past life, the people who lived in it, the person she had once been. What mattered now, the only thing that mattered, was that she should somehow crush her wayward emotions, her errant will, until she was fit to become a part of the community that had been willing to open its doors to so unpromising a postulant.

It had been such a struggle and she felt no happier for it, no more at peace; yet she supposed that it was a cause for thankfulness that she had come this far, to the point where she was to be admitted at last to the novitiate. 'Like spring coming after winter,' Louise had called it.

When Louise had come into the chapel for the ceremony of her Clothing, Isabella had been almost shocked by the joy that had shone from her face; no bride on her wedding day could have looked more radiant. But then, Louise had been a bride, and for her it was a wedding day as joyful as – no, more joyful than – that of any worldly bride.

Now Isabella's own day had come, the day she had longed for, and she felt not the faintest stirring of joy in her heart. Was that to be her punishment, justly deserved because of the enormity of her sin, that even a proper spiritual joy should be denied to her? Was that the only way she could be emptied of self, so that God could take up His rightful place in her heart? She had to remind herself that the whole purpose of these months of preparation had been to begin on the task of breaking her heart and her spirit. If Louise was able to feel joy, then that was because God had long been enthroned in her heart, accepted and welcomed. Isabella was still very far from wholehearted acceptance. Without it, she could not hope for that celestial joy.

Louise had come to her Clothing in a gown made for her at her family's expense, an exquisite confection of silver and gold. Her family and friends had all been there in the chapel to share in the great moment with her. Isabella would have no one, but the nuns had made her a gown as pretty as any girl could have wished for, of creamy silk trimmed with ribbons and gauze. Louise – now Sister Sainte-Anne – was among those who helped her to dress, laced her into the gown, brushed her hair, which was left to flow loose, in heavy golden-brown waves over her shoulders.

She was given a lighted candle. She saw how her hand shook as she took it, watched the tremulous flame as she walked into the chapel, surrounded by the high clear singing of the nuns; on up to the choir where she knelt before the priest.

'My child, what do you ask for?'

'Father, I ask God's mercy, the charity of my sisters and the holy habit of religion.'

'Do you ask these things of your own free will?'

'I do, Father.'

The Superior confirmed that she was acceptable, and she was led out of the chapel to the room where the habit waited, folded amongst flowers in a basket. She heard the outer grille of the chapel slam shut, with a noise at once emphatic and final.

The nuns helped her to dress, putting on the white robe and the wimple, and then she was led back into the chapel, to kneel before the Superior. Reverend Mother took scissors and cut Isabella's hair, putting the discarded swathes aside in a silver basin. Isabella thought how strange her head felt, how light; but only for a moment, for very soon sash and scapular and crucifix were put upon her, and the white veil of the novice was laid over her head. Then, crowned with flowers, she heard the words of acceptance and rebaptism. Henceforth she was Sister Sainte-Marie-Madeleine. Isabella Milburn had ceased to exist.

There was a celebratory meal after the Mass that followed the Clothing. Still with flowers crowning her veil, the new Sister Sainte-Marie-Madeleine walked to the refectory beside Sister Sainte-Anne, who momentarily broke the rule by raising her eyes to her companion and smiling, with all the happiness she clearly expected the new novice to feel. Isabella returned the smile, before bending her head again, as discipline demanded. She felt a sudden sharp sense of isolation. In another place, at another time, she would have welcomed Louise as a friend, been cheered by her company, confided in her; they would even, perhaps, have giggled together over the most trivial things. She had not wanted to confide in anyone for a long time, but she felt a sudden regret that never again would she be able to do so. No nun must ever seek friendship or any other kind of intimacy with one of her fellows. Friendship, like triviality, had been put behind her. Her only friend now was God Himself.

They filed into the refectory, heads bent, silent. From the streets beyond the convent walls, sounds reached them: the clatter of running feet, voices shouting. Such noisy intrusions were common enough, situated as they were in one of the

busiest districts in Paris, where it was never wholly quiet. They
had learned that when the world forced itself so much upon
their attention that they could no longer ignore it, then they
must pray for it the more earnestly.

The sounds increased, as if a crowd of people were running
through the streets, crying out some urgent news, summoning
others to join them. The clatter of feet became a thundering, the
shouting a roar. The noise intruded on the long grace before
they sat down, and formed an uneven accompaniment to the
mealtime reading, but no one appeared to take any notice of it.
Isabella heard it without curiosity; even now there was nothing
exceptional about it. In this year of hunger there had been many
days of noisy protest and even a number of full-scale riots.

Later, she decided that this was yet another riot, brought
about perhaps by the ever-increasing problem of bread prices.
The noise grew as the afternoon passed, sometimes near at
hand, sometimes further off, but swelling as if many more
joined the crowd as the hours passed – if it was a crowd.

By nightfall, the Faubourg St Antoine was still in uproar; and
not just St Antoine, perhaps. From across the city they heard
the rattle of musket fire. Later, when darkness came, the high
narrow windows of the convent were filled with red. Somewhere, something was burning.

A few hours later, as they made their way in the dawn light
to the chapel for Prime, a new clamour broke out, drowning all
other sounds – a sudden wild desolate ominous ringing of bells,
as if almost every tower and steeple in Paris was rocked with
sound, echoing about the roofs of the city, along its alleyways
and boulevards, vibrating through its very foundations. It was
nothing like the joyous ringing at the high festivals of the
Church ... Isabella was not the only one to come to a halt,
struck with a sense of terror and awe, listening and wondering.
It was a moment or two before discipline reasserted itself, and
the soft footsteps resumed in the passages, as each nun went on
her way.

Isabella's body was doing as it should but her mind could not
shut out the sound, for it went on and on, apparently without

end, only growing in strength as yet more bells joined it, tolling and tolling into the lightening dawn; and then the drums began, thudding out a strong insistent rhythm beneath the tolling bells. She could no longer suppress her curiosity. This was more than a riot, it must be! She longed to know what it meant. She felt afraid, yet excited too.

At Mass they heard the priest pray for the peace and safety of France, which only confirmed Isabella's sense that the bells had some ominous significance. She felt irritated that they were given no other clue to what it was, and then immediately prayed for forgiveness for her moment of rebellion. To wish to know more than she was told was to put her will before God's – she who had sworn she would never wish for anything ever again. How could she begin to keep that vow, if she was so unready, even here in the convent, to submit her will to God's control?

The bells did not cease all day, nor through the following night. Beneath their echoing clangour the other sounds continued – shouting, the rushing of feet, drums beating, shots being fired and, further off, the sound of cannon fire, joined, as the hour came for the Great Silence, by a distant rumble of thunder. Hard though she tried, fiercely though she prayed, Isabella's wayward mind would not submit to her attempts to control it. She would find herself, at every moment when she was supposed to be absorbed in silent prayer, wondering what it all meant, going over the little she knew of recent events in France.

That there was hunger and distress, she knew well enough. But earlier this year, she remembered now, they had been asked to pray for the Estates General, assembling at Versailles. She remembered dimly that her uncle had spoken to her about it: France's Houses of Parliament, or some such thing, summoned by the King to facilitate the levying of new taxes. But Uncle Henry had said something too of the high hopes in France that, once summoned, it would bring about greater changes than the King expected ... Just a few weeks ago, Reverend Mother had directed them to pray that the deputies of the Estates General would remember always their loyalty to God and to their King. Could the noise on the streets of Paris have anything to do with those other happenings at Versailles? Isabella was sure that out there in the summer rain great events were taking place, of which only the faintest whisper reached them here. She wanted furiously to know what they were. She felt, oddly, uncomfortably, as if the tolling bells had somehow aroused her from a long and dreary sleep. She tried to force herself to pray, for the King, for his subjects, for the Church, but the questions kept burrowing through the ordered words, sending them scattering, so that it would take even longer to reorder them again.

At Mass the next morning the priest said, 'Let us offer this Mass for our troubled land of France. Let us pray that the people of this city may be brought back to a true and dutiful submission to the laws of this kingdom, and to their most tender and good monarch, King Louis. On this day when we give thanks for the life of the great Saint Bonaventure . . .'

Isabella heard no more. The Feast of Saint Bonaventure! How could she have forgotten? She should have known, she should have been prepared. Each day of their lives here was ordered, marked out with the name of one saint or another, as the Church had decreed. If she had not been so wrapped up in worldly curiosity, she would have realised; then she could have prayed for strength to face this moment . . . July 14th, the day when, just one year ago, her child had been born, into a world devastated by storm. Now, a year later, a storm of another kind had driven that memory from her head; until this moment when it seared her very soul, making her catch her breath for the pain of it.

She could see the child at her breast, the soft downy head, the dark blue eyes, smell the newborn smell of her, a smell like no other, feel the tug of the sucking mouth, the little fingers splayed on her flesh . . . Oh, if only the infant had indeed been the monster she had dreaded, and not the tiny perfect dependent creature for which her whole body still craved!

What was it her confessor had said, when at last, two months ago, she had dared to speak to him of the longing that so tormented her? 'The child you bore was a child of sin. You have put the world behind you; put her behind you too, for she is of the world. When these sinful thoughts come to you, offer prayers to the Mother of the Holy Child, ask for her help, remember the sinlessness of that Child, and of His birth. Beg forgiveness for the corruption that surrounded the birth by which you are tormented; pray for all women tempted to sin, that they may not fall as you did.'

Sometimes that advice had helped her; but not today. She tried, with a kind of desperation, to wrench her thoughts and emotions into some kind of order, to force her mind to prayer, while on and on the bells and drums of the angry city mocked her efforts with their din.

If only the bells would be quiet, if only the city would return to something approaching its normal busy murmur! How could she hope to surrender herself to prayer with this endless clamour filling her aching head? How could she subdue her wilful self, while her every nerve was set on edge by the noise? She looked about her, and saw that none of the other nuns seemed to be affected by it. But then an observer looking at her might not have seen any outward sign of disturbance or unhappiness.

She could concentrate on nothing that morning, not the tasks she had to do, not the prayers, not the words of the Office. Some time around the middle of the morning, the bells quietened at last, not suddenly, but fading gradually, as if one by one the ringers realised the time had come to stop. It was an enormous relief, but Isabella did not find that she was finally able to order her thoughts. Other noises continued, the shouting and running, guns firing and drums beating, intermittently, but never ceasing for long.

When the hour of Recreation came, about midday, she longed to talk to one of her companions, tell her what she felt and ask her advice. But talk of so personal a kind was not permitted. The only confidants they were allowed – apart from God – were their confessor and the Superior. If any nun were to try to confide in anyone else she would be overheard and reprimanded, with reason.

Sister Sainte-Anne, sitting near her, said, 'It seems so wonderfully quiet, now that the bells have stopped.'

Isabella was about to reply, with something suitable restrained, when a great booming reverberation shattered the temporary lull, setting the whole building shuddering.

'That was close, very close!' Sister Sainte-Anne was white faced, all her serenity gone.

'The guns of the Bastille, it must be!' said another sister. And in the path of those guns lay the crowded streets of St Antoine . . . Isabella felt her heart thud painfully.

Volley after volley of musket fire rattled into the momentary silence, and then the cannon fired again. They could hear snatches of shouting, the cries of men fighting and dying, the lamentations and fury of their women. Isabella's own pain evaporated, a triviality against what might be happening out there. Perhaps someone would come to tell them what was going on, or reassure them. But the bell simply rang for the end of Recreation and they had to make their way again to the chapel, where only the words of the Office guided their prayers.

When the bell went again, the nuns dispersed to their domestic tasks. It was Isabella's turn to work in the garden, where the Community grew as many vegetables as the confined space allowed. Out there in the heavy heat of the summer afternoon, the sound of conflict was louder than ever, unmistakable. Risking a forbidden glance upwards, she could see the towers of the Bastille beyond the high wall of the garden, the tiny figures of men crowding the battlements, pikes and guns jutting sharply black against the grey sky. Now and then a tiny puff of smoke swelled out from the walls, and a moment after the noise of firing would crack into the air, to be answered by shots from below. Beyond her sight in the street, marching feet clattered rhythmically past, towards the fortress . . . More soldiers to defend it, or to reinforce the attackers? What men would be mad enough, or desperate enough, to attack a fortress so impregnable that even the fabled King Henri IV, with all his soldiers and all his military skill, had failed to take it? As she bent to pull at the weeds, Isabella prayed for those foolish, desperate men, for those of them who would die today, for those who would – surely, inevitably – suffer cruel punishment afterwards, for their temerity. She tried not to think how vulnerable she was, and the sister working with her, out here in the garden, exposed to a stray shot or even a cannon ball. She was relieved when the bell summoned them indoors for vespers.

More cannon fire, more musketry, more shouting; and then a sudden abrupt silence, just as the nuns were making their way to Compline. Isabella dared not raise her eyes to see whether the others showed any sign of listening as she was doing for a clue to what was happening. They filed into the chapel, and the chanting began, soft and sweet. And then a new sound, swelling into the hot air, broke into their short-lived tranquillity: the sound of cheering, ragged at first and uncertain, and then wild, joyful, full throated, as if a thousand voices were raised at once in a great shout of victory – only it went on, rippling out along the streets, past the convent, into the city; and with it came triumphant singing and the rhythmic clatter of clogged feet, dancing along the street outside, coming nearer, passing, moving on into the distance and fading away, the voices of the dancers singing out the tune to which their feet moved.

In the streets of St Antoine the sounds of celebration continued through the night, as if the happiness that filled the city was too great to allow anyone to sleep, as if something so momentous, so wonderful had happened that every single man and woman and child had to show his joy, to share in the great festival of rejoicing that had engulfed the city. Every man and woman and child, Isabella thought, pondering the matter, except she and her sisters here in the convent. They did not even know what there was to celebrate; or if for them the thing that had happened would have quite a different significance. She lay awake that night, through the Great Silence, not in the concentrated prayer with which she ought to fill hours of wakefulness, but listening to the sounds and wondering.

After Mass the following morning the nuns were summoned to the parlour and there the Superior addressed them.

'My sisters, I have grave news to impart to you. You cannot fail to have heard the tumult that has troubled this great city during the past days. It is, I fear, a city in rebellion. The deputies of the Third Estate at Versailles have set a most lamentable example of insubordination, they who should be first in service to their King. Seeing what was done by their betters, the people of Paris, forgetful of their duty, stirred up by agitators, have dared to rebel against the action of the King, who chose to dismiss the minister on whom they had hung their foolish hopes. News reached them that His Majesty, concerned to restore his slighted authority, had gathered troops to march on Paris. The worst sort among the people of Paris, rather than submit as they ought, rang the bells to summon the city to rebellion. I regret to say, their rebellion has been met, so far, with some success. I have learned that the Bastille has fallen into their hands. Monsieur de Launay, its governor, has been cruelly murdered, and other innocent men also, men who were simply seeking to serve their King and, through him, their God. Pray for their souls, my sisters.'

The silence in the room as she paused had a special quality, awed, frightened, yet tense with expectation. What she had told them was beyond belief, thought Isabella; but it must be true, for the Superior, always slow to allow news of the outside world to reach them, would not otherwise have told them of it.

'We live, dear sisters, in times that have many dangers for people of goodwill. Our prayers are needed more than ever they have been, that peace and order may be restored to this land. We shall now make our way once more to our chapel, there to offer special prayers for the King's Majesty and for France. We shall remain there until it is the hour for Compline. We shall abstain from all fleshly nourishment today, offering the discipline of our fast for the sins of France.'

# Chapter Seven

Isabella had thought that once she had entered on the novitiate she would find a kind of peace.

Certainly the desperate misery of the first months after the birth had subsided, returning only occasionally to overwhelm her with sudden tears. Most of the time, it had become no more than a dull ache, like that of a diseased tooth liable only now and then to flare into agony.

But misery had given way not to peace or acceptance, but to a troublesome restlessness. She found it hard to direct her thoughts as she ought, to surrender herself to prayer. Unanswered questions nagged at her, stray memories that she had thought she had put behind her, trivial anxieties. Increasingly dreams troubled the short hours of sleep, sometimes the old nightmare, sometimes dreams of the lost child. Often she would dream of some scene or incident from her childhood, something long forgotten but returning with painful clarity to her sleeping vision. Now, though, the figure at the centre of these remembered scenes was not little Isabella Milburn, but quite another child, her nameless infant grown to girlhood.

She was not sure if she imagined it, but she thought that something had changed too in the outwardly serene atmosphere of the convent. Sometimes there even seemed to be a fleeting expression of anxiety on the face of the Superior, glimpsed by means of a furtive, forbidden raising of the eyes. Since the fall of the Bastille no more definite news of the outside world had been given to them, but there were daily prayers for the King and for France, carefully worded pleas that the deputies of the Third Estate, 'now calling themselves the National Constituent Assembly', should be brought to their senses and return to their true allegiance, and that peace and order should be restored to the countryside. More startling still, there were prayers for the safety of the King's brother, the Comte d'Artois, and others who, like him, had fled the country.

Outside the convent, the city seemed to have returned to something approaching normality, though there was more singing than before, more dancing, as if everyone was in a continual state of celebration, lessening perhaps, but never quite suppressed. Then a new sound began to punctuate their days; a constant deafening hammering noise, with a rhythmic accompaniment of song, as of a hundred men joyfully at work on some massive task of demolition. The next time she took her turn in the garden, Isabella saw that only empty sky filled the space above the walls. The towers of the Bastille had disappeared.

The days grew shorter, the air fresher, summer gave way to a gentle autumn. There were prayers now for rain, to power corn mills immobilised by the long drought; and the usual prayers for the poor and the hungry. Early in October the bells rang out in the city again, to call the people not to worship but to riot. Once more, they were followed a few days later by the now familiar celebratory noises. From the prayers at that time, Isabella gathered that the King had come to Paris, for some reason taking up residence with the Queen and the royal children in the Tuileries, rarely used in the hundred years since Louis XIV built his great palace at Versailles. She could only deduce from the tone of the prayers that the move had been made against his will. There was a more mystifying prayer, too, for the women of Paris, that they might not throw off the feminine qualities of humility and gentleness, revealed to them in the nature of the Blessed Virgin herself. As so often lately, Isabella felt a twitch of rebellion, that she could not ask questions or in some other way satisfy her curiosity about what it all meant.

A few weeks later, she was working in the kitchen, preparing the last of the peas for the soup that was to be their evening meal. The light was fading fast, for it had rained incessantly today (one prayer had been answered at least, for October was washing itself away in daily torrents of rain). As she worked, she could have had her thoughts on any number of suitable subjects: her Lord a child at the carpenter's bench at Nazareth, or turning water into wine at the wedding at Cana; His Mother engaged perhaps in some domestic task. Or she could have prayed for the world's needs, for the hungry, for peasants and farmers who grew the crops that fed the cities.

Instead, she suddenly saw the kitchen at Blackheugh and its great fireplace, where she used to sit with Jamie, eating some good thing fresh from the oven, begged from an indulgent cook ... The heat of the fire, songs and stories; wonderful tales of dreadful deeds, many committed by her own forebears, for revenge or gain – no wonder Tynedale lads were barred for centuries from being bound apprentice in Newcastle ... Jamie laughing, his head thrown back, the light of the fire only half as bright as his hair ...

'Sister Sainte-Marie-Madeleine, Reverend Mother wishes to speak to you.'

Astonished, she let a pea pod fall to the floor, and had then to stoop to pick it up, promising herself to perform some small penance later for her carelessness. She could not stay for that now, because one did not keep Reverend Mother waiting. Why was she summoned? Had the Superior somehow come to learn of her restlessness, her lack of ardour, her endless small failures?

She stood with bent head in the Superior's office, her trembling hands pushed into her sleeves. She waited for the words of rebuke.

'My child, you are to be offered the great privilege of making your final, solemn vows before the usual time.'

Only with a great effort did she prevent herself from breaking the Rule and looking up into the face of the woman at the other side of the table. She tried to take in what had been

57

said, and then stammered, 'But, Mother, it's only three months since I entered on the novitiate. That is not even half the time.'

'Then you are especially privileged.' She could tell from the voice that the Superior was smiling.

She said nothing. What should she say? That she was further than she had ever been from the state of holy acceptance that should go with the moment of Profession? That her thoughts were more often concerned these days with what went on in the world than with the state of her soul? She was shocked that such objections should come to her, even for a moment. After all, what more could she ask, but to be allowed to take that final irrevocable step into the religious life, to die to the world, to dedicate herself fully to God? Often enough in the past her spirit had chafed at the long time of preparation that lay before her . . . but not lately, not since she became a novice.

And why – why should this gift (for such it was) be offered to her? She could think of no possible reason. 'I don't understand. I have done nothing to deserve—'

'Ah, if we had our deserts! But no, my daughter, it is quite another matter. You see . . .' Reverend Mother paused, as if she too were searching for the right words. 'I think you had better sit down,' she said at last, waiting until Isabella had seated herself on the stool before the table. 'Here, I fear, I must explain to you something of the machinations of sinful men. We who live apart from the world are yet touched by it, and sometimes in ways that we do not expect. Things are happening out there that I think none of us could ever have dreamed of in our worst nightmares. But God's will be done.' She paused again, as if for a moment of prayer, and then resumed: 'Bear with me if my explanation must be a little long. You know that the Estates General was summoned at the behest of his Majesty the King?'

'Yes, Mother.'

'You know that the members of the Third Estate, the representatives of the common people, set themselves against the wishes of the King and indeed of the major part of the other two Estates, the clergy and the nobility – that they have set themselves up to devise a constitution for France, as if the customs and laws of centuries were not of sufficient merit in their eyes?'

Did she know that? If nothing else, things she had certainly known began to fall into place. 'Yes, Mother.'

'It seems to me that a love of novelty is what guides them, and not the well-being of France. Further, I fear there are among their number many men whose love for Mother Church is not what it ought to be, who regard it even with suspicion. Their deepest suspicion is for the monastic life, the contemplative orders most of all. Tales of forced vocations and idle and luxurious living are commonplace among them, and believed, strange as it may seem. Of late, within the Assembly, a subject of much discussion has been the legality of the vows taken by all religious. It seems only too likely that a decree will go out forbidding the taking of any solemn vows.'

Isabella forgot herself enough to glance once, sharply, at the lined face opposite her, before lowering her eyes again. 'Can they do that, Mother? Is it not a matter for the Church?'

'Even here, enclosed away from the world, we have always been subject to the King as well as to the Church. Render unto Caesar ... though who now is Caesar I would find it hard to say. It is certain that the King would never willingly agree to such an assault upon Holy Church; but it may not be in his power to prevent it. It may be that before very long painful choices will be forced upon us, in the defence of our religion.

'But what concerns me now is to avoid the position where any member of our community has to make such a choice, between the laws of God and those of man. If we have no one in our community who has not taken her final vows, then that is one difficulty the less. Sister Sainte-Anne has expressed her joy that she should be given this privilege, but then she has spent more time in the novitiate than you. Of course, I have no wish to hasten any novice into taking her vows before she is ready, but in your case I feel ...' She broke off, and Isabella saw what was implied.

Acceptance, humility, the wonderful grace given to Mary,

who had bowed her head and said, 'Be it unto me according to thy word,' – that, now, was what was asked of her. Not to listen to the tiny protesting murmurs of what was left of the girl who had been lost forever on an autumn night two years ago, but to take the next step in this life she had chosen, resting on the loving support of God, who had shown her the way and would continue to do so. After all, what difference did it make whether she made her Profession now or in a few months' time? Better indeed that it should be the sooner.

'Then,' she said, 'I accept what you offer, Mother, unworthy as I am.'

There were no flowers for the two novices at their Profession, no joyful singing; only the mournful chanting of the *Dies Irae* and a shroud to cover them as they lay prostrate on the chapel floor. It was the burial service for everything that had bound them to the world, all that yet remained of their old selves. By the laws of France – by the laws of the old France, at least – they were no longer persons, but as unequivocally deceased as if their corpses had been buried in one of the many crowded Parisian graveyards.

Afterwards, alone in her cell with a short time for reflection, Isabella knelt to meditate on what had happened to her that day, on the solemn vows she had made, surrendering herself to a lifetime of poverty, chastity and obedience. The vows had seemed once to offer her hope, to offer all she could ask for in this life. But now that they had been made she felt no joy, no relief, no peace. Another quite different emotion filled her, setting her heart thudding, making her shiver uncontrollably: fear.

She had taken her chosen path. Her future was here in this place, the rest of her life was to be dedicated to prayer, to the obliteration of self, to the search for God. Yet over and over a small voice whispered in her head, 'What have I done? Oh God, what have I done?'

That night as she lay drifting at last into an exhausted sleep, she was jolted suddenly awake by the desolate wailing of a child, very near, as if it was just outside her cell, or even inside it. She sat up, listening; but could hear only the familiar night sounds. Had she imagined the crying? Had she been dreaming? Had the child (if there was one) simply been soothed to quietness? She could not tell. She only knew that it had seemed as clear, as real, as any sound within the convent.

She began, silently, to weep.

# Chapter Eight

'**M**y sisters, I have something very grave to communicate to you today.'

It was clear from the Superior's voice that she did not much relish her task. Isabella, as always, wondered guiltily if she had committed some grave fault for which she was to be reprimanded. She knew quite well that every day she committed many small faults – no, not faults but sins, and no sin was anything but grave. She must not trivialise her own wrongdoing. On the other hand, Reverend Mother did not usually approach such matters in this way.

'A new decree has been issued by the National Assembly. It has taken upon itself to order the suppression of all monastic orders.'

In the pause before the Superior spoke again the shiver of dismay that went through the company could almost be heard. Some even lost control so much as to murmur aloud.

'My sisters, we are more fortunate than our brother religious. The monasteries are to be closed, without exception. But we nuns are to be allowed to remain within our convents, for the time being at least. For that we must thank the benevolence of our new masters.' Isabella did not think she had ever heard sarcasm in the Superior's voice before; but then nothing like this had ever happened before. Except long ago in England . . . Was this how English nuns had heard the news of King Henry VIII's dissolution of the monasteries?

When the Superior resumed, it was with a hint of rare

emotion, so that her voice was husky, the words faltering a little. 'I ask your prayers, my sisters, for all those our brothers who will be turned out into the world, to live as best they may. Pray that in the midst of all their temptations they may remain true to Holy Church and to their vows. And pray for me, my sisters, that I may have the strength and wisdom to guide this community through unknown and uncharted waters. Pray that we may not founder in the storm that threatens us. Pray that we may be brought at last to a safe haven and a sure rest.'

The very earth on which they lived out their lives had trembled; yet afterwards nothing changed, on the surface at least. The daily Office continued, the round of prayers and tasks, the fasts and the discipline, everything was as it had always been. But Isabella was more unsettled than ever. It was hardly new, that she should feel like this, except that now a sense of insecurity was added to her other distractions. She might not be at one with the routine of the convent, but she dreaded the possibility of being turned out again into the world. On the other hand, the dismay she had felt at the moment of her Profession had not given way to resignation or peace. On the contrary, she chafed at almost everything that was asked of her, found little satisfaction in anything she did, and saw no point in much of it. Whatever spirituality she had possessed seemed to have vanished; she was dried up, barren. Her confessor treated the matter calmly, when she told him of it. She was being tested, that was all. She must keep her feet firmly on the path, persevere, and in God's good time all would be well; spring would come to her soul, after long winter. Isabella thought of Louise, on the day of her Clothing, but was not comforted. Louise – Sister Sainte-Anne – seemed to find joy in the dreariest task.

It was a long time since any of the nuns had been in the same room with any man who was not a priest.

There were two here today, seated at the far side of a long table, which had been brought into the Chapter House for the occasion. After one furtive glance Isabella had not looked at them again. She did not want to look. One man had an appearance of great severity, the other looked both contemptuous and assured, and she was reminded only too well that men were not to be trusted. She was glad that she was not alone, but supported by the company of all her sisters gathered here at the Superior's summons. She was the last to be called to the table.

'Be seated, sister.' She sat on a stool, her arms folded in her sleeves. The June sunlight, hot and bright, fell on her bent head from the small window high in the wall behind her.

Reverend Mother had spoken to them all this morning before the men arrived. They knew already that the National Assembly had ordered an inventory to be made of the property of every religious establishment in France, and had despatched commissioners to that end. It brought home to them all that they had merely gained a respite in being allowed to remain where they were. In due course the female religious, like the men, would almost certainly be turned from their convents so that the buildings could be sold.

The commissioners had in fact been in the convent for several days now, listing its furnishings and examining the archives, while the Superior had taken care to ensure that the majority of the nuns saw nothing of them.

But they had a further duty to perform, so the Superior said. Convinced apparently that few nuns could have chosen voluntarily to take the veil, the National Assembly had empowered the commissioners to remind every nun that the law permitted her to abandon her vows, should she so choose. The law of the new France did not recognise binding vows of that kind. To remain in the convent, each nun in turn must make an individual declaration that such was her wish, freely made. 'Many convents have already been visited,' Reverend Mother had told them, with obvious satisfaction, 'and the commissioners have been gravely disappointed by the results. They expected to be welcomed with gratitude. They expected to be met by oppressed nuns eager to be rescued from a mournful fate. Instead, they have found everywhere women who are happy with the choice they have made and who swear that they will remain faithful to their vows until death. I know that such will be their reception here.'

Already, this morning, the Superior and thirteen other nuns had declared aloud, with pride and happiness, that they had no greater wish than to remain where they were, obedient to their vows and the rule of their Order. Now it was Isabella's turn.

'Your name, madame?'

It was strange to be called 'madame' ... 'Sister Sainte-Marie-Madeleine.'

'Then you are Madame Isabella Milburn?'

A long time too since she had heard her old name. 'Yes, monsieur.'

'Your age?'

For a moment she could not remember how old she was. Her birthday used to be in May; it was now June. She stammered, 'Nineteen, monsieur.'

After each reply, one of the men wrote something on a paper in front of him; a further pile of papers lay at his elbow, and a volume that Isabella knew contained the names of all the nuns in the convent and the date of their Profession.

'You know that you are free, should you so wish, to leave this place? The law no longer compels you to remain.'

'I never was compelled,' she said. 'I entered freely.'

'And now, madame, should you wish, you may go freely.'

Up to that moment there had been something mechanical, automatic about the exchange. He must have used much the same words many times before now. She had already heard him repeat them over and over this very morning. Yet, she did not know why it was, but what he said suddenly seemed heavy with an implication far deeper than was suggested by the facility with which he had spoken.

She felt as if she had been seized and lifted up to hover like a bird high above the convent walls, where for the first time in months she could see the outside world laid before her. It was sunlit, so bright that it dazzled her eyes, so that she could only just pick out the tiny distant figures of people below, little moving dots of colour, bustling in the streets, singing and dancing, drinking and eating and laughing. And further off still, almost beyond her sight, a little girl danced too, all alone in an empty square, turning endlessly round and round with her small arms outstretched at either side ... She had dreamed something of the kind one night, and then been woken again by the crying. She had heard it often since the night of her Profession.

Our Lord Himself had been lifted up to a high place, and offered what must for a moment have seemed right and good. But it was the Devil who had tempted Him ...

She came back with a jolt to the present, to the men waiting for her answer, the sisters silent, a little tense, because she had said nothing for so long.

It was clear enough: no functionary of the government could release her from her vows, for only God Himself had power to do that, or His representative the Pope. The words had changed nothing.

'I wish to stay, monsieur.' She felt the relief and thankfulness among the nuns, and perhaps a momentary disappointment on the part of the commissioners. Would she have been their first apostate nun, had she answered differently? She knew that there had never really been any danger of that.

She signed the declaration the man wrote out for her and returned to her place among her sisters.

That night the crying woke her again.

There were no storms at all to mark the second birthday of her child. Instead the air was full of song, as if not just the whole city but the whole of France, the whole world, had joined together in happy celebration.

Isabella supposed there was some festivity for the anniversary of the fall of the Bastille. Within the convent, they only prayed, once again, for France to return to a proper subordination to her King and her God. Isabella strained her ears to hear the singing, and the sounds of dancing feet that seemed endlessly to clatter past the convent, echoing between high walls, harmonised with laughter and yet more singing. There was one song that came more often than any other, its vigorous tripping rhythm lingering on in her head for hours after the streets were silent. One day she picked out the most frequently repeated words: '*Ah, ça ira, ça ira, ça ira!*' – 'All will be well.' She tried to tell herself that the words had a message for her, of acceptance and trust; but there was something almost savage in the vigour of the tune, something so utterly unspiritual, that she could not take it as a spiritual message. Once she caught her feet tapping to its rhythm, and was horrified; and the next moment found herself remembering the dancing at Christmas in the kitchen at Blackheugh: Jamie sword-dancing with the men, then a wild country dance when he swung her round and she laughed and danced until she was dizzy. She had loved dancing once. The dancing master who came to her convent school had been voluble in her praise. She had thought she would have many years of dancing before her, once school was left behind . . .

She tried to force her thoughts into some more proper channel. If the daily life of prayer and mortification could not hold her, then there was the thought of the eternal life that might one day be hers . . . Would there be dancing in Heaven? Would a little girl come running to meet her, arms outstretched, as she entered the heavenly city? Surely not, for she would never have known her mother . . . Would it all be right, one day? If only she could believe that it would.

It had not seemed hard, on the day the commissioners came to the convent, to give her answer. She had known very well that there was only one answer she could give. She had only hesitated for a moment, she was not sure why.

Yet in the months that followed she found herself, time and again, wondering if perhaps she could have given another answer. To renounce her vows was the greatest possible sin that a nun could commit, a mortal sin. She would then be dead, not to the world, but to all eternity. Only if she were given a dispensation could she leave her convent, and even then it would be a grave matter. She would know she had failed, by turning her face towards what could only be second best.

In any case, Isabella's family had rejected her; she could not return to them. At a purely practical level, a girl alone in a foreign land, far from family and friends – indeed, with no family or friends who would ever now acknowledge her – would be foolish in the extreme to leave the shelter of a convent, even if she were unhappy there. And Isabella was not unhappy, or not more than she would be outside, she was sure. Except for the one thing . . .

She must not even think of it. Outside the convent she would quickly starve, even if she had only herself to support. She had no skill or experience to which she could turn as a means of earning her living. As for the child, what could she offer it, even if she were to find where it now was? Hunger and suffering, shared with its mother? Surely Uncle Henry would have made sure that it was well provided for. Better by far that it should be left in peace. It was only selfishness, sin, that made her want to seek it out – her interests, not the child's.

No, she must drive such evil thoughts away and give herself with new ardour to her life here. She turned to the most helpful passages of bible or breviary, and sometimes they gave her a short-lived consolation, or briefly renewed her will to go on. At other times, she came close to despair.

Then they heard confirmation of what until now had only been a rumour. All nuns, whether within the convent or outside it, were to be provided with a pension, at the state's expense. How much it would be and when it might be available, they did not yet know. For the other nuns it was a matter of supreme indifference, except that it ensured that they would have enough to live on. For Isabella it brought a new turmoil of doubt and hope.

She took her trouble at last to the Superior. 'Mother, I cannot stop thinking of my child.'

It was some time before the Superior seemed to grasp what she was talking about. Then she was clearly shocked that Isabella should even have thought to speak of it. 'You have put all that behind you, my sister. You have made a solemn vow to renounce the world.'

'I know that, Mother. But I want only to be sure that she is well. What if she is ill used, or sick, or hungry? She has a mother still living, who could care for her as a mother should.'

'No, my sister, you are mistaken: she has no mother in the world.' It was a rebuke, sternly uttered.

'I don't want to live in the world. I don't want to break my vows. I have no wish to be anything but chaste.' The thought of any relationship with a man could still make her feel sick and afraid; and however much the world outside might distract her and arouse her curiosity, she knew that the reality of it would be frightening and full of danger. 'It is just that one thing. If I knew all was well with her, then I would be at peace.'

'You must renounce your anxieties with everything else you have renounced – or should have renounced.'

'Would you grant me leave just to go out for as long as it takes, to find the child? Then if all is well with her, I shall come back and you will never hear me speak of it again.'

'And if you are not satisfied that all is well?'

'Then ...' She faltered, hesitated, then went on in a sudden burst, 'I should wish to leave and be a mother to her.'

There was a little silence, then the Superior said, 'You have failed in both trust and obedience, my child. No, you may not have leave of absence for such a purpose, even for a short time. Remember, the child is in God's hands. Repose yourself on that, trust in His mercy. It may not be easy, but you have not chosen an easy path. The way must often be narrow and thorny, but you must persevere with courage. Set your heart on God alone, empty it of carnal feelings, and in time you will find healing.'

'Yes, Mother.' She felt a dull sense of rebellion and disappointment, but there was nothing more she could do or say. There were only two choices left to her: fidelity to her solemn vows, or eternal damnation. It was not really a choice at all.

'Offer your trouble to God, my sister,' Reverend Mother concluded. 'Pray for all foundlings, all women who fall into sin, all penitents. Remember always, you are called to pray for the world, not to live in it.'

In October that year the pensions for members of religious orders were finally decided upon, and the commissioners were instructed to make further visits to convents, in case any nun, faced with a concrete financial inducement, wished to change her mind and renounce her vows after all.

The Community had been given warning of this second visit while they sat at Recreation. Afterwards, Sister Sainte-Anne turned to Isabella and murmured, 'I shall pray for you, my sister.'

Isabella glanced at the other nun. What instinct had told her how troubled her companion was? Had she any idea what kind of thing troubled her? She longed to tell her all that was in her mind, to seek advice and comfort, but she knew she must not. There was at least some comfort in the thought that someone so holy was praying for her. If anyone could call down the strength she needed, then surely Sister Sainte-Anne could.

This time the commissioners demanded to speak to each nun individually, one by one, and not in the presence of the whole community; to rule out the possibility that any of the nuns might have pressure put upon them to conform, Isabella supposed. But it did not need the company of her sisters to keep any of them faithful to their vows. Isabella was glad at least that the Superior insisted that each of them should be chaperoned during the interview, by another nun. She had no wish at all to find herself alone with the men.

In fact, there was only one man waiting for her in the parlour, when she answered the summons to appear; she supposed his colleague must have been called away. He was quite different from the two who had questioned her in the summer, a large kindly-looking man – fatherly, she supposed some would have described him, except that he was nothing like her father. He leaned across the table towards her (she heard old Sister Sainte-Agathe stir anxiously behind her as he did so) and said gently, 'Now, madame, we wish only to be sure that you have considered all the possibilities open to you.'

She was about to make the usual, the expected reply, when he went on, 'There will be a pension for sisters of your convent of about five hundred livres per year, paid quarterly from January 1st 1791 – that is, in two months' time. Not a fortune, but enough for a woman to live frugally. Many raise families on less than that. And for a young woman such as yourself, madame, the possibility of an early marriage must not be overlooked.'

He went on talking about marriage for some time, which did not interest her in the least. The very idea of marriage was repugnant to her. That was not what drew her even to consider taking what he offered, though it would mean turning her back on every solemn vow she had ever made and risking eternal damnation.

Five hundred livres – about £20 in English money, twice what the cook at Blackheugh was paid, but then she had her board and lodging on top of that. Not a fortune, but enough, Isabella thought, if one was careful.

'How would I live until then?' But she must not talk as if there was even the remotest possibility that she would accept his offer.

'You may take with you what goods you have in your cell, and any other personal effects.'

Isabella smiled ruefully. A hard plank bed and a rough blanket would not offer much sustenance in the streets of Paris, and would not make much if sold.

And then she thought suddenly of what Reverend Mother had said one day, speaking of their uncertain future: 'God will provide.'

'I wish to leave, monsieur. At once.' She heard herself say the words, without being aware that any decision had been made. She glimpsed the smile on the man's face, and at the same moment felt the dismay and distress that flowed from Sister Sainte-Agathe.

What had she done? Yes, God would provide for the convent, He would provide (she supposed) for her child; but would He also provide for the material needs of an apostate nun? Of course He would not. Reverend Mother had told her to trust in God's mercy towards her child; that should have been enough. It showed a deplorable lack of faith and obedience for her even to consider taking this step. And there was still time for her to change her mind and tell the man she was mistaken. Then she thought: 'If I can just see for myself that my child is well, then I can come back here and face my punishment.' It would most certainly be a severe punishment, but not as severe as the one that would await her in the afterlife if she were to leave and never come back.

She was thankful that the man, whatever his sense of triumph, treated her request with great matter-of-factness. He seemed quite unperturbed by the whisper of frightened prayer that came from Sister Sainte-Agathe. 'Very well, madame. Now let me see . . .' He took a pen in his hand and then paused to look at his notes. 'Your name is Isabella Milburn. Do I understand that you are English?' He sounded surprised. 'May I compliment you on the excellence of your French, madame? I should not have known. I suppose you will wish to return to England?'

She felt a sense of horror. 'No – no, never! No, monsieur. My family would not have me back.' A new possibility struck her. 'Am I not eligible for a pension then?' Without it, there was no point in leaving the convent. If she were to find that her child needed her, then she must know she would have the means to support them both.

'I cannot see that there will be any difficulty about that, madame. There are other English nuns in French convents, though I have not had dealings with them. I shall need to make inquiries. But what will you do? Have you friends in France?'

She did not know what impulse made her tell him precisely what she wanted to do. It must have been a wise one, for he heard her in a sympathetic silence, and then said gently, 'Perhaps the best course would be if I were to – er – adjust your record. A French name, perhaps – Isabelle . . .' He hesitated.

Isabella thought hard. Milburn . . . mill stream; in French that was *ru du moulin*. No, that would not do . . . The French for mill was *moulin*. Yes! Aloud, she said, 'Isabelle Moulin.'

He murmured the name as he wrote, the sound of pen scratching on paper mingling with the continuing mutter of Sister Sainte-Agathe's prayers. He filled two pages with writing, scattered sand on them to dry the ink and then handed one to Isabella. 'You will need this as proof of your identity, when you come to claim your pension. Keep it safe.'

She looked him full in the face. What did such immodesty matter, when she had set her foot on a much darker path? 'Thank you, monsieur.' She folded the paper and tucked it into her sleeve.

He rose to his feet. 'Now, Mademoiselle Moulin, we must convey word of your decision to the Superior. Do you wish me to come with you?'

For fear that even now she would be refused what the law afforded her, though the Church forbade? No, she had to face this alone, for it was her choice. Besides, now that it was done, the kindness that had helped her through it seemed somehow less innocent, more calculating. There was something almost conspiratorial in his manner, as if he and she were joined in an alliance against everyone else in this place and had been brought into a greater intimacy because of it. She was grateful to him, but she did not want him to think he had any claims upon her.

'Then I shall wait for you here,' he said, when she refused his offer, 'in case you need me. I shall not leave until you are safely on your way.'

As Sister Sainte-Agathe moved to accompany her out of the room, Isabelle saw that there were tears running down her lined cheeks.

Reverend Mother did not hide either her distress or her anger. Isabelle had to endure a lengthy and passionate appeal to her to consider what she was doing, to change her mind and repent, before it was too late; to realise what must be her fate if she were to persist. It shook her, more than she hoped the Superior could see, but it did not make her change her mind, though she wondered for the first time if force would be used to make her stay. They could justify it, as necessary for the safety of her soul – even she could see that.

But in the end, Reverend Mother acknowledged defeat. In a grim silence Isabelle was led to an unoccupied cell, where the two extern sisters brought her some clothes: a coarse chemise, a drab woollen skirt, a bodice of some harsh homespun material, a grimy linen cap and neckerchief. Slowly, she pulled off her habit, and the sisters folded each item carefully and laid it aside, averting their eyes while she dressed in the rough clothes, pulling the cap quickly over her shorn head, slipping on the wooden sabots, which were a little too small, so that they quickly rubbed her feet. Then a blanket was put into her hand, rolled about a pewter plate and spoon and cup.

She felt oddly naked as she took the fateful step through the grille into the hall; naked and very alone. The commissioners were waiting for her. There were two of them now; she wondered if she would have made the same decision if they had both been there at the outset. The other man looked much less approachable.

Her interviewer came towards her, and instinctively she shrank from him. He himself seemed quite different now that she was alone with him, without the concealing folds of her habit shrouding her, or the protective company of her sisters – no longer her sisters, for henceforth they must reject her, as she had rejected them.

She saw the man put his hand in his pocket and then bring out something folded in his palm. 'For you, mademoiselle. A small gift, to mark this day of liberty.' With a shaking hand she accepted the coins he gave her. Just for a moment their hands touched, and she felt a shiver of distaste. 'Thank you, monsieur,' she said, though her voice came in a whisper.

Then the other man opened the convent door and she was released alone into the street.

# Chapter Nine

The din of the city, so long a distant distraction, closed over her head. It seemed to lash her, break in waves against her, until she felt battered and dazed. Everywhere people gossiped and shouted and exclaimed and sang and cried and muttered and yelled, and pushed and shoved, or dodged to escape some missile from above, or suddenly stood still in her path, or fought or embraced. Among them donkeys brayed, dogs barked; horses' hooves and the wheels of carts clattered and rattled. In her memory, the streets of Paris had never been like this. But then she had rarely passed through them on foot, and never alone.

Crossing a side road, Isabelle emerged from the crush of people so exhausted and dizzy that she had to lean against the nearest wall for support: its stonework was almost obliterated by layer upon layer of posters, as clamorous as the street, arguing for this, declaring that, informing and urging – though quite what they urged she was too bewildered to find out. She stood there, trying to get her breath and accustom herself to the strangeness of her situation.

She dared not look at the passing crowd, fearful of catching someone's eye; they might be able to read in her face the enormity of what she had done. Instead she looked up, expecting still to see the massive towers of the Bastille filling the sky above the roofs, but there too, as in the convent garden, there was only an absence, a great expanse of empty greyness from which a shadow had departed. It had really gone then, as if it had never been.

Later, when she had taken a deep breath and forced herself to walk a little further, she realised that it had after all left something behind, for she came to the place where it had stood – a great open space, bordered with a battered trellis, from which remains of greenery hung, and ribbons faded and torn, and lamps swaying in the wind. She thought it had the look of a dance floor. Then she realised it was indeed a dance floor, and even on what she supposed was an ordinary working day (she could not remember what day it was) a handful of people were dancing there, in spite of the intermittent rain and the cold, laughing and swinging each other round as they sang. She had heard the songs before, from inside the convent; the *Carmagnole*, an old dance with new words, the *Ça ira*, which had haunted her so often.

She stood watching the dancers for some time, awed again that anything but a mighty army and a long siege should have brought about such a change. It was more than a year since the great fortress had fallen, but it did not surprise her that the joy in its going seemed as strong as ever. Looking round, she saw that here and there archways and openings in the ground gave way to steps that led down into darkness. The dungeons in which prisoners had been held were still standing then, perhaps as a reminder of what had been destroyed on that momentous July day. As she watched, a group of people emerged from one of the openings, their faces sober, as if they had briefly relived the ordeal of some forgotten political prisoner whose life had dragged by in the depths below. One of the women was carrying a child, who suddenly began to cry. The mother rocked the baby and then began to sing to it, a soft monotonous lullaby that quickly soothed it. Isabelle felt a sudden fierce pang of renewed longing. She should not be wasting time here, when there was her child to be found.

On leaving the convent that had been the one thought in her mind: to find her daughter. Now she realised that she had thought no further ahead than that, as if all she had to do was to step through the convent doors and there the child would be. Out here in the clamour and bustle of the streets she realised it was a great deal less straightforward than it had seemed. What made it worse was that the noise seemed to scatter all her thoughts, so that she could not concentrate on what she was doing or what she ought to do. For a long time she stood where she was, trying to bring to mind what she knew of her child's possible whereabouts, and how she should set out on what now began to seem an immensely complicated task.

It was a painful task too, for she had to force her mind back to the time of her child's birth; and, worse, to the dreadful moment when her uncle had snatched the baby from her breast ... What was it he had said, as he had scolded Toinette? She did not want to remember, because even to think of it now after two years brought an anguished lump to her throat, but she knew it had to be done ... '*To the curé!*' Yes, she thought that was what he had commanded; or if not that, something very like it. Later, in a hysterical outburst of weeping – one of many in the days that had followed – she had shouted to him to tell her what had happened to her baby, but he had refused to say anything. She could only suppose, looking back, that the curé had agreed to make arrangements for the care of the child.

That then was where she must go to find her – to the curé of the little town where she had been born. The only trouble was that Isabelle could not now remember the name of the town; in fact she doubted whether she had ever known it, for the matter had seemed of supreme indifference to her then. All she knew (and she could not even be certain about that) was that it was not far from Amiens.

Even this first part of her journey was discouraging, for she was not at all familiar with the streets of Paris and had only a vague idea that Amiens lay somewhere to the north – or was it the west? Trying to remember, braving the pain of all those memories, she thought back to the August day when she had arrived in Paris and tried to recall which gate it was by which they had entered. The Barrière St Denis perhaps? She was not at all sure, but maybe if she were to make her way there she would recognise some landmark and know that she was on the right road. After that, she would have to rely on asking her way to Amiens, in the hope that she would somehow be able then to find the little town not far from there.

She could have asked the way to the Barrière St Denis, but she shrank at the prospect of deliberately approaching a stranger in these threatening streets. She walked on in what she hoped was the right direction, feeling horribly alone and exposed even when she reached one of the boulevards, wide and tree lined, which encircled the heart of the city and where the crowds were less dense. She had never walked anywhere before without a chaperon; more often in the past she had not walked at all, but travelled in a carriage. Protected from all possibility of unpleasantness, she had not then thought of herself as wealthy – indeed, she would have described her family as poor – but she now realised how privileged and protected she had been. There was no one now to keep her from harm, no money except what the commissioner had given her (she had not yet taken it out to count it, for fear someone, seeing what she was doing, should snatch it from her), no possessions except the sparse mementoes of the convent, no food, no means of transport but her feet, already feeling sore from the ill-fitting sabots. She was, like so many of those around her, the poorest of the poor. Yet she did not feel at one with them. They frightened her, those confident women with children in their arms, laughing and talking; the men, large and small, yet all strutting, assertive, looking her over with a calculating brightness of eye that frightened her. What should she do if one of them were suddenly to approach her?

She had meant, for ease, to follow the boulevards round until she reached (as she surely must eventually) the rue St Denis, which bisected the northern half of the city. But suddenly ahead of her she saw a large group of men noisily drinking at one of the bars that edged the boulevard. Panic filled her. She could have crossed to the other side of the street, beyond the trees, and hoped to pass unnoticed, but there seemed so many of them, their voices so loud, some singing with raucous enthusiasm, others fondling and embracing one or other of a handful of women who formed part of their company. The fact that some of them were in uniform did not make them look less threatening, for the blue coats faced with red were unfamiliar to her. She knew that she would sooner die than walk past them.

She stood where she was for a time, her heart thudding, her mouth dry; and then she turned and plunged into one of the narrow streets that led off the boulevard, almost breaking into a run, wanting only to get as far away as possible from those threatening males.

She found herself very soon in a maze of narrow streets, overhung by high walls that scarcely let in the daylight. She stumbled on through mud and filth, beside stinking open drains that ran, deep and murky, down the centre of each street, and began to realise that she no longer had any idea which way she was going. Sometimes, she would bump into someone, bringing on herself a torrent of abuse; sometimes she would be shouted at for no reason at all that she could think of. She began to regret the space of the boulevard, for even to pass the men would have been less terrifying than to walk alone and lost in this place.

At last she realised not only that she was completely lost, but that if she did not pull herself together and ask for directions, she would never reach her destination. It was foolish to allow panic to govern her. She halted, drawing deep breaths to calm herself and looking about her for a sympathetic female face.

She was distracted by the sound of furious shouting from somewhere above her head. The next moment a nearby door opened and a woman came rushing out, face bruised and cut, blood streaming from an ugly wound in her forehead. Isabelle cried out, ready to run to help her, when the girl turned and began to pour out a fluent stream of abuse at the house, at the top of her voice. At school, Isabelle and her friends had exchanged swear words, in whispers, when the nuns were not listening, and she had a considerable stock of French vulgarities; but she knew they were innocent indeed against the words

81

that now filled the street, incomprehensible to her, yet clearly
dragged from the gutter.

She had scarcely had time to take in what was happening
when the swearing came to an end, and the girl looked about
her, catching Isabelle's eye and grinning suddenly. 'Bastard!
No man treats me like that!' The blood was flowing faster than
ever, streaming over the girl's thin freckled face. Isabelle
pulled off her neckerchief and reached out to staunch it. 'Not
here,' said the girl quickly. 'Out of sight.' She led the way
round the corner into an alley, darker and more unsavoury even
than the street they had left. 'Tell me if he comes.' She leant
against the wall, holding the neckerchief to her forehead.
Isabelle kept anxious eyes on the street they had left. She
thought she was probably even more frightened than the girl
appeared to be. Before long, she saw a large man stumble
drunkenly along the street, not even glancing their way. 'Was
that him?'

'Yes.' The girl grinned again. 'I cracked a bottle of wine over
his head. Serves him right. Pity his head's so hard. Stopped him
drinking any more though. May he rot in hell, if there is one!'

'He did this then?' Isabelle asked, putting the bundle of her
belongings down on the ground, while she took the cloth and
tried to give the wound some more methodical attention. She
felt that any girl who suffered at the hands of a man deserved
her warmest compassion.

'Aye, among other things. Fine enough when he's sober, but
drunk – well, you can see. I'll not be going back to him, that's
for sure.' As soon as Isabelle had secured the neckerchief as a
bandage about her head, the girl straightened. 'I'd best be off,
before he thinks to try this way. Thanks for your help.'

She was about to move on, when Isabelle caught her arm.
'Wait, one moment please, mademoiselle. Which way must I
go for the Barrière St Denis?'

As if really seeing her for the first time, the girl examined
Isabelle in silence for a moment, a certain curiosity in her sharp
green eyes.

'You're a fair way off still,' she said. Then: 'I'll come with you. I might as well go that way as any other.'

They set off, quickly, for the girl clearly knew her way very well round these streets.

'You a country girl then? I can tell you're not Paris born and bred.'

'Yes,' said Isabelle slowly. Her French was fluent, but she was not sure how far her accent would give her away.

'You going home then? But you sound like a southerner. St Denis is the wrong way for the south.'

'I'm not going home,' she said, a little curtly.

She saw the girl give her another of those speculative looks, though she asked no more questions. After a moment she said suddenly, 'You're not wearing a cockade.'

Isabelle stared. Then she saw that the girl wore in her cap a rosette of red and blue and white; and she realised that almost everyone they passed wore one too, somewhere about their person. She felt the colour spread over her face. 'I ... Must ...?' No, she could not ask whether she ought to wear one; it was obvious enough, she supposed, and it would simply show how ignorant she was of what was passing in these streets. Eventually, she put her hand up to her cap and said, a little unconvincingly she thought, 'Isn't it there? I must have lost it.'

Fortunately the girl seemed to accept the explanation readily enough, for she made no comment. The next moment, as they passed a baker's shop, she said, 'I'm starving. You couldn't let me have a couple of sous ...?'

The smell of the bread was very enticing, and Isabelle realised that she was hungry too. She pulled the money from her pocket and spread it on her palm to examine it. She felt the girl lean closer and crooked her fingers, half fearful of an attempt to snatch it.

'Ah, good, four whole livres!' Another of those sharp looks, the eyes scanning her quickly from head to toe, as if trying to reconcile her shabby appearance and hesitant manner with the possession of so much money; and also with the odd assortment of goods she clutched under her arm. 'So that's why you've no cockade. You're an aristocrat!' There was hostility

in every inch of her body, every inflection of her voice.
'Running away – you're an émigrée!'

'What's an émigrée?'

The question clearly puzzled the other girl, temporarily
holding her suspicion at bay. 'The nobles who flee the country,
for fear of the people's wrath. They go in disguise, some of
them. To Austria, or England, so they can plot to destroy the
Revolution.' Then, the hostility lessening just a little, 'Where
have you been all these months, not to know that?'

'In a convent,' said Isabelle quietly.

'My God! No wonder! Were you forced into it?'

It seemed as if everyone made that assumption. Was she?
Once she would have been sure of the answer. What was it she
had said to the commissioner? 'I entered freely.' She had said
it with a certain pride, believing it to be true. But that was
before she had decided to risk everything by leaving. Now, she
was not so sure where the truth lay. There had been no overt
compulsion. She had believed that only her own conscience
had induced her to take the veil. She had recognised that it was
a privilege that someone in her condition should be allowed to
do so. She knew, too, that if her child had indeed been born
horribly deformed, or had died at birth, then she would have
had no hesitation in remaining in the convent. Yet still, looking
back, it seemed to her as if all the time she had been half asleep,
allowing others to guide her, accepting all they suggested.
Now, she was awake – or waking, slowly, after long troubled
sleep to a new life in a new world. 'I thought I went freely,' she
said.

She gave the girl one of the coins and then waited a little
anxiously until she emerged again from the baker's shop with
bread for them both and a small pile of change. Isabelle felt a
little guilty that she should have been so mistrustful; but then
it was probably wise not to trust too much. Trust had never
done her any good.

They began to walk on, eating hungrily. 'Then you're going
home now?' the girl asked after a while.

'No, I have no home any more. I'm going to find my child.'

After that, she found herself telling something of her story, piece by piece, disjointedly, while the other girl questioned and listened, sympathy and indignation growing in equal measure.

'And the man – the child's father – where's he been in all this, the bastard? Left you in the lurch, I suppose.'

The child's father – she had never thought of him as such, could not begin to do so now. He was hardly a person even, but a memory of horror and pain the very thought of which made her feel sick. 'I don't want to talk about it.'

The girl slid an arm through hers. 'Don't blame you. They're all the same, these men.'

Anxious to change the subject, Isabelle said, 'How far is it to Amiens, mademoiselle, do you know? How long will it take?' She felt uncomfortable at the other girl's closeness, and was glad when her arm was released. For too long now she had been warned against the slightest gesture of affection.

'I'm not mademoiselle, I'm Marianne. Don't be so formal. Amiens, you say?' She stood gazing at Isabelle, and shook her head. 'You think to set out without even knowing where you're going! You'll be lucky to get there in one piece. I tell you what, you'll get on better if you have some food with you, and you'll need a cockade. I've a friend just along there.' She gestured vaguely in the direction of a street to their right. 'Thérèse'll have what you need. And if she doesn't know the way, she'll know who to ask. You'll get on better for it.'

Still a little mistrustful, yet wanting to trust, Isabelle went with Marianne along the street, and several more beyond it, to a house where, on the fifth floor, a florid woman on the edge of middle age, well rouged, bejewelled and amply perfumed, opened the door to them, welcoming Marianne effusively, including Isabelle in the warmth of her full-bosomed embrace.

When the greeting was at an end, Marianne explained to Thérèse why they were there, and then they waited while she flew about her two untidy rooms, gathering up a bewildering assortment of objects – ribbons and needle and thread, bread and cheese, a bottle of wine, two apples, a leather purse, a nearly new neckerchief, even a pair of shoes, a little battered, but almost exactly Isabelle's size – chattering away while she did so. Much of what she said was wholly mystifying to Isabelle, who gathered only that the woman was an actress and that much of her talk consisted of theatre gossip. She had never met an actress before and was both awed and a little uneasy. By the very nature of her work Thérèse had put herself outside the Church, for all those connected with the stage were automatically excommunicated. But then who was Isabelle to judge her for that?

Thérèse sat down at last, inviting them with sweeping gestures to do the same, and then, still talking incessantly, rarely waiting for a reply, began to shape pieces of ribbon, red and white and blue, and stitch them together. 'And you, poor little thing, shut up in a convent for life! I had enough of nuns when I was at school. It must have been terrible for you! What lengths those fanatics will go to! But thank God those days are over.' She bit through her thread and reached for more ribbon. 'Mind, the men are set to make a mess of it, if we don't keep an eye on them. Time we women had a say, don't you think, Marianne? Who was it got the King to Paris, after all? Leave it to the men, and he'd still be at Versailles, and the Assembly with him. If you want anything done, ask a woman. You haven't been along to our club lately, Marianne.'

Marianne shrugged and managed to insert a reply in her own defence. 'Oh, you know how Antoine was – jealous as hell if I was out of his sight for a minute. But now he can whistle for me. I shall please myself. Don't know why I stayed with him so long. I was a fool.'

'You've left him then? Best thing you could do, mark my words. There now –' She held out what Isabelle now saw was a shiny new cockade, much like the one both the other women wore. Marianne took it.

'Let's pin it on.' She fastened the cockade to the place where the crisp white neckerchief crossed at the neck of Isabelle's bodice. Then she swung Isabelle round. 'There – that's better, don't you think?'

Isabelle found herself staring at her own reflection in a

mirror. It was two years since she had seen a mirror, longer still since she had studied her own appearance in one. What she saw now was a fresh-faced girl, slender yet womanly, the curves of her body given emphasis by the close fitting bodice and the round neck that, even with the neckerchief folded over it, seemed indecently low. Worse, she was sure that the bright cluster of ribbons would draw every eye to the clear fair skin above – and below – the neckerchief. She pulled the snowy linen higher about her shoulders and heard Marianne laugh behind her.

'Do that, and they'll know you're straight from a convent!'

Isabelle took off the cockade. 'I'd prefer it in my cap, like yours.'

'As you wish.' Marianne reached up and pinned the cockade just above the deep frill that shaded Isabelle's face. It looked festive and showy, drawing an immodest sparkle from the gold-flecked brown eyes beneath it. In spite of herself, Isabelle smiled; and the uncertain young woman suddenly came alive, a normal girl setting out upon an adventure. Then she asked the question she had not dared to ask before. 'What does it mean, the cockade?'

She heard the exclamations – brief and astonished from Marianne, voluble and scandalised from Thérèse – then the younger girl said, 'It's the mark of patriotism. No more fleur de lis, no more Bourbon white, except that little bit. Then there's red and blue for the city of Paris, because we made the Revolution.' She was silent for a moment, neither she nor Isabelle taking much notice of what Thérèse was saying. Then she spoke again, gravely, into the momentary silence occasioned by the actress's pause for breath. 'You know so little, you'll get yourself into trouble. How would it be if I came with you?'

Isabelle stared at the reflected green eyes, watching her in the mirror. 'Came with me?'

'To Amiens.'

'It's not Amiens, it's somewhere near. If I can find it.'

'All the more reason to have company on your way.'

'But why should you? You hardly know me.'

The girl shrugged. 'I've nothing else to do. It's something different. And you might have some chance of getting there if I'm with you.'

Isabelle turned and looked the other girl full in the face. Slight and fair, with her gold earrings dangling on either side of her sharp freckled features, her clothes in their showy poverty marked her out as a world apart from Isabelle in experience and expectations, as did her speech and her manner and everything about her. Isabelle recognised that to Marianne the journey was simply a chance for excitement and adventure, a diversion, no more than that; for Isabelle it was her whole life, a journey that carried all her hopes and fears, and might end in disaster and grief. Did she want for her companion someone she scarcely knew who could not begin to understand what she felt?

Then she knew that she did. Why that should be so, why she should feel a sense of relief, even of joy, at the thought that this stranger from the Paris streets should offer her companionship, she did not know. But so it was.

She smiled suddenly. Her mouth was still unused to smiling, and felt strange and stiff. 'I'd like that,' she said.

# Chapter Ten

'We just stay on the main road until we get to Amiens,' Marianne said when they had parted, with much embracing, from Thérèse. 'Simple.'

They left Paris by the Barrière St Denis, which looked nothing like the impressive customs post that Isabelle dimly remembered from her journey three years ago. Now, the buildings were a blackened ruin, already softened by weeds. A couple of men in the uniform she had seen on the boulevard stood there, muskets in their hands. 'National Guards,' explained Marianne. They were so deeply engaged in conversation that they could not possibly have been keeping an eye on what was passing. Carts and wagons and carriages rolled by, without any attempt being made to halt them and demand the dues that once would have been levied on any goods entering the capital. 'That's all done with now,' Marianne said carelessly, when Isabelle asked her about it.

Slowly – with an unbearable slowness – they made their way through the suburbs, with the heights of Montmartre on their left, scattered with windmills among a patchwork of woods and vineyards, and little fields that in spring would be planted with vegetables and flowers for the markets of Paris, but which now looked sad and brown, brightened only by the occasional tattered green of late cabbages or leeks. It seemed an age before that landscape was behind them and they were at last on the wide empty road beyond the capital. In a coach the distance would have been quickly covered; on foot, Isabelle realised now, it would take them days rather than hours to reach Amiens. That was hardly a startling discovery, but it was something which had not, until now, occurred to her. In spirit she had already flown over the leagues to Amiens, or to whatever place held her child. In fact, after less than an hour, she could feel her legs, unused as they were to steady walking, beginning to ache. She realised too that even these new shoes were not a perfect fit. They would give trouble before very long.

The sense of frustration passed. Isabelle grew accustomed to the gentle pace, and even, after a time, began to think they made quite good progress. It was (for once in this wet autumn) a fine afternoon, and she was out in the open, with no routine to bind her, no one to tell her what to do, and a companion at her side whom no rule forbade to make her friend, if she so chose. She had set out at last on the journey to which all her thoughts had been directed for so long, and for the moment at least she was certain that, having begun so well, it must end at last in success. Success would mean that she found her child, not in misery, but in circumstances that made it only right that she should take responsibility for her. She did not really believe that she would be faced with the need to keep her conditional promise to return to the convent.

Well into the afternoon, they halted by the road to eat a little of the food that Thérèse had provided for them. Isabelle felt her spirits lift, filled with a sense of holiday. She sat on the grassy bank and savoured the sheer sensual pleasure of being able freely to raise her face, eyes closed, to the sun, and then to eat good fresh bread, white and crusty, and salty cheese and an apple, crisp and sweet, with no more than a first faint passing sense of guilt at her delight in their flavour, and in satisfying her hunger. Best of all she had the company of a friend: after nearly two years of enforced friendlessness, that went to her head more quickly even than the coarse red wine they drank. Still shy, still unsure of herself and of her companion, she caught Marianne's eye, and they exchanged grins, and happiness ran through her, warm and intoxicating.

'Have you lived in Paris all your life?' Isabelle asked. The words sounded rather stiff and awkward, for how could she begin to put into words what she was feeling? Would it even be wise to do so, when she knew so little of Marianne?

'Yes, though my mother came from Lorraine. What about you? Where are you from?'

Isabelle cursed herself for having introduced the subject of origins, and considered her reply. She already felt instinctively that she could trust this girl, but she had learned long ago that instincts were unreliable. After all, who could you trust, if not your own cousin?

'All right, don't tell me then!' said Marianne at last with a shrug, returning her attention to her apple. She sounded genuinely irritated, and Isabelle regretted her caution. After all, she owed her new friend a good deal already.

'I come from England.'

'England!' Marianne let her hand fall and stared at Isabelle. 'Are you English?' Isabelle nodded. 'Why did they send you to France? Don't they have convents in England?' She spoke teasingly, as if the concept of a country without convents was laughable.

Isabelle tried to hide her surprise at such ignorance. 'England's a Protestant country. Catholics have been persecuted there for a long time.'

'Like Protestants in France?'

'I suppose so.' The ignorance then was not all on one side. 'There were convents in England once, but King Henry the Eighth had them shut down and took all their lands.'

'And now the Assembly's shutting them down over here. Good thing too . . . You don't sound English.'

'I was in school in France. My father wanted a Catholic education for me, you see. Catholics aren't allowed to run schools in England. Besides, I have French relations.' Still, she felt the sickness rise in her at the merest thought of them.

'Why not go to them now then? Wouldn't they help you?'

'What, when I've left the convent? Of course not; they're good Catholics. Besides—'

91

'Besides what?'

She wanted to tell, to be free in some way from the burden of her secret knowledge, but somehow she could not. It was to expose herself, to reopen the wound again – though she knew it had never fully healed, and probably never would. 'Nothing,' she said. Then, 'I've finished. Let's go on.'

As she rose to her feet she remembered what Marianne had said about the émigrés and wondered if her aristocratic cousins had fled from France. She could not imagine they would wish to remain in a country that no longer looked on aristocracy as something deserving of automatic respect. But where would they go, if they fled? To their cousins in Northumberland? That was only too likely, and a horrible thought. It was also strange to realise that she was so cut off from any news of her family that such shattering things might have happened to them without her knowledge. She had thought that in the convent she was shut away from the world and its concerns; now she knew that she had never been as isolated there as she was today. No one from her past knew any longer where she was or what she was doing, or had any means of finding out. She even had a new identity. For the first time in her life she was free to do exactly as she chose, utterly free. It was a thought at once terrifying and exhilarating.

So many things on this journey came to her with the freshness of the unfamiliar. Small things, like the bustle of a market in a town they passed through, or the noise of people talking or singing, no longer seemed overpowering as they had in the first moments of leaving the convent, but interesting and exciting. And after years when the only company she had known was that of women, to see children again was both a delight and a heartache, reminding her of the child she was seeking, and holding out a promise for the day when she was found at last. For two years now the only children she had seen were the painted Infants in the arms of the painted Virgins in the convent chapel. These children were real, noisy and dirty and squabbling, barefoot and ragged, or prettily dressed and bright eyed with health. She remembered how in the past she had been struck, sometimes with pity, by the affected children of well-to-do families, dressed like little adults, in stays and brocade and lace, with powdered hair, the little boys with miniature swords at their sides. Nowhere now did she see such children. But then even the most prosperous-looking of men and women seemed to have abandoned their stays for softer, more flowing clothes, and many of the men wore their hair not only unpowdered but cut short. Few women now painted their faces with rouge or decorated them with patches. Everyone, everywhere, seemed to wear a tricolour cockade somewhere about their person.

It was, of course, a long time too since she had seen men in any number, and those men not made safe by vows of celibacy. She realised how thankful she was that she was not travelling alone. Two different men approached them that first day, perhaps wanting no more than to talk, but each with an expression of such admiration and interest that Isabelle had felt deeply alarmed. On both occasions Marianne rebuffed the man with a cheerful friendliness that had the desired effect without causing offence. 'I've had my fill of men,' she said to Isabelle, as if she needed to excuse such behaviour. 'We'll get on better for not encouraging them.' Isabelle could only agree, and was the more thankful that she did not need to give her reasons for doing so.

She had one anxiety, which she put to Marianne as the shadows began to lengthen and the air grew chill. 'What do we do tonight? I want to save the money I've got for my baby, if I can.'

'You'd be amazed what you can do without money.' At the look of doubt on Isabelle's face, Marianne grinned. 'I've got by without it most of my life. And when you need it, there are always ways. Just so long,' she added, 'as you don't worry too much about how you go about it.'

Isabelle felt uneasy. 'Do you mean stealing?'

'No, I mean surviving. I wouldn't be here now if I hadn't learned to do that. I was born with nothing, you see. If I hadn't learned to beg before I could walk, we'd have starved, my

93

mother and me. She was a servant before I was born. Then the master got hold of her, the way they do – or did, in the old days. Long live the Revolution and the end of masters!'

There had been a servant girl dismissed at Blackheugh for pregnancy, Isabelle remembered, though it was said she was immoral. Ritson the butler had been her partner in crime, but as he had been led astray by her wiles, he had retained his post. At La Pérouse, her cousins used to laugh about the servants, and how easy they were, how ready to oblige. Isabelle had accepted it all at the time. Now, she wondered. Were women always responsible for what happened to them? 'She lost her job then?'

'What do you think? Anyway, we survived, until I was old enough to fend for myself. Then she died. They had a round up of beggars one day and I was caught and sent to an orphanage. I ran away from there the moment I got the chance, I can tell you.'

'What did you do then?'

'This and that – whatever came to hand. I got work spinning; my mother taught me to spin. But then they couldn't sell enough cloth and threw a lot of us out of work, so I was back where I started. I've been a servant, once – never again if I can help it; slave would be a better word. Otherwise – well, there's nearly always a man who'll buy your next meal, if you know how to go about it. I don't mean whoring. I've done a bit of that now and then, but not often. Most of my men have been lovers, proper lovers. But not one of them I've wanted to stay with for long in the end. They're all the same. Can't do too much for you, till they're sure of you. Then you're just there to run about at their beck and call. That's not for me. Still, I keep hoping. Maybe somewhere there's someone different.'

Isabelle could not imagine a life more unlike her own, and much of what she heard repelled her. Yet she acknowledged that in two respects she and Marianne were alike: they had both, in one way or another, offended against what the world saw as respectability; and each of them now was setting out on a new phase of her life, without money or employment or the support of family or friends. They had one another, and that was all. As yet it was too tenuous a relationship on which to build trust or real friendship.

'What about you then?' Marianne was speaking again. 'Was your child's father the only one?'

'Oh yes!' She could not even bear to think that there might have been others. It astonished her that anyone should contemplate such a relationship so lightly, not simply from a moral point of view, but because what it demanded from a woman was so unspeakably horrible. Yet Marianne talked as if it might even offer the possibility of happiness; and Isabelle knew that there were men and women (a few) who lived together in contentment. It was puzzling, but not something she wished to dwell upon.

Isabelle was impressed by the assurance with which Marianne set about finding accommodation for the two of them that night. At the first farm they reached, on the edge of a village not far from Senlis, she bargained with a suspicious farmer's wife for a supper of soup and hard black bread, and a night's sleep in a hay loft. In return, Marianne undertook to spin some of the flax awaiting attention in the house, and Isabelle, lacking obvious skills, was directed to rock the cradle in which a fretful baby was whimpering, while her mother went out to help her husband attend to the beasts for the night.

Isabelle put her whole heart into her task, as if it were her own child lying under the woollen covers in the shabby wooden cradle. She sang as she rocked, humming a tune she dimly remembered from long ago. Perhaps once someone had sung it to her as she lay in her own cradle, though she could remember no words. But this child was loved and cared for. Somewhere her own child still lay bereft of a mother's love, without even the compensation Isabelle herself had known, of being loved instead by a dear grandmother. She had to fight an urge to leave the warm fireside and the good smell of soup and rush out into the darkness, to go on with her search without ceasing until she found her daughter.

They were shown the loft above a byre where a plough horse

and two cows were housed. It had the merit of being warm, sweet with the breath of the animals, but Marianne shuddered and edged past the horse warily, at a safe distance, keeping her eyes on it all the while, as if afraid that it might leap out and attack her. Isabelle paused to pat it and fondle its warm soft nose, a procedure which Marianne watched in amazement. 'I hate horses,' she said. 'I was kicked by one once, when I was little. I don't know how you can do that.'

'I used to like to ride, once,' said Isabelle, thinking sadly of Bonny, who was not unlike a smaller version of this great gentle animal. 'Pity we can't borrow him for the journey. He'd take the two of us.'

Marianne came to a halt at the foot of the ladder. Isabelle could see her eyes gleaming in the light of the lantern the farmer had lent them. 'If we left early, before they get up . . .'

'No!' said Isabelle firmly. 'What would they do without their horse? That would be wicked. Besides, I thought you were afraid of horses.'

'I'd get over it.' Then she shrugged. 'But you're right. They're not aristocrats after all. Or even bourgeois. Just stupid peasants.'

They climbed a narrow step ladder to the loft and settled down on the hay there, putting out the lantern with care, for fear of fire. Isabelle lay in the darkness, warmed by the food and the shelter from the brisk icy wind that had sprung up with the night, listening to the munching of the animals and the sound of Marianne shaping the hay to fit her body. For so long she had lain alone at night, alone with the unearthly wailing of her child and her futile prayers and her nightmares. Now, for the first time in years, she had a companion. She turned on her side to face the place where she knew Marianne had settled down, wanting to say something so that she should hear how close she was. In the end, it was Marianne who spoke first, her voice low and sleepy in the darkness. 'Tell me, which side of Amiens was this town?'

'This side, the Paris side, I think.'

'But you don't remember the name at all?'

'No.'

'Was there a foundling hospital there?'

'I don't know. There wasn't much. But I don't see what that has to do with it. She wasn't a foundling.'

'Where else do they send bastard children? I suppose we could try Amiens itself. There'll be a hospital there, for certain.'

'Why do you keep on about hospitals? My baby won't be in that sort of place, I'm sure. It's the curé we want to speak to. He'll know.'

Marianne was silent for a moment, then she said, with the first note of hesitancy Isabelle had heard in her voice, 'You know, we may find nothing – there may be nothing to find even.'

'I know,' said Isabelle, conscious that she was accepting in words what her instincts and emotions would not, could not, allow her to accept, that her child might be lost without trace, or (more likely) dead. 'But I shan't give up, ever, as long as I live.'

Marianne laughed softly. 'I might leave you to get on with it then.' She went on talking for a time after that, but Isabelle ceased to hear what she said. She drifted into sleep, and dreamed that the baby in the cradle she was rocking had opened blue eyes to look up at her, and was smiling; and then that she had lifted her up, and the small plump arms had closed about her neck, the little head with its soft curls of brown hair come to rest upon her shoulder.

It was bright enough when they set out next day in the crisp frosty dawn; but after a short time the frost began to melt and a dense raw fog settled over the landscape. Very soon they could see no more than a yard or two in front of them.

It was like being isolated in a tiny enclosed world, just the two of them cut off from every other human being, every place. They said little, partly because the muffling silence seemed to stifle the smallest attempt to speak. Isabelle remembered suddenly that at this time yesterday she had still been in the convent, a nun vowed to God's service, going through all the usual daily routine of the day. Now, so soon (yet it seemed a lifetime ago), she had turned her back on all that – but no, she reminded herself, she could still go back and face the consequences, if she were to find that her child did not need her, either because she was happy in her present home, or because – but no, she was not dead. Why otherwise would Isabelle have heard the cry in the night, or dreamt that she had her safe in her arms? And as for happiness, who could say that she would not, in any circumstances, be happier with her true mother than with the kindest of substitutes?

She noticed that Marianne was less talkative than yesterday, that she even seemed a little morose. She wondered if, like Isabelle herself, she too had rubbed and blistered feet, so that setting out this morning had been a painful business, and if she too seemed to ache more after her night's rest than she had before. Isabelle asked, 'What's the matter? Are you tired?'

'Of course not. Nothing's the matter. Why should it be?'

'You seemed a bit quiet, that's all.'

'Do I have to talk all the time? You want entertaining, I suppose. I'm not here to keep you amused.'

The ill-tempered reply astonished Isabelle. 'I know you're not. Anyway, I never asked you to come.'

'You want me to turn round and leave you then?'

'Of course not. I'm glad you came.' But she began to wonder. She had difficulties enough to face without having to cope with her companion's unpredictable moods. She re-membered now how little she knew about Marianne, and how that little ought to have warned her to caution rather than trust.

After they had walked for a time without any more being said, Marianne broke out, 'If you must know, my head aches and my stomach hurts.' She grinned. 'Just the usual. At least I'm not pregnant.'

Isabelle turned to her with a sudden impulse of sympathy. 'Did you think you might be?'

'I've escaped so far, but you never know. It would be just like him to leave a souvenir. Mind, if you know how, you can sometimes stop it happening. Before or after.'

Isabelle was so shocked by the shameless frankness of the remarks that she was silent for some considerable time. Now it was Marianne's turn to wonder at her companion's sullenness. 'Come now, why should men always get away with it, and women never? That's not just, is it? You should see that if anyone does.'

'I don't want to talk about it.'

'Suit yourself. Maybe you should have stayed a nun.'

They walked a little further, then Isabelle halted. 'Don't let's quarrel. My feet hurt and I'm tired and hungry and falling out will only make it worse.'

'Then let's eat and there'll be one less thing wrong.'

The truce lasted while they sat down and shared some of the black bread the farmer's wife had given them. Later, as they rose, reluctantly, to walk on again, Marianne asked suddenly, 'Why did you say that last night – about her not being at the foundling hospital? I thought you didn't know.'

'The curé was my uncle's friend,' Isabelle explained. 'I expect he found her a home with a good family.'

'What's a good family then?' Marianne's voice had a faint note of scorn.

'You know, respectable people with means, people who would give her a good upbringing.'

'Families like that don't take in unknown bastards. You might find a good kindly poor family who would, especially if they were given enough money. But respectable bourgeois – no! Besides, I thought no one told you anything. What gives you the idea the curé would do more for your child than he would for any other unwanted bastard?'

Isabelle winced a little at the tone. 'He would, wouldn't he? He knew who the mother was. He knew it wasn't – well, just any bastard.' Even as she spoke she wished the words unsaid. She had not meant to imply that her own child was more deserving than any other in her position, only that she supposed that the curé would have regarded her in that light; but even to her ears the words had an unpleasant ring.

Marianne looked at her sharply. 'Who the mother was?' then: 'You *are* an aristocrat – I was right after all!' She suddenly took hold of Isabelle's hands, examining them fiercely. 'Soft as soft! I should have known. These hands have never done a day's hard work.' Isabelle thought that her own hands were not markedly softer than Marianne's, and she could have argued that the final accusation was quite untrue, but she knew that was not the point. It was not the supposed soft hands that made her guilty, but what they represented. She felt herself colouring.

'Whatever I may have been once, I am Isabelle Moulin now, of no family and no fortune.'

'Aye well, maybe – that's what you say anyway.' The look of hostility that had sharpened Marianne's features increased. 'I bet you anything he sent her to the foundling hospital.' She said it, not as if simply expressing an opinion, but as one of Isabelle's schoolfriends might have spoken in a moment of deliberate spite.

At that level it worked, too, for the thought that her child might have been abandoned to an institution filled Isabelle with horror.

'What's the matter? Too good for that, is she, this aristocratic daughter of yours? Such places only fit for the common people?'

'That's not what I meant. You know it's not.'

'Do I? I don't know anything about you at all. You've made sure of that. You told me you weren't an aristocrat, and now I find you are – an English one too.'

'I didn't say I wasn't an aristocrat; I didn't say I was either. My family are poor enough. You don't get rich Catholics in England.'

'There are poor aristocrats. They're the worst. All they've got is their pride.'

Isabelle thought of her cousins, and could find no defence against that argument. She knew only too well how true it was.

'What about your French relations then?'

'What about them? I don't want to talk about them.'

100

'No, you expect me to tell you everything, but let me ask a few questions and you shut up. Don't trust me, I suppose.'

'The way you're behaving now, can you blame me?' Immediately, she regretted those words too, and said quickly, with a plea in her voice, 'I'm grateful you came with me, truly I am. And for your help. Don't let's quarrel over such a silly thing.'

'Is it silly? It's the aristocrats who tried to stop the Revolution, who would still destroy it now if they could.'

'I know nothing about the Revolution. You've seen that yourself. If it's destroyed injustices, then I'm glad. But I can't care about something I don't know about.'

'Then you can't expect me to care about you if I don't know about you.'

They trudged on in a bad-tempered silence for some time, footsore and cold and nursing hurt feelings. But Isabelle had never been of a sulky temperament. Where she hated, her anger burned fiercely, but she did not hate Marianne. She was simply irritated with her, and the irritation did not survive for very long. She said after a time, 'My family were thieves and robbers for generations, most of them. They've a little land, and a great many debts, and lately they've been pious enough. You can call them aristocrats if you like, I don't care. But I am myself. There's no mystery, nothing hidden, just what you see.' She was nevertheless conscious that the matter was not quite as simple as that.

Marianne glanced at her. 'And your French relations?'

'That's different.'

'No mystery, but you won't talk about them?'

'Oh, let it alone,' Isabelle retorted wearily. This time she could not summon the energy to try and cajole Marianne into a better humour. She knew her own patience was at a low ebb too, so she was simply glad that no more was said for a long time.

It was not until late in the afternoon that the fog lifted sufficiently to reveal that they were walking along a narrow muddy track through a dense wood. There was no sign in any direction of houses or inns or any settlement of any kind.

'This can't be the main road to Amiens,' Isabelle said, coming to a halt.

Marianne was silent for a moment, looking about her. Then she said, 'There's a crossroads ahead, and a signpost.'

But when they reached it Isabelle saw at once that the signpost made no mention of Amiens. She turned on Marianne. 'You said we couldn't go wrong! But we have, you can see that!'

'It's not my fault it was foggy,' retorted Marianne.

'Then where do we go now, tell me that?'

'How should I know? Which sign says Amiens?'

Isabelle stared at her. 'None of them – can't you see?'

'You don't suppose I can read, do you? I'm not an aristocrat.'

'Oh, don't be so touchy! ... I'm sorry,' she added grudgingly. Then she read the names to Marianne. 'Now, which one do we want?'

'I don't know. I've never heard of any of them.'

'But you came to show me the way.'

'I never promised that. I don't know any more than you do. I've never been out of Paris before.'

'But you said—' Isabelle was temporarily speechless.

Marianne shrugged. 'I said you'd never get there without me. Nor would you. You've as much sense as any fine lady. You need me.'

'That's nonsense. I'm quite capable of finding the way alone. I only agreed you could come because you wanted to.'

'You'd be lost in five minutes if I left you.'

'Leave me and see then!'

'I've a good mind to. I'd be safe and warm in Paris now, if it wasn't for you.'

'Then go back to Paris! I'm not stopping you.'

'Right then, I'll go. I was a fool to waste my time with an ungrateful aristocrat!'

She swung round and began to walk briskly back the way they had come, anger giving her a sudden renewed energy.

Isabelle stood watching her, feeling her own anger – born rather of sore feet and weariness than any real cause – dwindle as the figure of the other girl diminished and faded into what was left of the mist. But she fought any urge to call after her. If that was how she felt, better indeed to go on alone. She turned and went on her way, and tried not to recognise how much more weary she felt, how much more miserable.

After a time, she could bear the pain in her feet no longer and took off her shoes and walked on barefoot, though now the stones cut her feet. It was growing dark, and the cold was closing in again. She tried not to allow herself to be swallowed up by self pity, but she thought it was a long time since she had felt quite so miserable, physically at least.

A dog came running towards her along the road, barking with furious energy. She halted for a moment, and then continued, steadily, commanding the dog to be quiet. From somewhere in the haze behind it she heard a man's voice call, and then a large figure began to take shape: the dog's owner, coming to investigate what had put it on its guard. Isabelle was not afraid of dogs, but she feared men more than anything else in all the world.

She turned and walked at a brisk steady pace back the way she had come, until she was safely out of sight round a corner and the dog was no longer pursuing her. It had quietened now.

She stood where she was for some time, trembling. 'I must not let fear put me off,' she thought, 'I mustn't give up just because there's a man on the road.' But then she remembered that, since she was lost, it did not much matter which way she went. One direction was as likely to be as good as another – except that the most sensible course would be to ask someone which was the Amiens road. Someone, but not a man.

She had come a long way to this point, on a straight road that had seemed endless. It seemed longer still now, as she retraced her steps in search of the last side road she had passed. She had rejected it then as too small and narrow. Now, she decided she would go that way.

The road – more of a lane than a road – wound amongst

scrubby plantations of trees, where small streams trickled sluggishly by in the shadows, and then alongside open fields, grey and damp and cheerless. It was an undramatic landscape, not flat, but with only the gentlest of mounds and hollows. She passed through a small hamlet, but most of its population seemed to be absent or indoors. She stopped to ask a toothless, bent old woman the way to Amiens, and thought that the gesture that accompanied the mumbled reply indicated the path ahead of her, though she could not be quite sure. It renewed her confidence a little.

By now she was close to exhaustion, and hungry too. But Marianne had carried what remained of their food (which was little enough) and she had no intention of spending any money until she had found her child. She plodded on, through the hamlet and into a wood beyond, more dense and extensive than most of those she had seen so far. She tried not to wish that Marianne was still with her, though she could not help thinking that a little of the other girl's resourcefulness would be useful now, with night coming on. As for her companionship – no, she was better off without so irritating and irritable a companion; one, moreover, whose lack of morals (however useful) she could not condone.

Darkness grew and a wind blew up from nowhere, dispersing the last of the mist, swirling the dead leaves, bending the branches over her head. Then it began to rain, soon chilling her to the bone. There was no point in going on, for she could see almost nothing and she would soon be drenched to the skin. She turned off the road into the wood and huddled down in the partial shelter of a holly bush.

Through the din of the rain another sound reached her – a shout, repeated, and then the soft thud of running feet. She peered through the trees and could just make out a dark shape, whipped by wind and rain, coming along the road towards the wood; she could not tell whether it was male or female. She shrank back, hoping she would not be seen; and then heard the shout again, and this time knew who it was.

She stood up and moved a step or two closer to the road; and the shape turned its head just as the wind tore the cloud clear of the moon, and she saw Marianne's drenched figure lit by the cold light. She ran; and Marianne saw her and came to meet her and they hugged one another, laughing.

'Thought I might as well come with you as not,' Marianne said. 'Even if you are a fucking aristocrat.'

There was no malice in the profanity, and Isabelle simply laughed. 'Let's get out of the rain,' she said.

They huddled together under the trees until the rain had given way to a biting wind, and then they set out again along the road, and came at last to an abbey, its buildings gaunt and deserted in the moonlight, its already peeling walls covered with 'For Sale' signs flapping in the wind. There they found shelter in one of the vast barns, settling down to sleep on a heap of empty sacks with their arms about one another. Isabelle lay there forgetful of sore feet and aching body and exhaustion, happy because she was not alone any more.

# Chapter Eleven

The next day began clear and cold, with a bitter wind. Marianne and Isabelle shared the last of the previous day's black bread and then set out once more.

At the first village they came to they checked that they were on the right road. At the next village it was market day. The road was busy for some distance before they reached it with peasants in carts or on foot, leading cattle, driving geese, carrying great baskets of vegetables. Once in the village, it was easy enough for Marianne to mingle unnoticed with the crowd and steal a cheese here, fruit and bread there, from the goods laid out for sale on stalls or on the cobbled surface of the market place. Once they had enough to keep them going for a day or two, they left the village as quickly and unobtrusively as they had come. Isabelle thought with a stir of unease that she was already beginning to accept this life of criminality.

They went more slowly that day, because Isabelle's feet were so sore that she wondered at first if she would be able to walk at all. In the end, Marianne stole some stockings from a washing line and insisted that Isabelle put them on, and after that she felt a little more comfortable. Soon it began to rain again, heavily and purposefully.

'No point in sheltering,' Marianne said. 'I'm already wet through. Besides, if we wait for it to stop we'll never get where we're going. Wherever that is.'

'I don't think we'll ever get there,' Isabelle said gloomily.

'Oh, we will,' said Marianne. She seemed to have thrown off

every trace of her ill temper of yesterday and was relentlessly cheerful, sometimes irritatingly so. It was Isabelle who was in low spirits today. She felt as if she had been walking all her life, the hours passing in a long haze of discomfort, a journey without beginning or end. The purpose of it all seemed now like a dream, something unreal and pointless.

Late in the afternoon they reached a small town, grey and deserted in the rain. In the centre of its market place stood a tall tree branch, its withered leaves decorated with trailing ribbons of blue and white and red and festooned with garlands of paper flowers, their colours streaked and faded. 'A maypole,' said Isabelle. 'What's it doing still up in November?'

'It's a tree of liberty. They've put them up all over the place. Didn't you see the one on the edge of those woods we came past last night? They had one where the market was too, only that was a real tree, a poplar. People dance round them.' She did a little dance herself, there in the rain. Watching her, laughing, Isabelle's eyes were drawn past her, to the solid church on the far corner of the market place.

She felt a shiver run down her spine, and her hair lifted a little on her scalp . . . What chance was it that had led them out of their way to this place of all places? Could it be chance at all?

Marianne became aware that her companion had neither moved nor spoken for some considerable time, and ceased her dancing and came over to her. 'What's the matter with you?'

'This is the place, I'm sure it is!' Isabelle said, very softly.

Marianne studied her rapt face. 'Where she was born, your baby?'

Isabelle nodded. Then, her heart beating furiously, she led the way down a street on the far side of the market place and there, at its furthermost corner, found the house in the courtyard, weed-grown now, the gate rusting, but otherwise exactly as she remembered it. Was Madame Bertrand still there?

Marianne was about to knock on the door when Isabelle laid a hand on her arm. 'No, it's the curé we want. We must find him.'

'Maybe he's dead,' said Marianne warningly. 'Maybe he's emigrated, so he doesn't have to take the oath.' She had already explained that all priests would soon be required to swear allegiance to the new order of things.

'We shan't know if we don't ask.'

'I know. I want you to be prepared, that's all. Just in case. You think it'll all be easy now.'

Isabelle denied the accusation, while knowing that it was perfectly true. From the moment when she knew where she was, all her depression had fallen from her. She felt exhilarated and full of hope. 'Let's find him,' she said. 'Then we'll know.'

It seemed that her optimism was justified, for they found the presbytery easily enough, and were shown inside by an elderly housekeeper; and the man who came to them in the sparsely furnished parlour was the one Isabelle remembered, a little older and plumper but in every other respect the same.

Clearly he did not recognise her, though he welcomed them as warmly as a good priest should, faced with two poor women, drenched and tired and hungry. He would have insisted that his servant brought a change of clothes, while their own garments were dried, except that Isabelle told him that there was no time. 'Then sit here by the fire – let me make it up for you. Marie-Louise will bring something to warm you.' It was not until the woman had brought wine and cakes that Isabelle was able to explain her errand. She watched the curé's face as she spoke and saw recognition spread over it, and a sudden wariness that gave it a severe look, quite unlike the kindly concern of a moment before.

'But were you not to go into a convent?' he asked. 'In Paris, as I remember?'

A little awkwardly – for he was a representative of the Church after all – she explained her decision. At that he stood up, looking very grave.

'My child, I cannot tell you what you want to know.' She felt a chill settle about her heart. Marianne was right then! The child was dead. She had been a fool not to accept the likelihood of it ... Then she realised that was not what the curé was

109

saying; that his concern was of quite a different kind. 'You renounced all claim upon that infant at its birth. You went, freely, knowingly, to Paris, and there you took the most solemn vows before God. Now, today, I find you here in my house, those vows cast aside as if they were of no account, demanding to lay hands again upon that child. When you took those vows you died to the world. The child became motherless. She is nothing to you. I do not either confirm or deny that the child lives, but whether she does or no, do you think I would allow myself to take any step that would put a helpless infant into the care of a woman who so lightly discards her most solemn undertakings?'

Of all the things Isabelle had hoped and feared, she had never expected this. She sat there by the fire with a cake untasted in her hand, trembling, riven by a sudden shaft of guilt, staring at the accusing face of the priest. When he spoke again it was as if God spoke directly to her. 'Return now, before it is too late. Go back to your Order, do whatever penance is required of you for this terrible sin, resume your vows. It is your only hope. The other way, believe me, lies damnation!'

Still Isabelle sat there, not knowing what to say or do. She started when, suddenly, Marianne rose and laid a hand on her shoulder. For a moment she had forgotten that the other girl was with her.

'Let's go, Isabelle. We'll get nothing from this fanatic.' She spat on the floor at his feet and tugged at her friend's arm. 'Come on!'

Shocked, appalled, as much at her friend's behaviour as at the priest's words, in a kind of uncomprehending daze, Isabelle went with her, with the words of the curé echoing again in her ears as he called his warning after her, 'Do not further imperil your immortal soul! Go back to your duty!'

In the street she stood by the closed door of the presbytery, staring blankly at it. Then she heard Marianne say very gently, 'If he'd thought she was dead, he'd have said so. If I'd been him, I'd have said it anyway, even if it wasn't true. That would have made you go back, I guess. But I suppose he's honest, in his way.'

She was right; she must be right, Isabelle realised. And the shock of the meeting began to fade a little, driven back by a revival of her hopes, of her supreme purpose. God's will against hers – or was it? She did not know; she only knew that she had not come so far to turn round now, not while there was still hope.

'I always said I would go back, if she's better off left where she is,' she said stubbornly, as if the priest were still there to hear her defence.

'Then you'd be a fool,' said Marianne.

Isabelle ignored that. 'Let's try the house.'

Madame Bertrand was there still, but her wits had gone and she could tell them nothing, so the maid said; that explained the neglected appearance of the house. The maid was not Toinette, who, they were told, had married and gone to live in a village two leagues from the town, or so the woman thought. But she couldn't be sure, and she did not know anything about her predecessor's husband.

They found the village, but by then it was nearly dark and they knew they would only cause alarm, knocking on doors so late in the night. They tried to seek shelter at a farm, but the farmer threatened to set the dogs on them. In the end, they found a church porch and sat huddled together on the stone floor, snatching what sleep they could while the rain poured down outside.

The next day passed in an endless, fruitless trudge from house to house, farm to farm, in that and the surrounding villages. There was no sign of Toinette. One woman directed them (oh, let it be her!), to an Antoinette married to a blacksmith, but she was very young and prettier than Toinette had ever been, and knew nothing of what they were seeking. By nightfall they had to admit defeat.

'If no one can tell us what the curé did with her, then we have to work that out for ourselves,' Marianne said, as they sat exhausted by the edge of the road just out of sight of the last village they had scoured.

'I told you, he'd have found a good family to take her in.' In her weary state Isabelle was in no mood to listen to Marianne's endless and depressing speculation.

'I think we should try Amiens. That'll be where the nearest foundling hospital is.' She caught sight of Isabelle's expression and shrugged. 'If you don't want to, that's up to you. But we could at least try it. If they haven't got her they might know where we should look next.'

Isabelle was too tired for further argument. She knew that there was another cold and miserable night before them, without proper shelter, another day of walking and questioning, more of this endless searching. She felt the tears rise in her throat, and struggled to control herself. She must not give up, not when they had come so far!

They found another deserted abbey that night – there was no shortage of such accommodation in this area – and slept as best they could in another empty barn. The next morning Isabelle had no better suggestion to offer than Marianne's, so they set out for Amiens, silent and tired and depressed.

There were several hospitals in Amiens, and more than one took in abandoned or orphaned children. Most, however, only did so on a small scale and denied that they were likely to have taken in an infant in the position of Isabelle's child. They came at last to the Hôpital Général, where most of the foundlings in the area were provided for.

It was a grim-looking place. It must have looked grim enough when it was first built, with its high smooth walls and tiny windows and heavy doors. Now the paint was peeling, the windows grimy, the whole place looked ill cared for, and smelt strongly of sickness and dirt. They rang the bell at the gate and were eventually admitted by a harassed-looking nun, who took them to a small parlour.

'I will tell Reverend Mother you are here,' she said, and left them.

'I never thought they'd be nuns,' Isabelle whispered, feeling cold with apprehension. She could not expect any better reception here than she had received from the curé, particularly if by some chance he had told them her story.

'All these places are still run by nuns. There's no one else to do the work. At least they're some use. Not like the ones in your convent.' Marianne paused, studying Isabelle's face. 'They won't know anything about you,' she said reassuringly. 'Why should they, unless you're daft enough to tell them?'

Reverend Mother, when she came, was a large sensible-looking woman, a little breathless, as if she had hurried, as much as any nun ever hurried. Her manner was businesslike but friendly enough. 'How can I help you?'

Carefully, omitting any details that might give the woman cause to condemn her, Isabelle told her what they were seeking. 'You see, I think it is just possible that the curé brought her here.' At this moment, all her denials to Marianne had lost their force; all she wanted now was to be told that her search was at an end.

'It is very likely,' the nun agreed. 'Many of our infants are the fruits of immorality, poor little things.' Isabelle waited for her to make some move towards investigating her records, but she simply paused for a moment before saying, 'You must realise that if your child was committed to our care, then we will have incurred considerable expense in maintaining her during the past years. Further, we do not encourage mothers to retrieve their children. It only induces the feckless to abandon them, thinking that the decision can always be reversed at a later date.'

'I would never have abandoned her, if it hadn't been for my family,' Isabelle explained.

Another little pause; then: 'You realise, I suppose, that by the rules of this hospital we make a charge for the examination of our records? It discourages the frivolous and helps towards our funds, which are never adequate for the needs of our children.'

Isabelle felt cold. She had just over three livres. Would it be enough? 'How much, Mother?'

'Sixty livres to examine our records and a further sixty for each year that we have supported the child, to reimburse us for those costs.'

There was a silence. Isabelle knew that Marianne was as incapable of speech as she was, faced with this disastrous information. Had they come so far for this, to find that it would take nearly half her total annual pension to retrieve her child? What was more, even if she had been able to pay, the first sixty livres might simply have been wasted, if the child proved not to be here after all.

Not that it mattered much in any case, since even one payment of sixty livres was far beyond Isabelle's present means. She wondered briefly if she should say that she would come back when she had the money, but rejected that at once. She could not bear to think that she must go through all this again, without even being sure that she would succeed in the end. And the waiting would be unendurable.

She swallowed hard, trying to find the courage to speak. 'I have nothing like that.'

'Then how do you propose to maintain the child, when you have her?'

She could not tell the truth now. She was quite sure what reaction she would face were she to confess that she looked forward to a pension as a former nun. 'I have work in Paris.'

'Then go back and earn what you need.'

She forced down the tears. 'I could not. I have to live myself.' There was a small sound next to her and she glanced round and saw that Marianne was about to burst into one of her explosions of rage. She laid a hand swiftly on her friend's arm, urging her to silence. Then she rose to her feet, facing the nun. 'Please, Mother, I beg you – if I have to wait, the child may die—'

'She may already be dead. She may never have been brought here. Many such children are despatched straight to the foundling hospital in Paris. Have you tried there?'

Isabelle shook her head. 'I know she may not be here – but it is just possible she is, and I have come so far and hoped so

114

much. I want to make up for all the neglect of the past. I must find her!' She could feel the tears in her eyes and a great painful lump in her throat, so that her voice sounded hoarse and faint. She fought desperately against breaking down.

There was a further silence, and then the nun said, 'How much money have you with you?' Isabelle told her.

Again the nun was silent. She was biting her lip now, as if deep in thought. Then Isabelle heard her murmur something that sounded like, 'It would be most irregular ... We are in need of every possible source of funds ... I ought not to—' Then she looked up, suddenly brisk and matter of fact. 'Pay me what you have, and I will examine the records.'

Isabelle handed it over, wondering how she would feel were there to be nothing in the records, for this money was all she had in the world. But she did not hesitate for a moment. She was beyond prudence.

The nun left them for some time and at last came back with a large volume, which she laid on the table before her. She opened it and ran a finger down apparently endless columns, presumably listing the names of children taken in over the years: name after endless name of infants abandoned to the care of the institution, for all kinds of sordid or tragic reasons, many of whom, now, would certainly be dead. As she passed from one page to another she murmured this detail and that under her breath; until at last her finger came to a halt.

'The fourteenth of July 1788, you say? Yes, here – two names that day: Louis, Camille, both baptised here in Amiens. Both boys – but you say the child you seek was a girl?'

'Born on the fourteenth, yes.'

'Ah, *born* that day. Then perhaps she was brought to us at a later date.'

'The next day, perhaps.'

'Ah, here, the sixteenth, one Henriette, infant.'

Henriette, thought Isabelle – from Henri de La Pérouse? She shivered, and then realised that the child was more likely to have been named after Henry Milburn. If this was the child.

'Yes,' the nun went on, 'she was baptised by the curé of

Beaucourt la Bataille, on the fourteenth, so presumably that was the day of her birth . . . Bastard born to an English girl, one Isabella Milburn, father unknown. Left here by the curé with one hundred livres towards the child's keep . . . Ah, we did receive something then! . . . Put out to nurse at – what is this now? – Les Rosières. That would be with Jeanne Martin. But the woman died a year ago, at least. There is no record here as to what became of her charges. Arrangements will have been made, if there were any left alive. But I think I have bent the rules more than enough. All I can suggest now is that you ask in Les Rosières.'

Isabelle felt as if she had been raised up on a great rosy cloud, as if the world around her had burst into song, as if the sun had somehow lit up every corner of the dim and dingy room. Smiling, trembling, she rose to her feet. She even had to fight an urge to hug the Superior. She forced herself to some kind of calmness and said, 'Thank you, Mother. I can't thank you enough.'

There was a hint of a smile on the woman's large pale face. 'If you find her, my daughter, repay me by raising her in the fear and love of God. And may He go with you on your journey.'

Isabelle wondered, as she left the hospital, whether God could possibly go with her on this journey, when by setting out on it she had turned her back on Him. Just for a moment, she felt a tremor of fear, in case there might still be some punishment awaiting her, even in this world. Then she turned to smile at Marianne. 'Now, to find Les Rosières – and Henriette.'

The village, for all its pretty name, was, perhaps, the saddest-looking place Isabelle had ever seen, a cluster of damp and decaying cottages on low ground beside a sluggish river. The stink of poverty seemed to hang about it like a pall, as palpable as the stench of the middens that fronted the houses, amongst which ragged and barefoot children played. Suspicious eyes watched them as they picked their way from one house to another, enquiring for anyone who remembered Jeanne Martin. They found her husband at last, a desperate-looking man whose breath stank of cheap spirits. 'There was only one child left. I don't know the name. Someone took it. I don't recall who. They were bad times.'

A neighbour standing gossiping nearby had paused to listen to the exchange and now intervened. 'There were two children, madame. The curé found someone to care for them, but I don't know who. It wasn't anyone here. You'll find him in the next village, across the river.'

It seemed a miracle that the curé, inhabiting a decaying presbytery in a village little better than the one they had left, was warmly welcoming; and even more of a miracle that he remembered the children very well, and knew precisely what had become of them. 'Two little girls – one of them died that same winter, of a fever. It was the winter before last, a terrible winter. The other was sick too for a time, but she lived. Yes, she was called Henriette. You'll find her at the first house on the right, further along this road, with Suzanne Vaudricourt. Tell Suzanne I shall make it up to her for the money she loses, if you take the child.'

As they walked towards the house on this last stage of their journey, Isabelle felt Marianne's hand close about hers, sharing her apprehension and her hope.

The house was as bad as any they had seen today, its thatched roof green with moss and grass, its tiny windows unglazed. It was set in a wasteland of mud and puddles, where a few scrawny chickens scratched in the midden. A large boy with tousled hair emerged from the dilapidated outbuildings carrying a basket of eggs, and then halted to look at them with a mixture of puzzlement and suspicion.

'We're looking for Suzanne Vaudricourt,' Marianne said, and the lad mumbled something and gestured towards the battered door of the house.

There were chickens indoors too, in the single downstairs room, which was so dark that it was several minutes before Isabelle's eyes could make out anything in it, except for what lay in the area immediately round the meagre fire. The woman who bent over it was thin and weary-looking, and could have been any age from twenty to fifty; peasant women aged quickly, Isabelle knew. The only other person in the room was a child.

She sat on the earth floor in the furthest and darkest corner, leaning against the wall, silent and very still. Isabelle, her heart thumping so fast that she could hardly breathe, her eyes scarcely able to focus and yet held in that place, made out thin ankles and dirty bare feet, a dark dress, a white face and tangled hair of some indeterminate colour. The eyes gleamed in the shadow, but what colour they were Isabelle could not tell either. Part of her wanted to run at once and scoop the child up in her arms; another part hung back in fear – fear of what the child's reaction might be, fear, even, that this was not her child.

It was Marianne who found the words to explain their errand. And then any doubts they had left were dispelled. The woman turned her head. 'Henriette – come here.'

The child stood up and came slowly into what light there was: a thin frail-looking toddler, as dirty as everything else in this place, as starved-looking as the woman. Isabelle thought at first from her slowness and her silence that the child was frightened of the woman, but then she saw that there was no obvious fear on her small face. If anything, it was blank, empty of any expression.

'This is your mother, come to take you away.'

It was, after all, as simple as that. There was no struggle, no argument, not even the faintest sign of regret at parting from the woman who was, presumably, the only mother she could remember. The child came to Isabelle and stood at her side, very still, waiting to be told what to do next. Isabelle took her hand – it felt cold, and a little clammy beneath the dirt that crusted it – and then she and Marianne and Henriette left the house.

Outside Isabelle fell on her knees and gathered her daughter, dirty and smelly as she was, into her arms, as she had so longed to do, as she had dreamed of doing. But it was nothing like her dream. There was no response. Henriette simply stood there, neither accepting nor rejecting. Isabelle drew back and looked into her small face, its features made indistinct by the tears that filled her own eyes. Blue eyes looked back at her; not dark blue, as they had been at birth, but a clear summer blue, without brightness. The nose was straight, the chin rounded, the hair nearer fair than dark beneath the dirt. The face was too thin for that of a child so young.

Isabelle rose to her feet, fighting a desire to weep uncontrollably. She caught sight of Marianne's expression, and was struck by the pity in it. She looked quickly away.

'Well, let's go then,' she said, with enforced cheerfulness, and took the child's hand in hers. Henriette came with her meekly enough, as gravely docile as ever, questioning nothing.

'What now?' asked Marianne. And it was then, faced with the obvious question, which she had not thought to ask before, that Isabelle realised in full that this was not the end of a journey, but a beginning.

This reunion, so longed for, was not simply a matter of fulfilled love, or happiness; at present, in the circumstances, there was little enough of either of those things. No, what she faced now was a lifetime of responsibility. She had taken on, blindly and impulsively, the care of this small creature at her side, whose only tenuous link with her – and it *was* tenuous, she realised – was the fact that she had given birth to her, on a July day two years ago; and that care must last at least until the child was a woman. And it must begin now, had already begun when Isabelle took the child's hand in her own, though she had no money, no employment, no family or friends, except Marianne – and no safe shelter to which to take the child at the journey's end.

For a moment she felt a chill of apprehension, even a brief regret for the security of the convent, above all for the total absence there of any responsibility, any need to make decisions. She had thought it hard; now she saw it was easy, compared to this.

119

But she would face it, somehow. On the day she left Paris she had seen that she was free as she had never been before. As indeed she was, if freedom meant the ability to make what choices she wished. But choices, once made, brought consequences, and with them responsibilities. This little creature she had taken into her care tied her more surely even than the vows she had renounced; for Henriette had no one else now but the mother who knew nothing of mothering and had not even begun to learn.

'Back to Paris,' she said staunchly. 'Then I shall find work, and somewhere to live.' She did not look at Marianne as she spoke, for fear of seeing the scepticism in her eyes.

# Chapter Twelve

'What's the matter?' asked Marianne, looking round from the fire, where she had been warming a pot of coffee. 'You've got that look again.' It was not the first time in recent days that she had commented on Isabelle's expression of gloomy reflection.

'I told you. It's nothing.' She saw Marianne shrug impatiently, as if shaking off any sense of responsibility for her friend's moods, and she was sorry. But how could she begin to put into words what she feared, if only because to do so might somehow make it real, more than just a groundless fear? If it was groundless . . .

She looked down at the child sitting in the corner of the room where she spent most of the daylight hours. The passive blue eyes returned her gaze without interest.

Nearly a week now they had been in Paris, and there seemed to be no improvement. It was not as if she had not tried with all her might to bring about a change. 'She's not used to being loved,' Marianne had said, on the day they found her, when Isabelle had expressed concern at Henriette's unchildlike behaviour. In her experience (admittedly slight) children were noisy exuberant creatures who climbed trees and ran and jumped and skipped and sang, and drove the adults about them to exasperation with their boundless energy. She had been such a child, without being greatly loved by anyone except her grandmother. Perhaps that had been enough.

But Marianne's diagnosis had cheered her and she had set out to show her daughter how greatly her mother loved her.

Their first night together had seemed to offer confirmation of Marianne's verdict. In the hayloft where they had found shelter, Isabelle had taken the small unyielding body into her arms, where it had lain very still, as limp as a rag doll. Then, as drowsiness came over her, Henriette had moved closer, nestling against her mother's body with the instincts of any young animal. Eyes full of tears, Isabelle had held her close, her mouth on the dirty tangled hair. She had not slept much herself that night, for it had been enough simply to feel that small body relaxed against her own, taking its warmth from her.

The next morning, the responsive child of the night had disappeared without trace. It was the other child who seemed to be the real Henriette, the child who throughout the three days of their return journey to Paris had said nothing, neither murmured nor complained, nor shown any interest, however slight, in what went on around her. Sometimes Isabelle would ask, with great tenderness, 'Are you tired, my love?' – 'Are you hungry?' – 'Are you warm enough?' But each time the child would simply look back at her from those expressionless blue eyes, saying nothing, only nodding or shaking her head as the question demanded. She never admitted to any discomfort or need of any kind, though, given food, she would eat like one half starved.

Once in Paris, fed as well as their meagre resources permitted, kept warm and clean, given adequate sleep and fresh air, the child had quickly been transformed into a rosy little girl, with shining fair hair and, increasingly, a look of health and vigour. But the transformation was all on the surface. In her behaviour Henriette was no more like a normal child than she had been before. Isabelle put all her energy into trying to interest her in the usual activities of childhood. She took her for walks, drawing her attention to birds and animals and other children, she sang to her and played clapping games and danced, she told her stories and even gave her a pretty wooden

122

doll that Marianne brought home for her one day, without explanation as to its origins.

But there was no pleasure in singing to a child who simply sat and stared gravely back at her with what seemed to Isabelle all the cold disdain of someone watching the antics of an irredeemable eccentric. As for anything more active, the child would follow any instructions given to her, but always mechanically, with no sign of interest. When left to herself, she would simply sit on the floor in the corner, exactly as she had in the cottage, doing nothing. As she was doing now, today . . .

'Coffee!' said Marianne, carrying the pot to the table and pouring the hot liquid into the bowls. Automatically, Isabelle added milk to Henriette's bowl, from the supply Marianne had brought home yesterday. Marianne broke pieces from the coarse loaf and Isabelle took bread and coffee to the child in the corner. Then she sat and watched, her own breakfast untouched, as the child ate, no longer quite so much like a starving creature, but quickly, her eyes watchful, as if she feared that someone might try and take the food from her.

'It's her, isn't it?' Marianne asked suddenly. 'That's what's wrong?'

Isabelle turned her head, about to make the usual disclaimer. Instead, she heard herself saying through a painful lump in the throat, 'What if she's – well, not like other children? In the head, I mean. Slow.'

Marianne studied the child. There was some relief for Isabelle in realising from her thoughtful expression that she had clearly not considered such a possibility until now. On the other hand, she did not immediately dismiss the idea, and she was silent for some time. Eventually, she said, 'I don't think so. It's possible, I suppose.' She glanced questioningly at her friend. 'Would it make any difference? Would you wish you'd left her where she was?'

Isabelle could not answer that question; or perhaps she dared not. The worst part of it was that in an odd way she almost hoped that the child should prove to be slow in the head, not because she really wanted her to be, but because the alternative explanation was so much worse. If it was not Henriette's slow brain that made her unresponsive, then the fault was Isabelle's: quite simply she had failed as a mother. And if she could not be a good mother, able to win her child's love, then the reason for that seemed starkly obvious. She was not meant to be a mother, but a nun, free of human ties, giving all her love to God. By refusing to allow her to win her daughter's love, God was pointing out Isabelle's guilt and shame, demonstrating her worthlessness, indicating in the clearest possible way that only He could give her life any purpose. And if that were so then she did indeed wish she had left the child where she was, and remained in the convent. It would have been better for both of them.

But of course she could not now turn back. She had made her choice. Whether Henriette was retarded or normal, whether Isabelle was a good mother or a failure, she could not simply wish it all undone. She had to accept the consequences of the choice she had made, however disastrous they might prove to be.

'Come to think of it,' Marianne went on after further reflection, 'she knows what you mean when you tell her to do something. She's not stupid. No, I don't think she's wrong in the head. She's frightened—'

'Of me? How can she—?'

'She doesn't know any better. Maybe she's had good cause to be frightened, of everyone. Give her time.'

Isabelle felt, as if it were her own, the unknown suffering her child had endured in those two lost years. If only she could go back and start again; if only she had some idea what experiences haunted Henriette's memory and her imagination! She knew herself how crippling old cruelties could be. And now she was learning how very helpless she was to cure the damage that had been done.

There was silence for a time, then Marianne said, 'Come to the club tonight – why don't you?' She had urged Isabelle more than once to come with her to the Sunday evening club of which Thérèse was a leading member, but Isabelle was repelled by the prospect. She had no idea what form the club took. In England, clubs were for men, places for drinking and smoking and getting away from women, but this one, open to those who lived in their Section of the city, was evidently not like that, since it admitted both sexes on equal terms. But Isabelle shrank from any gathering which would take her among crowds, especially where there were men. Today, she merely said, 'I can't leave Henriette.'

'Bring her along. Everyone does. The place is full of babies. She's hardly going to make a disturbance, is she now?'

'I'd feel strange.' She began to clear the bowls from the table.

'I was going to ask Thérèse if she had any ideas about work. Better you ask her yourself.'

It was after all Isabelle herself who had brought that matter up.

It had been surprisingly easy to find accommodation in Paris, on the strength of Isabelle's future pension. They had found a baker, one Monsieur Picot, who had a room to let above his shop in a narrow street in one of the eastern sections of the city centre, near where Thérèse lived. Shown Isabelle's papers, he had readily agreed to wait for her rent until the first payment was made, in a month's time. That probably implied that the sixty-five livres a year he was asking for the single room on the fourth floor was rather too much, but Isabelle did not care. The room was quite large, with a bed just about big enough for three and a window looking out on the busy narrow street; it was also below rather than above the house's single privy, overused by all the lodgers, which made it more salubrious than the evil-smelling rooms on the upper floors. In fact, for much of the time it smelled agreeably of bread, and plump Monsieur Picot, who seemed fond of children in a slightly gushing manner, would sometimes slip a small loaf or a cake into Isabelle's basket, with a wink and a 'For the little one.' Marianne pointed out with what Isabelle thought was unwarranted cynicism that he only did so when his shop was full of customers, and he always spoke loudly enough to be heard by all of them.

Marianne, homeless herself since leaving her unregretted lover, had been happy to accept a share in the lodging, in return for what she could do to supply the needs of the household. Isabelle did not ask how she acquired the food or money she brought back to the house, for it was all there was between them and starvation, but she did not feel wholly at ease with her dependence on Marianne's dubious assistance. Besides, she suspected that even when her pension was paid, she would still need to have some other means of supplementing her income. After all, the pension was designed to support a single nun, not a mother and child.

Marianne had been cruelly blunt when Isabelle had expressed a wish to find work. 'What can you do?' she had asked.

It was not an easy question to answer. 'I can sew, a little.'

'There are seamstresses out of work all over Paris, the very best too.'

And she had never been more than mediocre. What else could she do? She could play the harpsichord, after a fashion; she knew a few songs, most of them probably outdated now; she danced quite well. But none of those accomplishments was much use in the present circumstances. She knew a good deal about horses too, but she had never heard of anyone employing a woman as a groom. Besides, she might be more knowledgeable on the subject than most women, particularly in France, but that did not mean she had much more to offer than the newest stable lad. 'Do you think anyone would want to learn English? I could teach that.'

'You need decent rooms for that. Anyone who could afford to pay would turn up their nose at this place.'

Then Marianne had suggested applying to Thérèse for advice, a suggestion that Isabelle had been glad to accept. Only she did not want to brave the club to do it.

'What do they do, at this club of yours?'

'Oh, it's like the Jacobins, but for poor working people . . .' She caught sight of Isabelle's expression and realised that another of her frequent explanations was required. Sometimes she showed a little impatience at Isabelle's ignorance of a world changed by revolution, but she was always ready to enlighten her. 'That's the club in the old Jacobin convent, in the rue St Honoré. The members are good patriots, but well to do, most of them anyway – deputies and such. They discuss the debates in the Assembly, and what laws there should be, that kind of thing. The men do anyway. Women are only allowed in the gallery. Our club admits men and women as equals. And you don't need money, like the Jacobins. You don't pay anything to join. Sometimes they read the papers. Or someone explains the laws, the new ones that are just made. And anyone who wants to change something can stand up and say what they think. Some of the best speakers go on afterwards to the Assembly or the Jacobins and tell them what we want.

'That's what's new, Isabelle – the best thing of all. Ordinary people, even women – we have a voice, even if we have no vote. We can make them listen, those smooth lawyers in the Assembly. We made the Revolution, and they know that if they don't pay heed to us we'll take up arms again, like we did last year, and make them do what we want.' Her eyes shone, and Isabelle began to catch just a little of her excitement and enthusiasm. Until now she had been too wrapped up in her concern for her child to care very much about anything else. In the convent she had longed to know what lay behind the sounds she heard from beyond the walls, but since then other things had become more important to her. 'Come tonight – just give it a try. Six o'clock in the old monastery, you know the one. Then you can see Thérèse for yourself. Better that than let me do it for you. And you might enjoy it, you never know.'

'I don't want to take Henriette anywhere like that, not while she's the way she is.'

'Maybe it would brighten her up. There'd be plenty going on.'

In the end it was that argument which persuaded Isabelle to accompany Marianne, after nightfall, to the hall of a disused monastery in an adjoining street. She carried Henriette in her arms, afraid that she might slip in the filth underfoot, or be crushed by the throng that was going in the same direction. 'So many of them!' Isabelle exclaimed softly. Across the street she glimpsed the Fournier family from the room next to their own, the young wife Claudine, heavily pregnant, and her husband Jean-Louis, a journeyman carpenter, with their two small boys. For Marianne had been right about the children: everywhere there were women carrying babies or holding toddlers by the hand, or older children helping the younger ones along. They chatted as they went, an animated noisy crowd, purposeful yet happy.

'There's one thing, it saves on candles and firewood, meeting like this,' said Marianne. Isabelle recognised a practical common sense about the necessities of life which she herself had scarcely begun to acquire. She had never before had to consider such things.

The hall, when they reached it, was already crammed with men and women of all shapes and sizes and ages, young men in jaunty 'carmagnoles', the short jackets named after the dance whose lively tune had hung in the air day after day since the Revolution had given it new words, older men unshaven, in clothes soiled from work; old women with their knitting, young women with babes at the breast or toddlers in their arms, sweethearts only a little distracted by one another from the seriousness of purpose that had brought them here. The air was thick with pipesmoke and chatter and the crying of children and the heavy odour of unwashed bodies. Above all, it was tingling with excitement and anticipation.

Marianne pushed a way through the crowd to the front, where Thérèse was engaged in vigorous conversation with two women and a large fair young man, who had a sheaf of papers under one arm. She embraced Marianne and then smiled at Isabelle. 'I can see you were never a nun at heart! Bless her, isn't she a little beauty?' She included them in the conversation without appearing to break off whatever it was she was saying to the others. 'Yes, I heard Etta Palm – magnificent! I'm going to speak about it ... Pierre, get them a place – we'll talk afterwards, Marianne . . . It's what every woman wants to hear, I can assure you . . .'

Isabelle was alarmed when the fair young man detached himself from the group about Thérèse and came over to them. He was massive, a square-shouldered young giant, with a red woollen bonnet pulled over his blond curls and a friendly grin that did not particularly reassure Isabelle, who found herself thinking, with a slight sense of unease of which she was ashamed, of Blackheugh's redcap. But then several other men in the hall wore red bonnets, symbol, so Marianne said with all the confidence of near ignorance, of freed Roman slaves. In the aftermath of tyranny and oppression . . .

'Follow me, mesdemoiselles!' said Pierre, and began to push his way through the milling throng, up to the back of the rows of benches. The way cleared as if by magic, though he did no more than walk steadily forward. Then he halted beside an apparently crowded bench. 'Move up there, friends. Let these lasses have a seat.' Isabelle and Marianne found themselves edged onto the end of the bench beside a fat market woman with elbows vigorously agitated by her knitting. Isabelle held Henriette firmly on her lap and wished she knew whether or not the child was frightened by all the noise and bustle. She showed no more emotion than usual.

'What I'd give for a pair of shoulders like that!' Marianne was saying to Pierre, with a knowing sideways look, unlike anything Isabelle had seen on her face before. 'Anyone got a claim on them just now?'

Isabelle felt hot with embarrassment. The young man grinned all the more. 'I'm a free man, mademoiselle – but then, aren't we all free now?' He seemed about to turn away, when evidently he had second thoughts and came back, pulling one of the small folded papers from under his arm. 'Today's *Ami du Peuple*, hot from the press.'

Marianne spread her hands, as if to indicate their emptiness. 'I can't pay.' Not, Isabelle noted, the more appropriate answer, 'I can't read.'

Pierre handed her the paper. 'Then owe me. I'll be round to

claim the debt.' He paused, then lowered his voice. 'You can always pay in kind.' They looked at one another in silence, smiling, as if neither of them wanted to be the first to look away. Eventually he gave a nod and then he left them.

Marianne watched him make his way smoothly back to the group now out of sight at the far end of the hall. 'Hm, tasty!'

'I thought you'd done with men,' said Isabelle, conscious that she sounded prim and disapproving; but then she felt a little disapproving. She could not understand anyone choosing to behave as Marianne had just done.

'I could always make an exception.' She glanced at Isabelle, her eyes bright. 'Well, a girl needs a man now and then, you must admit.'

Isabelle could admit nothing of the kind, but she decided she would be wasting her breath to say so. 'What's the paper?'

'Marat's paper – Jean-Paul Marat, friend of the people. The finest patriot there is. Want to have a look?'

Isabelle shook her head. 'Later,' she said.

It was clear that some attempt was about to be made to start the meeting, though people were still trying to find places. A thin girl even managed to squeeze on the end of their already full bench, and even then more people thronged the gangways, sitting on the steps, standing at the back.

At last someone unseen across the room banged a gavel and called for silence, though it was some time before the hubbub died down, to a murmur of coughing and infant whimpering.

Someone (still unseen) began to read a number of extracts from a newspaper, reporting debates in the National Assembly, mostly on law reform. They were not in themselves particularly interesting and at times they were scarcely audible, but the excitement with which they were received made up for any deficiency in their content. There were cheers, boos, stamping of feet, shouts of warning and encouragement, threats and laughter and a good deal of lively language. But for all their noisy exuberance, the members were clearly listening keenly to what was read, taking it in and considering it. Their noise was a response, not a random hubbub. Evidently there were heroes and villains among the deputies; certain names brought clamorous cheers, others an outburst of ferocious booing. Most of the names were unknown to Isabelle, though she had heard of the Marquis de Lafayette (scattered booing), a hero of the American war, who, like the Comte de Mirabeau (some modest cheers, one or two boos), had been spoken of in unfavourable terms by the Superior of her convent. Evidently he was now Commander in Chief of the National Guard. She noticed that neither of these aristocratic gentlemen was referred to by his title, but simply by his surname. Her cousins would have been appalled at such disrespect.

When the reading was finished there was some lively discussion, in which members of the audience participated as vigorously as the speaker at the front. Once a sudden disagreement between two men in the body of the hall threatened to flare up into violence, all those around them preparing to join in, shouting, waving fists, rolling up their sleeves. But the president hammered on the table until he had something approaching silence, and then he ordered them to make up their differences, and then the entire proceedings were interrupted while everyone in the hall embraced everyone else, in a mood of fervent reconciliation.

Isabelle was fascinated, her attention wholly absorbed by the points made, the objections raised, the fierce arguments brought forward for this view or that. Sometimes what was said seemed nonsense to her, at other times she heard ideas and proposals take shape that seemed to express things she had scarcely known she wanted or believed, which yet had been there, waiting for this moment. Then she would find herself cheering or shouting approval with the rest of them. Once or twice the fiery eloquence of a speaker moved her so much that she cheered with everyone else, only to realise that she did not agree with a word that had been said.

Thérèse proved to be a superb speaker, when her turn came. She recounted an incident observed at another club of which she was a member, where someone had dared to plead for women to have equal civil rights with men. She acted out the parts as she told the story: the audacious young man, speaking from the heart; the ridicule of the refined company about him, full of fine sentiments but unwilling to follow them to their logical conclusion; the female journalist, one Etta Palm, who had intervened with passion to defend him, routing all his opponents by her arguments. When Thérèse reached the end of her story, the women present cheered her to the roof. If any of the men had their doubts, then they were too entertained by Thérèse to voice them. Isabelle was so absorbed in considering the new and startling ideas the actress had raised that she missed most of what the next speaker said.

As for Henriette, she sat quiet and obedient on her mother's knee, making no move and no sound; except once, after someone, in passing, had mentioned the Queen. A great savage roar rose from the crowd, so full of hate that Isabelle had to hold Henriette very close to her, alarmed by the strained whiteness of her face. She did not know whether to be glad or concerned that for a moment the child actually clung to her, before reverting to her habitual impassiveness.

The meeting ended perhaps two hours later with a prolonged burst of singing, concluding with the *Ça Ira* and the *Carmagnole*, which brought the members stamping and clapping to their feet. If there had been room, Isabelle thought they would have danced too. The singing had scarcely finished before Marianne shouted in Isabelle's ear, 'Let's find Thérèse!' and began to push her way down to the floor of the hall. Isabelle suspected that it was not her wish to see Thérèse that gave such urgency to her tone, but she lifted Henriette in her arms and followed her friend. There was, she saw, no sign of Pierre among the group gathered at the far end of the hall. She sensed Marianne's disappointment as the actress came alone to meet them. 'You want work, Marianne says. Now, it may be I've just the thing for you. There's a group of women come to my place after these meetings, just to talk over some of the things we've heard, but more quietly. There are some feel a bit shy you see, talking among so many, with men there too.' Isabelle tried to imagine Thérèse feeling

---

shy and almost laughed at the idea. 'Well, some of them were saying last week they wished they could learn to read and write. There's a good many like Marianne you see – well, as you would expect, they've had no schooling, nor have their children. So I've been trying to think how we could set up a little school on Sunday nights, for the mothers and children – and any men who might be interested too. But I can't do it all alone. And now Marianne comes along saying you want work. You can read and write, can't you? Couldn't be better!'

'But I've a child.'

'Then bring her along. If she doesn't want to learn – she's a bit young, I can see that . . . But she can play. There'll be other little ones there. How about it? You'd not be paid much, but those who can afford it would give a couple of sous a time, and it may be the club would get a collection together.'

Isabelle felt a little overwhelmed by the suddenness of it all. Only a short time ago she had been living in solitude and silence. Now, suddenly, she was being drawn in to this close and noisy community, asked to play a part among these people she hardly knew. She felt excited and yet apprehensive. 'I'll think it over,' she said. But she knew as she spoke that she would agree to do what Thérèse suggested.

She left the hall in a daze, and scarcely noticed that they passed Pierre on the way, and that Marianne paused just long enough to exchange some remark with him.

The next morning after breakfast, Isabelle went to bring water from the well in the courtyard behind the house, leaving Henriette in her corner as usual. Marianne had gone out early, without saying where she was going; but there was nothing particularly unusual in that. Generally she would return later with some new item of food or clothing. Today Isabelle suspected that she might have some quite different motive, and she felt a little uneasy about it.

The dark and narrow stairs always seemed much steeper on the way up with a full bucket than they had on the way down.

Isabelle paused on each of the small landings to get her breath before going on again, and was thankful when at last she reached her own floor. She pushed open the door; and came to a halt there on the threshold.

Henriette was exactly where she had left her, sitting in her corner. But gone was the unnatural immobility of the frightened child. Instead, she had reached out for a pair of shoes that Marianne had left within her reach and was solemnly moving them about in front of her, talking softly and unintelligibly as she did so. She was so absorbed in what she was doing that she had not seen her mother come in.

She was playing, actually playing! Isabelle felt her heart leap and stepped into the room; and saw the flinching in the child's eyes as she looked up. Henriette pushed the shoes from her and sat very still, watching Isabelle as if she fully expected to be punished.

Isabelle put the bucket down and went to sit on the floor beside her, trying not to mind when the child shrank against the wall and then stiffened as her mother's arm went about her shoulder.

'Here, my love –' She pulled the shoes near. 'What are they – boats, is that it? Sailing on the river.' She had taken Henriette along the river bank more than once, and pointed out the boats to her. She moved one of the shoes along, rocking it up and down as if on a wave; then she made the other sail in the opposite direction, until 'Bang!' they collided. She made a noise of mock dismay and heard, unmistakably, the faintest ghost of a chuckle from the child at her side. She bent and drew her close and kissed her, and did not mind that there was still no response.

She got up, pushing the shoes back towards the child. 'There, you play with them, while Maman gets on with her work.' She began to wash the coffee bowls and tidy the room, singing softly as she did so. '*Frère Jacques; Frère Jacques . . .*' She peeped at the child now and then and saw how, after a moment or two of hesitation, she had begun to play with the shoes again, rather more timidly than before, and always

134

watchful for the still-dreaded rebuke from her mother, but gradually growing in confidence. In time, her murmurings began to run along, a soft refrain to Isabelle's singing.

# Chapter Thirteen

Isabelle was to look back on the six months that followed her return to Paris with Henriette as a time of increasing happiness. As the days went by the dark shadow of divine retribution receded to the furthest corner of her mind. She ceased to dread the possibility that she might have to face some sort of punishment in this world for her broken vows. As for the next world, she deliberately would not allow herself to think of it. It was this world and what it offered that absorbed her, and in particular her new friends, to whom the broken vows meant only freedom. She had never thought life could offer such richness, not since the carefree days of her childhood, when she had not known she was happy; but this, she thought sometimes, was even better than those days. Then she had been a healthy unthinking young animal; now she was a woman, with all the complexities that involved, and she had at last begun to learn about herself and the possibilities open to her.

The noisy life of Paris was no longer like a tidal wave threatening to drown her, stifling life and breath. It was as if, just as she was about to be overwhelmed, she had suddenly found she could swim, and now she was riding the waves, rejoicing in every swooping fall and rise, exhilarated by the power and energy that propelled and invigorated her. When she thought about it – which was not often – she found it odd to remember that when she had been part of a religious community she had felt isolated, deliberately cut off from those around her by the rules of the Order. There, all her thoughts had been concentrated on her own spiritual quest, so that they had seemed to be always turned inwards, yet with the aim of losing all selfhood, all individuality. Now she had no time to look inward, no wish to think of her inmost self. All she did, day by day, was done with and for those around her, and in that daily sharing she found happiness and fulfilment. She was no longer an outsider, listening in silence to distant music, but a singer, a part of the song.

She loved the Sunday evening gatherings at the club, with its sense of excitement, the fierce arguments and emotional singing, the sense of being at the heart of great changes. Even more she enjoyed the meetings afterwards in Thérèse's apartment, where she would often be asked to read some book or pamphlet to the other women. In this way, she came to know works she had scarcely heard of until now, or only as something forbidden to good Catholic girls, writings by Voltaire and Rousseau, for example. She found herself by turns entranced and excited and angered, so that often she would forget herself enough to join vigorously in the discussions that followed each reading. She was learning as much as the women who listened to her with such rapt attention – more perhaps, for she had not, as they had, lived through the events of the past two years. Her mind seemed to be awakening from a long sleep, along with her body and her emotions. It was as if at the end of her childhood she had been swallowed up by a nightmare from which now at last she was awakening to the full light of day, to develop with amazing speed into a mature woman with all her senses alive and growing and flowering.

Best of all, she loved the classes where she helped to teach, at first at Thérèse's apartment, later, when the numbers grew, in the empty monastery church beside the club meeting room. She enjoyed the company of the women and children and the handful of men who came to her for lessons. They were eager to learn, enthusiastic and grateful for her skills, which she had never particularly valued before, perhaps because, until she was tested, she had not known she had them. She loved to see how, as each person learned a little more, so he or she seemed to grow in dignity and self esteem. It was not just the teaching she enjoyed, but also the talk that went on before and after the lessons, the friends she made, the other young mothers who could give her advice or share their anxieties, the children who laughed at her stories and made her laugh with their own. Not once did anyone make her feel worthless or despised because she was the mother of a bastard, though at first she had braced herself for that reaction. Instead, she was simply accepted, and everyone made as much fuss of Henriette as they did of any of the other children.

She began to lose her fear of male company. She even grew to like one or two of the men who sat at the tables among the women and children and earnestly set themselves to read and write. Neither they nor any of the women treated her with the exaggerated formality of manners she remembered as the usual approach between men and women in the past. Some of them even dropped the ordinary 'madame' and 'monsieur', addressing one another merely as 'citizen' and 'citizeness'. Once she grew used to it, she liked their simplicity, their dignity and directness and honesty, and the uninhibited emotions that would suddenly erupt into anger or tears or a frenzy of fraternal embracing. She felt she knew exactly where she was, that they were hiding nothing, though she retained a certain wariness.

Then there was Henriette, who since the day when she had begun to play had steadily become more like the child she ought to have been. There were bad days, when she seemed to retreat into herself again, but the improvement was a progressive one nevertheless. When the classes began Isabelle took her with her, since she had no choice in the matter, but Henriette would not go and play with the other small children, refusing obstinately to move from her mother's knee. After being hampered for two lessons by that resistant weight on her lap, Isabelle put the child down on the flagged floor and commanded her to go and play. Instead of obeying with her usual meekness, Henriette behaved like any normal thwarted two-year-old and promptly had a tantrum, her theatrical screams rising effortlessly to the high vaulted ceiling of the

139

hall. The other mothers looked on in sympathy, some laughing, some making helpful suggestions, while Isabelle tried to calm the child, her distress vying with a sense of relief that Henriette was behaving so normally. In the end, she had to compromise and allow the child to play quietly on the floor beside the stool where she sat. Two weeks later Henriette went of her own accord to watch the other infants; and the next week began to join in their play. Before long she was indistinguishable at a distance from the rest of the chattering squabbling group.

By the end of January, after much walking from office to office and even more wearisome hours of waiting, Isabelle had her pension at last. She had thought it would be a simple matter: she would go to the municipal finance office, taking the papers given to her when she left the convent, and that would be that. It was not, of course. It took her some time to find the appropriate offices of the Paris Commune, a new body elected early in the Revolution to run the affairs of the capital. She went first to the Hôtel de Ville, where most of the Commune's business was carried on, but from there was directed to the Mairie, somewhere on the Île de la Cité, in the warren of ancient streets not far from the Cathedral of Nôtre Dame. Even after she had found the place, she lost her way in its passages two or three times before arriving at what would have been the right room – except that when at last her turn came to be interviewed, she was told she must have a certificate of residence before she could claim her pension. That vital document could only be obtained from the headquarters of her Section, the district in which she lived. But by that time of course, it was late in the day and every office in Paris was closing down for the night. Next day, she spent several hours waiting to be seen by an official at the Section headquarters (in yet another disused monastery), and by the afternoon was able to carry all the necessary papers to the Mairie – where they told her that the final arrangements for distributing pensions were not yet complete and she would have to come back in a week or so. She returned to the office three times before eventually receiving what was due to her for the first quarter of the year:

one hundred and twenty-five livres in assignats, the new revolutionary banknotes.

Conscious that she must make the money last, she was nevertheless able to buy new clothes for herself and Henriette, household necessities, food of her choice, though she found some shopkeepers suspicious of the new notes. One or two insisted on being paid in coins, others she suspected of putting up prices when confronted with the assignats. But at least she was no longer destitute, nor dependent any more on Marianne's dubious assistance. She was ready to offer generously to share what she could with her friend, but found that there was no need to make the offer: Marianne clearly assumed that she would do precisely that. Isabelle stifled a momentary resentment at being so taken for granted by reminding herself that she did after all owe Marianne a great deal.

In February, a group of women, impressed by Isabelle's success at teaching, asked her to consider taking a class of children each weekday morning. They would pay her one sou a week for each child, they said. They would be able to work much harder and earn more money during the absence of their children, and at the same time the children would receive a broader education than the Sunday classes could offer. They could be taught not only to read and write and do simple sums, but also to be good citizens of the new France, to understand the benefits the Revolution had brought, to recite the articles of the Declaration of the Rights of Man and to sing the revolutionary songs. Apprehensive at first, Isabelle at last agreed to what they asked. It was a new and exhilarating experience to feel that she could be useful, even successful, not merely as a mother (for she was beginning now to believe that was possible) but in other things as well.

So her days took shape, each morning given up to the growing number of children who came to the church to learn from her. Henriette soon joined the class, and spurred the slower children on by learning to form letters and recognise words more quickly than they did.

The afternoons were Henriette's entirely. Then mother and

child would go for walks or play games or Isabelle would read stories, or they would shop together, if the shopping had not been done early in the morning, while the markets were well stocked with food. Sometimes Marianne came with them. Once, at the end of May, the three of them went to the Assembly, to observe the deputies at work, on a day when they chanced to be debating capital punishment. As they took their places, a slight neatly dressed man in glasses was pleading with a kind of compelling monotony for the death penalty to be abolished altogether, as unworthy of a free nation. 'That's Robespierre,' Marianne murmured in Isabelle's ear. 'He's from Arras. A true patriot. They call him the Incorruptible. Mind, I think he's wrong this time.' So, it seemed, did the majority of the deputies, for in the end they voted to retain the death penalty for the most serious crimes. 'It'll be the same penalty for all, rich and poor,' Marianne said as they left. 'No more breaking on the wheel.'

It was only rarely that they had her company. More often she would be out on some errand of her own, or sleeping late after coming home in the early hours. Isabelle never asked her where she was going or who she had been with, but Marianne told her enough for it to be clear that her acquaintance with Pierre had grown considerably. He was, Isabelle learned, a printworker by trade, previously employed by the press that printed Marat's paper, but now single-handedly running his own small firm, at present meeting orders for others but any day now hoping to bring out a newspaper of his own. Reading Marat's paper, which combined a real passion for the injustices suffered by the poor with a demand for invariably violent remedies, Isabelle hoped that Pierre's ideas were of a more peaceable nature. She wondered too if there was any room for yet more newspapers, so many were there for sale in the new Paris. On the other hand, the demand for information and ideas seemed limitless. Pierre had one other significant quality. 'He's a conqueror of the Bastille,' Marianne said triumphantly one day. They, Isabelle had learned very early, were the élite among the revolutionaries, the men who had fought on that hot July day under the

142

shadow of the great state prison. It was odd to think for a moment that among those she had heard fighting so fiercely, so near yet so cut off from her, was that large, handsome young man.

, After the barrenness of her former life, it seemed suddenly full of a richness undreamed of. She had her beloved child, her friends, she was needed, even valued, as she had never been before. She found that she could do many things she had never imagined she would be able to do, that she had skills and resources she had never guessed at. She became confident in herself and her ability to control her own life. She shared the lives of her new friends in work and recreation, and out in the streets too, where festivals and celebrations followed one another almost as regularly as the old festivals of the Church, whenever anything gave the government an excuse to lay on a spectacle for the enjoyment and edification of the people.

On a grand scale in early April came the funeral of Mirabeau, the great orator of the National Assembly to whom, it was claimed, the Revolution owed a massive debt. Everywhere, there were signs of official mourning: black-bordered posters and journals, and reports in the papers of long debates in the Assembly, where it was decided that the dead man should be the first in France to be buried in the Panthéon, once the church of Sainte-Geneviève, which was to become the national burial place. Marianne observed all of it with a cynical eye. 'Pierre says he was in the pay of the Court,' she said.

In spite of that dismissal, they both stood with Henriette to watch the funeral procession pass. It was not the thought of the dead man, nor the respectful crowds, nor the grandeur of the draped coffin on its high carriage that impressed Isabelle, but the music, which was like nothing she had ever heard before; a new music, fit for a nation transformed by Revolution. The procession moved to a slow and solemn march, broken with aching pauses, like a sob of grief, before the sombre beat of drums resumed, and the harsh anguished brassy notes of the band. It seemed to reach into Isabelle's very soul, its desolate

143

sound bringing a lump to her throat and tears to her eyes. She felt at one with the silent crowd about her, sharing not only their sense of loss but the experiences that had brought them to this day, in which the dead man had played so large a part. She recognised that it was much more than just the mourning of a man, but also a time to remember all those who had died or suffered to build a new France; a solemn moment of recollection and rededication.

Two months later, silent crowds witnessed another slow parade, but this time there was no music and no magnificent spectacle, for this procession had not been planned or wanted.

It began on a hot June day. At breakfast time Isabelle promised Henriette that they would go to the Tuileries gardens, once school was over. It was one of the child's favourite places, even though it was some way from their lodging. There were trees to provide shelter from the intensity of the afternoon sun, and children at play, ponds with fish, dogs being walked, well-dressed ladies who made a fuss of Henriette and kindly old men who gave her sweets. Sometimes they would see the King or Queen walking there, with a protective escort of National Guards. Best of all, from Henriette's point of view, in a corner near the palace, fenced off from the public, was a small garden where the Dauphin, the six-year-old heir to the throne, could often be seen working with miniature tools, clearing weeds or planting seeds under the supervision of a devoted servant. Seeing how much Henriette longed for just such a garden of her own, Isabelle had spent precious money on plant pots and seeds and set them on the windowsill in their room, so that her daughter should have something of her own to grow. As yet, they had produced nothing more than unidentifiable seedlings, but Henriette cared for them tenderly and watched eagerly for any change.

But first there was school. On the way, Isabelle called at the room next door for Claudine's two older sons, who had recently become her pupils. Their mother came to the door to see them off, with her four-month-old baby in her arms, and Henriette told her eagerly about the afternoon's promised excursion. Claudine shook her head. 'I doubt you'll get in the Tuileries gardens today,' she said. Her eyes gleamed, in the manner of someone first with the latest news.

She was about to explain when Marianne, who had gone out earlier, came hurrying up the stairs towards them. 'I'm glad I've caught you,' she said to Isabelle, but she paused to get her breath and gave Claudine just time enough to get in first with, 'The King's gone – have you heard?'

Marianne nodded. 'From the Tuileries ... It's all shut up, guards everywhere. You can't get in the gardens. They've closed the city gates, though what use that is, God knows. The Assembly's meeting now – let's see if we can get in.'

'I can't – the children will be waiting.' For the first time ever, Isabelle regretted the morning's class. Claudine, freed of all but the baby, decided to go with Marianne. The two of them kept Isabelle company for the few yards that their paths lay in the same direction. 'Where's he gone?' Isabelle asked. 'Do they know?'

'Abroad, I reckon,' said Marianne. 'To the Austrians, if the Queen had anything to do with it. At least, that's what they're saying. Officially they've put it about he's been kidnapped. As if anyone could believe that! They do say Lafayette must have known.'

At the end of the morning, the mothers coming to collect their children from school were full of the news, and anxious to be home again as quickly as possible. 'Stay indoors,' Claudine advised Isabelle as they walked home together; she had little to report from the Assembly. 'You never know what's going to happen. They say he'll bring an Austrian army back with him. There'll be a massacre if he does.'

It was not until late in the afternoon that Marianne returned home. 'I was right. He left a declaration that everything he'd done had been forced on him, that he took it all back. Now we know the truth: every word he said in support of the Revolution was a lie.'

'What will happen now?'

'Who knows? Some people want the Duke of Orléans made

regent. I reckon we should have done with kings for good and all.'

Four days later Isabelle and Henriette and Marianne stood in oppressive heat and intermittent rain and watched, a part of the greatest crowd Isabelle had ever seen, as the King and his family, arrested at the frontier, were escorted back to Paris under heavy guard. The moment the royal carriage came into sight a silence fell, a strange eerie silence, cold and inflexible. Those who were nearest glimpsed the still figures in the coach, staring straight ahead, as if they knew they were in disgrace and dared not glance out of the window. In the streets no one moved, no man took off his hat, no child waved or asked questions. Only the carriage lumbered on, and the marching soldiers; the only sounds were the rhythmic tramp of their feet and the rumble of the carriage wheels. It was as if the whole city held its breath, the whole of France, knowing that after this nothing could ever be the same again.

'There has to be a republic now,' said Marianne as they turned to go home.

To Isabelle there was something shocking about such an idea, even after more than two years of a Revolution that had overthrown almost all that was familiar. True, the United States had set themselves up as a republic, spurning the British King, but then they had merely been a group of colonies, not, as France was, a proud and ancient kingdom. On the other hand, France, unmindful of the possible danger of contagion, had given every help to the rebellious colonies ... There was also a precedent nearer to home; except that when she spoke Isabelle felt as if she were referring to some scarcely known place at the other side of the world. 'England had a republic once, for a short time. About a hundred years ago.'

Marianne looked at her with interest. 'I never knew that. What did you do with your King?'

'My family fought for him. The other side didn't like Catholics.' Uneasily, she began to see parallels. She added, 'They cut off his head.'

146

'My God!'

'It didn't last, more than about fifteen years. They killed the regicides afterwards, those that were left.'

Marianne looked speculatively in the direction of the sombre procession, now out of sight. 'I guess they'll just keep this one under guard, until they decide what to do,' she said. 'They'll not have the stomach for – well!'

They made their way home through streets suddenly exploding again into noise. They passed a tobacconist's shop, where a man, supported on the shoulders of two of his friends, daubed mud over the word 'royal' above the door, to encouraging cheers from a group of passers by. At a street corner a little further on, effigies of the King and Queen were burning merrily, while a crowd danced round the impromptu bonfire singing the *Carmagnole*.

At the club the next day the angry voices continued. Like Marianne, everyone there was clear about one thing: King Louis had broken faith with the French people and must be deposed. 'We've had enough of kings!' someone shouted, and a great roar of agreement went up from every corner of the hall; from which another voice emerged, 'Put him on trial – that's what they should do!' It was that demand that was put into a letter to be sent to the Assembly.

'Not that they'll take any notice,' said Thérèse after the meeting. 'Look at them – laws to stop workers getting together to put wages up, no equal rights for slaves, closing all the public workshops, only rich men can vote for the new Assembly – and then they give out that the King's been abducted, when everyone knows he went of his own free will – or the Queen's free will anyway. No, the Assembly's bursting with self-interested scoundrels. You can count the good men on the fingers of one hand. Robespierre – now he's honest and cares for the people. And Pétion, his heart's in the right place too. As for the rest, they'd have let the King get all the way to Austria and march back to Paris with a foreign army, to murder all good patriots in their beds. No, for good men you have to look outside the Assembly – the Cordeliers Club, Danton,

Desmoulins and that lot; and Marat too.'

'Come on, Thérèse,' Marianne broke in, 'you know it's not men we need at all, it's women. We'd soon show them what to do.'

'That's right, so we should – and so we shall, if they go on like this.'

They laughed, arms about each other, reaching out to include Isabelle, who had been walking a short way behind, carrying Henriette.

The deputies of the National Assembly confirmed Thérèse's view of them by merely suspending the King and continuing to claim that he had been abducted. As for his declaration, that, they announced, had been dictated by his wicked advisers, whom he now repudiated. He himself was utterly without blame. 'They never think anyone will believe those lies!' Marianne exclaimed, when Isabelle read her the statement from a poster on a wall.

But if few believed it, many were prepared to behave as if they did, simply in the interests of public order and the progress of a Constitution which, if there were no King, would have to be rewritten. The greatest fear was that the Austrians, furious that the royal family was held in near captivity, would invade France to free them.

The Cordeliers Club, largest and most vociferous of the clubs open to ordinary men and women, took the lead in getting together a petition that a republic should be declared, and decreed that the signing should take place at the altar of the Patrie on the national parade ground of the Champ de Mars, on July 17th, the Sunday following the celebration of the fall of the Bastille.

The 14th of course was Henriette's third birthday, and the first that mother and daughter had been able to celebrate together. Isabelle wanted it to be as special as possible. There were no classes that day, as, even in these uncertain times, it was a public holiday, and they went to watch the ceremonies on the Champ de Mars. 'Nothing like last year,' Marianne said disparagingly. 'Now that was something. They thought they'd never get the ground ready in time, so everyone came, to wheel barrows to shift the earth for the stadium – rich and poor, whores and fine ladies, even nuns – not you I suppose?'

'Mine was an enclosed Order.' Isabelle spoke reluctantly, for she still felt uneasy whenever she thought of the convent.

'Oh well, you missed a great day. It was hard work and it rained, but everyone was singing and working together. National Guards came from every corner of France to swear the oath to the King and the nation. Afterwards there was dancing all over Paris, for days, and feasting. You'd have had to look hard to find anyone who'd admit to being against the Revolution then, even the King maybe. The trouble is there are too many of them think the Revolution's over, that there's no more to be done . . .'

'Will there be horses, Maman?'

Isabelle smiled down at Henriette's eager face. Three days before, on July 11th, she had taken her class of children, braving the mud and threatening rain, to watch the procession carrying Voltaire's ashes for reburial in the Panthéon. She had carefully explained the significance of the occasion to the older children, who had listened respectfully: the man whose remains were to be carried to the national burying place was one of France's greatest thinkers, whose writings had been an inspiration for the Revolution.

The younger children, of course, Henriette among them, had barely listened to what she said, being far more interested in the marching ranks of the National Guards and the curious classical costumes of other participants – 'Those men are wearing dresses!' one little boy had exclaimed. And then the strange antique-style carriage had come into sight, on which a waxwork model of Voltaire lay above the coffin, and it was at that moment that Isabelle had felt at last that Henriette was truly her daughter.

'Horses, Maman!' she had cried.

Certainly, they were beautiful horses, perhaps the most beautiful that Isabelle had ever seen; twelve perfectly matched greys pulling the massive carriage. She had held the child up so that she could see better, and she had watched herself, delighting in the way the animals moved, their power and grace, the great working muscles of their necks, the flowing manes and tails, the delicately stepping hooves, perfectly in time to the solemn music.

*Oh to be riding in the border hills, with the wind in her face and the hooves thudding on the rough grass and the curlews crying overhead, and the burns rushing in the valleys . . . !*

*Or to be lifting Henriette onto her old pony, for her first lesson, with Jamie encouraging the child, making her laugh, her grandmother watching from the door, proud of the child's fearlessness . . . Her great grandchild; would she ever see her? No, of course she would not.*

She was in Paris, with a group of children in her care, and the procession was nearing its end and she must get them back to their parents without allowing them to add too much to the mud that already clung to their clothes and shoes.

*What was Jamie doing now, and her grandmother? Once Jamie had taken her birds' nesting and she had fallen from a tree and come home with her clothes torn and filthy, a shoe lost, her knees grazed and covered with bruises. Her father had been furious. Her grandmother had hugged her. 'A true Tynedale lass, that's what you are, my hinny,' she had said. 'I'm proud of you.' . . . Would Henriette ever learn to climb trees and watch birds and animals?*

She had pushed aside the sudden sense of heartache and regret, as sharp as it had been unexpected. She must regret nothing, for she could never have returned to Blackheugh with Henriette; could almost certainly never have returned at all, under any circumstances. And she knew now that Isabelle Moulin could live a rich and fulfilling life here in Paris. There was no alternative that would not have involved leaving Henriette in the squalor of Les Rosières, or herself in the constriction of monastic vows.

There were horses on the Champ de Mars on July 14th too, but they were ordinary horses, ridden by National Guardsmen.

Fortunately, Henriette seemed content with that. But for all the fine weather and the crowds, it was nothing like the joyous day that Marianne had described so enthusiastically. How could it be, when many people, outraged at the King's betrayal, had refused to take part in a ceremony that included an oath of allegiance to that very man?

'On Sunday we'll go out to the Bois de Boulogne, if it's fine,' Isabelle promised Henriette as they walked home. 'That will be your birthday treat.' She liked Sundays in Paris, for then most of the population – so many of them country people by birth – went out to the suburbs and country areas on the fringes of the city, where they would eat at cafés in the open air or picnic under the trees in large parties with families and friends, playing music and singing and dancing.

'I'm going to sign the petition on Sunday,' Marianne said. There was a certain aggressive note in her voice, as if she were rebuking Isabelle for frivolity and at the same time expecting disapproval from her friend.

'We can do that on the way home,' Isabelle said.

'Oh! You are going to sign then?'

'Of course,' said Isabelle serenely. 'Remember, they're only asking for a new Assembly to work out a new constitution. That's the least anyone could ask for.'

'But it's a republic they want. Everyone knows that.'

'I know. I believe we should have one. That's why I'll sign. But I can sign without joining the march first.' She paused, then went on, 'You don't have to come with us, you know.'

Marianne grinned. 'Of course I'll come.'

It was one of the happiest days Isabelle could ever remember, that day in the woods with Henriette and Marianne. Marianne was in one of her liveliest moods, and Isabelle did not know that she had ever laughed so much. They dined extravagantly on a fine savoury tart and a salad and a special expensive cake that Isabelle had bought that morning. They watched the fashionable riders exercising along the woodland tracks. They danced and sang and played games, they walked for miles, they jumped the child high in the air until she was crimson with giggles. When at last the time came to make their way back to the city, they went with regret.

They were singing as they reached the Champ de Mars, in a holiday mood like many of those still moving in great numbers towards the high dais where the altar of the Patrie stood. There were family groups, couples, single people, young and old, some returning from a day in the country, others marching from their homes in more organised groups. Marianne's eyes scanned the crowd. 'There's Pierre!' she said suddenly. She must, Isabelle supposed, have arranged to meet him here, for he did not look in the least surprised as he edged his way towards them. But she could not resent his intrusion, when he began by ruffling Henriette's hair and telling her how grown up she looked, now she was three years old. Then he gave his attention to Marianne, and his smile vanished. 'The red flag's up on the Hôtel de Ville,' he said. 'I saw it as I came by.'

The words meant nothing to Isabelle, but she saw Marianne glance sharply at him and was struck by the gravity of her expression. 'What does that mean?' she asked.

'Martial law. Trouble.'

'Two men were killed this morning,' said Pierre. 'They were found hiding under the altar. To blow it up, it seems. It'll be just the excuse they were looking for, Lafayette and his lot.'

The sun suddenly seemed to lose its power, the cheerful clamour of the crowd dwindle to a menacing murmur.

'Let's get done here and be off home,' Pierre added, in a tone that frightened Isabelle. She wished people would move more quickly. They were still some way from the dais.

The petition, when they reached it, already consisted of several pages, thick with signatures, though many, like Marianne's, consisted of no more than a cross. Isabelle signed herself, and then turned to go, lifting Henriette up so that she should not stumble on the way down the steps.

Before them lay the great field, densely crowded still between the earth banks that enclosed the area. Above the banks could be seen the rural heights of Chaillot in one direction, beyond the river; in the other, the grand façade of the École Militaire. And just coming into view through one of the eastern openings in the earthworks was a troop of mounted soldiers in the blue, white and red uniform of the National Guard. Behind them marched infantry and an artillery troop.

The distant thud of hooves reached the crowd gathered on the dais, and the sharp bark of shouted commands. The troops halted. Someone, high on the earth bank near the soldiers, threw a stone; one or two others did the same. The next moment, horribly, a volley of shots rang out.

'Run!' shouted Pierre, and Isabelle ran, holding Henriette close to her, down the steps, across the field, pushing westward through the now panicking crowd. She heard more shots as she ran. Near her, someone fell, moaning; a woman screamed. She heard the noise of horses riding into the crowd behind her, coming her way. She ran as she had never run before, her breath shuddering in her aching lungs, on through the nearest opening, and then on and on, along unknown streets taken at random, until all sound of conflict was left behind.

When she halted at last to get her bearings she knew she had long ago lost Marianne and Pierre; but then they had no child to protect. She had to ask her way before she knew where she was, and even then it took her two hours to reach home. She thought she had never been so glad of anything as she was to set Henriette down on the floor and close the door of her room behind her.

She did not know how long it was before she heard steps on the stair outside. By then it was fully dark, and Henriette had long been asleep.

Marianne was safe, but she was not alone; Pierre was close behind her.

'I said he could stay here, just till it all dies down. They're arresting everyone they can get their hands on. He had word – they've raided his print shop.'

Isabelle looked at the one bed, thought how many there were already in this room, wondered how a man could possibly be accommodated; and repressed her fear at the thought. How could she turn him away, if his life might be in danger?

'He's welcome,' she said, but she did not mean it.

# Chapter Fourteen

What came to be called the massacre of the Champ de Mars ended Isabelle's time of unclouded happiness. As fear and repression gripped the city, clubs closed, newspapers ceased publication and patriots kept quietly within doors, or went overseas, or into hiding like Pierre, so a new bleakness came over Isabelle's life too.

She liked Pierre well enough, as far as she could like any man; or she had done when she only met him occasionally, in passing. Now he was a large and constant masculine presence in her room, scarcely ever leaving it, except for the shortest time, so that she could never be alone with Henriette, never be off her guard. His presence affected Marianne too, but in a different way. It seemed as if, with Pierre there, she forgot that there was anyone else in the room at all. Their liking for one another was only too obvious, and they had little restraint about showing it. They exchanged not only meaningful, teasing glances and words – that she could have endured – but caresses too, uninhibitedly at times. The fact that Henriette, used now to caresses herself, seemed not to notice anything, did not mollify Isabelle. It was no suitable example for an innocent child. She determined to say something about it to Marianne, but could not seem to find the right words or the right moment.

Once, she had been happy to go out for walks or to her classes, and as happy to come home again afterwards, to the place she had made her own. Now she spent as much time as she could away from the room, returning only when she must. At least it was summer time, and warm enough even for a young child to take her meals out of doors and go for long walks. But Isabelle dreaded the approach of winter, noting each hint of an autumn chill in the air with apprehension. There would not even be the club to provide a refuge on Sunday nights, for it had been forced to close, with so many of its members in prison or in hiding.

There was a further problem too. Pierre no longer had work to supply him with an income, so that he, like Marianne, became another drain on Isabelle's already overstretched pension. That August, the price of bread began to rise suddenly and steeply, and it grew progressively more difficult to feed so many on the money she had, particularly now one of them was a large and hungry man. There were no more little treats for Henriette, no new clothes for any of them, because there was nothing left over when they had all been fed. As things got worse, they scarcely ever ate meat or anything but bread. To make things more difficult, Isabelle's pension was often delayed, and their landlord, who had seemed generous enough in the early days, became surly and impatient. He tried to insist that now there was an extra lodger in the room he should be paid an additional ten livres a year in rent. Isabelle had refused indignantly, and had won her argument (rather to her own surprise), but after that there were no more little gifts of bread or cakes from Monsieur Picot, now that they really needed them.

That September, in a moment of temporary truce – unspoken, like the hostilities that had preceded it – Isabelle and Marianne went with Henriette to the Assembly, to observe one of its final sessions. Pierre, unable to go himself, was anxious to hear their reports of what happened. The King had given his assent to the Constitution – that flawed Constitution, which the doomed petitioners had hoped to see put aside – and elections had been held for deputies to the permanent Legislative Assembly that the Constitution decreed.

'Let's hope we get something better from the new lot,'

Marianne said, without much optimism, as they made their way home afterwards. 'The trouble is, all the best men have gone underground. That only leaves the dregs to stand in the elections, and they won't have our interests at heart.' Then she added, 'Pierre says they should lay down maximum prices for bread. He reckons the aristocrats are plotting to starve us into submission, so they can march an army in and bring back the old régime.'

Isabelle thought that Pierre was managing to achieve that end quite well himself, at least as far as the starving went, without any help from aristocrats, but she merely murmured some words of agreement, keeping her thoughts to herself. It was, she supposed, not his fault that he had no work. She wondered if the retirement of the present government – none of whose members was eligible for the new Assembly – would make it any safer for him to venture out in search of new work, but she did not put that thought into words either. When the time came, then she would speak to him, if he showed no sign of leaving. It could not come soon enough for her.

The baker's shop was empty as they passed its door. Their landlord stood in the doorway, looking out on the street, as if seeking some amusement in these idle times, now that all excitement was at an end. They told him where they had been. 'Well, that's the Revolution done with,' he said. 'Now we can all settle down and get on with our lives in peace.'

'He'll be the first I string up on a lamp post, if I get the chance,' Marianne muttered, as they mounted the stairs. 'Stingy bastard!' Then they reached the room, and she went to wrap herself around Pierre again. The truce was at an end.

Two nights later something suddenly jolted Isabelle out of a deep sleep. She had no idea what it was – some sound perhaps, in the street outside, or upstairs.

But it was not outside. It was in this very room and it came, she realised, from close by, from somewhere near the dead embers in the hearth, where Pierre lay at night rolled in her old convent blanket; and it was not one sound but a succession of

157

sounds unlike anything she had ever heard before. She lay still, tense, listening, puzzled, and then increasingly afraid. For the sounds were not after all unidentifiable. They held echoes in them of the horrible sounds that had haunted old nightmares, and memories she had thought long buried came flooding agonisingly back. There was a moment only before she knew what was happening, and then she lay, rigid, heart beating fast, hearing it all yet wishing she could shut out the sounds. They seemed to go on and on – like that other time – animal noises, grunts and gasps, rhythmic and incessant. Then Marianne was crying softly, ecstatically, 'Oh yes – yes – yes!' How could she find pleasure in it? How could she bear it? ... Please God Henriette did not wake and hear them and question her mother, or cry out in fear!

Then it ended, with a soft whispering laugh, and murmured words quickly broken off; and a little later Isabelle felt Marianne creep back into the bed beside her. Her warmth was tangible, and the smell of her. Isabelle felt sick. It was a very long time before she was able to sleep again.

Marianne was out of bed first the next morning, singing happily to herself as she made coffee. There was by then no sign of Pierre; he had gone down to buy bread, with money from Isabelle's purse, presumably. In a cold fury, she dressed Henriette and set her playing with some toy and when she was fully occupied, happy and absorbed, said abruptly, 'Marianne, I want him out.'

Marianne broke off her singing and stared at her. A little colour spread over her face. Did she guess then that Isabelle knew what had happened in the night? 'Out? But he's nowhere to go. You know how it is.'

'I know, oh yes, I know. When I said – well!' She could not put it all into words, though the anger and hurt boiled inside her, that Marianne should be capable of such a betrayal.

'You wouldn't just turn him out? You can't do that!' She came and slid her arm through Isabelle's. 'You know I love him, Isabelle. Don't tear us apart, please!' Her voice was coaxing, wheedling.

Isabelle pulled herself free. 'I don't care what you do, so long as you don't do it here.'

'Then I'm to go too, is that it?' Marianne's eyes were sparkling with anger, her mouth set in a thin line.

'You know that's not what I meant!'

'Oh, I can stay here then, so long as I live like a nun, like you!'

'I'll not have my child corrupted!'

'It's corrupt then, to love! First I knew of it!'

'Outside the bonds of marriage – like that – yes!'

'Who are you to preach chastity?'

'It wasn't my choice! How you could—!'

'You frigid bitch – I pity you! But you'll not dictate how I live, I tell you.'

'Then you can live somewhere else!'

'Fine! If that's what you want, you can have it!' And she turned, began swiftly to gather her belongings (and Pierre's) into a bundle and marched from the room. Isabelle turned her back, hearing what she did but saying nothing. Marianne had said too many harsh things for her to want to call her back. And there was last night – she could not condone that.

It was Henriette who cried for Marianne, when she realised she had gone for good, though she was soon comforted by a series of treats. Isabelle felt an astonishing sense of release, of liberation. Just the two of them, the whole room to themselves, nothing and no one to intrude after the higgledy-piggledy life of the past weeks – it felt wonderful. What was more, she actually had a little money to spare again, at last.

They met Marianne only once after that, one sunny Sunday in December as they walked through the arcades of the Palais Royal, the Duke of Orléans' pleasure gardens. She was alone, but looked happy enough; until she saw them. She halted then, her expression caught between surprise, awkwardness, coldness, warmth. Then Henriette ran to her and she bent and caught her up before looking at Isabelle, her colour fiery. 'You're well then, both of you?'

'Yes.' Isabelle's voice was cold, but even after what had

happened she could not repress a faint pleasure at this meeting, however awkward it might be.

'I'm living with Pierre now. He's found a good place, off the rue St Martin.' She paused, as if hoping for some response, and when none came, said brightly, 'Do you think there'll be a war?'

Isabelle's thoughts were very far removed from the current incessant debates as to whether or not war should be declared on the European powers that harboured the hordes of émigrés. 'Robespierre's against it,' Marianne added, when Isabelle still said nothing. 'I heard him at the Jacobins. Brissot and his lot are all for it though. But they say the Queen is too, and that's a bad sign.'

Isabelle tried to collect her thoughts, to frame some reply. It was the more difficult because she was not sure precisely what she felt about her former friend. All she knew was that the arguments of politics had nothing to do with those problematic feelings.

Then, before she could think of any response, Marianne lowered her voice and said carefully, 'I thought you wouldn't hear. We tried to be quiet.'

Quiet! The noise had been clamorous to Isabelle's ears.

'Oh, I know maybe it wasn't the place, but it happened. I'm sorry.'

Isabelle had never heard Marianne apologise before, for anything. For a moment she was almost ready to forgive her, completely and ungrudgingly. But then she remembered those horrible animal noises in the night, and the reviving warmth died in her. 'It's done,' was all she said. Then: 'I'm glad you've found somewhere.' Then she called to Henriette and they went on their way.

# Chapter Fifteen

There had been drums beating in the streets last night. In the early hours of August 10th the bells woke Isabelle, sounding the tocsin, the call to arms.

For weeks now the atmosphere in Paris had been tense and electric, like the air before a storm, full of menace and excitement. Now Isabelle knew that the storm was about to break.

War and hunger and internal enemies, and a government few trusted, made an explosive mixture. July and August had brought National Guards to Paris from every corner of France, among them men from Marseille, who had marched into the capital to the rhythm of a new song that had spread like fire in a high wind, until within days it was heard everywhere, on the lips of children and of volunteers marching to battle, in parlours and wine shops and theatres, in parks and gardens, in the revived clubs, in the Assembly itself. It seemed to put into words all the anger and fear and hope of a people faced on every side with defeat and betrayal at the hands of those they had trusted, from the stubbornly uncooperative King to aristocratic army officers whose hearts were with the enemy. Now, in the hot August dawn, Isabelle heard the song again, coming in snatches through the clang of the bells and the beat of the drums and the rush of hurrying feet. *Allons, enfants de la Patrie – le jour de gloire est arrivé!*

It was useless to try and sleep again, with that noise outside. She slid from the bed, gently, so as not to wake Henriette –

though if she had not woken by now, then probably nothing would disturb her. It was too hot to have kept the fire alight, and not economical to light it so early, though Isabelle would have liked some coffee – except that she was used to sugar in her coffee, and sugar had been both scarce and expensive since last summer's slave rising in the Caribbean colony of St Domingue. She was getting used to doing without, but it was not the same. It was just one of the many things she had been forced to give up, not simply because prices were so high, but also because her pension for this quarter, due at the end of June, had still not arrived, in spite of constant tramping from office to office. Today would be one day when she would abandon her search, she decided. Nor would there be any lessons. The people of Paris had other things on their minds and had done for weeks, as the sans culottes took power into their own hands. 'Sans culotte' was a new word, meaning 'without breeches', used to describe working men like Pierre and his friends, who wore trousers rather than the knee breeches usual to the well-to-do. They were the men who, with their wives, had poured onto the streets at every decisive moment of the Revolution, and would do so again, whenever the need arose. Now they were swelling the ranks of the National Guard, in spite of rules that excluded them, and taking over the Commune of Paris and the Section assemblies, replacing men who shrank from doing what had to be done. Isabelle almost felt sorry for the King, but then he had brought it on himself.

There was a rush of sound in the street outside, and she ran to look out on the red-bonneted heads of men and women pouring along it, home-made pikes in their hands, the harsh vigour of their singing rising into the hot air. It was the *Ça ira!* they sang, the old tune with new words, full of threats and blood. They were like a river, not separate individuals but one single mass, moving so fast and with such grim purpose that anyone in their way would have been trampled heedlessly underfoot. Isabelle knew that all over the city other such crowds were hurrying just like this one, steadily, inexorably, towards the well-guarded palace of the Tuileries.

Above the noise from outside, some other sound caught Isabelle's attention. All was quiet in the room, Henriette still sleeping peacefully. She moved away from the window and heard it again: a soft scratching at the door, too soft to be heard by anyone deeply asleep. She opened the door, and found Claudine standing there. Sensing her fear, Isabelle moved aside to let her neighbour in and then closed the door behind her. Claudine sat down on the stool near the empty hearth. Even in the dim light, Isabelle could see that she was trembling.

'Is he out with them then?'

Claudine nodded. She did not need to explain any further. Her husband Jean-Louis was a vociferous republican who had already taken part in several demonstrations this year. Isabelle had seen the pike he kept propped in a corner of their room, ready for the call to action when it came.

It was no time for scruples about economising. Isabelle lit the fire, as quietly as she could, and made coffee for them both. Claudine had a little sugar, which she brought across for them to share, so her neighbourliness was rewarded. They sat drinking quietly, and then Claudine said, 'It has to be done, but I'm so afraid.' Isabelle looked at her with grave sympathy, but said nothing. She felt that there would be a kind of presumption in anything she might say; after all, she had no man to fear for. 'It's not just this, today. If they fail, even if he escapes with his life ... with the Prussians so near ...' Claudine broke off, shuddering. The troops of the allied forces of Prussia and Austria had been massing on the eastern borders of France for nearly a month now. 'Even if they win today, if the enemy get through ... They said there'd be no mercy for ... "Exemplary and forever memorable vengeance," they said, if there was any threat to the King.'

'They won't get through,' said Isabelle soothingly. 'Our soldiers will drive them back.' Since their soldiers, many of them raw, ill-equipped, scarcely trained recruits, had already retreated some considerable distance and were led by officers of doubtful loyalty, even she did not believe what she said. She hoped she sounded more convinced than she actually was.

'They have right on their side,' she added.

Claudine continued as if she had not heard a word Isabelle had spoken. 'It's not just the enemy out there. In the prisons, all those priests and aristocrats ... They hate the Revolution. And there are so many of them. They have friends too, even in Paris. They've only to get together and break out – they'd take over in no time. Then the enemy could march in unchecked. When all the men have gone to war, we'll have no one left to protect us.'

Isabelle reached out and laid her hands over Claudine's. She had heard these fears before. The Paris prisons were full of priests and monks who had refused to take the oath required by the law, and had shown themselves in other ways opposed to the new order of things. It was widely believed that they were scheming with aristocrats still at large in the city to overthrow the elected government and restore the King to all his old powers. Isabelle had no means of judging how well founded these fears were, though she could imagine how deeply the Revolution must be hated by people like her cousins, or indeed the nuns of her former convent, people who might well risk anything for what they believed in. And at this time when the allied armies were advancing ever further into France, under leaders who had threatened Paris with savage reprisals if any further moves were made against the King ... Sometimes at night she would lie awake, haunted by terrors, fears for her own safety and that of her child. There would be no mercy for a renegade nun if the forces of the old order captured Paris, and she had heard what dreadful things invading armies could do. But she had no intention of allowing Claudine to see that her fears were shared.

'They'll win today,' she said confidently. 'We'll have a republic. And then we'll beat our enemies, every one of them. You just wait and see.'

'How can you be sure?'

'Because our soldiers are free men, fighting for liberty.'

It all sounded very fine, and after a time her repeated assurances began to have some effect on her troubled neigh-

# Candle in the Dark

bour. Later, when day broke, Claudine brought her three boys into Isabelle's room, and the children played together while the women kept one another company through that anxious time. All morning, the noise of musket and cannon fire reverberated over the city, but no news came.

It was well into the afternoon when they heard distant cheering. Isabelle smiled at the relieved face of her companion. 'You see! I said they'd win.'

'You don't know who's cheering. Maybe it's the Swiss Guards. Listen!' They were silent again, hearing the continuing gunfire.

Then, a little after, there came the noise of singing out in the street. They rushed to the window, and Isabelle found herself staring down at yet another mass of running men and women, and, directly below her eyes, something which at first she could not identify, something grey, partly covered with a sticky red matted substance . . .

Then she saw that it was a human head, stuck on the end of a pike. There were others too, and pieces of scarlet cloth like scraps of some kind of uniform, and the people were cheering as they moved along, and chanting the *Ça ira*. Isabelle shrank back. She was trembling now; but Claudine was smiling. 'You were right. They have won.' She took Isabelle in her arms, embracing her with relief; and then, sensing some resistance, paused suddenly, looking her in the face. 'What's wrong?'

Isabelle forced a smile. Marianne had told her how heads of slaughtered men had been carried on pikes on the other great days of the Revolution, but this was the first time she had seen it for herself. It was different somehow, to see that horrible featureless thing that had once been part of a man, not in her imagination, but there in all too tangible flesh before her eyes. Yet it was obvious that Claudine thought nothing of it.

And nor must she, for dreadful though it was, it meant that the day had ended in triumph. She told herself that there had been worse things done by her ancestors, in search of plunder on some border raid; she had sung about their deeds often enough . . .

165

*'They mangled him most cruelly,*
*The slightest wound might caused his deid,*
*And they hae gi'en him thirty-three.*
*They hackit off his hands and feet*
*An' left him lying on the lee . . .'*

Just songs they had been then, appealing to the bloodthirsty enthusiasm of a child who had never known real pain. But this, today, this was real; this was the boiling over of rage after too much pain, too much suffering. Where there had once been tyranny, redcap took up his place, dyeing his bonnet in human blood . . .

She reached out to hug Claudine. 'Nothing's wrong,' she said.

It was almost dark when they heard the clatter of feet on the stairs, and someone calling for Claudine. She rushed out onto the landing, Isabelle behind her, and there she halted, and gave a great anguished scream. 'Jean-Louis!' Three men were coming towards her, half carrying between them the slumped figure of her husband, his clothes drenched with blood.

There was a time of confusion, while the men got their wounded comrade into his room and his bed, and Claudine wept over the blood-soaked bandages that bound his chest, and asked endless frightened questions, and Isabelle tried to do what was needed to calm and distract the children. She heard one of the men say, 'The surgeon saw him at the Tuileries – he's done what he can. Time and care will do the rest.'

It was only when all was calm again, and it was clear that the wounded man was not as imminently in danger of dying as his wife had feared, that Isabelle was able to ask for news of what had happened that day.

'We got into the Tuileries this afternoon,' Jean-Louis's friend said. 'Went through the place from top to bottom. No looting, mind. Our work was honest work. They'll find every piece of the Austrian woman's jewellery accounted for, every one of her expensive gowns, all the knick-knacks they've hoarded over the years while the people starved. The King took refuge in the Assembly, with his friends there, like the coward he is. He left his Swiss Guards to do his work for him. They resisted every step of the way, curse them, turned their cannon on us and mowed us down. But we overcame them at last – though our losses were heavy, many killed and wounded. They paid with their blood for that. We cut them to pieces.

'There's one thing certain now: Louis the Sixteenth of France is Louis the Last. There'll be no more kings in France after this, ever again.'

Things happened so fast in the following days that it was hard to keep pace with them. The Assembly decreed the suspension of the monarchy, a compromise that made no one happy, and the royal family became virtual prisoners in the ancient tower known as the Temple, a few streets away from Isabelle's lodgings. Better than that, new elections were announced, in which all men, even the poorest, would be able to vote for a National Convention that was to draw up a new Constitution. It was obvious enough that it would be a republican Constitution, even if no member of the government actually said so. Then the popular leader of the Cordeliers Club, Georges Danton, was made Minister of Justice, scattering minor government posts to all his friends and inspiring the nation to energetic defence with speeches of a ferocious eloquence, which eclipsed all the pallid efforts of his fellow ministers. But from further afield the news was grim in the extreme. Lafayette had shown his true colours at last and gone over to the enemy; and then that same enemy marched easily into France, and took the fortified border town of Longwy. The vengeance of the émigrés was frighteningly near.

Jean-Louis was very ill for many weeks, and Isabelle found herself taking on full charge of the little boys, so that their home, now become a sick room, should be quiet. The question of her pension nagged at her, especially now that there were extra mouths to feed and Claudine had only the charity of neighbours to depend upon, but everywhere in Paris the old officials (or those who were left of them) were being thrown out and new men put in their places and it seemed wiser to wait until everything had settled down before resuming her quest for that elusive money. By then she might no longer have so many children on her hands. She told herself that as long as she had a few sous left in her purse, she would manage. She was relieved when, after a few days of uncertainty, classes began again, since that assured her of some sort of income; though two children, fatherless since August 10th, ceased to attend, and others had to be taught free of charge, since their parents, like Claudine and Jean-Louis, had no means to pay for lessons any more.

Sometimes in the afternoons Isabelle would play with Henriette and the boys or tell them stories, or read from one of the increasing number of works provided for good patriotic children, full of improving moral tales. At other times, she took them for walks, to Henriette's favourite haunts, along the river, to one of the many public gardens. There were new entertainments for inquisitive children, who were happily unaware of the tension that stretched beneath every part of their daily lives, tautening each day. It was as if vigorous activity kept fear at bay. In the squares of the city gangs of men were toppling every royal statue, to enthusiastic cheers from the watching crowds. Along the boulevards, small groups of volunteers marched on their way to the armies, their women carrying their muskets for them, with sausages or bread speared on the bayonets, all singing as they marched. There were executions too, Isabelle knew, three of them that August, by means of a new and reputedly painless machine, nicknamed the guillotine and erected in the Place du Carousel, near the Louvre. Those she carefully avoided. In France, as in England, children were often taken to watch executions, but she had no wish to inflict such sights on any child in her care, even as a warning of what might happen to those who had links with the enemy. She hoped that the new free France would become a nation of humanity and kindness, unstained by the cruelties of the past.

There was one day of excitement which they none of them appreciated, when the house was subjected to a search, from roof to cellars, by a detachment of men from the police committee of the Section. It was Danton who had ordered the searches, requiring the disarming and arrest of all suspects. Isabelle did her best to calm the children while the men banged and clattered their way through the house, apparently over-turning the contents of every room. She waited in terror for them to reach her, but found them more considerate than she had expected. They examined her papers, questioned her briefly, exchanged jovial, if largely unappreciated, remarks with the children, and then left her in peace. From the room above they led away a quiet elderly man of whom the other lodgers had seen little, who, it turned out, was a refractory priest. When they had gone, Monsieur Picot, who had stood by in silence while they went through his house, complained bitterly about the disruption.

Then one morning early in September Isabelle woke to an empty purse. Claudine had promised her that if ever she found herself without the means to feed the boys, then she would help her somehow. But when she went to collect the children from the room next door, Claudine greeted her with the assurance that today at least they could stay at home; Jean-Louis was very much better and wanted their company. Claudine was grateful for all Isabelle had done, and assured her that if ever a favour was needed in return, she had only to ask, but Isabelle could not quite bring herself to ask for money to feed herself and Henriette. Claudine needed all she had to feed her own family.

There was only a crust of hard black bread left from yesterday, which they ate for breakfast, inadequate though it was, and then she went with Henriette downstairs to the baker's shop. Henriette's presence was essential, for since Pierre and Marianne left Monsieur Picot had begun now and then to resume his small gifts to the child and even sometimes to allow her mother to buy bread at less than the full price.

But this morning, in spite of a shop full of customers avidly listening to every word, the baker was in a far from accom-modating mood. 'No, madame, I can't help you. I've been soft long enough. All you do is take advantage of my good heart.

May I remind you, you owe me six weeks' rent. If you want bread, then you pay for it. If you want a roof over your head, then you pay for that too. I'll give you one more week, and then I want to see that rent. Otherwise, you're out in the street, you and the child both.'

Isabelle understood then exactly how Marianne had felt when she had said she would like to string Monsieur Picot from the nearest lamp-post. As she felt at the moment, Isabelle would have helped her with great enthusiasm. She tried pleading, reminding him of her dependent child and the troubled times, but to no avail. 'It's not my fault this country's going to rack and ruin, woman,' he said harshly. 'It's not taking me with it, that's all.'

The only course open to her then was to go once more in search of her elusive pension. It was a Sunday, but Isabelle knew that both the city and sectional assemblies had been meeting in permanent session for more than a month now. It was just possible that even today she would find someone who was prepared to attend to the mundane matter of keeping a former nun from starvation.

When she and Henriette reached the Mairie, they found everything in chaos. Men were hurrying about, or standing talking urgently in corners, papers in their hands. There was a feeling of purposeless activity, as if no one knew precisely what he ought to be doing, but everyone wanted to appear to be usefully occupied. When at last she found a man standing idly in the corridor and asked for directions, he proved to be a bewildered visitor, like herself. Eventually, a harassed-looking clerk showed her into a dusty waiting room, with the assurance that someone would attend to her soon. In fact, she waited for more than an hour, before she was summoned to the familiar office where a man she had never seen before was seated at the desk, writing busily. After a moment or two, during which he gave no sign that he knew she was there, she said, 'I have come about my pension, monsieur.'

He looked up, frowning, pen poised to write the next word. 'Your pension, citizeness? This is no time to be talking of pensions. France is in mortal danger.'

'France won't be saved if her children are starving,' Isabelle retorted, though her heart beat faster with anxiety. She had an uneasy sense that this was a complete waste of time, that no one had any intention of helping her.

Apparently unmoved by her argument, the man wrote a little more, and then at last laid down his pen and examined her papers. He took some time over it, and at the end shook his head. 'These won't do.'

'What's wrong with them? There's never been any trouble before.'

'Times have changed, citizeness. You now need a certificate from your Section, guaranteeing your good citizenship. When you have one, come back and I will see what can be done.'

By now it was early afternoon and everyone seemed to be going home for dinner, or gathering in cafés and restaurants, but there was none of the usual dinner time calm. Careworn faces bent over tables, and men and women talked sombrely while they ate. There were anxious groups on street corners, reading papers and arguing, but Isabelle scarcely noticed them, so absorbed was she by her own worries. In her hurry she collided with someone. Drawing hastily back, apologising, she recognised one of Jean-Louis's friends. He said, in the manner of someone so full of dreadful news that he could only find relief by pouring it out to everyone he met, 'You've heard, citizeness? Verdun's fallen. The road's open to Paris.' She stared at him in silence, feeling the horror of what he said.

Then she stammered, 'I had not heard. That's bad,' and went on her way, her determination overlaid with a sense of panic. If the enemy was nearly at the gates, then it was the more urgent that her child should be fed, before the whole world fell apart, while there was anyone left to listen to her pleas.

At the Section headquarters it seemed as if few people had taken time off for dinner. The building was echoing with noise and bustling with activity. Men and women hurried in and out of its arched stone doorway, or stood talking in its dim vaulted passageways. Isabelle pushed her way in, looking for a familiar face; and almost at once found one, that of Sanson Benoît, a cobbler whose daughter was one of her pupils. He was talking to two or three others, but broke off for long enough to direct her to a doorway. 'That's where they're meeting,' he said.

Beyond the door was a large room, hazy with pipe smoke, noisy with vehement argument. To one side were the public benches, where men and women were crammed together, noisily observing their representatives ranged on the tiers of seats filling the room, smoking, listening, embracing, arguing. One had a sword propped at his side, another a gun laid across his lap. In a corner pikes were stacked, with a heap of other miscellaneous weapons on the floor nearby. Two men, facing one another across the ranks of their fellows, were deep in fierce discussion, if it could be called that when neither listened to the other. At a far table a man shouted in vain for silence and order, while at his elbow a clerk wrote busily in a large volume, presumably trying to make some record of the proceedings, though quite how he hoped to extract anything coherent from the chaotic scene Isabelle could not imagine. As she stepped into the room, a man near the door jumped up and tried to make himself heard too. Meanwhile, the rest of the company talked and argued amongst themselves. Isabelle stood gazing in bewilderment, trying to make out the subject of the meeting, if there was one, and wondering how she could hope to attract attention through the clamour.

Then one of the speakers – a large man in the obligatory red bonnet of the militant sans culotte – gave a violent exclamation, left his seat and marched towards the door. She realised that she had seen him before, at the now defunct club, she thought; though his expression as his eyes fell on her was not particularly friendly. She stepped forward, barring his path, and quickly explained why she was there.

She was relieved that he halted, giving her some at least of his attention. When she had finished, he said, 'Come with me.' She followed him, glad that at last someone seemed to be taking her seriously.

He led her to a nearby office, where he slouched on a chair

behind the table, watching her with eyes whose expression she did not much like; it had something combative in it, even angry, though why she could not imagine. He did not ask her to sit down, but she did not mind that; he was sitting so low on his chair that she would not have been able to face him comfortably if she had been seated, and she would have felt still more at a disadvantage.

He stuck his pipe in his mouth, sucking on it in silence for some time, and then, pushing it to one side, said, 'Citizeness Moulin, isn't it? Now, tell me again. What is it you want?'

A little reassured that he recognised her, she held Henriette's hand firmly in her own and repeated her account of her predicament.

When she had finished speaking there was a momentary silence, while he seemed to be considering what she had said. Then he took the pipe out of his mouth and asked, 'Have you taken the oath?'

She gazed blankly at him, not knowing what he meant. His expression – simply aggressive until now – turned to a sneer.

'Look at her, standing there in her snowy white Royalist apron, all aristocratic airs and graces! She's not for taking any oaths, this one-time nun. And we all know why not. Your heart's not patriotic, never was, never can be, no matter how jauntily you wear your cockade in your cap. Too much the fanatic still – that's it isn't it?'

Before she could say anything he had risen and come round the table to stand close to her: his breath stank and it was some time since he had shaved. She shrank a little, and at that he reached out and closed his hand on her arm and pulled her near. 'Fanatical and rotten, that's what you all are. Whoever thought we'd make good sans culottes of women like you, all fanaticism and pride on top and whores under? Miss your priests do you, all those sessions in the dark with your confessor? But no, you're in league with them still, plotting to get them out of jail and murder all good citizens in their beds.'

'That's a lie!' Her voice sounded faint and frightened, and she heard him laugh.

'Prove it then! Let me get between your legs.'

To her disbelieving horror he pushed one sweating grimy hand down the front of her bodice, groping roughly, while the other began to pull at her skirts. She seemed to see in his face those other horrible features, the candle going out, what came after – the terror that she had hoped was leaving her at last. She wanted to cry out, but could find no voice. She felt his face against hers, bristly and evil smelling, and his wet mouth. It was happening again, and she had thought it was over, in the past; and she could do nothing, nothing to stop it. She heard Henriette whimpering with fright.

'Citizen!'

She felt him push her away from him. She fell, gasping, shaking, sobbing in dry coughing sobs, against the back of a chair, bending over it for support. She was only dimly aware of angry voices in altercation behind her, too caught up in horror still to know what they said. Then a hand touched her arm, and with a little cry she recoiled, sharply. She found herself looking into the face of another man, quite a different man; a face both stern and dismayed.

'I beg your pardon, citizeness – in the name of the Section, I offer you the sincerest of apologies for the disgraceful conduct you have had to endure. You can be sure that Citizen Command will be called to account for it.'

He was apologising to her, actually apologising – and in a voice that was quiet and calm and gentle, as well as full of sober feeling. Her assurance and self confidence, so carefully built up, so suddenly and completely obliterated by that moment of utter terror, began slowly to return to her. Her assailant was standing by the table, looking on with only a shadow of his former bluster, while the second man – her rescuer, she supposed – began, slowly, to take shape before her.

'I don't understand,' she heard herself stammer. 'About the oath. What oath is that?'

'The oath of liberty and equality,' said Command. 'Ex nuns who won't take it don't get a pension.'

174

'The oath applies only to men,' the other man rebuked him. 'Female religious are exempt.'

'Not if they teach.' Commard took a step nearer to her again, and there was a note of triumph in his voice. 'And this one teaches. I know, because she taught my wife – fanatical bitch giving her fancy ideas, making her neglect her domestic duties!'

Isabelle had a dim recollection then of a thin anxious woman who had been her pupil for a short time, soon after she began to teach. She had shown signs of growing in confidence and self esteem; and then she had suddenly ceased to attend the classes, no one knew why. Now Isabelle understood.

The newcomer cast an angry look at Commard, who fell silent, though his expression was far from conciliatory. Then the younger man turned back to Isabelle. 'Come with me. We will discuss this further.'

'It's not your department, Duvernoy!' Commard retorted, but Isabelle felt the touch of a hand on her elbow and followed the second man from the room, with great relief. Henriette had stopped whimpering, though she was very silent and Isabelle could feel how she trembled. With a kindness that made her warm to him still further, Duvernoy looked down at the child. 'What is your name, little citizeness? Henriette? That's a pretty name.'

Isabelle felt her heart beat more quickly as he opened another office door and gestured to her to go through. He had rescued her, but she had no wish to be alone with any man, ever again; and especially not so soon. On the other hand, it seemed she had no choice but to trust him.

He pulled up a chair near one of the three desks with which the room was furnished, and gestured to her to sit down. 'Let me introduce myself; Jérôme Duvernoy, assessor to the Section Justice of the Peace. As Commard so rightly says, the issue of civic certificates does not concern me, but these are difficult times and it seems to me you are in need of assistance. I take it that's why you are here – for a certificate?'

She explained her problem to him and then he asked to see

her papers and questioned her at some length, writing her answers down as she gave them. She watched him as he wrote, interested in spite of herself.

He was about medium height and slightly built, with soft dark hair cut too short to tie back, in the style becoming popular with the more extreme revolutionaries. She thought he must be a little older than she was, in his mid twenties perhaps. His face was high cheekboned, with wide grey eyes, very clear and direct when he looked at her, set beneath straight black brows angled so that they gave him a permanent look of slight surprise. He was dressed with the casualness that went with the loose unpowdered hair, but somehow still managed to look elegant. Isabelle was just thinking that he had beautiful hands when he looked up again, and she felt herself colouring, as if caught in some misdemeanour.

If he noticed the blush, he gave no hint of it. 'Is there any citizen who could vouch for you? Other than Citizen Commard, of course.'

She remembered how she had met Benoît in the corridor and gave his name, hoping he was still in the building. Duvernoy, who evidently knew him, thought he might be found in the Assembly hall and went in search of him. When he had gone, Henriette said, 'Can we go home now, Maman? I'm so hungry!' She leaned wearily against her mother, and Isabelle was troubled by her pallor.

'Very soon, my love,' she said, and was relieved when Duvernoy returned, accompanied by Benoît. Better still, he was carrying a portion of bread, which he handed to Isabelle. 'I thought you might not have had time for dinner,' he said tactfully.

She tore off some bread for Henriette, looking up to offer Duvernoy the warm thanks he deserved; and her words froze unspoken on her lips. From far off across the city came the dull roar of cannon fire, and then the bells began to ring. Isabelle's heart thudded; she felt cold and afraid. Henriette gave a cry, and she lifted her into her arms, holding her close.

'The tocsin,' Duvernoy said quietly, as if conscious of her

fear, 'calling men to arms – but this time for the defence of France against her enemies. Danton has asked for sixty thousand volunteers.' Then he turned to Benoît and began to question him. The other man readily confirmed that Isabelle had brought great benefits to the children in her care, with no possible trace of fanaticism and every mark of a good citizen.

When he had gone, Duvernoy finished noting the details of his affirmation and then said, 'Do I understand that you are unwilling to take the oath?'

'Not at all,' she said. 'I hadn't heard of it, that's all.'

He nodded, and wrote again. 'It seems to me that if you are teaching the Section's children, you ought to take it. There must be no doubt of your patriotism.' He rose to his feet. 'You can swear now, before the Assembly. They are about to disperse, I think, so let us be quick.'

He led her back through the incessant clangorous ringing of the bells towards the noisy hall. She went with him, not thinking of anything much, except her relief that help was at hand and her search nearly at an end. This was just one last formality. She hoped that afterwards there would still be time for her to take her certificate to the Mairie before it closed.

Duvernoy went to the presiding official and spoke to him, and the man demanded silence; and, astonishingly, got it at last, after much banging on the table and shouting. Then someone handed Isabelle a paper. 'There, citizeness – say the words, good and loud.'

She cleared her throat and opened her mouth to read. And then she closed it again.

There were no solemn rituals to mark this moment, no prayers or music, nothing but the sound of bells and a smoky room full of noisy men sitting beneath a framed copy of the Declaration of the Rights of Man. Yet she was about to swear an oath with as little thought as she had sworn the other oaths in her life, because it was expected of her and circumstances had led her to this moment, not because she had freely and consciously chosen to do so. In the end, she had broken those other vows she had made. Was she to take this one lightly too, unthinkingly, only to break it when circumstances changed?

All over France, men and women had refused to speak these words, or others much like them, at risk not only to their pensions but also, in these uncertain times, to their freedom as well. The city prisons were full of refractory priests who had put faith before expediency and refused to swear, because the Pope had forbidden them to do so. Isabelle did not want to risk imprisonment, she did not want to put her pension at risk, or her duties as a teacher, still less did she want to turn her back on the means of sustenance for her child; but she did not want ever again to take an oath she could not keep.

She had glanced at the words once, not taking them in. Now she began to read them again, slowly and carefully, in silence. She sensed the impatience around her, heard one man say, 'Citizeness, read!', but she looked up and said, 'I want to understand what I swear to, citizen. An oath should not be taken lightly.'

That seemed to impress them, and they were silent, waiting. What, she wondered, would be their reaction if she were to decide against the oath? It would, at the least, not be a kindly one.

'*I swear to be faithful to the Nation and to maintain Liberty and Equality or to die defending them.*' . . . Could she promise something so vague and yet so complicated, so potentially demanding? She had chosen to make France her country, because the land of her birth had rejected her, and France had offered her a haven. In return, she accepted that she owed her adopted country a debt that she would gladly repay, if the need arose. The bells warned her that the moment of repayment might not be long delayed. If foreign armies should reach Paris, she knew she would do whatever lay in her power to defend not only her child but also her friends. That kind of faithfulness she could give instinctively. But to maintain Liberty . . . ? It was in the name of Liberty that she had left the convent; in the name of Liberty that she hesitated now, before taking this oath. Liberty meant the freedom to choose, but also the need to accept the consequences of her choices. And was it truly compatible with that other great principle, so lightly coupled with it, as if they belonged naturally together?

Equality implied an end to many of the things she had grown up with, an end to pride of birth, to great differences of wealth, to valuing a man or a woman by what he or she could buy. It meant that the freedom of the rich and the powerful must be controlled or even destroyed, so that the many might be liberated. It meant that Marianne and Claudine and Pierre were as important, as valuable in the eyes of the state – in her eyes – as her cousins in their château, as Louise the nun. It meant that the single mother of a bastard child was as worthy of care and nurture and acceptance as the most respectable married woman.

She saw, clearly, that Liberty alone and uncontrolled was like the lawlessness of the old border raiders, where the strong preyed on the weak and the poor could only suffer in silent misery. The two principles were after all necessary, one to another, Liberty tempered by Equality. The God she had rejected had taught it as surely as these men, many of whom had no belief in God and sought their inspiration from Rousseau or the classics or simply from their own instinctive sense of justice.

'I am ready,' she said at last. And then she held the paper high, and steadily, clearly, read the words into the attentive silence of the room. Afterwards, as directed, she signed her name.

She realised that Duvernoy was at her elbow again. 'Come to the office. I am authorised to give you a small sum to keep you going, until such time as you can claim your pension. You would be wiser to leave it for a few days, I think.' The remark puzzled her a little, but before she could ask him to explain it he said, 'I thought for a moment you were going to refuse the oath.'

'I had to be sure I could mean every word,' she told him as they made their way along the passage again. 'I broke one oath, you see. I don't want to break any more.'

'What made you do that? Leave the convent, I mean. I know

there were very few nuns who did, in spite of what was expected.'

'I left because of Henriette,' she said, and explained what had happened as simply and briefly as she could, and with little emotion. If he saw a wayward girl led astray by passion and then forced by her family to take the veil, then she said nothing that might suggest it had been otherwise.

'Then if you broke your vows for her sake, could you not take this oath for the same reason? Make no mistake, I don't suggest you ought to have done. I am interested, that is all.'

'I think,' said Isabelle slowly, conscious that his grey eyes were watching her with great intentness, 'that some things are even more important than making sure she has food to eat. I could not have broken my religious vows if I had thought what I was doing before I made them, if they had really been freely made. But then if I had known what I was doing I would never have allowed them to take her from me. Now, though, I am responsible for more than feeding her and clothing her. I have to give her a good example too. And that means that sometimes I may have to do things that would seem to be against her interests, just because they are right.' Even as she spoke she knew that she would have found it very hard to face the consequences, had she believed she must refuse to take today's oath.

She wondered if Duvernoy thought her lacking in maternal instincts, for he merely observed her thoughtfully, saying nothing. She was conscious that she wanted him to approve of her, though quite why she should feel like that she could not have said.

Back in his office he handed her ten livres, for which she had to sign a receipt. 'I know it's not much,' he said. 'I suggest I come and speak to your landlord. A word in the right place may convince him to be patient a little longer, in case your pension is further delayed. You can give him a little to keep him quiet.' Isabelle knew that the Sections' Justices of the Peace, and the assessors who were their deputies, were among the most highly respected of the Revolution's innovations, responsible as they were for settling, free of charge and without formalities, any minor disputes that might arise. Her own dispute with Monsieur Picot was not even in that category, of course, but she thought that if anything could mollify the baker, then an approach from so respected a figure as Duvernoy would do it. She thanked the young man warmly, full of relief and gratitude.

By now, the corridors were crammed with men making their way outside, pikes in their hands, guns on their shoulders. Duvernoy went ahead, making a path for her through the crowd to the door, where they came to a halt. Men jostled past them, pouring from the building to join the greater flood that hurried along the street. She saw Commard among them, his pipe still stuck in his mouth, his face dark and purposeful. He did not seem to notice her.

'They can't all be volunteers,' said Isabelle.

'No.' Duvernoy's expression was grim. 'Their purpose is internal security.' Seeing she did not understand him, he added, 'The prisons, and – justice –'

She frowned, still not understanding, but before she could ask anything further he said quickly, 'You should be at home, citizeness. This is no time for women and children to be about.' Then, taking advantage of a lull in the passing crowd he steered her into the street, skilfully moving against the flow of men, finding some doorway or alley in which they could wait when the throng became too great.

The streets near her lodgings were quieter, and there they could go more slowly. She wanted to ask him what he had implied by his cryptic explanation of the crowds they had seen, but she sensed that he would not tell her. They turned into her own street, and she noticed how carefully he ensured that she walked against the house walls, where it was less dirty underfoot, apparently heedless of the effects of the filthy gutters on his own neat polished shoes. 'I live there,' she said, indicating the high narrow building half way along the street. 'That's Monsieur Picot's shop.'

'Citizen Picot,' he corrected her gently. 'He is a man like any other, no more and no less.'

181

Her landlord would not like that, Isabelle thought; he was convinced of his own superiority, at least to those who rented his rooms. She smiled a little maliciously, and Duvernoy smiled back at her; and she felt as if her legs had lost all power, as if she could not breathe, as if something inside her had turned right over.

It was a moment or two before he said, 'I think you should be present when I speak to him.' He sounded as if he too found breathing difficult, Isabelle thought.

They went into the shop, where Duvernoy asked for a word in private, and the baker led them into a back room. Isabelle was greatly impressed by the conversation that followed, by the tact and fluency of the young man's manner, and the charm that acted with surprising swiftness and ease on the baker's truculence, even overcoming his obvious distaste for the 'citizen' with which nearly every sentence ended. In a short time he had agreed to accept three livres on account, and to wait for the rest until Isabelle had her pension. She handed over the money, and they left the shop.

Outside again, she said, 'I can't thank you enough.'

'It's my job, that's all,' Duvernoy said, though with a certain pride beneath the modest words. Then he added, 'Stay safe indoors for a day or two, citizeness. Leave your pension until the streets are calmer. But if you need any further help, send for me.'

'Thank you,' she said again. For a time he did not move, but simply stood looking at her. She found she could not take her eyes from him, while a turmoil like nothing she had ever felt before swept through her. Then he bent his head, in a gesture that had in it an echo of an old-style bow, and left her. She stood watching until he reached the corner, and felt her heart leap when he turned and raised his hand to her before he disappeared from sight.

That afternoon the massacres began in the prisons, and went on for five days and five nights.

# Chapter Sixteen

In her dream she was at Blackheugh, in the pele tower. She opened the door in the dark and the redcap was there, bent over the fire; but when he stood up she saw he was tall with blond curls, like Pierre. He pressed his bonnet down on his curls and the blood that drenched it dripped from his hair and ran in rivulets down his face, while he smiled and smiled.

She woke sharply, into the darkness of the early morning, and knew, as usual, that she had many sleepless hours before her, and that they would be worse than the nightmare. Even in the daytime, while she was occupied, distracted by Henriette or her pupils, the thoughts still troubled her endlessly, but at night, in these long dreadful hours before dawn, they were at their most intense and tormenting.

'*Internal security,*' he had said: '*Justice . . .*'

But what sort of internal security was it that allowed a frightened and angry population to run unchecked, killing as it willed? What sort of justice was it whose only gesture of legality, that she had heard, was to scratch together makeshift citizens' courts in the prison yards, to pass a hasty judgement on hundreds of defenceless prisoners? That there had been acquittals excused nothing, for more than a thousand had been slaughtered. And such slaughter . . . She had lain awake night after night haunted by what she had heard of men and women hacked to pieces, dying horribly. Friends visiting Jean-Louis had talked of their 'work'; she knew that many had the blood of that work on their hands, coming in tender concern for their sick colleague straight from the killing . . .

> They mangled him most cruelly,
> The slightest wound might caused his deid,
> And they hae gi'en him thirty-three . . .

*Justice . . . Jérôme Duvernoy, assessor to the Section Justice of the Peace.* How could a man working for justice speak so lightly of something so terrible, so totally opposed to any true meaning of the word justice? It was the barbarism of primitive hate, in this most civilised capital of a civilised country. She thought, looking back, that had she known what was about to happen she would never have taken that solemn oath before those men who all too soon would be butchering prisoners. It was not that kind of liberty she had sworn to uphold, nor the equality of men who had behaved more savagely than animals, and their women who applauded them. There had been killings in other years, ever since the Revolution began, but somehow they had been understandable, even excusable, the work of an oppressed people desperate for their freedom, enraged by hunger or betrayal, caught up in the heat of battle. But this – this was something quite different, quite new. It was bad enough that it had been done; worse, that it had been done by people she had thought of as her friends, and excused, before it had even begun, by a young man of such kindness and courtesy. For that he had known what was going to happen she was quite sure; as sure as that he had done nothing to stop it. When they had parted, she had wished that they might meet again, had even had some thought of seeking him out as he had hinted that she might. Now she hoped she would never see him again.

She longed for a friend in whom she could confide. If only Marianne had not gone! But Marianne had betrayed her, and besides she – or Pierre at least, if she was still with him – was as likely to have been involved in the killings as anyone. There was no one she knew who was untainted by them, no one to whom she could confide feelings that those around her would have seen as sentimental and unpatriotic. She continued to take her classes, but she avoided the company of others as much as she could. She went to claim her pension at last, and settled her rent, and did what shopping had to be done, but otherwise, once school was over, she stayed at home, fearful of what she might see in the streets, afraid of meeting people she knew and having to talk to them, with her mind full of the knowledge of what they had done, or might have done. Once she had felt a part of this crowded community of people, at one with them. Now a great gulf seemed to have come between them.

Two weeks had gone by and it was Sunday again. Wakeful in the dawn, Isabelle wondered whether she should take Henriette into the country today, or even to walk in the tree-covered grassy space of the Champs Elysées, full of doubtful characters after dark, but safe enough in daylight. The child was looking pale and weary for lack of exercise and fresh air. But she could not go anywhere without being haunted by the thought that those around her might have blood on their hands, and, besides, these days it was not always easy to leave the city, even for the simplest and most innocent of purposes. The enemy were very near the capital and the barrières were well guarded. She thought with regret of the happy Sunday spent in the country with Marianne and Henriette, and wished that time of innocence had not gone without trace ... Though that day too had ended in a massacre.

She lit the fire, while Henriette watered her rows of plants; they had flowered well this summer. She heard steps on the stairs, getting nearer – a visitor for Jean-Louis perhaps, for they came to a halt on the landing outside. She waited for the distant knock, and was startled when it was not distant at all, but close at hand, on her own door. She straightened, standing very still by the hearth, afraid, though she did not know why. It was not until it came again that she went to open the door.

She had forgotten the effect he had on her. She had thought of him as a guilty man, without a heart. Now she found herself confronted by those grey eyes and she felt the world stand still around her, everything that was essential gathering together in this one place, where she stood and he stood, two people held in silence, enclosed, alone.

Then he cleared his throat. 'I was concerned, in case you have still not had your pension.' She said nothing. His voice was husky, youthful, with something in it that seemed almost caressing. She had heard the words, but she was conscious only of the voice. 'I hope there has been no more trouble with Citizen Picot,' he added.

'No, thank you.' She supposed that was the right thing to say. What now? One did not invite strange men into one's room, not if one was wise; and she had every reason to want to be wise. He was a stranger, even if he made her feel as no stranger had ever done, or anyone else for that matter. But to close the door and let him walk away . . .?

'It's a beautiful morning. May I invite you and the little one both to take a walk with me?'

How it was she did not know, because she had no recollection of having agreed to what he said, or even of having wanted to do so, but she found herself walking down the stairs in front of him, Henriette jumping the steps beside her. She was acutely conscious of his nearness, seeing, though her eyes were not on him, the soft hair under the broad-brimmed hat, the loose long dark coat, the breeches clinging close to his legs. Then she was out in the street and the hazy smoke-sweet September sunlight, walking along she had no idea where, with the young man at her side and Henriette holding a hand of each and skipping happily along between them, as if she did this every day and Duvernoy was an old friend.

Only then did Isabelle remember that she had not wanted to see him again, and why. The day seemed to darken, she felt a chill little wind insinuating itself under her shawl, through the coarse cloth of her bodice. Her steps faltered and slowed, until at last she came to a complete halt. Duvernoy turned to look at her, smiling; but the smile faded when he saw the look on her face.

'You said it was justice,' she said.

'I don't understand.'

'The killings, in the prisons.'

'Oh! That!' His expression gave nothing away. He glanced round at the throng of passers-by, shoving against them in this narrow street. 'Not here – let's find somewhere quieter.'

They went to the Luxembourg gardens, which a few months before had been like some relic from the past, unchanged since the days of the old régime, thronged with priests and aristocrats – military men and civilians – and assorted foreigners, dressed as if the old world was with them still, deep in low-voiced talk; conspiratorial talk, everyone had said. For that reason Isabelle had avoided it, fearful of meeting some acquaintance from her schooldays. Now it was virtually empty, a sunny and tranquil place. If royalists and priests still conspired in Paris, they did so out of sight.

They halted by a pond, where Henriette crouched on the edge, looking for fish, with Duvernoy's hand firmly holding the edge of her skirts. Already Isabelle's indignation and disgust were slipping away and it was hard to recall them; but she made herself do it and said reproachfully, 'Why did the National Guard not stop it?'

'We are at war, citizeness. The people were afraid of a prison plot. They would not march to defend France while they believed their families were unprotected.'

She digested that in silence for a moment – it was after all something she already knew – then she said, 'Do you believe there was a plot?'

'I believe that it is what people feared.'

'But to allow it, and do nothing—'

'We have had no government in France for months now. Brissot and his friends got us into the war, but once in they could only make fine speeches. They are so afraid of any curb on liberty that they put that before the very safety of France. What power there is lies in the hands of the Commune and the Sections, and they are controlled by the people. And it was the people who wanted justice done in the prisons—'

'How can you use that word, about what happened?' She was finding indignation again, forgetting – almost – the man who was speaking to her, in dismay at what he said.

'In the state of Paris as it was, no one could have stopped it. Even the Brissotins did not try. The only course was to control it as best one could. And trust that the new government will prove more effective, when it is fully established.'

She knew that the newly elected National Convention had been meeting now for more than a week. 'Is it going to be more effective?'

He shrugged, in a way that reminded her faintly of Marianne. 'It remains to be seen. There is one thing – since the massacres men have poured into the armies. Their minds are at rest, so they feel able to go.' He must have seen that he had not convinced her in the least, for he went on, 'No, it wasn't justice, it was anarchy: I know that. But it could not be avoided, in the state of things. We need a government that will hear the people and work with them before they will listen to what their representatives say. Well, Paris has its own men in the Convention now, Danton, Robespierre, Desmoulins, Marat. It may be that things will change, if they can get a word in through the empty eloquence of Brissot and his friends.' He paused again, then added, 'Your feelings do you credit. But don't let your heart rule your head. The Revolution is not over yet. I hope there is no worse to come, but we cannot be sure.'

That another possibility stared them starkly in the face Isabelle knew very well. 'Do you think the Prussians will reach Paris?'

The surprised brows had drawn together in a frown, their angle accentuating the severity of his expression. 'Our troops have fallen back on Châlons. It is not so many days from Paris. But with so many new troops—'

'Untrained—'

He smiled suddenly, his eyes sparkling. 'But with the fire of liberty in their bellies. Is that not worth something, against the mercenaries of a despot?' He looked around him suddenly, his gaze settling on Henriette, as if he found comfort in her untroubled play. 'Trust in the Being who made us, and who is our strength in times of trouble.'

She was astonished to hear so confirmed a revolutionary talking in such unequivocally religious terms, and wondered how his 'Being' compared with the Catholic God who might yet punish her for her apostasy. Very little, she thought, for she suspected Duvernoy was a Deist, one of those near-atheists condemned by every priest she had ever come across, for rejecting the divinity of Jesus and the reality of sin. He bent then to talk to the child, and Isabelle saw how easily she responded to him, with a fearless simplicity. It was a mark in his favour, for Henriette did not always take readily to new people. His manner was gentle yet unpatronising and it moved Isabelle greatly. There was something about tenderness in men that was very attractive, she thought.

He had returned his attention to her. 'Before you went into the convent, where did you come from? You're not a Parisian I think.'

The question was so unexpected that she coloured. 'No.' What could she say? She had no intention of admitting to being English. Most certainly she did not know him well enough to trust him with such information. Besides, she was no longer English, but French. 'I was at school in Paris,' she said. 'I was in Brittany too for a time.'

She was relieved that he seemed to accept that and quickly turned the enquiry on him before he could ask anything more. 'You are a Parisian, I suppose?'

'No – I come from Burgundy.'

'What brought you to Paris?'

'The usual – work. No, to be more truthful, it was that other old story: I could not agree with my parents. They had my career mapped out for me – a training in law, working my way up in the office of the notary of our village, marriage to his daughter, a pretty but frivolous girl, unbearably affected. It was my father's dream, and my mother's because it was his, but not mine. We had never got on well. Besides, I had no love for country life. In the end I could only escape the fate they had in mind by coming to Paris. After all, in the old days the father ruled the family.'

189

'Then you never see them now?'

'No, never. Nor do I wish to. They have my older brother. He was always the dutiful one. He never asked any more of life than to stay at home and tend the vines – my father has vineyards, you see. They will have forgotten I exist, I imagine.'

Isabelle smiled suddenly, moved to reminiscence. 'I had a dutiful older brother too. I hated him.'

He stood smiling back at her, and his eyes on her face had a look in them that turned her bones to water. 'I've never met anyone like you,' he said suddenly, his voice very soft. 'I don't know what it is. You are very simple and direct, or you seem to be, not like most young women. Yet there's something remote about you, out of reach. That's why I came back. I couldn't get you out of my mind, not since we met.' He paused, then said, with an awkwardness, a hint of shyness he had not shown until now, 'Henriette's father – do you see him?'

She shook her head with vehemence, sick in the pit of her stomach, all the magic of the moment gone. 'No. I hope I never do, ever again. He doesn't even know she exists. And don't ask me about him, please!'

'I'm sorry, I did not ...' He looked concerned. 'Is there – forgive me if I am intruding – is there anyone else, any man?'

She looked at him, her feelings in turmoil. To deny it would be to concede the possibility that he might be admitted to a special place in her life. But she had never for a moment considered that there was such a place, for any man, ever. She had no sense of any vacancy waiting to be filled, or a need unmet. That she might ever be tempted to break her vow of chastity – as she had broken those of poverty and obedience – was unthinkable, not so much from principle as because she could not bear even to imagine it happening. Yet to admit any man to a special place in her life implied that possibility.

In the end, she avoided the question. 'I am not in need of a man,' she said, and then immediately wondered if she would regret that answer. She did not want to admit him to any special place, but she wanted to go on seeing him, somehow.

190

'Were I to offer you my friendship then, that and nothing more – would you accept that?'

She smiled, as if he had solved all her difficulties. 'Yes,' she said, and immediately wondered if it was possible for a man to be simply the friend of a woman. She could not somehow imagine it. Jérôme Duvernoy had been kind in a moment of trouble, had shown concern for her, much as Marianne had done; but what she felt in his presence was nothing like the easy companionship of her relationship with Marianne, before that had been broken. She had an uncomfortable feeling that in saying 'yes' to his friendship she was in fact admitting him to something quite different, even to the possibility of the very thing she had rejected.

They walked on, and in the gateway were met by a rider on horseback. Isabelle paused to watch him pass, and then realised that Duvernoy had halted too. Henriette, excited, was jumping up and down. Duvernoy laughed. 'I see your daughter has a good eye for a horse.'

'Just look at the way he arches his neck and lifts his feet! Have you ever seen such a beautiful creature?'

'Very rarely, it has to be admitted.' Isabelle saw that his eyes were warm with amusement. 'I see where Henriette gets it from. Do you ride?'

She caught her breath. 'Oh, not for so long now, not for years! But once, yes I used to. Nothing like that, but I loved to ride. I think it was the thing I loved most in all the world.'

There was great tenderness in his expression, as if with everything she said, every change in her expression, he liked her the more. 'Did you not find it very hard in the convent, shut away from all that?'

'Yes. But I thought it was right, then.' It all seemed so long ago, as if it had happened to another person. But then she thought she had become another person, for so much had happened in the brief fraction of her life that had followed her rejection of the convent, she had learned so much, that Isabelle Moulin now had little left of Isabella Milburn; and still less of Sister Sainte-Marie-Madeleine.

191

'Next Sunday, shall we ride? I could hire two horses, quiet horses. You could take Henriette up with you.'

She was enchanted, and simply stood gazing at him with all her joy naked in her face. At that moment she would have given him anything he asked, admitted him to the most intimate place in her life; or almost. 'Oh!' she said, and then could think of nothing more to say. When she did find words, she thought they sounded almost ungrateful, 'I have no riding habit.'

'Does that matter? Do you mind what people think? Or can you not ride in ordinary clothes?'

'I can ride in anything,' she promised him, though conscious that riding in the Bois de Boulogne was not quite like cantering her pony over Hareshaw Common.

Next Sunday morning he was at her door early, but she and Henriette, each as excited as the other, had already been up for hours.

The sun was shining and two good things had happened in the past week, as if leading up to this great day in her life. First, news had come that the invading Prussian army had been held at bay and then turned back at the hill of Valmy, east of Paris; and yesterday the National Convention had at last unequivocally declared the end of monarchy and the inauguration of the Republic.

Jérôme kissed Henriette and swung her in the air. 'There now, little citizeness, do you know what day this is? The very first day of the very first year of our very own French Republic! And to celebrate, you shall ride a horse.'

Henriette gurgled with laughter, and Isabelle watched with delight and wondered if in caressing her daughter he was in an oblique way paying court to her.

The whole world seemed to be in celebration that day. The ride was wonderful, and Isabelle did not mind at all that she rode in her striped linen skirt and red bodice among the fashionable equestrians who still enjoyed parading their skills and their horses in the Bois; she did not mind that the animals Jérôme had hired were sturdy unshowy beasts. His post as an assessor was unpaid and he did not earn a great deal from his

192

everyday employment as a clerk to the Paris criminal court, so
that he could not afford anything better, but he had chosen their
mounts with as much care as he could and they were good
tempered and trustworthy. Henriette showed no fear at all and
loved every moment of the ride and Isabelle did not think she
had ever been so happy in her life before.

Afterwards, Jérôme saw them home and at the door he
kissed Henriette, who clung to him, her small arms about his
neck. Then he set her down, though she continued to hang on
to his hand, jumping around him. He simply stood very still,
looking at Isabelle in silence. She was aware with great
intensity of his face, above all of his mouth, thin yet expressive.
She did not know how it was, for she made no choice, took no
decision, but she knew they were moving closer together, that
he had bent his head, that she had raised her face to his. She
saw his eyes, darkened and soft, felt his breath on her face, very
rapid, and then his mouth touched her own, warm, gentle yet
firm. For a tiny instant she felt some surge of feeling within her,
responding; then his hand took hold of her arm and she pulled
herself away, shivering and cold and sick. She saw the
puzzlement and hurt in his eyes, and was sorry; but there was
nothing she could do about it.

'I beg your pardon,' he said, a little stiffly, his voice still
breathless. 'I thought ...' He cleared his throat. 'I was not
mistaken was I? You seemed to like me, I thought.'

'You were mistaken,' she said, her voice trembling.

A shutter seemed to close over his face. She knew he was
hurt, and offended too perhaps. 'Very well. I apologise. Good
day.' He turned away, and she felt as if the world had
abandoned her. A little cry burst from her.

'No, don't go!'

He glanced back, surprised, his expression still cold, but
questioning too. She was relieved that he came to a halt.

'It was not – you were not ... It's too soon, that's all.' She
struggled for the right words, the ones that would induce him
to remain her friend but at a safe distance, without making any
other demands upon her. 'This morning – it was wonderful. I

have not been so happy for a long time. Thank you.'

He stood looking at her, and she could not interpret his expression. She waited for him to speak, but as the silence continued thought miserably: *It's over; he will never forgive me.*

Then suddenly he took a step back towards her. 'May I – will you ride again, next week? I ask nothing from you, until you wish . . .'

She knew that she had only put off the thing she feared, not extinguished it altogether, but she would not let that spoil her happiness.

# Chapter Seventeen

Isabelle sat on the bed, oblivious of Henriette's demands for a game or a story, gently repulsing her without knowing what she was doing.

She had not known it was possible to feel like this. It was as if Jérôme had seeped insidiously into her being, to take possession of her, mind and body. She thought of him endlessly, constantly – no, that was wrong: she did not *think* of him at all, or not most of the time. Thinking was too conscious, too controlled a concept to be applied to the obsession that consumed her. It was simply that he was there, present in all she said or thought or did, waking or sleeping. There was no room for anything else, anyone else, scarcely even for the child she loved so much. She could not sleep properly and had little appetite, for these things no longer mattered to her. Tasks were neglected, or done in a dream. Only Jérôme mattered, only he was real. It frightened her a little, in that part of her that still had any conscious awareness of her old single self, for it was so overwhelming. Sometimes it made her wonderfully, deliriously happy, as she had never been happy before, so she could not keep still but had to sing and dance. At other times she was so torn by longing to be with him that she could not endure it, and then the restlessness was worse than ever.

Yet when they were together, as they were on every Sunday that he was free, there was so little for an outsider to see – walks, talks, rides, a few games with the child, with no word or gesture passing between them that could mean anything more than appearance suggested, or not at least after that difficult moment of parting at the end of their first ride together. Did he suffer this same inner turmoil, this fever of the blood and mind and heart that burned but did not consume, could not be quenched? She did not know. He liked her, of course, enough to have wanted, once, to kiss her. But his manner since that day had always been calm and easy and friendly. It was not the manner of a man overwhelmed by the torments of passion; but then she knew that her own manner belied the intensity of her own feelings. She fought a constant battle to hide the depth of her longing for him. She was afraid above all that if he once guessed what she felt, then he would expect from her what she could not give, and she would lose him for ever; either that, or she would yield to him against all her instincts and allow him to tear aside the curtain that covered the dark place in her mind where lurked a too well-remembered horror.

Better then to leave things unspoken and unacknowledged between them than to destroy what happiness they had. Yet some instinct told her it could not be as simple as that, or not for much longer; that he would not allow it to rest there.

Oh, if only she had someone to talk to – a mother, a sister; a friend –!

*I'm living with Pierre now. He's found a good place, off the rue St Martin...*

Could she go to Marianne, after all that had happened? And if she did, would she be able to talk to her, would she find an answer to her predicament?

'Let's go and see Marianne.'

Henriette, happy at last, skipped beside her out of the room, down the stairs, into the street.

The rue St Martin, like the rue St Denis, bisected almost the whole of the northern half of the city, forming at one point the boundary of their own Section. Isabelle supposed that Pierre and Marianne no longer lived in the Section, for she had not seen them about, or glimpsed Pierre at the Section Assembly in September, as she surely would have done had he still lived nearby. There was, she supposed, nothing for it but to make her way northwards along the whole length of the road, walking down each street that led off it, until she found the place. It might well take her hours, if not days. The one consolation was that there were not a great many print shops in that part of Paris.

In fact she found the place very quickly, in an alley on the northernmost edge of the Section, a narrow two-storeyed building on the corner where the alley met the rue St Martin. Through the small grimy window she could see two men at work, but neither of them looked like Pierre. A third person, talking to one of them, was a woman: Marianne herself. Isabelle's heart began to thud painfully. She took a deep breath, held Henriette's hand in a firm grasp, and then pushed open the door into the shop. 'See to it then,' Marianne was just saying, and seemed to be about to turn away from the men, perhaps to mount the narrow stairs that led up from one corner of the room. Then she saw Isabelle and came to a complete halt. The two women stood there, with the length of the room between them, saying nothing. Henriette began to run to Marianne, but then, conscious of some awkwardness in the atmosphere, stopped again and stood looking from one to another of the women, unsure where to go next.

'If it's not convenient, I'll go,' Isabelle said at last. A part of her wished she had not come, could not think how she could begin to put into words, however faltering, what had brought her here, and hoped that Marianne would give her the excuse she needed to extricate herself from the situation. Another part of her begged in silence for Marianne to welcome her.

Very slowly, Marianne took a step towards her. Then she held out her hands to the child. 'I've always got time for my little Henriette. Come to Marianne. Tell me what you've been doing.'

Happily, Henriette went to her. Isabelle stayed where she was, watching in painful suspense as her daughter chatted to Marianne, and Marianne answered her, all light laughing good humour. She felt hurt. Was Marianne going to exclude her altogether, using her child as a means of rebuke for the old ill feeling between them?

Marianne lifted the child into her arms, and then suddenly

197

she looked straight at Isabelle and, through the continuing stream of chatter, said carelessly, 'Come upstairs then.'

Relieved – yet nervous too – Isabelle followed her up the narrow ladder-like stairs to a simply furnished living room, from which she glimpsed an adjoining bedroom. A further ladder led into a room above, presumably an attic. Marianne had gone up in the world then, to be in possession of two rooms on the first floor.

Standing in the middle of the room, looking about her, she felt awkward and unsure of herself. 'Where's Pierre?' she asked, more for something to say than from any particular curiosity.

'Gone to the front,' said Marianne.

'Oh!' The word came with a warm rush of feeling, mingling sympathy and concern. 'I'm sorry, that must be hard for you. When did he go?'

'A month ago, once the prisons were dealt with.'

Isabelle did not allow her mind to dwell on the implications of that remark. 'Then you run the business?'

Marianne nodded. 'Oh, I know I can't read, but the two down there can, and I can count up the money and haggle with the customers as well as anyone.' She paused, studying Isabelle's face. 'Sit down then,' she said. 'Or aren't you stopping?' She sat down herself on a chair by the hearth with Henriette on her knee, and Isabelle sat facing her, managing a faint, unconvincing smile.

'Something's happened,' said Marianne.

Isabelle coloured. 'What makes you think that?'

'You wouldn't be here otherwise,' said Marianne, without apparent rancour. Isabelle felt disappointed. She had hoped that somehow Marianne might have been able to read in her face something of what had brought her here, so that she would not need to put it into words. As it was, she did not know where – or how – to begin.

After a silence that seemed to last an uncomfortably long time, Marianne said, 'You're still lodging with the high and mighty Picot?'

'Yes.'

Silence. Then: 'Still teaching?'

'Yes.'

'I see Thérèse sometimes.'

Another silence. Then they both began to speak at once, then broke off laughing – 'You first!' 'No, you.' Then Isabelle burst out, 'I've met someone.'

'Ah ha!' Marianne looked triumphant. 'So that's it! So my cold English friend is not so cold after all! Tell me about him.' She was all warm eagerness, but the curiosity, natural enough, that underlay her warmth, and the assumptions implicit in her tone, jarred on Isabelle's nerves. She should not have come. It was foolish to think Marianne could help, with her careless acceptance of life in its most sordid aspects. She had already shown what kind of friend she was, how lacking in morality.

'It's not like that,' said Isabelle, colouring still more and not entirely sure what she meant by 'that'.

'Oh no?' Marianne studied her visitor's face. 'What is it like then? Who is he?'

She could not bring herself so to expose Jérôme before Marianne, to set him up here, name and age and history and all before the critical knowing eyes of the other girl. 'A man,' she said.

'A Frenchman?'

'Yes.'

Exasperated yet laughing, Marianne put the child off her knee and came to take Isabelle's hands in hers. 'Oh, tell me now – all about him! You are in love, that's it, isn't it? I can see it in your face.'

'I – perhaps – I don't ...' But it was true, only too true. If she had not given it a name, even to herself, it was not because she did not know what it was but because she feared the implications of that knowledge. And it was they that had brought her here today.

She was on the point of accepting defeat, acknowledging that Marianne, so practical, so down to earth, who saw love –

bewilderingly – as a casual and straightforward matter, was not the person who could begin to understand or to help.

And it was then that the smile left Marianne's face and she said with sudden gentle gravity, 'What's wrong? You're not happy. Tell me!' This time it was not curiosity, not even simple friendliness, but genuine concern and compassion that was in her voice. And Isabelle found all at once that she could speak, as freely as she so much needed to do.

'Yes, I love him. I think he loves me too—'

'Then where is the difficulty?' It was asked quietly, acknowledging the fact that there was a difficulty which could not be dismissed.

'When people love they ...' Why were words so faltering and inadequate?

'Like me and Pierre, you mean?' Another time Marianne would have spoken more directly, using blunter terms, but some instinct made her tactful. 'Or marriage perhaps – is that what you have in mind?'

'Not necessarily.' She was surprised herself at that admission. Yet she knew it was not the legality of it that troubled her. 'For you, it was easy. But for me – it isn't.'

'Because of the vows you made once – chastity and all that?'

'No, no not that.' She looked up into Marianne's grave face and said suddenly, 'I am afraid. I do not want it again, ever. Not after ...' Her eyes moved to Henriette, who was watching them, without (Isabelle hoped) understanding anything of what they said.

Marianne glanced at the child too, and then looked back at Isabelle. She seemed to be pondering what might be meant. 'Did you have a bad time when she was born?'

'Not especially.'

Another little silence. Then Marianne said, 'You never told me who he was, the man who – well ...'

Isabelle did not know what instinct had made her friend avoid the word 'father', but she was grateful for it. She did not want Henriette, ever, to associate that word with the man who had been responsible for her existence. 'He was my cousin. Is still, I suppose.'

'You loved him?' There was doubt in her voice, as well there might be, when there was only a kind of repressed harshness in Isabelle's face and voice; but then that could have been caused by a sense of betrayal.

'No! Never, never, never!'

Marianne pulled up a stool and sat beside her, stroking her hand. 'Tell me what happened, all of it.'

So she did, slowly, with difficulty, her voice harsh, sometimes scarcely audible, sometimes too loud, while she searched for the words that would bring into the open the thing that for so long had been shut up inside her; trying always to choose words that the child would not begin to understand. It took a long time, with many halts and hesitations, many painful bursts of feeling. At the end she was shaking violently, from head to foot. Then she began to weep.

Marianne heard her in complete silence, and at the end said only, 'Bastard!' and put her arms about Isabelle and held her, rocking her as if she and not Henriette were the child. Isabelle clung to her, grateful for the comfort, the warmth, above all for the silent understanding. She even reached out an arm to draw Henriette near too, conscious that the child looked troubled at her mother's strange behaviour.

Isabelle stopped weeping at last, and drew back a little, reaching for her handkerchief. Marianne, still holding her, said, 'That was the only time then?' Isabelle nodded. 'And you think it will always be like that?' Another nod. 'It won't, Isabelle. I promise you it won't. Rape is one thing, love quite another.'

'Rape.' She had never even thought of it in those terms before, with all its implications of cruelty and violence and compulsion. Until now, her own connivance in what had happened had seemed undeniable; and her guilt too, as a consequence.

'And never think it was your fault. It wasn't, not one tiny bit. Men who rape don't do it from passion or love. They do it from hate, hate for women. That's my belief. I'd geld the lot of them.

This man you've met, if he loves you, really loves you, it won't be like that, it couldn't be.'

'But I – I can't forget. I'm afraid.'

'Then you know what you must do – you must tell him, this man you love.'

'Tell him!' She stared in horror and amazement at her friend.

'What you've just told me, yes.'

'But what if – if he ... Oh!'

'If he loves you, then he will understand and you will know you have nothing to fear. If he thinks nothing of it, if he treats it like a joke or says it doesn't matter, then you have no more to do with him. He's not worth it and he'll only make you unhappy.' She grinned suddenly. 'There! That's my advice. I'm right too, you'll see.' Then, grave again, she said, 'I know now why you were so angry about – that night ... Friends again then?'

'Friends again,' said Isabelle and kissed her.

'Now, when do you see him next?'

'Tomorrow. That's why I ...'

'Then bring Henriette here to me before he comes. You'll find it easier to tell him if she's not there. Besides, you might—' She caught the questioning expression on Isabelle's face and broke off. 'No, perhaps not.'

Isabelle felt strange as she walked home later that day, weary, drained almost, yet with a sense of peace that she had not felt for a very long time. Only now did she realise what dark bitter misery had lain inside her, even when she thought it had gone. It was still there; it would take more, after so long, than an hour or two of talk to disperse it. But a little light had been admitted, a fresh wind had begun to blow, the clouds were beginning to break up.

For the first time since it had all happened she allowed her mind to dwell on that time, even deliberately made herself think of it; not now of the one incident, so soon over, yet never at an end, but of what had gone before and, above all, what had followed. Until today, the months between what she had now learned to call the rape and the realisation that she was pregnant had been obliterated as if they had never been. Now, all kinds of things came back to her, clearly recalled, as if daylight had suddenly been admitted to a once shuttered room.

She remembered how, when he left her there in the dark (no word, no sound, just his steps going away, a door closing, the cold fastening its hold upon her ...), she had crawled, shivering, sobbing, to her feet and then groped her way back to her room. She had been bruised and aching, her clothes dishevelled and torn, hanging half off her body; but that had not been the worst of it. She had known then that she was dirty, soiled beyond cleansing. She had tried to cleanse herself, pouring water, scrubbing every part of her. Later, in the dark, she had gone out to where a stream ran along the side of the neglected yet formal garden and plunged into the icy water. She had lain in it, put her head back, felt the water run over her, cleansing, yet not cleansing. Would she be clean, she had wondered, if she let it run right through her, into nose and mouth and lungs? Would death cleanse her?

Why she had not let herself drown she did not quite know, now or then; but she had at last returned chilled still more to the château and made her way to bed, where she had lain huddled under the bedclothes, shivering and drenched in horror, for what remained of the night.

She had not wanted to go downstairs next morning, soiled as she was. They would see it, smell it, as surely as if she were smeared with excrement, she had been sure of that. And he would be there.

He was, at the far side of the room, beyond the chattering figures of his sisters. He had glanced once at her from those cold eyes, as one might look at horse droppings in the street, the better to avoid treading in them, and then he had turned away to give a sharp command to one of the servants standing nearby. It was the only time for the whole two weeks that she remained at La Pérouse that he had come anywhere near to acknowledging her presence. Before that night, he had scarcely

203

spoken to her, but he had watched her. Afterwards, he had no more use for her.

She saw now that it had never occurred to him for a moment that she would betray what had happened; nor had it occurred to her. She knew why. No one would have believed her, still less believed that she was not responsible for what had been done, if only in part. She herself had not believed it.

*Men who rape don't do it from passion or love. They do it from hate.* So Marianne had said. Isabelle had not consciously imagined that love was the motive for her cousin's action, yet some part of her had always thought of love and what had happened as somehow close to one another. To see it not as love at all, but as hate – that gave her a new and startling perspective. Yes, he had behaved as if he hated her; hated and despised her, as if she had no existence except as a convenient object to be used and then discarded. But then he had shown little warmth to anyone, even his brother or his sisters or his parents. She had realised one day, overhearing some talk, watching a face, that the servants hated him. She thought, now: *Were there other women he used like that?*

It was, somehow, a startling thought, an important one. She was looking suddenly at someone else overpowered and used by her attacker, as she had been. Innocent, unsuspecting, a life ruined by a man's whim – no, she would never call that woman guilty, but rather a victim, to be pitied and consoled. Not punished, as she had been punished.

For it had been a punishment, she saw that now. That was not how she had seen it at the time, nor had her father, she thought. In his view, as in hers, to enter a convent was a privilege, not a punishment. For her it had been an especial privilege, because she, above all others, deserved punishment. Her sin and her guilt had been so great that only a lifetime given to God could buy her any hope of forgiveness.

How dared they! Anger shot into life, anger such as she had not felt for years. Her own father, above all, who should have protected his daughter, cherished her, comforted her – not once had he spoken kindly to Isabelle, offered her any word of

204

sympathy or love. If someone did that to Henriette, she thought, I would kill him with my bare hands, without a second thought. And I should teach her that she must feel no guilt for what had been done to her against her will.

Of course, until today she had told no one apart from Father Duncan precisely what had happened or who was responsible; and he had simply given force and focus to her sense of guilt. But did her father really know her so little, that he could accept without question that she was responsible for what had been done to her? More than once, in the stormy weeks after she had told them of her condition, she had assured her father that she had not wanted it to happen. Perhaps her own sense of guilt had made that assurance sound unconvincing, for even she had not quite believed it. But her father was a man, who understood a man's nature and had years of experience behind him; and she had been little more than a child. Why had he not held her in his arms, as surely her long-dead mother would have done, and said, 'Tell me, Bella – who did this to you? We shall believe you. We shall not blame you.'

But no one had done that. Perhaps her grandmother would have done so, had she been able to. Looking back, Isabelle thought that she alone had understood more than she had ever admitted, or been told. But it was her son's house and Isabelle was his daughter to use as he chose and she could not interfere. Very likely, she had been ordered not to interfere. Everyone else had assumed her guilt. They were not unique in that, of course. It was the way of things. Looking back, she remembered gossip overheard in kitchen or drawing room. 'Well, she must have asked for it . . .' – 'It takes two, you know . . .' But not always, not inevitably. Today she had realised that at last. And it was those who should have loved her most who had prevented her from discovering the truth until today, when a young woman they would have despised had shown her an understanding and sympathy she had never received from any member of her own family.

She did not sleep a great deal that night, but this time it was anger that kept her awake, a furious anger at what her family had done to her; and through it all a new and searing hatred for her cousin. She had not been able to hate him unequivocally before, soiled and guilty as she had felt. She had blamed herself too much to blame anyone else. Now, freed of guilt, she was able to hate him, as he so richly deserved.

Strange, she thought: in the land of her birth, hate and anger had for centuries fed violent and bloody feuds. But through it all, family and tribe had always come first – Milburns and their kin before the world. The enemy of each bearer of your name was your enemy too, hated with an implacable hatred into eternity. Now, she was faced with the truth that her enemies were her own people, her own flesh and blood. It was they who had ruined and oppressed and wronged her beyond words.

Well, she was free of them now, freed by a cleansing anger. She had left Tynedale behind, and the Milburns, for they had driven her out. Now her land was France – or at least this corner of it – her family was where she chose it to be, where she loved. Henriette, Marianne – and Jérôme?

He called the following morning, to lure her into the misty autumn sunlight for a walk. She was glad they had not planned to ride today, because it would be easier to tell him on foot, somewhere quiet and beautiful, away from crowds, free from interruptions. It would not be easy, because she knew that in his reaction to what she said would lie the key to her future, their future, if there was to be one. But she knew that Marianne was right, and that this was the only way forward.

'Henriette's with a friend today,' she told him in answer to his question. 'You see, I want to tell you something.'

He was clearly curious, but he asked no more questions, talking of nothing in particular as they made their way out of the crowded city streets and on into the Bois de Boulogne. Then, when Isabelle was ready, he listened quietly as she began with a fact which had nothing much to do with the essentials of what she had to say, but which she wanted him to know all the same. There were, she decided, to be no more secrets between them. 'There's something I haven't told you. I was born in England, to English parents.'

She dreaded his reaction to what she had not yet told him, but she had not expected the look of dismay with which he received this piece of information. 'How can you be? You have no accent. You were a nun – or was that a lie?'

'Oh, it was true.' She felt her heart thud at the tight anger on his face. If he was reacting like this to something so trivial, how would he react to what really mattered? 'What's wrong? We're not at war with England.'

'No, not yet . . .' Then he broke off and looked at her intently and a sudden smile lit his face, in the way she loved. ' "We", you said – "We're not at war with England." Not "You".'

'You see, I said I was born of English parents. But France is my country now.'

'All because of your tiresome elder brother.' His voice was gently teasing.

'No,' she said, unsmiling. 'No, not because of him. That is what I must explain.'

He heard her story without a word, sitting very still beside her on the fallen log where she had suggested they rest for a while. She told him everything, calmly, but with indignation giving force to her words. Today there were no tears.

When she came to an end he did not, as she had feared, put his arms about her as Marianne had done. For a moment, though she was thankful for it, she feared it was from disgust or indifference; then, after what seemed a long silence, he said vehemently, 'I'd like to kill that man! For him, I'd bring back torture . . . Has he emigrated, do you know?'

'I don't know. I expect so.'

She knew what he implied and wondered what he would have done if her cousin had been within his reach. Perhaps the savagery of the sans culottes was not so alien to this courteous and principled young man as she had thought; perhaps it was simply a measure of what he felt for her.

Then he said, his voice suddenly very gentle, 'I understand you now, the things I didn't understand before. Forgive me if

I hurt you. You know that what happened then – that has nothing to do with what I feel for you. You know I love you?'

With each step she had taken since that November day two years ago she had moved further from the beliefs and principles by which her family had lived, set herself outside all they would have regarded as permissible and right. She had scarcely had time for a sense of guilt, wrapped up as she had been in her search for the child and her attempts to build a new life for them both. In any case, what guilt she had felt had been rooted in one single event over which, she saw now, she had had no control. Now at last, with Marianne's help, she had been brought face to face with her feelings, with all that had happened to her, and in doing so she had deliberately rejected all that her family had imposed upon her, even the guilt of her apostasy, for what guilt could there be in rejecting vows made under the duress of a misplaced contrition? In doing that, she was free of them as she had never been before, and of all they stood for. Henceforth, she decided, she would take her life firmly in her own hands and live it on her own terms, reaching out for her chance of happiness without hesitation, without looking back, without regrets. It would not be easy, she knew. The very next step she would take would perhaps be the hardest of all, but she would take it all the same, because unless she took it she could not move on, out of the past.

'Yes,' she said. 'And I love you.' Then, her eyes never leaving his face, she reached out and put her hands in his.

There was a long silence. She could hear that his breathing had become more rapid and uneven; he was even trembling a little, as if with some intensity of feeling fiercely constrained. At first, he smiled at her with great tenderness, but then the smile faded; he even looked a little severe. At last, in a harsh undertone, he said, 'Will you allow me to kiss you?'

She felt her own breathing quicken. She was afraid – would she ever be free of fear? – but conscious too of some more pleasurable excitement. She nodded, unable to speak through her ragged breathing. He leaned towards her, and she closed her eyes.

'No, love,' he whispered. 'Open your eyes. Look at me. Then you will see that I love you, that there is nothing you need to fear.' She opened her eyes, and saw how near he was. Then he was nearer still and she felt his mouth touch hers. It was soft, warm, very gentle, just brushing her lips, a gentler kiss even than that first kiss at the door. All kinds of strange new feelings came alive in her, wild unexpected sensations too much for the shivering remnants of her fear. When he moved away, just a second or two after, she heard herself cry softly, 'Oh!' There was dismay in her voice. Then she laughed and moved towards him. For an instant she saw him hesitate – to hold himself back from some more impetuous response? – before he brought his mouth to her again. This time his lips moved over hers, nuzzling, exploring. It was like nothing she had ever felt before. He was still holding her hands, but she freed them and the next moment felt her arms move, slowly, hesitantly, then in a sudden rush, to close about his neck. Then, gently, his own arms closed about her. For a moment she stiffened, drew back just a little, and she saw the question in his eyes, and then she laughed and kissed him again, her kiss, given to him, freely and in love, because she wanted it.

They stood there she did not know how long, kissing, touching, always gently, never more than a kiss and a loving embrace, without force or harshness. And it was not Isabelle but Jérôme who brought it to an end. 'That's enough, my darling. Enough for today, or it will be too much.'

They walked on under the trees, hand in hand, and Isabelle had never felt so happy. She was scarcely aware of what lay around her, except as a part of her happiness, as if singing birds and hazy sunlight and the blue of the sky glimpsed through the tangle of fiery branches overhead were all an essential part of the happiness that was in their linked hands and his tenderness and the drawing back of fear and darkness.

# Chapter Eighteen

'The tricolour is blue and white and red . . .'

Isabelle looked down with affection on the black bullet head of Robert Griffard, bent over the page along which his grimy finger moved with steady persistence as his voice growled out the words. It had taken a whole year to get him to this point, a year during which she had wondered, often, if he would ever sit down for two minutes together, let alone give her his attention once he had done so. She knew he had long been the despair of his parents. Louis-Robert he had been at the start, but the Louis had been dropped after August 10th. His father was now toying with the idea of adding 'Brutus' to his name, so his mother had said this morning. There might be a certain grim appropriateness in the symbolism of giving the child the name of Julius Caesar's assassin at this time when 'Louis the Last' was on trial for his life before the Convention, but Isabelle thought it would be asking for trouble. Robert was quite difficult enough already. Still, it was that very difficulty that made her love him, more than many of her more biddable pupils; and even more now that he was at last beginning to read and write and learn his numbers.

His little sister Victoire, watching him with solemn eyes as round and black as his own, was an angel, and could read fluently already. Strange; though they were so different in temperament they were astonishingly alike to look at, un-mistakably brother and sister. But then they shared the same parents on both sides. Isabelle glanced at Henriette, who was imaginatively if not very accurately 'reading' a story to three other children. Would there be much resemblance if only one parent was shared . . .? No, she must not think of that now.

She was glad when the class ended and it was time to go home. She felt desperately tired today and it had taken all her willpower to concentrate on what she had been doing. Once all the children had been returned to their mothers she set out with Henriette through the cold January afternoon, pausing to buy bread on the way. She was hungry, but feeling too sick to enjoy what she ate.

The greyness of the day reflected her mood. She did not want the weeks of happiness to end. If only she could be sure that they were not about to do so. Dread filled her.

Jérôme had become the centre of her life, and to lose him would be like tearing the very heart from her body. He had given her so much, best of all the gift they had first shared on a wet November afternoon in her room . . .

Isabelle had taken Henriette to spend that Sunday with Marianne, as she did very often, to the satisfaction of both of them. Any unease Isabelle might have had at the frequency of the arrangement had soon been dispelled. She had realised one day, with a sense of surprise, that Marianne, who had declared once that she was done with men, loved Pierre as much as Isabelle loved Jérôme, and missed him with something close to desperation, made worse by fear for his safety. For her, Henriette's company was a buffer against loneliness and fear. So Isabelle had taken the child to her that day without hesitation.

By then the hesitation had all been on Jérôme's side. From the day he had first learned the truth about Isabelle he had treated her always with a tender consideration that had even, in the end, made her impatient with him. Never had he asked more of her than she wanted to give; almost always, he had asked less. Yet bit by bit, caress by caress, he had wooed her, kissing her in different ways and different places, stroking her neck with a soft lingering finger, on her hand or her arm, murmuring loving words in the voice that was itself like a caress. Even now, to remember those times made her shiver with delight.

There had been long days together when Isabelle had wanted Jérôme with every part of her, when she had felt that neither fear nor horror nor anything in her past could destroy her longing or prevent her from finding peace with him. But it had been nearly two months before Jérôme had at last accepted her invitation to come to her room, and then she had wondered if he had accepted simply because the rain was too heavy for them to do anything else. They had bought something to eat from the cookshop on the way, Isabelle could not now remember what, except that it was hot and savoury. At the time she had not noticed either, being too full of desire and apprehension to care about food. For she had known that then, that very day, she would take the last step and end her fear by confronting it openly and completely. She wanted to take it, the driving need of her body had told her that; and her mind, and Marianne's reassurance, and Jérôme's, told her that this would be nothing like that other too well-remembered time, that rape was not love and had nothing to do with true passion. Yet the fear was there still and a lingering conviction that there was no difference and the horror of that day would only come back to her with all the dreadful freshness of repeated experience. She could not quite shift that conviction; she knew that it would not shift until – or unless – she had taken the last step and discovered for herself where the truth lay.

So there they had been, in her room, with Jérôme standing at the table preparing a salad to go with the food that she was transferring to plates with hands trembling so much that she spilt a good deal on the table. She thought that neither of them had been able to eat very much. They had drunk, though, or at least she had. Jérôme had bought a bottle of the sparkling wine of Champagne, too good to drink diluted, he had assured her, so she had not added water to it, as she usually did when she drank wine, and he had filled and refilled her glass, almost without her noticing. Only afterwards did she realise he had scarcely drunk at all, though she herself, unused to drinking very much, had quickly felt reckless and light headed.

Then she had gone to close the shutters, though it was still only early afternoon. Jérôme had caught her arm. 'No, leave them. We're not overlooked. We're private enough. This is for the daylight, my love, not the dark. There is nothing between us that need ever be hidden away.' Then he had held her shoulders gently in his hands and turned her to face him.

The lash of the rain on the window had formed a gentle background to what came after. Ever since then the sound of rain would bring that afternoon fresh to her mind, as if she were reliving it. Rain and joy, linked for ever in sweet association.

They had kissed, and her passion had been as great as his, as eager. Gently, caressingly, he had undressed her, garment by garment, letting each one fall to her feet, every unlacing and unbuttoning done with such tenderness that it was an intrinsic part of the seduction, moving her more intensely with longing and desire. In the end, before he had slipped the chemise from her warm and trembling body, she had been so aching for him that there was no fear left in her, nothing that could link this moment with the horrors of the past, only a consuming need to be joined with him. It was she who had pulled him to the bed and drawn him onto her. What had followed had not been a possession, but a union of two people drawn by equal passion, coming together as their need demanded. And so, that day, the past had been driven out for ever, set apart from the present sweetness that had nothing whatsoever to do with what had happened before. She knew at last that there had been nothing to fear. She had heard herself cry out as Marianne had done that night in her room, from the final throes of longing, and then from joy and delight and completion. He had cried out too, his groans of exaltation mingled with the tenderest of endearments.

Since then there had been many such times, shared afternoons of passion, or mornings or evenings, whenever Marianne would have Henriette with her. By now Isabelle was almost as familiar with Jérôme's body as she was with her own.

But in two days it would be Sunday and they would meet again, and she must tell him; and she dreaded the possibility that their happiness might end there. She had thought she trusted him completely, but there were still some things she could not be sure about; and this was one of them. Ever since she had realised the truth, whenever she thought of telling Jérôme, she had felt an unpleasant churning in her stomach, mingling with the constant sickness that had first warned her of what had happened.

She mounted the stairs slowly, wishing she did not feel so sick and so weary. It did not make the anxiety any easier to bear, that she felt so unwell. Henriette chattered away as they went up, but she did not hear what was said, making non-committal murmurings at what she hoped were appropriate intervals.

There was someone on the landing, standing leaning against the wall outside her door. Just as he came into sight, he strode to the top of the stairs to meet her, and she saw who it was. 'Jérôme!' She felt more sick than ever, and yet glad too. Better perhaps to get it over with sooner.

Always when they met he had a kiss for her and for Henriette. This time he simply halted, facing her, and said with a sombre note in his voice (she could not see his expression in the dimness of the landing), 'They voted for the King's death.'

She too came to a halt. She shivered. 'When?'

'They are debating now whether to defer the sentence, but I think they will decide against. If so, then he dies on Monday.' As if suddenly recollecting where they were and who she was, he put an arm about her. 'Come inside.'

They went into her room, and he closed the door and set about reviving the fire. She watched his face as he worked. 'Are you sorry? Do you think they're wrong? To condemn the King, I mean.'

He shook his head. 'No.' Then he went on, as if trying to put before her all the arguments that he had heard, all that he had thought; perhaps because he needed to look at them clearly himself, 'I think they can do nothing else. Louis Capet has

215

proved himself a deceiver in everything he has done. He has always worked against the Revolution, whenever it lay in his power. We know now that he even bought Mirabeau. With one hand he has done one thing, while always pretending to honour what the people's representatives decided. He is guilty. To say he is not, that would be to say that everything the Revolution has achieved is wrong. Either we are guilty, or he is; it's as simple as that. But to imprison him for life would be to leave open the possibility of a rescue by foreign powers, or conspiracy within France, both with the aim of taking us back to all that we have thrown off. To exile him would do the same. He has to die. But it cannot be a matter of rejoicing, that it should be necessary.'

'No.' It was strange to look at what was happening now in France, and to remember how her own ancestors had fought to save King Charles the First. Many had regarded his execution as the ultimate sacrilege, for which the perpetrators could never be forgiven. Now she was on the other side, allying herself with the regicides. 'Cruel necessity' was what Cromwell was said to have observed of King Charles's death. There was just that note now in Jérôme's voice.

'I will tell you what did make me shiver, though – when I heard Philippe Égalité speak for the death sentence.' Isabelle knew that Philippe Égalité was the erstwhile Duke of Orléans, the King's cousin, who had allied himself with the most extreme group in the Convention, those they were calling the Montagnards – Mountaineers – because they sat in the highest seats on the left. 'No one would have censured him if he had asked to abstain. On the contrary, it was expected that he would. But to hear him speak out as he did – I tell you, I have never seen such universal disgust as there was on every face there.'

Even here in this Revolution that prided itself on mapping out a new world, the ties of family still counted for something, Isabelle thought, with a sense of surprise. There had never been love lost between the King and his cousin, yet it was expected that in the end blood would mean more than expediency.

'There is another thing. After this, there is no turning back. We are committed for ever to the Republic. That is not a thought to be taken lightly. I have always believed I would give my life for it. Now I know that this is something that could be asked of any of us who have supported what has happened this day, not just those who voted openly in the Convention, but all those who agree with them.'

In England the monarchy had been restored and then the regicides had suffered the cruellest deaths, those who had already died being subjected to appalling degradation, their supporters hounded until the end of their days. No, it was not something to be taken lightly.

Some of Isabelle's apprehension must have shown in her face, for Jérôme reached out his arms and then held her, reassuring her. 'There was never really any doubt. It has to be. Only when it's done can we move forward. As Robespierre said, "Louis must die that the nation may live." There was never any question of his guilt. The vote for that was overwhelming. As I see it, as all right-thinking men must see it, the rest follows without question.' He was about to return his attention to the fire, when he seemed to remember something else. 'There is one thing that is certain now, if there was ever any doubt about it – this will bring England into the war.'

Ever since the victory of Valmy it had been said that the British Prime Minister, William Pitt, was taking steps that were clearly designed to lead to war with England's old enemy. 'I see,' said Isabelle.

Jérôme gave a final poke to the fire, which set it blazing, and then rose to his feet. 'It seems to me there is an inescapable conclusion to be drawn from that.'

'Oh?' The fire seemed very far away and feeble as yet, for she was shivering.

'That we should be married, then you will be unquestionably and unequivocally French.'

She felt the colour flood her face, while words seemed stifled in her throat. He had taken her breath away by putting before her what she had seen merely as a faint and distant hope, probably rash and unfounded, to be banished from her thoughts before it led her to a foolish disappointment.

'What's wrong? Don't you want to be my wife?'

'Oh – oh yes!' Then words came. 'There was something I had to tell you. I think I'm pregnant.'

All the sombreness left his face. He came and hugged her and kissed her, delight in every touch of his hand, every change in his expression. 'Oh my love, what more could we wish for than this?'

'Can we marry without anyone's consent?'

He frowned a little. 'How old are you?'

'Twenty-one.'

Relief cleared his brow. 'Then we can. Let it be as soon as possible, in six days' time. We can go and give notice at the Hôtel de Ville this afternoon.' He held her in his arms and kissed her gently. 'But first, let's go and eat.'

They went out to a restaurant they visited sometimes, where the decor was severe and the prices low, but the food and the company good. Isabelle suddenly found her appetite again and happiness went to her head like wine, of which she drank little. Jérôme was at his most vivacious and charming, and they laughed at everything. There was one more sober moment. Half-way through the meal Jérôme abruptly laid down his fork and put a hand on Henriette's head, while his eyes remained on Isabelle's face. 'There is one thing, my darling. I should like Henriette to be my daughter, in law, beyond all argument. I love her already, but she must have the same legal right to that love as this new infant will have. Would you agree that I should adopt her, when we marry? Then, whatever happens, no one else will ever have any claim over her.'

Isabelle looked at Henriette, who was watching them both with a mixture of inquiry and gravity, as if she realised, without quite understanding it, that something momentous to her welfare was being discussed. Jérôme said, 'Would you like me to be your father, little one?'

Henriette nodded, her lips pressed close together but her eyes very bright, as if the idea pleased her. Isabelle reached across the table and laid her hand over Jérôme's. 'Thank you, my love.'

'She shall have a true Republican baptism!' Jérôme went on, in a sudden burst of enthusiasm. 'A new name – something worthy of the day on which she was born.'

Isabelle thought of Robert Griffard, who might very soon be renamed Robert Brutus Griffard, and was not at all sure. She had never liked the name Henriette, which, with all its associations, was not one she would ever have chosen, but she had grown used to it and so, most certainly, had the child herself. 'You'd better ask Henriette.'

He turned to the child. 'Tell me what you think, little one. At present you only have one name – most people have more than that.'

'Have you got two names, citizen?'

Jérôme coloured; Isabelle realised he was faintly embarrassed by the question. 'My first name is Louis, but I don't use it. Jérôme is enough for me. But now that you're going to be my little girl, would you like to have another name – then you can choose which one you want to be called by?'

Henriette gazed back at him, clearly giving the matter some thought.

'Shall I tell you what I think?' he went on. She nodded. 'You know that your birthday is on a very special day, not just for you, but for France. July the fourteenth was the day when the sun of Liberty rose over our nation. Don't you think you should have a name that reminds people of that?' She nodded again, though Isabelle doubted if she understood very much of what he was saying. 'What do you say to "Aurore", sunrise?' He looked down at the child. 'Shall we call you Aurore, little one?'

She gave the matter careful thought, repeating the name softly, as if trying out its sound. Then she nodded again, and broke into a sudden smile.

All the way to the Hôtel de Ville she repeated the name over and over in time to her skipping feet. 'Aurore; Aurore; Aurore . . .'

219

*

They were strange, those winter days of early 1793, days of alternating sombreness and joy, in which shafts of sudden brilliant light seemed to burst through the grey of the winter sky, illuminating every colour and awakening every fragrance; only to be gone again, almost as if they had never been, yet leaving a memory behind.

Isabelle and Jérôme gave notice of their intention to marry, showing the necessary papers, and Jérôme took steps to register 'Aurore Henriette Moulin, father unknown', as his adopted daughter. The child began immediately to insist on being addressed by her new name, refusing to answer to anything else, to Isabelle's amused exasperation. 'You've a lot to answer for!' she chided Jérôme tenderly.

Afterwards they had their supper at a café, rather early, and then they walked slowly home and Isabelle did not feel the cold or see the greyness that obscured the sun.

But it was grey the next Monday, and cold. The streets swarmed with soldiers and National Guardsmen, marching, drawn up in ranks, watchful, and columns of sans culottes with pikes in their hands, prepared to repel any attempt at an eleventh hour rescue of the king.

A heavy silence hung over the city from the early morning, broken only by the sounds of marching feet and the distant beat of drums. It reminded Isabelle of the silence in which Paris had greeted the King's return after his flight, only this was more oppressive, more sombre, reaching even into her room, where she sat trying to keep Henriette amused and distracted, so that she should not ask too many questions about what was happening on this day when there were no lessons and almost everyone they knew had gone out to watch the long, slow procession to the Place de la Révolution, where the guillotine had been set up, beside the broken foundations of the statue of Louis XV, after whom the square had once been named. Jérôme had suggested that they should go with him to watch the cortège make its way along the boulevards, but Isabelle had refused. If the new world of the French Republic was to bring in a kinder time then the children of this new world must not be taught to celebrate any death, however just. Jérôme heard her argument with gravity, and seemed to accept it.

Late in the morning a ripple of sound spread towards her through the city, growing in volume, the sound of thousands of voices raised in defiant acclamation. 'Vive la Nation! Vive la République!' The King is dead, she thought; long live the Republic. With some old instinct never quite extinguished she found herself sending up a silent prayer for the unknown future, and then wondered if there was anyone to hear it, or indeed, should God exist, if He would listen to the prayer of an apostate nun on behalf of a regicide Republic.

Later, Marianne came to see her. 'You missed nothing,' she said. 'You couldn't see what was going on, for the soldiers.' Then she began to talk of Isabelle's wedding, to which she was to be a witness, to her immense satisfaction. 'It's all my doing,' she insisted, and Isabelle had to admit there was some truth in that. She also, obliquely, had Jérôme to thank that her friendship with Marianne had been restored to her.

Three days later there was another sombre procession, this time for the funeral of a Montagnard deputy, the ex-noble Lepeletier de Saint-Fargeau, murdered by a Royalist because he had voted for the King's death. There were more solemn drums, and cannon fire too, as if to warn the distant armies of France's enemies that such deaths would be avenged. Then this, the corpse of the Republic's first martyr, was buried in the Panthéon, alongside the now discredited Mirabeau. That day, Isabelle and Henriette carried their few belongings to Jérôme's two good rooms above a florist's shop a few streets away, and moved in with Marianne for the last night before the marriage.

The next day the clouds did not matter, nor the bitter wind and rain. Isabelle and Henriette dressed in white muslin beneath large enveloping shawls, with tricolour ribbons in their hair and at their waists, and a few expensive hot house flowers supplied by Citizeness Didier, Jérôme's landlady. Henriette

221

was unbiddable with excitement, Isabelle nervous yet happy. They set out in good time with Marianne, calling for Claudine on the way, to meet Jérôme at the Hôtel de Ville, where he was waiting on the steps with two of his friends, Nicolas Lefèvre and Pierre-Joseph Crespy, both fellow clerks.

The ceremony was brief and simple, a matter of exchanging vows and signing documents before a municipal officer in a tricolour sash. Afterwards, Jérôme kissed Isabelle, and then Henriette, and then all the witnesses embraced the newly married couple; and then with much laughter and arms about one another the group of them went to a restaurant near the Hôtel de Ville where they ate and drank well, joined soon by Jean-Louis and Thérèse and a number of other friends. The waiter had news for them as he brought their wine. 'England's expelled our Ambassador,' he said. 'That's just the first step. Give them a day or two, and we'll be fighting them too. But what of it? We can beat the whole of Europe, no question of it.' Isabelle felt Jérôme put a consoling arm about her, and then the celebrations enfolded her again.

A week later, anticipating the inevitable, France declared war on Britain and Holland. She was now ringed with her enemies, her people and her armies inspired by the defiant speeches of Danton and Brissot, threatening to set Europe ablaze with the flames of liberty. But in Belgium the tide of victory began to turn, and in the western department of the Vendée there were savage peasant revolts against military service; while in the Convention the squabbling between Brissotins and Montagnards, temporarily submerged by the King's trial, broke out again with renewed and apparently limitless venom. Hunger came back to Paris with the spring.

But Isabelle was happy. She put aside the small and scarcely discernible ache inside her at the knowledge that the land of her birth was now at war with the land of her adoption. She and Jérôme and Aurore were together in their new home, a tender and loving family. It pleased her that Aurore seemed as happy as her mother was, delighted to have her own room and

222

someone she could call 'Papa', who bought her treats and made her laugh and sang to her and told her stories. He took her riding too, sometimes, leaving Isabelle at home. 'No more riding for you until the child's born,' he told his wife firmly, and she had to agree. Much as she missed the rides, she wanted Jérôme's child too much to risk doing it any harm. Sometimes, looking at Aurore, she shuddered to think how before she was born she had longed for some accident to rid her of that burden. Now only one small fear remained: that this second child, conceived and born in love, would mean more to her than did her firstborn. And then she would hold Aurore in her arms and think she could love no child as much as she did this daughter she had lost and found again.

# Chapter Nineteen

Isabelle stood looking out on the little garden behind the house, where Citizeness Didier's hens flapped and scratched in the dust in their enclosure and plump Marguerite Didier, fifteen years old, was cutting the last few roses for her mother's shop, now that normal supplies from outside the city could not always be relied upon. The window was open and a warm breeze set the flowers in Aurore's pots swaying gently and stirred the loose tendrils of Isabelle's hair. Her fingers tapped an impatient rhythm on the window sill. It was so hot and time dragged by so slowly! It would be hours yet before Jérôme was home. His new work was far more demanding than the old, often keeping him away from Isabelle until late in the night, even though he no longer had the extra duties of an assessor to perform.

She could have taken Aurore out for a walk. The child had clamoured this morning to be allowed to go and see the sight Jérôme had told them about, the pigeon that had nested under the folds of the robes on the statue of Liberty, erected in the Place de la Révolution for the first anniversary of August 10th, which had also marked the acceptance by referendum of the new Constitution. The pigeon had been part of the celebrations too, released with hundreds of others to symbolise peace and plenty, which it had evidently found, rather sooner than the spectators were likely to do.

But Isabelle did not want to go out. In these last days – weeks – of her pregnancy she had felt disinclined for any activity, slowed down by a heavy and sluggish body. Aurore, fascinated, loved to lay her head against her mother's belly and feel her small brother or sister kicking against her cheek. She too, like her mother, was longing for the child to be born, impatient because, so the doctor said, the due date had already passed, perhaps as much as two weeks ago.

All through the hungry, turbulent spring Isabelle had been cosseted, insulated from the fear and anger of the streets as she had not been since the days of the convent. But this was a different kind of protection, born of love and care for her. She had revelled in it, delighted to lean on someone after so long during which she had only had herself to rely upon. Of course, she had been glad enough then to be free to make her own choices, proud of her independence and the success she had made of her life. Yet it was good to be able to take a rest from that freedom, to know that there was someone else who, ultimately, felt himself responsible for her and Aurore and their well-being, and that of the child in her womb. Jérôme had insisted that she give up her teaching, something she had done with mixed feelings, but in the weary sickness-burdened early days of her pregnancy it had on the whole seemed preferable to continuing. Later, as the sickness went and her energy returned, she found she still had few regrets. She had more time now to give to Aurore, and time in which to prepare for the baby's arrival, to sew and shop for what was needed.

And when Marianne needed her, she had been there. It had been on a morning in May that her friend had come running up the two flights of stairs to her rooms with her face shining with happiness and a torn and stained letter in her hand. 'It's from Pierre, I know it is – I couldn't ask the men to read it, in case he said – well . . . Read it to me, Isabelle!'

She had sunk panting down on the chair by the hearth with her eager eyes on Isabelle's face as her friend unfolded the paper and quickly scanned it. 'Go on!' she had urged, when there seemed to be too long a delay. Then: 'It is from Pierre, isn't it?' For the first time a note of doubt had crept into her voice.

'Yes, it's from Pierre,' Isabelle had said. There had been another silence before she said gently, 'He's at Valenciennes, in hospital.'

Marianne gave a choked cry and pressed her hand to her mouth. 'Where's Valenciennes? I must go to him!'

'It's in the north somewhere, I think, on the border. But let me read what he says. He's well enough to write, remember – that's something.' She spread the page on her knee and began to read, conscious almost of intrusion in so intimately worded a letter. *'My beloved, I think of you every day, even in this hell-hole where I'm lying now. They took off my leg last week.'*

Again, that stifled cry from Marianne, but Isabelle did no more than pause until her friend was quiet again. *'Thank God it's no worse than that. I count the days until I can come home and show you that your one-legged lover is as much a man as ever he was. In fact, I only wish I could come to Paris now and sort out those buggers in the Convention. If you could see how the armies of France have to fight, you'd weep, my love, from pity and rage. No shoes, no boots, no sabots, no uniforms to know our soldiers by – you know them by their rags, the little bits of cloth tacked together to cover them as best they can against the weather, never mind blue, white and red, they're all colours of the rainbow, like a band of gypsies. Anything worthwhile we ever had has been sold long since. As for food, we're lucky if we see a few ounces of mouldy bread in a day. We're never paid, of course. At night, there's often nothing between us and the ground, or the sky, come to that. It's only the fire of liberty in our bellies that's led us to victory, and now even that's not enough, for we're led by traitors who are all the time in the pockets of the despots and the émigrés.*

'Are there no true sans culottes left in Paris, that they don't march on the Convention and set things in order there? If I were fit and back home, I'd soon get some of the good lads together and tell them the truth. We must have an end to all the faction fighting, all the threats against Paris. Paris made the Revolution – just let the Brissotins remember that. If they go on as they are, the nation will fall apart. It's half-way there *already. Once that happens, the enemy will march in with no one to stop them, and that will be the end of liberty. It must not happen, my love. No more factions, no more squabbling, we must have unity. Every French man and woman and child has to be made to serve France to the last breath. The Montagnards are our only hope, with the sans culottes to put the boot in. Get the lads to work, put out some leaflets. Show Hubert this letter. He'll know what to do. He'll pass the word around too, and you must do the same.*

*'Curse this useless leg of mine, and the fever that's shaking me up! If it wasn't for them, I'd be back with you already and taking things in hand. As it is, I trust you as I would myself, to act for the good of the people, and their soldiers who will perish if help does not come soon.*

*'I am angry, and then I think of your sweet body, your sweet little breasts, your mouth, and I'm fit to sob like a baby. But it strengthens me too, to think of you, for I long only to be well and return to you, as surely I shall very soon. Let the fire of patriotism burn in you, as does the love that we share. Vive la République! Your Pierre.'*

When Isabelle had at last raised her head, she had seen that Marianne looked as if she had aged ten years since the start of the letter. The freckles on her face stood out sharply against the drawn pallor beneath; yet in spite of the tears filling her eyes, there had been a look of resolution about her mouth.

'I shan't fail him,' she had said. Then she had embraced Isabelle. 'Tell Jérôme what Pierre says. He knows who are the best people in the Section, to get things moving, that is. But Pierre's wrong if he thinks no one cares or that they're doing nothing. They are and they will. What's more, we've been putting out leaflets for weeks already.'

On May 31st the tocsin had signalled another day of action, and the people, organised by the Commune and the Sections, had marched on the Convention and demanded the removal of the eloquent but ineffectual Brissotins. Within days, it had been done, though many of the threatened deputies simply left Paris to go and stir up rebellion in their home territories against the

supposed dictatorship of the capital and its militant revolutionaries. At a time when Marseille and Lyon as well as the west
were already in a state of revolt that was no light matter. And
then, in July, Marat, closest friend of the sans culottes within
the Convention, had been murdered. The Republic had its
greatest martyr, and the most extreme among the sans culottes
had lost the one representative they trusted, whose guidance
they would – sometimes – accept. There was yet another
sombre and magnificent funeral, organised as usual by the
painter David.

But at least the Montagnards (of whom David was one) were
now in power and by August there had been many changes. The
Committee of Public Safety, a new body set up in April to run
the war effort, initially under Danton's direction, was strength-
ened, its membership increased to twelve, and experts in
military matters were added to it, along with Robespierre,
formerly one of its bitterest critics, who began to see some
purpose in it after all. It was soon after his election to the
Committee that Jérôme was recruited to its growing bureau-
cracy. 'I got to know Robespierre when he was with the court,'
he said casually, by way of explanation.

Unfortunately, increasing signs of efficiency had not yet
solved the problems of the war, whether internal or external.
Great regions of France were still in rebellion against the
government and the allied forces marched daily further into
France. Valenciennes had long fallen to the Austrians, and
Marianne, bereft of news, feared that Pierre was now their
prisoner. All her instincts urged her to go in search of him, but
she remembered the work he wanted her to do and stayed
where she was, supervising the print shop and coming often to
see Isabelle, to share her fears and be comforted and consoled.

She came again that afternoon, running up the stairs as if
some urgent business brought her. Isabelle, recognising the
step, glad of some distraction, went to open the door to her.
Aurore, who, conscious of her mother's mood, had been
occupying herself with a book, ran to be swung into her arms.
Then they sat down about the table, chatting inconsequentially

for a time, until Marianne said suddenly, 'How old's Jérôme?'

Startled, Isabelle said, 'Twenty-five.'

'Then it's a good thing you married.' She smiled at the questioning look on Isabelle's face. 'It's just been announced. They're going to call all single men between eighteen and twenty-five to the armies.'

'What, every one?'

'That's what they say. I suppose if they're needed for something else, they'll be let off.'

Isabelle was silent for a moment, trying to imagine such vast numbers of young men as that implied. When necessary, armies had always pressed men randomly into service, in England as elsewhere, but this massive summoning of every young man to serve his country was something new and strange.

'I heard Barère's speech,' Marianne went on. 'A fine stirring one it was too. I wish Pierre could have heard it – he'd have cheered with the rest of us. Did Jérôme tell you what he was going to say?'

Barère was one of the twelve members of the Committee of Public Safety, but if he had discussed his speech in the hearing of the secretaries, Jérôme had been discreet about it. Isabelle shook her head.

'All the French, both sexes, all ages are called by the nation to defend liberty, he said.' Isabelle could hear the note of exaltation in Marianne's voice, caught perhaps from the well-known eloquence of the speaker. 'Young men are to fight, married men make weapons and see that the soldiers are fed and clothed, old men must encourage the young ones, women make tents and work in the hospitals, children tear up linen for bandages.' She leaned across the table. 'Thérèse is getting a group together to sew and make bandages. I go when I can—'

'But you hate sewing!'

'So what? I have to do what I can, we all do. Besides, the talk's good. Will you join us, when the baby's born?'

'Of course.' But she felt as if that time would never come. She seemed to have been waiting all her life for this birth. She had been impatient before Aurore was born, but this was different, though the impatience was as great, because this child was wanted and longed for as Aurore had never been.

Today Jérôme was home earlier than usual, rushing into the flat as if afraid he might find that the child had arrived in his absence. He embraced Isabelle with his usual tenderness. 'Still nothing?'

'Not the least twinge,' she said, feeling all her weariness and boredom ease in his presence. With renewed energy she set about preparing a meal, helped after a fashion by Aurore. She went through the usual routine of asking Jérôme how his day had gone, probing a little in the hope of being told something of what his work entailed. He was so near the men who, in practice at least, ruled France, that she was curious about it. But, as always, his answers were brief and evasive. 'I'm at home now,' he said. 'I've left work behind.' He took Aurore on his knee and began to talk to her, nonsensically, until she was squirming with laughter.

That evening Nicolas and Pierre-Joseph, both bachelors, came to pass the time lightheartedly in playing the flute (Nicolas had brought his own instrument) and singing and talking, clearly enjoying the domestic comforts of Jérôme's home and the company of his pretty wife. Isabelle assumed that Pierre-Joseph at least, whom she knew to be younger than Jérôme, was liable to be sent to the front, but she supposed he must be glad of an excuse to lay aside all thoughts of revolution and war for a little while. It was only when she returned from putting the child to bed that Isabelle found the young men deep in some earnest political discussion, concerning the evils of 'federalism' (of which, she knew, the Brissotins were said to be guilty) and the equal danger of pressures from the more extreme sans culottes.

'With Marat gone, it seems there's no one they'll listen to,' Jérôme was saying. 'Something has to be done, or we'll have another May the thirty-first on our hands, and they'll be after the Montagnards this time.'

'Today's speech must go some way to keeping them quiet,'

said Pierre-Joseph. 'They've been asking for measures like that for long enough.'

Isabelle came in quietly, unnoticed by the young men, and sat down with her mending.

'And a good deal else besides,' she heard Nicolas say. 'Price controls, the death penalty for all traitors and speculators, so on and so forth. Why can't they see that it's their representatives that rule France? Rule by the people doesn't mean the people individually can dictate every single thing that's done. The people speak when they cast their vote. After that, it's up to the men they voted in to see that their will is carried out.'

'That's the trouble,' Jérôme said. 'Half of them want direct rule or nothing. The rest want the Constitution implemented at once.'

'Won't it be? It's been accepted by a large majority—'

'What, risk elections with the country in its present state? That would be madness!'

Isabelle saw that the other two men were staring at Jérôme, as if his last words had disclosed some information unknown to them yet astonishing in its implications. She supposed, as presumably they did, that he had inside information. 'You know something,' she said.

He turned then and saw her, and his tender careless smile lit his face. 'I didn't hear you come in, my love. Is Aurore asleep?' Deftly he moved the talk to lighter matters, and the mood of the earlier part of the evening returned, charming and lighthearted and casual. The time passed pleasantly enough, but Isabelle only felt irritated by it.

When the other men had gone, she said to Jérôme, 'Why do you never talk to me as you did to your friends tonight? You changed the subject as soon as you saw I was there.'

'Perhaps I was in danger of being indiscreet,' he admitted. He caressed her cheek.

'But if I'd not been there, you'd have said something more, wouldn't you? I know you would. I've noticed it before, the way you talk of politics and such things with your friends, but never with me. It wasn't always like that.'

'There was a time when you accused me of bloodlust – I could hardly let that pass. But that was different.'

'In those days I went about among people, I heard the news and took part in things. Now I never go to clubs or hear the debates in the Assembly.'

'Of course not, my love, nor would anyone expect you to. Such things are best left to men.'

She felt a surge of irritation. 'I never thought I'd hear a Frenchman talk like that! It was one thing I always liked about France. In England, when dinner's over, all the women leave the room and go to chatter about nothing much in the parlour, while the men talk politics and drink themselves under the table. I know how my school friends used to laugh at that when I told them. They thought it very strange. They said English men obviously didn't like women, or they'd never let the sexes be separated like that.'

'Nor would they, my love. But remember too, that was under the old régime.'

'What difference does that make?'

'Simply this, my love – in the old France no one ever discussed politics, for there was no politics to discuss. The King and his ministers decided, and that was that. If you have no say in government, then there is not much point in talking about how it should be done. Now, under the new Constitution, every man has a vote, so it must be talked of.'

'Then why shut women out of it? Are we not citizens too?'

'Most certainly, but not as men are. You know I'd never want to turn you out of the room for any reason. I grudge every moment that we're apart. But when we have to separate for any reason, then that's when I can talk with my friends of things that aren't your concern. It's as simple as that.'

'But why shouldn't they be my concern? Women aren't shut away from the world and what happens in it. Look at Marianne – her life's changed completely, because of what's happened to Pierre.'

'But you don't have the power to change what happens, with your vote.'

233

'Then perhaps we should.'

He stared at her, as if astonished to hear such views expressed at his own fireside. 'You surely aren't one of those Amazons who want women in the Assembly?'

'Why not? What's wrong with the idea? After all, until the Revolution no one even thought all men should have the vote. In fact, until last year, most of them didn't. In England I expect people laugh at such a thing even now, just as you laugh at the idea of women voting. But I don't see there's any difference.'

'I should have thought it was obvious, my love, especially to someone so familiar with the fanaticism of the Catholic Church, as you've had cause to be. Women are too easily swayed by their emotions, too subject to the pressures of priests. Not you, perhaps, but many women. Furthermore, matters of government require clear and logical thought, of a kind difficult for women.'

Isabelle was tempted to say that logical thought seemed to have been conspicuously lacking in the Convention during the first year of its existence, despite the fact that its members were all men, but she could not at the moment think of any specific examples to put before Jérôme. Instead, she said, 'Perhaps all women need is good education. After all, it's the one thing most of them have never had.'

'I am all for better education for boys and girls alike. But I don't think you'd find it would turn your sex into more rational creatures. Women are not made for the public realm, but for the tender and private one of the mother and wife and sister.'

'But if mothers are to bring their children up to be good citizens, should they not understand what that means?' Isabelle was afraid that with everything she said she was only somehow reinforcing Jérôme's argument, by showing how lacking in rational thought she was herself. Yet her every instinct rebelled against what he said.

'No, for every virtuous woman has a sweet and natural impulse towards what is right; that is all she needs to make her a good mother and to bring up her children to be good citizens.' He kissed her gently, small soft kisses all over her face. 'Your realm, my love, is here in this house. Here you rule your husband and your children with love and tenderness, a little autocrat indeed. What need have you of any other sphere?'

Isabelle looked round the room, and felt momentarily stifled, imprisoned; but that was ridiculous, for did she not have all she could ask for in Jérôme's love? Yet, though she did not argue any more, she had never felt so at odds with him as she did at that moment.

An instant later, he had driven all thoughts of the disagreement out of her head. Going to put the music away, he said suddenly, 'Your cousin was Henri Antoine de La Pérouse, was he not?'

She was surprised at the shudder that went through her then; she had not after all wholly thrown off her fear of him. 'Yes,' she said, a little unsteadily. 'Why?'

'A man of that name has turned up in the Vendée, leading a counter-revolutionary mob. He was taken prisoner briefly at Luçon, but got away. The General responsible for losing him is under arrest, which is how I know of it: we had a report before us today. What makes the case more serious is that La Pérouse's rebels were afterwards guilty of many appalling cruelties, not only against captured Republican soldiers, but also civilians, women and children among them.'

'Then he's still free?'

'Unfortunately, yes.'

'What will happen if they catch him?'

'What do you think?'

A rebel captured in arms against the Republic; there could be no doubt . . . 'Then I hope they find him soon,' she said.

She was glad that she had Jérôme's arms about her in bed that night. They helped to keep at bay the revived memory of the man who had done her such harm, who was after all still alive and active, and still in France. She could no longer feel resentment against Jérôme for the slight matter of a difference of opinion. What he had given her must always and for ever outweigh trivialities of that kind.

It was at dawn the next morning that the first birth pains

came at last. By mid morning, after a swift and easy labour, Isabelle was delivered of Aristide Fraternité, a fine healthy infant with powerful lungs and a soft black down over his small head.

There was no anguish to follow this birth. The child, washed and wrapped, was brought to her to be fed, and then Jérôme came in with Aurore, who scrambled up on the bed to peer at her new brother. Isabelle put out an arm to draw her near and looked up into Jérôme's proud and happy face, and was filled with a great swelling sense of joy. If ever there was happiness, this was it, here and now in this room with the three people who meant more to her than any others in all the world. She thought she could ask for nothing else from life as long as it lasted.

# Chapter Twenty

Isabelle woke again, soon after midnight, and lay in the dark staring at a cheerless future. She was glad when Jérôme suddenly reached out to hold her, as if he had dreamed that she had gone, only to wake with an urgent need for reassurance that she was still at his side. She clung to him, comforted a little by the anguished fervour of his embrace. How could she ever have doubted his love? 'I wish today was over,' she said. 'Even if the worst happens, I want to know.'

The worst: imprisonment, separation, an end to her happiness. Was this her long delayed punishment, falling on her after all, just when she thought she was finally free of the past?

She had been so wrapped up in her home and her children, happy and untroubled, though always with time to share the troubles of her friends, like Marianne. Pierre had come home a few weeks ago, transformed by a ferocious-looking moustache, and a wooden leg whose inconveniences drove him to frequent bouts of fury. Marianne bore with his ill temper as best she could, though Isabelle knew patience did not come easily to her. Yet now Isabelle found herself envying Marianne. At least Pierre was alive, and they were together. Would she and Jérôme still be together after today?

It was last week that he had come home with news of the proposal put forward by Robespierre in the Convention, and passed enthusiastically by his fellow deputies, ordering the detention for the duration of the war of all English residents in

France. The original motion had simply been to ban the importation of English goods, their proliferation and cheapness a cause of resentment since long before the Revolution. But that day a report had reached the Convention of the execution of the mayor of the great port of Toulon, which had been betrayed into the hands of the British fleet two months before. It was not British merchandise that the French Republic most had to fear, so the deputies agreed. The British government was known to be giving encouragement to the rebels in the Vendée. It was said that British spies were everywhere, working even at the very heart of the new Republic, seeking to undermine her from within, and that at a time when the federalist rebels, led by disaffected Brissotins, still held Bordeaux and Marseille and Lyon and many other places. France was bleeding internally, and something had to be done to staunch the flow, so that she could find the strength to defeat the foreign armies on her borders. To seek to detain all potential agents of her greatest enemy seemed an obvious move, when even her own citizens could not always be trusted. The Committee of Public Safety had been asked to work out the detail of the new law, which the Convention would then vote upon.

At first, on hearing the news, Isabelle had simply been glad that she had concealed her origins. She had put her arms about Jérôme, puzzled by his sombre expression, but supposing he was simply anxious in case the truth should somehow emerge, a possibility that Isabelle entirely discounted. Only he and Marianne had ever been told her secret, and she knew that Marianne had not even confided in Pierre. 'Don't worry, my love,' she said. 'No one knows about me. And you know I'm no spy.'

Jérôme's expression did not lighten at all. 'That's not the point,' he said. 'Don't you see, it would be wrong of us to seek to protect ourselves, if the law is passed, that is? No one else may know the truth, but you do, and so do I. The fact that we know you are wholly to be trusted makes no difference. It is our civic duty to be open about it, and face the consequences, however terrible they may be.'

Isabelle had let her arms fall and stood staring at him, seared by a burning sense of hurt. How could it even occur to him to do such a thing, when his every instinct should be to protect and care for her? Was that what his supposed love for her was worth, that he could put civic rectitude before her happiness? All her trust in him, all her sense of security, seemed to turn to ashes in that moment.

He must have seen something of what she felt, from the way she stood and the way she looked at him, but he did not relent, only sought again to make her understand. 'It is not what I want, of course it is not. It would tear the heart from my body to lose you, even for a little while, even knowing you were safe and well. Every moment I am away from you, even at my desk with the work piling up around me, there is scarcely an instant when I do not think of you and long to be at home with you again. But—'

'You don't trust me, you don't, or your wouldn't even suggest such a thing! How can you pretend to love me?'

'Did you not swear once to serve the nation with your very life?'

'That's not what this is about.'

He took hold of her by the elbows, holding her though she tried to break free, his grey eyes very intent on her face. 'Think, Isabelle! If you found, say, that Citizeness Didier downstairs was English, but had kept her identity a secret, what would you suppose? That she must be a spy, of course, for why else would she do it?'

'But you know why I did it. That's why I still don't want it known. If you tell, then what's to stop my family finding me, and trying to—' She could not at present think what they might do, but there was one fear that was very real. 'Or if my cousin — you said he's in France. If he came to claim Aurore . . .'

'He couldn't. He's a rebel. He'd be arrested.'

'You don't know him. If he wants something . . .' She shivered.

Jérôme held her close, stroking her hair, though she refused to lean on him as he clearly expected her to do. 'He will never

239

again hurt you or Aurore, I promise you that.' Then she knew that her argument had not moved him in the least, for he went on, 'I understand, of course I do. I would be content to keep your secret to all eternity, so long as we did not break the law by doing so. But if this law is passed, then by saying nothing we are seeking a privilege that the law does not allow us. That cannot be right. You must see that.'

Rationally, coldly, objectively, she supposed she did see it, but all her instincts protested that it made no difference, that his love for her ought to come before every other consideration, especially when by keeping silent it was unlikely that anyone would ever know the truth. When she said nothing, he went on, 'Isabelle, I work right at the heart of the government. I know that many of those in my position are only out for what they can get. They have fed off the Revolution, they seek only their own advantage. But, as I see it, if there is corruption at the heart of the government, then the whole nation is in danger of being destroyed from within. I cannot put my own happiness, or even yours, before the well-being of the Republic. Rather, I must sacrifice even what I love most, if need be, for the sake of France.'

A tiny part of her was struck with awe and even admiration at the staunchness of Jérôme's principles. It was an unbending purity of soul of just this kind that had led her forebears to martyrdom, yet Jérôme had no ardent belief in another world to guide him, but only a passionate conviction that a perfect order of things would one day be established here in France, if only everyone would act with an equal purity of motive. It was terrifying and disturbing, and still she felt hurt by it, yet she could not love him the less because of it.

'Isabelle, we're not being asked to sacrifice everything.'

'I know,' she said. 'But it feels like it.'

'Yes.' It was a relief to see grief rather than austerity on his face. 'Pray that it won't come to that. If the law is not passed after all, then there is no reason why we should speak out.'

And this very day the new law was to go before the Convention, and Isabelle planned to be there when it was debated. Its main provision, Jérôme knew, was still the banning of English merchandise from France, a matter which was of no interest whatsoever to Isabelle. Other than that, he had no further information, and in any case the law was as yet no more than a proposal, subject, in theory at least, to debate and amendment, and even the possibility of rejection.

Now, in the darkness before dawn, they lay in one another's arms, knowing that each was thinking of the same cruel prospect, and flinching at it, Jérôme because to him there was no choice, Isabelle because she knew that in this her husband would not be swayed by common human feelings.

'Did Claudine agree to look after the children for you?'

Isabelle did not want to go to the Convention cumbered with children, who might prevent her from hearing the vital discussion, so she had asked her former neighbour to mind them during her absence; if a little reluctantly, since she had never been parted from Aristide before and did not really trust anyone but herself to care for him.

'She wasn't too happy about it. She wanted to go to the Widow Capet's trial. In fact, she thinks that's where I'm going. She said it was only fair I should have a turn.'

'I think it will be her execution today, not her trial,' said Jérôme. 'They were close to a verdict last night.' Isabelle felt more than ever overwhelmed by a sense of darkness and misery. If she thought her own troubles were hard to bear, then this reminded her that for another wife and mother things were far worse.

There had never been any doubt as to the outcome of the trial of the former Queen. Hated as she was, her fate was perhaps more certain even than that of her husband had been. Yet in spite of everything, Isabelle could not but pity her, though she knew there were few others who did. The trial must have been a terrible ordeal, for the most appalling allegations had been laid against her, not just the old and inevitable ones of her misuse of funds, her malign influence on her husband, her links with the enemy and her constant opposition, both open and concealed, to the Revolution, but also the assertion that she had been guilty of sexual relations with her young son. So anguished had been her reaction to that claim, Isabelle had heard, that many women in the court (Claudine among them) had made sympathetic protests. There had even for a moment been a doubt whether her accuser had gone too far, so that the jury would be moved to acquit her. But most people were ready to believe anything of the 'Austrian woman', and in the end there had been no doubt of the verdict. Isabelle remembered the young and beautiful woman she had seen years ago at Versailles, carefree and uncaring. Foolish she had certainly been and selfish too, and without doubt she had done all in her power to destroy the Revolution, but did she really deserve such a fate as this? Claudine said her hair had turned completely white, though she was not yet forty. She had aged as quickly as any peasant woman.

Jérôme was right, and the former Queen had been condemned to death in the early hours of the morning, perhaps at much the same time as Isabelle had woken from sleep. By the time she made her way to the Convention, feeling a little as if, without Aristide in her arms, she had left a part of herself behind, the crowds were hurrying towards the Place de la Révolution, anxious to ensure the best places for the day's spectacle. Isabelle heard the talk among those who passed her, the ribald jokes and obscene remarks, and wondered at the depth of hatred that lay behind them. There had been no comments so venomous, none of this vicious sense of triumph, when the King went to his death. But then much had changed in the few months since that ominous day.

It was hard now to remember what it had been like in the early days, just after she left the convent, when it had seemed almost unthinkable that France should not be ruled by a King, or that the Catholic Church, even brought under the control of the state, should not be at the heart of most people's lives. Now, many churches were closed altogether, the figures of saints that had once adorned them smashed to pieces. If people still worshipped, it was in secret. Many of the sans culottes said that superstition was dead, and reason alone had power to guide

242

men's actions. It was a view Pierre shared, and Marianne too. Jérôme shook his head over it, and said that such excesses only turned people against the Revolution, and besides nothing could disturb his own belief in a Supreme Being. Isabelle, perplexed, did not know what she believed. One day perhaps she would find time to think about it.

There were few people in the gallery of the Convention today, with such a strong counter-attraction outside, and Isabelle found a place easily, with a good view of the proceedings below. She wished Jérôme could have been with her, to share this time, or Marianne, the only other person who knew of her origins. But Jérôme was at work in another part of the Tuileries, and Marianne and Pierre would almost certainly be at the execution.

After some routine business, Isabelle recognised the frigidly elegant figure of St Just, youngest deputy in the Convention, stepping onto the tribune with a sheaf of papers in his hand, and she felt sick and afraid. Less than a week ago the same speaker (heard by Marianne, who had supported a bad-tempered but stubborn Pierre all the way to the Convention) had declared that the Constitution was to be put aside for the duration of the war, for the government was to be declared 'revolutionary until the peace'. He was known for his ruthless devotion to the Republic, and his ardent support for whatever means were necessary to nurture it. He was also known to be close to Robespierre. Isabelle thought it was unlikely he would urge leniency towards the Republic's potential enemies. The best she could hope for was that it would all be decided quickly, or she might even have to leave before the vote was taken. Aristide, recently fed, would not sleep for more than a few hours.

She strained her ears to hear every word, yet long passages of both speech and discussion were lost to her. St Just's voice was resonant enough, but some of the others, facing away from her, were inaudible. She would find her mind wandering, and time and again had to force herself to concentrate, to take in the detail of the speech, and follow the arguments and disputed

243

points brought up from the floor. At other times cheers and applause drowned what was being said. All she understood was that the English were the enemy, and she, now, was one of them; she seemed to feel the very words 'English' written across her forehead for all to read. Any moment she thought she would feel a hand on her shoulder and hear a stern voice declaring her to be under arrest.

Then she realised abruptly that St Just was speaking of those who had long ago sought a refuge in France; like Isabelle Moulin, watching in anguish from the gallery...

'Whatever cause has driven a man from his native soil, his heart clings to it as a tree clings to the earth, or else he is depraved ... The love of his birthplace is the last virtue that leaves the heart of ungrateful men...'

There was no escape then. In the eyes of these men she was irrevocably and for ever English at heart. She wanted to cry out that it was not true, that this was her only homeland, that her roots were firmly established in French soil, but instead she stood leaning on the parapet, gazing at the upright figure at the tribune and listening to the words that doomed her.

'The detention of these foreigners must deprive them only of the means of corresponding with their country and causing us harm. That detention must be pleasant and comfortable....'

But, however pleasant, it would cut her off from Jérôme, from her friends, perhaps even from her children. She tried to tell herself it was something she must accept, that it would not be for long, that it could even be to her advantage, for if the war ended in defeat (a terrible possibility, which she could hardly bear to consider), then those detained as aliens would not be subject to the vengeance of returning émigrés, and their husbands too might be spared.

But all she felt was a great weight of misery about her heart. Her happiness was at an end.

There was more discussion, which she did not hear; then the speaker moved on. 'There can be no exception other than that which comes from nature herself: mothers have no other homeland but that of their children, and the wife of a

Frenchman is not a foreigner . . .'

She caught her breath. Did that mean what she thought it meant? Was she safe after all? She waited, listening, through the final paragraphs of the speech, until at last the three articles of the new law were put before the deputies.

'Foreigners, born subjects of a government with which the Republic is at war, are to be detained until the peace.

'Women married to Frenchmen before the decree of the eighteenth of the first month are not included in the present law, so long as they are not suspect or married to a suspect.'

The eighteenth of the first month – what did that mean? The first month was January; she had been married on the 25th . . . But no, of course, there was a new calendar now, just brought in. The revolutionary era was said to have begun on September 22nd 1792, the day when the Republic had been declared. It was now the second year of that era, but they were still in the first revolutionary month, which, like all in the new calendar, had thirty days. So the eighteenth day of the first month had been that day last week, October 9th old style, when the new law had first been proposed; and at that time she had already been married to Jérôme for more than eight months.

She did not hear the final article, nor the voting that passed the proposals into law. She had heard all she needed to know. She was safe, and Jérôme too. There was no need for awkward disclosures. Even in the eyes of the government she was no foreigner, but a Frenchwoman, the mother of French children. She wanted to shout aloud, to tell someone, to run at once in search of Jérôme and share her relief and happiness with him. But that would be to betray everything, to draw unwanted attention on them both. She must return quietly to her children, hugging her joy to herself until she saw Jérôme again.

On the way home it struck her, sharply, that there was an implication to the new law that she had not thought of before. There had been no mention of English men married to French wives. Presumably they were no more exempt than any others of their countrymen. That meant that in the eyes of the law, a woman adhered to the beliefs of her husband, where a man did

245

not. Pliable, biddable, dutiful, the good Republican wife; as unlike as possible to the late Queen who had brought shame on her husband and sought to bend him to her will ... Then she smiled to herself, amused at the foolishness of feeling offended by a distinction that had spared her from imprisonment.

It was obvious as soon as Jérôme came home that he had heard the results of the debate. He took Isabelle in his arms and his embrace expressed all his relief, and the depth of the fear that it had replaced. As they ate their meal, his eyes scarcely left her face, and he kept leaning over to touch her hand or stroke her cheek or kiss her. She knew that if the children had not been present then he would have carried her straight to bed.

That had to wait until the evening, when he returned from work and supper was over and the children asleep. Then they closed the shutters and locked the door and tumbled together, arms about one another, onto their bed. Jérôme had never been so tender as he was that evening, or so passionate, so full of small caresses that set Isabelle's body alight, arousing pleasure and desire in ways she had never dreamed of. Afterwards, as they lay side by side, satiated and content, she said, 'How do you know what to do – all those little things? I'd never have thought of them. But—'

Though it was dark, she knew that he was smiling. 'Well, I suppose I was well educated.' His voice was slow with the indolence of satisfied desire.

She leaned over to touch his face, running her finger down the length of his nose, across the prominent cheekbone. 'Who by, then, that's what I want to know.'

He laughed softly and held her and kissed her. 'Too much curiosity, my darling.' As she struggled, laughing, to form the question again he pressed his mouth on hers, silencing her. Then those enticing, exquisitely exploring hands began to stray again over her body, and the kisses moved from her mouth, following where the hands led.

Much later she returned to the subject. 'Very well,' he said, 'then I shall tell you. But don't you reproach me with it afterwards. You see, I was very innocent when I first came to Paris. A pure-hearted country boy. Though perhaps it was from lack of opportunity, who knows? However, in Paris I found work in the office of a lawyer – a dry old man he was too, very tedious. But he had a pretty wife, younger than he was. She was still old enough to be my mother, just. Turn by turn she took all of her husband's clerks . . . under her direction, shall we say. I think she saw it as her duty to initiate them. Perhaps for the sake of the women that were to come after her. My turn came at last – and as you see, she taught well.'

Isabelle was silent, reflecting on the possibility that she owed her present happiness to an unknown woman of dubious morals. She was not sure how she felt about that. But when Jérôme anxiously challenged her silence, she turned to him and laughed and then put the matter out of her mind. What did the past matter, so long as they had one another now? 'Maybe you'd better give me a few lessons too,' she said. 'After all, I might want to pass them on some day.' He fell on her with mock outrage and then, a little later, proceeded with a delicious enthusiasm to do precisely what she had suggested.

# Chapter Twenty-One

There was a new word in Paris in this early spring of 1794, the year Two of the Republic One and Indivisible: 'queue'. The word for 'tail' had been appropriated to describe the daily experience of most Parisian women and many men, as they stood patiently in a long line outside bakers' or butchers' shops, waiting for their daily ration of bread or meat.

Today, as usual, Isabelle stood in one such queue outside Citizen Picot's shop, had been standing in it since first light, with her basket on one arm and Aristide on the other, well wrapped against the cold. She had to bring him with her, because he was likely to need feeding during the hours of waiting. She was growing used to putting him to the breast while standing in the street, as did many other women around her. Aurore, on the other hand, was left safely with Marguerite Didier, since her mother's household had a servant to do the queuing for them.

Sometimes Isabelle almost enjoyed the waiting, at least when it was not too cold, for there was an atmosphere of cheerful comradeship among the people there, all suffering the same inconveniences, all making the best of them; and Aristide won particularly friendly attention. At least at the end of the waiting they were all sure of something, however little, and at a price they could afford. The bread might be dark and hard – the 'bread of equality', rather than the fine white bread that the wealthier citizens had once been used to – but at least no one went completely hungry.

People chatted as they waited, sharing jokes, discussing family matters or local gossip, of a general and innocuous kind. Sometimes there were comments on the war, at last showing signs of turning in the Republic's favour, or the latest speeches of Barère or some other member of the Committee of Public Safety; generally mentioned in terms of approval, since to do otherwise was inadvisable. There might be Royalist spies listening, for Paris was said to be full of conspirators. Alternatively, there were always sharp-eared neighbours who might carry tales to Section committees if one said anything that could be construed as unpatriotic.

Isabelle's turn came at last and she bought her bread – showing the necessary papers to do so – and left the shop, exchanging encouraging remarks with those she knew among the citizens still waiting. She set out for home at a brisk pace, anxious to be back in the warm.

'Citizeness Duvernoy.'

She turned, expecting to see some acquaintance close behind her, though she did not immediately recognise the voice.

For a moment she thought him a stranger: square-shouldered, fair, a large man in the prime of life, his manner and appearance at odds with his rough clothes in a way she could not quite define; but then that was not unusual in these days when to dress too finely might draw unwelcome attention on oneself.

'Do you not know me?' Still she stared at him. 'Your cousin ...'

She felt her heart miss a beat and then begin to pound, thunderously ... Her cousin, François, the brother of her attacker. He had always been a coarser and more human version of his older brother, both in looks and character, even when dressed as she had seen him last, in wig and lace and silks. Henri Antoine had been every inch the aristocrat, tall, fine boned, fair haired, blue eyed. There was none of his brother's cold pride about François, none of the unthinking arrogance, above all none of the contempt and disregard for women. She did not know him particularly well – it was his sisters who had been her friends – but what she knew she had no reason to dislike, except by association.

She tried to gather her thoughts, make sense of what was happening. It seemed so unreal, that he should be standing here, facing her like any ordinary acquaintance in a Paris street, so casually, as if they had last spoken together only yesterday. When had they last spoken together? On the day she left La Pérouse . . .

'I thought you would have emigrated,' she said. Like him, she kept her voice low, though there were few people about and the disused church beside which they stood had no immediate windows or doors to overlook them.

'So I did. So did we all, as soon as the mob were permitted to take the Bastille. It became clear then that His Majesty had lost control and that he would need friends overseas. We lived at Blackheugh for some time, but my sisters and my mother now have a small house in the south of England, where the climate suits them better.' He studied her, as if waiting for some comment. She was wondering how much he knew of her story, if anything. Presumably her family had at least told him that she had taken the veil, if not perhaps the reason why. Had his brother been at Blackheugh too? Presumably, before he went to the Vendée. 'You do not ask how they all are.'

'I don't wish to know. They are nothing to me now.'

'That I cannot believe, my dear cousin!' He looked very grave and she thought perhaps she had shocked him. 'Your brother was in good health, when I last heard; his wife too.'

She was on the point of asking after the one person she cared about, the one he had not mentioned: Grandmother Milburn. But he had already moved on. 'They were very much distressed to learn of your apostasy.'

'How do they know about that?' She had thought she had covered her tracks so effectively. Not effectively enough, in any event, for François was here, speaking to her, talking of people she had thought never to see or hear of again.

'Your Superior wrote, with great regret I may say, to tell your uncle of it. He is in good health too, by the way.'

It seemed as if he were talking of some age long past, some life that no longer had anything to do with her. And yet here he was, facing her outside the empty church in the spring sunlight, and in some way she had not yet confronted threatening the whole new life upon which she had embarked, for which she had cut herself adrift from the past that he embodied. He was standing with one hand resting on the feet of the statue of a saint, smashed in the dechristianising fervour of last autumn, before such things were officially frowned upon. With a shiver she seemed to see a kind of symbolism in his stance, as if he were warning her that the past – her past – could not so easily be destroyed.

'There have been many prayers offered that you may undergo a change of heart and come to repentance,' he added. 'From the little I know of you, I must admit I find it hard to understand why, having taken so solemn a step, you should then renounce it all so lightly. I suppose it was something to do with this man to whom you are now married. I understand your elder child was born outside wedlock – or what passes for it in this new ungodly France.' Then he had not been told why she had entered the convent, that was evident, and he seemed to suppose that Aurore was Jérôme's daughter. She was very thankful she had left the child behind today and hoped he never had cause to find out how old she was.

But it was clear that he already knew more about her present circumstances than she liked. 'How did you find me?'

'By chance, I suppose – or as I like to think, the workings of Providence. I saw you one day walking in the Luxembourg gardens, with the man whom I understand to be your husband. There was another man with you, who soon took his leave. As he passed me, I asked who you were. Of course, the name was not one I recognised, except for the Isabelle. But I was certain then.'

She could not tell from that whether or not he had come to Paris expressly to find her, sent by her family perhaps. 'I

252

suppose they all know then – my brother, my uncle, every-one?'

'Not as yet. Do you wish them to know?'

She shook her head vehemently. 'No, never.'

'Then I shall not tell them, until such time as you change your mind. You need have no fear of that. They do not even know where I am.'

'Then why are you here?'

He smiled faintly. 'Perhaps I should keep that to myself, cousin. Are you not an ardent Jacobin? Or do you leave such matters to your husband?'

She did not answer. It dawned on her now that this man she was speaking to, this cousin of hers, was almost certainly in Paris on some counter-revolutionary business. An enemy of the Republic . . . She wished now that he had never found her.

He was speaking again, his voice very grave. 'You know about Henri, perhaps?' She saw that there were tears in his eyes. Whatever he thought she might know, it was clearly far removed from anything she did in fact know about his brother.

'I – I did hear he was in the Vendée. With the Royal Catholic Army.' There was a deliberate irony in her voice, which he appeared not to notice.

'He was murdered there, most foully, last November, ambushed by Republican troops, all his followers massacred with him.' His head went up then, and there was pride in his voice and his expression. 'He died for his King and his country, a martyr for that great cause. I would not ask for it to be otherwise. Except that he was my brother, and I mourn his loss.'

She did not. Oh, how she felt her heart leap, what a sense of triumph rose in her! And relief too; for he had gone, he no longer had any power to harm her, even in thought. She was wholly free of him at last. But why had Jérôme not told her? Had he not heard? She was careful to allow none of her true feelings to show.

'After that, when we heard the news, I knew I could no longer sit in safety in England. I saw that honour demanded

253

that I too must give my all to the cause for which he died. So here I am.' Admitting as clearly as he could that he was plotting against the Republic . . .

'What made you renounce your vows, cousin? Am I right to suppose it was for love of this man, this Jérôme Duvernoy?'

'I had my reasons,' she said. 'They are my business. But I do not regret it. I am very happy.'

He frowned slightly. 'That you share your husband's political views, I cannot believe.' There was a hint of a question in the statement.

'I do not disagree with him,' she said, a little cautiously. She had begun to suspect that he had some motive in what he said, and until she knew what it was she did not want to give too much away.

'No one would ask that of a wife, even the wife of such a man.'

She said nothing, and he then appeared to change the subject completely. 'However greatly you may have cut yourself off from your family, however deeply you have sinned not only against them, but against God Himself, I know that at heart you cannot have changed. There are certain virtues that are a part of our heritage, and have always been so – loyalty to our own, a sense of honour, courage.'

Yet more resounding principles, held up to her as paramount: Mother Church, the Republic, now Family and Honour – all demanding whole-hearted sacrifice; except that they were mutually exclusive, each of the others. She smiled faintly. 'You pay me a great compliment, cousin. Perhaps now you'll tell me what you expect from my courage and sense of honour?'

He coloured very faintly, as if she had found him out in some subterfuge. 'When your own kin call, I know you will answer that call. I know that you cannot fail to wish almost as strongly as I do for vengeance on those responsible for the death of my beloved brother, your dear cousin.'

Vengeance – oh yes, she had wanted vengeance! The fierce blood of her border ancestors had cried out for vengeance, from the moment when she had recognised what it was that Henri had done to her. It was that blood that had shouted for joy at what François had just told her. She felt almost sorry for him, that he should have appealed for her sympathy on such delusive grounds, that he should hold in such veneration so unworthy a man as his brother had been, but she had no intention of telling him how mistaken he was.

'My family are not any longer those of my blood,' she told him instead. 'You are wrong when you think I am in any way like the Isabella Milburn you used to know. I have changed beyond words. I wish you no harm, but I can have nothing to do with you now.' A small voice whispered to her that the good Republican did not allow family ties to stand in the way of civic duty; and civic duty required the informing of the authorities of the whereabouts of any enemy of the state. But she told herself that she did not know for certain what François was doing in Paris. All she wanted now was to escape from him before he revealed anything more decisively incriminating.

He looked as if he were deeply disappointed in her. 'Very well, cousin. So be it. Perhaps we shall meet again.'

'I think not,' she said, and turned and left him. Once she looked back. She could no longer see him, but the feeling stayed with her that she was being followed.

Isabelle was home in time to prepare dinner, before Jérôme came in from work, but then of course the presence of the children made private conversation with Jérôme almost impossible. Today, as on many occasions lately, Jérôme gave most of his attention to Aurore, talking to her about what she had read, about her walks and her toys and her games, almost, Isabelle thought (a little resentful for their son), as if Aurore and not Aristide was his own child. She felt irritable and anxious, troubled as she was by this morning's meeting. Perhaps if they had been alone together she would have told Jérôme what had happened, but as it was she said nothing, thinking she might have an opportunity this evening.

He came home very late, when Aurore had long been in bed. Aristide, fed some time ago, had fallen asleep in Isabelle's arms, but she had continued to hold him, reluctant to return him to the cradle for which he was already growing a little large. She loved to feel the warm weight of his body against her, savouring the sweet sensations of motherhood that had been denied her when Aurore was a baby.

Jérôme, coming in, kissed her, but looked faintly disapproving. 'That son of ours should be in his bed by now.'

Isabelle said nothing, but soon afterwards laid the infant in his cradle and brought Jérôme's supper to the table. She would not tell him about this morning, she decided. By now her unease had receded a little, and in any case she sensed that he was not in the most mellow of moods. One thing she did say, however, when he had finished eating and was sitting by the fire with a final glass of wine in his hand. 'Did you ever have any more news of my cousin?'

'No. But then I'm working on other things now. I'll enquire, if you like.' Next day he brought her the news she had heard from François; that Henri was dead, killed in an ambush by the comrades of some of the very men he had previously tortured and killed, among whom was the lover of a girl who had been raped and murdered. No, Henri was no martyr, she thought, but a brutal monster whose life and death brought no credit to any cause he served.

Two mornings later, the day's queuing being at an end rather earlier than usual, Isabelle and the children went walking in the Luxembourg gardens with Marguerite Didier. The girl, fond of Aurore, threw a ball for her to catch, their game taking them further and further from the secluded seat, full in the sunshine, where Isabelle sat with the baby. She did not follow them, being content to dance Aristide on her knee, enjoying his chuckling delight in the attention, wrapped up in him. She did not see someone approaching her along the path, until a shadow fell across her and she looked up suddenly to see her cousin standing there. There was something in his expression that put Isabelle on her guard, something that had not been there the other day.

'We must talk, cousin. I will meet you in the Tuileries

gardens, at five. Do not fail me. You may have cause to regret it if so.' Then he was gone, before she could say anything.

She considered what he had said. She could not see how he, who had every reason to conceal his identity, could be any kind of threat to her, unless he were to be accidentally discovered. Perhaps he felt that he was safe from betrayal by her, for that very reason. On the other hand, he was an enemy, and as such his plans must be thwarted. If she were to meet him she might be able to find some way to thwart them, without putting him – or herself – in any danger. It was not a prospect she relished, but it convinced her to leave the children with Claudine that afternoon and dress in her plainest clothes and make her way to the Tuileries gardens.

It was some time since Isabelle had been there. Apart from anything else, they were uncomfortably close to the Place de la Révolution, which she had avoided since it became the place of execution. Since last autumn many people accused of various crimes against the Republic had gone to their deaths there: not only the hated Queen, but also Philippe Égalité, whose vote for his cousin's death had not saved him, and many of the Brissotins. But today there were no executions and few people about.

Large areas of the Tuileries gardens – like those of the Luxembourg – had been ploughed up, ready for planting with potatoes, by order of the Committee of Public Safety, concerned that the capital should be fed in this time of war and shortages. The trees were still there, showing the first tentative green of spring, and Isabelle kept close to them, hoping that she would not be seen from the windows of the palace, in one of whose graceful pavilions the Committee of Public Safety was housed. She had no wish at all to be faced with questions from Jérôme as to what she had been doing there; or, worse, whom she had been meeting.

She had half hoped that François would not come, but he was already there, standing under one of the chestnut trees near the river bank, at the further end from the palace. She knew that he had seen her, but he simply stayed where he was, waiting

257

for her to come up to him. Perhaps he too wanted to avoid observation, though why in that case he had suggested they meet here she did not know.

'I am glad you have enough family feeling left to keep our appointment,' he said, unsmiling.

'I think you know it's not family feeling,' she said, with equal gravity. 'And this isn't a good place. Please tell me quickly what you want.'

'I intend to appeal to your sense of honour; for I believe you still have such a thing, in spite of everything.'

'I told you, my idea of honour is not yours. We no longer have anything in common.'

He paused, studying her face. Then he said, 'Do not confuse honour with sentiment, cousin. The two are not the same. I believe you love your husband; you risked your immortal soul for his sake, after all. But that has nothing to do with honour.'

'I know that. But I told you, I have changed. I love my husband, but I also love France, as he does. I am not English any more, but French, more French than you are. After all, you left your country when she most needed you. I am proud to be a citizen of France, not the old dead one you deserted, but the new France. I am proud to belong to a nation that seeks to bring liberty and equality to all its people, to give them all a voice and to bind them together with bonds of true fraternity. I know there will be difficulties and failures, as there have been already. No one supposes it's easy to build a new order of things. But I believe it will be done and all I ask is to play my part as best I can, if only by raising my children as good citizens of the Republic.'

He studied her face in silence for a moment, then he said slowly, 'Did you hear what was done to helpless prisoners in Nantes, by one of your fine nation's representatives on mission, one Carrier? Priests, women, children even, crammed into boats, shut in so they could scarcely breathe; bound together with bonds of true fraternity, as you might say. Then the boats were pushed out into the Loire and sunk. I suppose it was equality, too, of a kind; equality in death. They're very good at enforcing that, your Republican friends.'

She stared at him, suddenly aware of how cold it was, and how quiet. 'You're lying.'

'I'm surprised you hadn't heard. But I see you're not so lacking in decency and honour as I feared. Ask your husband if you don't believe me. I'm quite sure he knows. I've heard it talked of in Paris, so it's no secret, that's certain.'

'I don't wish to hear any more. If all you can do is slander all I believe in, then truly we have nothing in common.' She turned away from him, but he caught her arm.

'Wait, cousin. Don't be so hasty. You forget the inconvenient fact that we are blood relations.'

'I owe you nothing,' she said. 'I have no family now, except my husband and children.'

'Perhaps then we should allow the Surveillance Committee of your Section to be the judge of that.'

She stared at him. 'Do you think I believe you'd go to them?'

'An anonymous note would be sufficient, I believe – to cause them to begin an investigation at least. It is not generally known, is it, that you are, by birth, an English aristocrat, with relations who are émigrés? For instance, does that blood-guzzling husband of yours know?'

'I have no secrets from him,' she said steadily, trying to keep herself under control. He must not see how he had frightened her.

'Ah, but what secrets does he keep from his masters? And what would they say, if they knew?' When she said nothing – she wanted so much to make a defiant reply, but could find no words – he went on, 'Jérôme Duvernoy is, I believe, employed in some capacity by the Committee of Public Safety. He is then, presumably, privy to many of the conferences and decisions of that powerful yet secretive body.'

'I wouldn't know. He does not talk politics to me.' That at least was largely true. If he ever told her anything of what happened at work, it was only what was already generally known; such as, for instance, the fact that Robespierre was

259

unwell and had not attended committee meetings for some time; or that St Just had returned a week ago from a successful mission to the armies in the north; or that Jean Bon Saint-André had just departed on mission to the naval base at Brest; or that all the committee members worked phenomenally hard, often throughout the night, which was why Jérôme and his colleagues were often kept so late at work themselves.

'You expect me to believe that, after the eloquent harangue I have just heard? No, my sans culotte cousin, you cannot fob me off so easily. This is what I require – all possible information, any information whatsoever, concerning the plans, actions, discussions and the like, of the Committee. More than that, any information about the twelve men who constitute it – their principles, aims, alliances, above all their friendships and their enmities. In short, whatever there is to know. We know that your husband has visited Robespierre's lodgings on more than one occasion. We also know that Nicolas Lefèvre, who is a frequent visitor at your house, is a close friend of St Just's secretary.'

Then he had been watching them! She felt indignant and afraid, but she did not speak at once, concerned that her answer should be the right one.

'Why do you want to know all this? What possible use can it be to you?'

'To lay our own plans successfully, we need to know the plans of the Committee. Further, if, as we hope, we are to retain the support of the British government, we need any evidence that will convince them that it is worth their while to support us – in particular anything that demonstrates the weakness of the revolutionary government. Unfortunately, the British have this awkward insistence that there must be some popular support for any restoration of Christian government in France – as if the most sacred monarch of France required the acclamation of the rabble before he could take his throne! But they must be humoured, of course. At least they see well enough the dangers of democracy, that many-headed monster.'

'And what if there is no weakness in the government?'

260

'The blindest fool knows of the divisions that have torn them apart for years now. Look how many former deputies of various assemblies have gone to their deaths over the past months. It can only get worse. In that is our hope. But we need solid information – who might be brought round to our point of view, who is the most dangerous to our hopes and so forth.'

'And you honestly think I can or will give you such information?'

'You have no choice. It is that, or exposure, for you and that husband of yours.'

*You have no choice.* The words chilled her, though her mind resisted them. 'He will never tell me,' she said, while her mind ran from one possibility to another, trying to find some final unanswerable argument why she could not do what he asked.

'Then you'd better find a way to make him,' said François. She wondered that she could ever have thought him likeable or harmless. In his way he was as deadly, as much a threat to her as his brother had been. 'I shall expect to receive your first information here at five next Friday afternoon – or whatever they call it now, in that ridiculous new calendar.'

Isabelle did a hasty calculation. 'Tridi – the third Ventôse.'

'As if the names God gave were not good enough for the new France!' Then he added, with a sudden softening of the expression which for a moment gave her a faint hope that he might lessen his demands, 'I cannot understand how someone brought up as you were, in true religion, with a sense of honour, could have fallen so low. It is passion, I suppose – a dangerous guide. All I can say is that one day you will be glad you helped me in this, when the Revolution has crumbled into ruin and France has returned to her true allegiance. You will not be alone then in seeing where it all went wrong.'

'Good day, cousin,' she said, weary of his moralising.

He had one last parting shot. 'Ask him about Nantes!' he called after her, in a low voice.

She walked away briskly enough, but once out of sight of him she slowed her step, feeling weary and miserable. What could she do? Whichever way she looked there was betrayal.

She recognised that she could do what he asked, if with some difficulty. There were many ways in which she could coax information from Jérôme without his realising it; not a great deal perhaps, but enough to satisfy her cousin. More than that, she could turn herself into a real spy, listening at doors when his friends came to the house, so as to hear the things he would not tell her. It would be underhand and despicable, but it would enable her to give François the information he asked for.

But she did not want to give him any information; he was working for a cause that sought the downfall of everything she had come to believe in, all she held most dear. Yet what alternative did she have? The good citizen, as she knew very well, must put family feeling aside and inform the authorities of anyone suspected of conspiring against the nation, as François so clearly was. Yet if she were to do that, her relationship to him would emerge and put not only her own life in danger, but threaten Jérôme's too. Worse, if she were to do nothing, the danger would be exactly the same, but made more certain by her failure in citizenship.

Things seemed no better when she reached home. Aurore came running to meet her, full of chatter, Aristide woke as she picked him up, and demanded to be fed. She sat by the fire with the baby at her breast and Aurore curled up beside her, and knew that Jérôme would soon be home for supper. On the surface, nothing had changed. But beneath the familiar simplicity and happiness lay a dark abyss that was about to open and swallow it all up, destroying every trace of her happiness and security.

When Jérôme came home he knew at once that something was wrong, but she fobbed him off with some talk of a headache. Later, in bed, while he slept beside her, she lay trying not to move – he needed his sleep, with the hard day before him tomorrow – but with an ache of restlessness in every part of her and her mind unable to find any peace.

What could she do? Ignore François and hope that somehow he would be unable to expose her? But then he would try and find his information elsewhere, might even succeed, and would go on to plot against the Republic, until perhaps he might do some greater damage. What if someone died because of what her cousin had passed on to his masters? The very least action could have vast and unpredictable consequences, their end unknown. Yet looking, purely selfishly, at the possible consequences to herself, and to Jérôme too, the safest course would certainly be to do as her cousin asked, and discreetly and cautiously to feed him small pieces of information, in the hope that they would make little difference and that, in time, he would go away and leave her in peace. Could she do that, and still live with her conscience afterwards?

What, oh what should she do? Perhaps she should meet her cousin as arranged, refuse what he asked and instead tell him everything she knew about his brother, revealing how unworthy he was of François's veneration. But she knew at once what her cousin's reaction would be. He would refuse adamantly to believe any wrong of his brother; as she had done when he told her about Republican atrocities. *Ask him about Nantes* ... The words repeated themselves in her head, insistently, beating out the rhythm of her uncertainty and doubt.

In the end, unable to lie still any longer, she got out of bed and went to crouch over the fire, staring into its last faintly glowing embers, as if she might find some solution there. In spite of her caution, she must have disturbed Jérôme after all, for he woke suddenly and, finding her absent, sat up and saw her. 'Isabelle, my love, what is it?' He climbed out of bed and came to her, taking her into his arms. How she managed not to tell him everything at that moment she did not know; the longing to do so was so strong. She knew what the result would have been. To him, her duty would have been utterly clear; he would have insisted that she go to the authorities, whatever the consequences to themselves. He would have hoped that somehow they would have been able to ride them and come out unscathed at the far side. He trusted the justice of the revolutionary courts, as she knew she ought to do.

Yet even if she had been sure of that, she was still faced with

263

the painful knowledge that in doing such a thing she would be sending her own cousin – a young man of her own blood who had never done her any harm – to certain death. She could not deny that, if any deserved death, then those who conspired against the Republic in this time of war were the most deserving. But then she had never before been faced with the realisation that one of those spies was someone she knew, someone of her own blood.

'Tell me, my darling!' Jerôme insisted.

She groped instead for the other dreadful thing that haunted her. 'I heard some talk today,' she explained. 'They were saying Citizen Carrier drowned prisoners in Nantes, priests and women and children.'

'Not children, at least not as far as I know.' Then it was true! 'I'm surprised you didn't know; it was no secret. Poor darling, has it been keeping you awake? Terrible things have been done in the Vendée, and not only by the enemy. Our own people have been driven to cruel revenge. It is no excuse, I know, but the drowned prisoners were rebels, taken in arms. The fact that they were mostly priests does not make them less guilty – on the contrary, they have been the most fanatical in encouraging rebellion.'

'But to do that to them, whatever their guilt! And a representative – Carrier's a deputy, sent by the Convention ...'

'And just recalled to Paris. I shouldn't be telling you this, but there are many who, like you, are uneasy at what has been done.'

'It's not just that – there were all those people shot at Lyon, after it was retaken; then the whole city destroyed. And the things Fréron did, and Barras, at Toulon. Oh, Jerôme, how can they be right? Doesn't it just make people hate the Republic even more?'

She could see by the dim light of the candle that he was troubled. 'The Republic is fighting for its life. It cannot afford to be lenient to its enemies. Time enough for that when it is firmly established. Remember the September massacres? Remember the hunger that autumn and winter, and how near we came to defeat and invasion? That is what happens when there is no firm government.'

'But surely you can't make people better by treating them so harshly? What sort of example is that?'

'Once the Republic is established, with good Republican schools, when our children are all brought up from infancy according to Republican principles, then there will be no need for repression, because no one will ever want to set himself against the law. It is just that centuries of despotism have destroyed men's natural virtue. The Republic will restore it to them.'

François, like all her family, would have said that humankind was naturally sinful and only the fear of God and of those in authority could keep them from savagery. Were they right, or was Jérôme, with his trust in the eventual triumph of man's natural goodness? Neither view seemed to have had much lasting influence for good so far, but Jérôme's had as yet scarcely been tried. Perhaps it should be given a chance.

She allowed Jérôme to caress her and talk softly to her until, even strung up as she was, she felt a little more at ease; and then they went back to bed, where they made love. Comforted, Isabelle slept rather uneasily until it was time to get up. 'You let things worry you too much, my darling,' Jérôme said at breakfast. 'All will be well, I promise you.' The fact that he himself had a careworn look did not make it easier to accept his reassurance.

That day she performed all the usual daily tasks without ever really noticing what she was doing. All the time her thoughts were occupied by the dilemma with which François had confronted her.

She had no illusions at all about what his aims were. Once he and his friends had overthrown the Republic and, presumably, meted out an appropriate revenge on all its supporters, the monarchy would be restored. And it would not be a limited constitutional monarchy on the British model, such as many of the early revolutionaries had sought, until the King's intransigence defeated them, but an absolute monarchy buttressed by all the old hierarchy of nobility and privilege that had been a part of the old order. His France would be one where young nobles could return to drive fast through the streets of Paris, injuring whom they pleased, not because the law said they might, but because even the law must give way to nobility, whatever its vices; a world in which men like Jérôme or Pierre, women like Marianne, must bow and scrape to another human being because his birth set him in authority, however unworthy he was of such an honour; a world in which the poor had no voice, and depended once more on the charitable whim of the rich. True, the new world was as yet far from perfect, but the changes were coming, the new order was being put in place, so that one day there would indeed be a juster, kinder world for all people. Even now, with all its faults, all its savagery, it was better than the old, she was sure of that. She knew herself, from her own small experience, how hard it was to start afresh from nothing at all, when all the bridges to the past had been broken down; and her little world was a simple matter, set against the creating anew of a great nation.

She was faced with the need to choose, and whatever choice she made there would be painful consequences, for herself and for her family. She had to weigh one good against another, one evil against another, knowing how great a risk she ran both for herself and all those she loved. Acknowledging that, then she knew she could only choose by setting aside all personal considerations and trying to make the choice that accorded with everything she believed to be right.

The next morning, after another sleepless night, she queued for the daily bread and meat and then went with her basket still on her arm to the Section headquarters; and there she made a statement that she had been approached by a man she thought to be a spy, and that they would find him at five in the afternoon in the Tuileries gardens on the third day of Ventôse, where he would be waiting to meet her. She also gave them a full description of her cousin, when they asked for one. She did not tell them that he had any connection with her. She supposed it would come out eventually, but there did not seem to be any point in making it known before it had to be. She was thanked with grave approval for her information, notes were taken, and she was free to go. She should have felt relieved that the decision had been made and was now out of her hands; but instead she felt miserable, as if she and not François were the traitor.

All that now remained was to tell Jérôme, this evening, what had happened, and then it would be over, at least as far as any choices of hers were concerned. But when he came home that night she saw at once that he had something on his mind, something so grave that he gave her no more than the most perfunctory of kisses and scarcely spoke to her at all until the children were in bed. She was about to ask him then what she had done to offend him, when he burst out, 'Le Bas sought me out this afternoon, to warn me.' Philippe Le Bas was, with the painter David, one of the few friends Robespierre had on the Committee of General Security, the Republic's police committee. 'He said Citizen Command had denounced you to the Committee of General Security, first thing this morning. He claimed that you had been seen in conversation with a man whom he knew to be a returned émigré, a Royalist, and probably a spy. He claimed furthermore that the man was your cousin.' Jérôme cleared his throat, his voice becoming more painful by the minute. 'Le Bas asked if I knew anything of this and I had to say, of course, that I did not. I could only say that I was convinced of your loyalty and patriotism ... It seems they had also heard that you are English.' Then he cried, 'Isabelle, tell me what I fear is a delusion, not the truth – tell me it is only Command's malice!'

She went and put her arms about him. 'It is true.' She felt him pull away from her, but would not let him go. 'No, love, hear me! I went to the Section headquarters today, to report that François had contacted me, in the hope of gaining information to be used for Royalist purposes. I told them where they could find him.' And thank God she had! It was the one defence she had against Command's denunciation, against the blot of her concealed origins and her émigré kin, that she had put her duty first.

She told Jérôme the whole story and he heard her in silence and then held her close. 'No wonder you were unhappy. I wish you had told me.'

'I had to be sure what was the right thing first.'

It was not over; they still had to face the consequences. But her greatest relief now was that she could have done nothing to prevent her cousin's arrest, even if she had not reported him, for someone else knew the truth. It was a comfort to know that his blood would not be on her hands; or not on hers alone.

'I gave Le Bas my word that we would go to answer questions tomorrow, both of us together,' said Jérôme, and they clung to one another, afraid, and yet comforted by the knowledge that they were united in this time of trouble.

# Chapter Twenty-Two

For weeks after that time Isabelle would wake in the early hours of the morning in a cold sweat, imagining herself once again in the palatial austerity of the Hôtel de Brionne, the large mansion between the Tuileries palace and the Louvre where the Committee of General Security had its headquarters.

They had been dreadful, those hours of questioning, alone in a room with a group of hostile men – the number varied, though there was always one who questioned her, assiduously, insistently – not knowing where Jérôme was or what he was saying to the questions they were asking him. 'Just tell the truth. That is all you need to do,' he had assured her. She had thought that he was very calm and unafraid, but often since then he had been her companion in wakefulness, rolling over in bed to hold her tight, and she had known that he too was remembering the fear of that time.

She had told the truth, because it seemed the obvious thing to do; the whole story from the beginning, the convent school, what Henri had done to her, the pregnancy, the child snatched from her, the convent. And then the moment when she had decided that she must be French, that only by cutting herself off completely from her family and the past could she hope to find her child and support her.

Because they were the kind of men they were, they had accepted her story, once they had checked every detail as best they could, with witnesses from her Section who could confirm her Republican credentials. She learned afterwards that they had even questioned Aurore, briefly and discreetly, to be sure that she had been correctly instructed by her mother.

She did not think she would ever forget the moment when, abruptly, they had told her she was free to go. She did not know whether the sun had been shining that morning, but she had felt that the world was bathed in gold, and out in the brilliance of the day beyond the dark heavy doors of the mansion Jérôme had been waiting, to embrace her with a passion that demonstrated as nothing else could the depth of the fear and apprehension he had shared with her. They had walked home hand in hand, collecting the children on the way from the ever-obliging Claudine.

They did not at any time, then or later, discuss what had happened to them, as if by silent mutual agreement they wanted to put it behind them. But in bed that night they made love with the abandonment of two people who have just learned how sweet life is, and how fragile.

The end of that time did not bring an end to fear. One real anxiety haunted Isabelle: that she might be called to the revolutionary tribunal as a witness against her cousin. The prospect of facing François in court and being forced openly to give the evidence that would condemn him was one that filled her with dread. But the weeks passed and no word came and Jérôme said he thought perhaps the Public Prosecutor had evidence enough, without hers. She began to wonder then if she would ever know precisely what had become of François; not that there was really any doubt of his eventual fate, though with the prisons so full of suspects it was likely to be some time before he was brought before the tribunal.

For others there was no delay. In mid March – towards the end of Ventôse – there were mass arrests of members of the radical Cordeliers Club, along with other extreme revolutionaries. Accused before the tribunal of implication in a foreign plot, they were speedily sent to the guillotine.

Foremost in urging their arrest had been Danton and his

friends, now crying for an end to revolutionary government and terror, and the return of a freer régime. Within a month Danton himself was under arrest.

Isabelle, hearing of it, was astonished. 'Danton arrested! But why? What can he have done?'

She thought at first that Jérôme was going to refuse to discuss the matter with her. He tried to change the subject, but when she persisted, sat down at her side on their little sofa. He was frowning with concentration, trying to gather his thoughts, and also perhaps to understand quite what they were.

'He has been speaking out for an end to the Revolution. He wants to see a halt to executions – as God knows so do we all – but also to all the other constraints we live under. He does not seem able to see that to end it now, when the Revolution is only half made, when the institutions of the Republic are not yet in place, when the country is full of foreign spies and counter-revolutionaries and the enemy are still on our borders, that would be to destroy everything we have striven for, all our hopes of a new world. But then, everyone knows he's made a fortune since the Revolution began, and it may be his heart was never really in it. Whatever his reasons, I don't want to go back to the state of things we had before, where hunger marches beside riches, and corruption and immorality are as common in public figures as they ever were, where men rise by trampling on the weak, where nothing matters but each man's self interest, each man's ambition. That was not why the Bastille fell, nor why the King died. If that is all we aimed for, then we might as well not have begun. All those deaths, all that pain, could have been avoided, for they were without purpose.'

She saw what he meant and was in sympathy with it. Yet when she heard by what a travesty of a trial Danton was condemned, before the very tribunal he had himself established a year before, she felt anguished that the régime which she supported could stoop to this. Yet she knew that if Danton had escaped with his life, then it would have been his opponents – Robespierre, the other members of the Committee of Public Safety, all those who shared Jérôme's vision, who would have gone in their turn before the tribunal.

But she did not disclose those final troubled thoughts to Jérôme. He was busier than ever now, for the Committee of Public Safety had purged the Commune of Paris of its more extreme members and replaced them with men it could trust; among whom was Jérôme himself, appointed to represent the Section on the Commune's General Council, from which he was selected as an administrator of the city's department of Public Works. No longer was the Commune to be in a position to call the Sections to arms against the Convention; in fact, the powers of the Sections were curbed too. Piece by piece the Committee was gathering all the threads into its own hands.

Pierre ceased printing anything that might prove controversial and confined himself to producing suitable publications for the edification of the armies. 'The Montagnards are the only ones we can trust, and I suppose Robespierre's the best of them,' he said, a little grudgingly. 'I'll not do anything to upset things, not yet at least.' There was perhaps a warning implicit in the last remark, but it was carefully veiled.

It was a strange time, that spring and early summer of 1794, a time of suspicion and fear through which ordinary life somehow continued, with its moments of happiness and long days of contentment or frustration. There were assassination attempts on members of the Committee of Public Safety, followed by swift execution of the culprits. Treason reached even into the heart of the Committee, and one of its number himself went to the guillotine, found guilty of passing information to the enemy. A new law laid down that all suspects from every part of France were henceforth to be brought to Paris, to be dealt with under the watchful eye of the central government, ensuring severity without excess, so Jérôme said. New prisons were opened in disused monasteries and mansions, to cope with the swelling numbers of suspects. Yet at the same time, laws were being put into place to ensure primary schooling for every French child, and to inaugurate a comprehensive welfare system for the poor and the old and the sick. There were schemes to supply the needs of orphans and unmarried mothers and provide pensions for disabled soldiers and their widows. Slavery was abolished in every part of the territories of France. Metric measurements were being devised, care of the insane and the deaf improved, all the small steps by which the new world order was to be brought about.

Isabelle and Jérôme watched their children grow, saw how Aurore's skills in reading and writing became ever more fluent, saw Aristide pull himself into a sitting position, and then go on to develop his own distinctive shuffling crawl. Sometimes they had time to spend a day together in the country, on the Décadi, the tenth day that had replaced Sunday in the new calendar and gave resentful working people a less frequent day of rest. It was to replace Sunday in other ways too, for at Robespierre's instigation the Convention decreed that the French Republic 'recognised the existence of the Supreme Being and the immortality of the soul', and not only were all discreet and peaceable forms of worship to be allowed, but regular festivals on the Décadi were to mark the Republican year.

The new civic religion was to be inaugurated on twentieth Prairial – June 8 by the old calendar – with a Festival of the Supreme Being to be observed in every commune in the land. 'Catholicism by the back door, that's what it is,' complained Marianne, though quietly, not wanting to be accused, however justly, of the new crime of atheism. 'You know the twentieth Prairial is the day the fanatics call Whit Sunday? Robespierre for Pope, that's what they'll be saying next.' She was not usually so open in her opinions these days, generally confining herself to non-controversial personal matters, though Isabelle knew she did not approve of many of the things that had been done. It made her uneasy to feel that Marianne did not trust her; not just Marianne either, but Claudine too, and even Thérèse. The actress had suffered a brief spell in prison earlier in the year, for making disparaging comments on the government's decision to close down all women's clubs – in the words of Amar, of the Committee of General Security: *A woman ought not to leave her family for the purpose of interfering with affairs of state.* On her release, it was clear that the Terror had

273

done the impossible, and subdued her natural volubility. She had become almost discreet. If Isabelle ever found herself regretting the caution of her friends, she would ask herself what she would have done had she heard any of them expressing the kind of views good citizens were supposed to disclose to the authorities. She could only be thankful that none of them risked putting her in that position.

For days before the festival Isabelle attended Section meetings, where they were coached in the various songs and hymns, and instructed in the order for the procession – an order which was liable to sudden reversals when David, the inevitable organiser of the festival, changed his mind, as he often did. At home, like other families in Paris, the Duvernoys did their best to meet the injunction to decorate their windows with flowers and ribbons and banners. Aurore cosseted her geraniums, so that they might compete adequately with Citizeness Didier's magnificent shop-front display.

They were up before dawn on the twentieth Prairial. Aurore, excited and nervous, dressed in her best white muslin, skipped from foot to foot as Isabelle tried to tether the circlet of flowers to her flowing fair hair and tie the tricolour ribbons about her waist.

When she was dressed she went to show herself to Jérôme, who studied her with careful gravity for some time, and then smiled and hugged her. 'My little daughter will be the prettiest of all the girls in the procession today. And the one I love the best.' Aurore giggled happily and, once freed from his arms, did a little dance about the room, and then went to show her finery to her friend Marguerite.

When she had gone, Isabelle, struggling single-handed to dress a restless Aristide in his crisp white robes, said to Jérôme, 'Anyone would think Aurore was your only child. Sometimes I think you love her more than you do me and Aristide put together.' She spoke lightly, but the hurt beneath the words was not lost on Jérôme.

'What could possibly give you that idea?'

274

'The time you spend with her. The fuss you make of her.'

Suddenly he looked very grave. 'If I do, then it's only to make up for what you don't give her.'

'I don't understand. I love her as much as I always have.' Yet an understanding of what he meant was already stirring in her conscience, while she fought with it.

'Do you know what I saw when I came in yesterday, at dinner time?' he went on. 'You were there by the window with the baby, with eyes for no one but him. And Aurore was in the corner, like you told me she always used to be, playing all by herself. I don't know how long she'd been like that, of course, but it's not the first time it's happened. You know that as well as I do.'

She felt her colour rising. 'I have to care for Aristide. He's only a baby.'

'But he was asleep. He didn't need you at that moment.' He reached out and took her hands, his voice low and imploring. 'My darling, don't let your love for Aristide's father get in the way of your love for your daughter, just because she was not conceived in love. It's not her fault, who her father was.'

'I know.' But did she know? Was he right, and had Aurore come to take a poor second place in her heart? She would have liked to deny it vehemently, but honesty would not quite allow her to do so. 'I love her, of course I do! How can you doubt that, when you think what I went through to find her?'

'Then let her see it. Let her know she is not second in your heart, but equally first, with her brother.'

She was silent for a moment, then she said, 'Do you not love Aristide more?'

'I don't know,' he said. 'I feel different things for each of them. But I loved her as my daughter before our son was born, and I am determined that she shall never feel she has a lesser place in my heart. But then I am only her father.'

Her stepfather, Isabelle thought; who yet saw more clearly than her own mother. She felt ashamed and alarmed, and perhaps Jérôme saw it, for he was quick to reassure her. 'There's no harm done. Just have a care, that's all. You know,

275

as I do, how poisonous jealousy can be between brothers and sisters. Better not give it cause to grow at all.'

She saw it all clearly then, in her memory: the neglected infant, blamed for her mother's death, while her brother was cherished and loved and praised. Was Aurore to grow up as Isabelle herself had done, knowing that her very birth had been a destructive and painful thing? No, she must never think that, never have any cause to believe it, not for one moment, as far as it lay in her mother's power to prevent it. 'Remind me, when I need it,' she said to Jérôme.

He kissed her with great tenderness. 'As you will tell me, when I do wrong,' he said.

She could not imagine Jérôme ever falling short of perfection; at least not in her eyes. But, gravely, she gave him the assurance he wanted.

He called Aurore to come and help them dress Aristide. The baby, like the rest of them, had his share of tricolour ribbons; even his leading reins were of blue and white and red. Isabelle wore her wedding muslin, newly trimmed, and she too had flowers in her hair. It was some time before Aurore was satisfied with Jérôme, whose clothes were, she thought, disappointingly sombre; but ribbons tied in a rakish bow at the waist of his dark blue coat, and a new cockade in his hat, satisfied her at last.

They set out at five in the morning, as instructed, for the Section headquarters, where there was some last-minute practising of the songs and final instructions before the company was somehow, with much confusion and laughter, got into line – boys and men on one side, women and girls, posies in their hands, on the other. Jérôme carried Aristide proudly in his arms, with some difficulty, since he also had the obligatory oak branch to carry. The baby looked about him with solemn grey eyes, now and then breaking into a smile at some appealing sight. Isabelle, conscious of her new resolution, smiled once at her menfolk, and then gave all her attention to Aurore.

They marched to the music of a band to the Tuileries Gardens, beneath a sky of a blue so pure, so transparent, that

276

looking up into it was like gazing into eternity. Washed in clear summer sunlight, Paris was a mass of colour. Every window-sill, every balcony, every doorway was hung with garlands and banners; scents drifted in the air, caught momentarily and then lost, before fresh perfumes flowed in to set the senses alight. There were roses everywhere, not just on balconies and window sills, but in the flowing hair of girls, in women's bonnets, in men's buttonholes, in posies carried by children; and carnations and fronds of lilac and honeysuckle, and lilies and marigolds and nasturtiums and flowers whose names Isabelle could not even guess at, some brought in from the warmer south, some plucked from gardens or window boxes. She felt a great lump in her throat and tears prickled her eyes, moved by the music, the flowers, the beauty of the day, the laughter and songs of those around her, the whole lovely feeling of a people united and happy in praise of the Being who made them. Today she could believe easily in Jérôme's loving and benevolent Supreme Being, in a humanity returning to its natural state of goodness.

In the centre of the façade of the Tuileries, facing on to the gardens, a dais had been built, to accommodate the ranks of deputies gathering there, their dark coats brightened by tricol-our sashes, nodding tricolour plumes in their hats. Among them, Robespierre, in sky blue, a posy of flowers in his hand, took his place as president of the Convention, to which position he had been elected for the current fortnight. He looked, Isabelle thought, like a man in a trance of joy, as well he might, for she knew from Jérôme that the theme of this day was the one that formed the bedrock of his revolutionary faith. There was a silence as he stepped forward to speak. For once the speech was short, and his voice carried well, as if fervour gave it unaccustomed strength. 'The author of nature has bound all mortals together with a chain of love and joy; let the tyrants perish, who have dared to break that chain . . .'

A band broke into solemn music, while Robespierre took a torch and stepped down to set light to an image of Atheism set below the dais.

'... Being of beings, we must not come to you with unjust prayers: you know the creatures sent forth from your hands; their needs do not escape your gaze, any more than do their most secret thoughts. Hatred of bad faith and tyranny burns in our hearts alongside the love of justice and our homeland; our blood flows for the cause of humanity: that is our prayer; those are our sacrifices; this the worship that we offer you.'

The bands struck up again, the marshals brought in for the occasion set about directing operations, and the procession formed up to march to the Champ de Mars, cavalry, trumpeters, drummer boys, deputies of the Convention, members of the Sections. Behind Isabelle's own group a carriage followed, filled with children from the Blind School, singing a hymn to the Deity. Their sweet young voices were almost unbearably moving.

At the Champ de Mars a huge symbolic mountain, topped with a Tree of Liberty, had been built, up which the deputies climbed before the singing began; hymns and songs, and the final mass outpouring of the Marseillaise, whose well-known chorus brought every man and woman and child into full-throated unison. Jérôme, carried away with exaltation, came to throw his arms about his wife and children, friends embraced one another, babies were danced in the air, and there were happy tears in the eyes of the most sober citizen. Isabelle felt as if a seal had been set upon her new resolution, and on her love for her husband and her children.

Two days after that celebration of joyful humanity, the disabled deputy Georges Couthon appeared before the Convention in his wheelchair and, speaking for the Committee of Public Safety, laid before his fellow deputies a law to speed up the processes of the revolutionary tribunal. Almost every means of defence was to be abolished, and there were to be only two permissible verdicts: acquittal, or death. There were protests from some of the deputies, but the law was passed all the same.

# Chapter Twenty-Three

The Convention made only a half-hearted attempt that year to organise festivities for July 14th, though in many of the Sections people organised their own fraternal banquets, with dancing until dusk. Perhaps the deputies felt that in the grim and frightened atmosphere of the city, large-scale celebrations would have seemed a mockery. Jérôme told Isabelle that many deputies, from guilt or fear, no longer lived at home but had gone into hiding, to avoid arrest. Quarrels split the ruling committees, so openly sometimes that they could not be hidden. On a hot day in June citizens passing the Tuileries had heard Robespierre's voice clearly, raised in such furious anger that a crowd had gathered to listen in fascination, until someone discreetly closed the window. Soon after that the Incorruptible ceased to attend the Committee's meetings at all. The uplifting mood of the Festival of the Supreme Being had vanished without trace.

Isabelle wondered if the men who governed France had lost all touch with reality, if indeed they knew anything of the ordinary lives of ordinary people in the back streets of Paris and the towns and villages of France. At the end of June the French armies had at last won a decisive victory over the allied powers, at Fleurus in Belgium, and the tide of the war was finally turned. Yet there was no sense of relief in Paris. It was almost as if everyone had become so accustomed to betrayal and terror that they could no longer remember how to live without them. Did the deputies of the Convention really think

279

that by suppressing all free expression of thought and opinion they were ensuring the greater safety of the Republic? Did they really believe that all the men and women dragged before the revolutionary tribunal were in fact guilty of the crimes of which they were accused, of counter-revolution and spying and corruption? True, there were acquittals, but even so nearly every day forty or fifty people went to their deaths. Long columns of tumbrils trundled with relentless monotony from the prison of the Conciergerie towards the place of execution – now in a more distant square near the Barrière de la Trône Renversé, since the residents of the Place de la Révolution had complained about the smell and the threat to public health.

It was impossible now to avoid any contact with the executions, unless one stayed constantly indoors. Often while returning from shopping, taking Aurore for a walk, visiting Marianne, making her way to the disused church where she and the other women worked at sewing uniforms and preparing cloth for bandages, Isabelle would glimpse a passing line of tumbrils or hear the talk of people returning from watching an execution – not that so very many went to watch these days, so commonplace had death become.

It was still a shock one hot and overcast morning to find her eyes drawn to a tall figure in one such tumbril and realise she knew him. For a moment she almost thought it was the hated Henri Antoine de La Pérouse, hair cut, shirt collar torn away, hands bound, yet still full of disdain, as if he regarded himself as superior even to those who shared his fate, still more the watching rabble. Then she realised it was François, grown thinner and somehow resembling at this moment of death the brother he had been so little like in life. She knew then, with relief, that she had not been needed as a witness against him, perhaps because, these days, so few proofs of guilt were required. Then she felt a pang of regret, though it was brief enough. She might have doubts about some of the executions, but this one, in truth, she could not deny to be just; if any were.

Three days later another tumbril gave her a much sharper jolt. A jeering crowd was running along beside it, and she saw that it contained only women, dressed plainly, all deep in quiet prayer. There was something about their demeanour which told her that they were nuns – which she could have learned too from the shouts of the observers. Then with a shock she realised that one or two of the faces were familiar; one above all, whose delicate and lovely features were unmistakably those of Louise de Rochefort, Sister Sainte-Anne, who had made her Profession at the same time as the apostate Sister Sainte-Marie-Madeleine.

Two young women who had set out on what had seemed the same path, come to such very different ends ... Isabelle felt a great sadness, a great pity. Yet Louise's face was radiant, in spite of the jeering and the coarse comments, which she must have heard; in spite of the fate that awaited her at the end of the jolting indignity of this last journey. Isabelle knew instinctively that if offered the chance to change places with the young mother watching from the corner of the street, Louise would not have taken it. She was dying as she had lived, with her whole will surrendered to God, a martyr for the faith that suffused her being. For the first and only time since she left the convent Isabelle felt something approaching a sense of loss. When, sooner or later, death came to her, she would not be able to face it with that serenity and joy, that confidence that at last all would be well. She almost found herself envying Louise.

But the feeling that lingered with her as she made her way home was one of sadness that the Revolution should have come to this, where the execution of a group of women who, in normal times, could surely have offered no threat to the security of the Republic, had become a necessity of state. Her cousin had in a sense deserved his death; but she could not believe that Louise and her fellow sisters were equally guilty.

She put that to Jérôme when he came home for dinner, looking tired and strained. He was unsympathetic to her protests. 'They had been corresponding with émigrés and harbouring spies,' he said. 'Don't waste your sympathy on them.'

She had to accept the assurance, but still she felt uneasy

about it. She wondered sometimes if Jérôme himself always believed what he said.

These days, when he came home, she sensed the intensity of relief with which he closed the door on the outside world, the profound thankfulness with which he came to embrace her and take the children on his knee. He would sit among them, talking of simple trivial things, and she would see the strain fall from him, returning only to disturb his sleep when they lay together through the night hours. He rarely laughed now, and he talked very little. Whatever it was that haunted him, he would not tell her of it, though she tried to wheedle it out of him. Perhaps he had found that once at home he could somehow pretend that it did not exist, and to speak of it might have destroyed the illusion. He had to find comfort from her in less obvious ways.

Often in the early hours of the morning she would feel his hand slip between her thighs, gently rousing her; then a little after he would slide into her and they would slowly make love, finding peace together in that sleepy intimacy. One morning, lying in one another's arms after one such time, Jérôme said thoughtfully, 'As soon as this is over, we'll move out of Paris. Find some land and a little house, and live there quietly. It will be better for the children.'

'When do you think it will be over?' She did not ask him what he thought might soon be over; the Terror she supposed.

'When the war is won, abroad and at home; when the Republic has no more enemies; when only virtuous men speak for the people.' It sounded a hopelessly idealistic aim.

'We could wait for ever,' she said.

'Then we might as well not have started.' He sounded utterly despondent. Perhaps he too was wondering what had happened to all the dreams and aspirations that had carried him to where he was today.

She held him closer, stroking his hair. 'I thought you didn't like country life.'

'I was young then.' He spoke as if he had centuries of experience behind him. 'Maybe I've learned sense. It would be better for the children, wouldn't it? And for you. You are a country girl by nature. And I would so like the peace of it, the physical labour, sound sleep at the end of the day. It seemed boring once. Now I think boredom has something to recommend it. No, not boredom, but peace.'

'We'll do that then,' she said, soothingly, conscious that it was a dream like everything else and perhaps as little likely to be realised.

After a silence, Jérôme said, 'Let's take a picnic into the country the day after tomorrow – no, it's tomorrow now, isn't it?'

'Aurore's taking part in the festival,' Isabelle reminded him, with some regret. 'Had you forgotten?'

That brought to mind that the Catholic Church was not alone in being able to inspire martyrs to its cause. The Republic had its martyrs too, men and women who had died gladly for their faith in the Revolution and what it represented; and children, one of whom was Joseph Bara, killed by the Vendéen rebels, who was to be celebrated with a festival of his own on the very next Décadi, the tenth Thermidor, along with another boy who had suffered a similar fate, Agricol Viala. Aurore was to take part in the festival, with some of the other children from the Section. She had been learning the specially composed hymn for some days now, singing it as she went about the house.

'Of course,' said Jérôme. 'Another time then.' Citizeness Didier's cockerel began to crow. 'There, it's already time I was up.'

That day Jérôme came home at dinner time in a state of breathless dishevelment. 'I can't stay long, my love,' he said. 'Maybe you've heard – there's turmoil at the Convention. They're saying Robespierre's been arrested. I'll get something at a cook shop and eat it at the Hôtel de Ville. We are needed there. God knows what's going to happen.' As if to emphasise his words, the distant sound of beating drums began to throb in the hot air.

She clung to him. 'I wish you'd rest and eat, love. Surely they can manage without you for a little longer. Look, your dinner's ready.' She gestured towards the table.

In the end he agreed to sit down, though he made a hasty enough meal, eating little. Isabelle had scarcely taken a mouthful herself when he was on his feet again. 'I must go.' He kissed them all quickly and went out again.

Not long afterwards Claudine called to tell Isabelle what Jérôme had already said, that Robespierre had been arrested, after a stormy session at the Convention, along with his brother Augustin, St Just, Couthon and Le Bas. They were accused, so it was said, of conspiracy against the Republic. 'The Commune's called the Sections out, to free them,' said Claudine. 'Jean-Louis said he wouldn't go, not after they brought in that maximum on wages.'

The drums continued to beat sporadically, and towards evening a few bells rang out, though only briefly and without conviction. Isabelle thought it was unlikely that Jérôme would be home for many hours, with things so uncertain. She gave the children their supper and put them to bed, singing to them and telling them stories, as much to calm herself as them.

When it grew dark and Jérôme was still not home she went to bed, though she lay awake for a long time, listening to the sounds from outside, unusual sounds for these days when anyone out after eleven was liable to be questioned by the National Guard. There was nothing very near at hand, but a distant noise of shouting, horses' hooves, running feet, something that might have been gunfire. At last, very late, she drifted into sleep.

She woke with a jolt and realised that it was full daylight, and that Jérôme's side of the bed was still empty; and that someone was hammering on the door. She scrambled out of bed and pulled a shawl about her and went to open it.

The officials and guardsmen outside pushed their way in. 'Get dressed, citizeness. You are to come with us.'

'But why? I don't understand – what are you doing?' For they were walking about the room, opening drawers, looking behind books on the shelf; then they pushed open the door into the adjoining room and Aristide began to cry, woken by his sister's terrified scream. Isabelle ran to comfort them.

'Dress them too, and hurry up. You're under arrest.'

With a sense of unreality and hands fumbling because of the shaking that had seized them, she dressed herself and the children – fortunately the soldiers allowed her to do so discreetly, in the children's room, with the door shut. Then two of the men led them downstairs to a waiting carriage. From windows and doorways across the street and on each side, neighbours watched in silence.

They took her, rather to her surprise, to the Section headquarters. She felt a little reassured as she stepped into the familiar building, for she was sure that there would be someone here who knew her and would realise that there had been some mistake. At the very least, she could hope for an explanation.

But she was simply hurried along a passage she had never seen before, meeting no one on the way, and ushered into what was clearly a prison cell. It contained a bed and a stool and nothing else. The door was slammed shut and firmly locked. Aurore looked about her. 'Why are we here, Maman?'

'I don't know, my darling,' said Isabelle, trying to force down a rising panic.

'Will we get out soon? We'll be late for the festival.'

'I'm afraid we shall have to miss the festival,' said Isabelle, at which Aurore began to cry.

It was only after several hours that the child asked the question that had been haunting Isabelle from the moment she awoke, 'Maman, where's Papa?'

'I don't know, my love,' Isabelle answered, and struggled to swallow the tears that were fighting for release.

# Chapter Twenty-Four

Isabelle and the children were left for two days in their cell with only the periodic interruptions of the jailer who brought their meals to break the monotony. He was so dour and so heedless of Isabelle's questions that she even wondered if he was deaf. The children had no toys or books, the one window was too high and too small to allow any view, except of a patch of sky – overcast for most of the time – and Aurore quickly grew bored and irritable.

Even so, any relief Isabelle might have felt when three men at last appeared in a purposeful manner at the door of the cell quickly disappeared. 'You are to come with us,' one of them said. She stooped to lift Aristide into her arms, and the man added, 'Not them – just you.' Isabelle stood there, cold with shock. 'They'll come to no harm. Citizen Barbot here will keep an eye on them.'

She had neither seen nor heard anything of Jérôme for more than two days, not a word; and now they wanted to separate her from the children and take her God knew where . . .! She picked up Aristide and held him close, while her free hand rested protectively on Aurore's head. The girl clung to her skirts.

'You'll be back here within the hour,' the man said. 'There are questions to answer, that's all.'

When she refused to move he gave a signal to the other men and the children were dragged from her and she was roughly

287

marched away, with the sound of Aristide's wailing echoing horribly in her ears.

They took her along several passages, some of which were familiar, and came at last to a hallway she knew well, and a door that brought memories flooding back. In this room, nearly two years ago, she had first met Jérôme. A sudden hope sprang up in her that he would be here now, perhaps a prisoner like she was; better still, come to protest at her arrest and insist on her release.

One of her guards knocked on the door and then entered the room, leaving the door half open behind him. Isabelle heard a murmured exchange inside, going on for several minutes; and then at last a voice said clearly, 'Right, bring in the Widow Duvernoy.'

It was a moment before she realised that they were speaking of her; and then she felt as if someone had drenched her suddenly in a deluge of freezing water. She stood where she was, unable to move, feeling all the warmth and life drain from her. *Widow* . . . No, they could not mean it!

She heard her voice come from somewhere, whisper, 'Jérôme!' A hand tugged at her arm. 'Come, citizeness!' Somehow her legs moved, but only just, unsteadily. There seemed to be no strength in them. When the man suddenly let go of her arm, she swayed and almost fell. Someone pulled up a stool and she sank down on it. The faces across the table swam in a kind of watery vapour, distant and grotesque, marred by black apertures that formed themselves constantly into new shapes . . . Their mouths, she realised after a time, speaking to her. But she could not understand what they were saying. Her brain seemed to have ceased to make any sense of anything around her. All she heard was a clamorous blur of sound, angry and harsh, washing against her and receding again.

Slowly, one face began to emerge from the amorphous mass and come into sharper focus, a large-featured unshaven face, with a pipe stuck in the corner of its mouth. Perhaps it was a figment of her imagination, a trick of memory, because she had seen it the first time she had come into this room. Citizen

Command, who hated her . . . She rubbed her eyes. No, he really was there. Then she understood. What had been said, it was all a ploy, a cruel ruse to make her admit to things that were not true, in the belief that Jérôme could no longer be hurt by them. He must be a prisoner then, for some reason she could not yet grasp, or at least in trouble of some kind. She struggled to bring her mind to clarity. It was important she should do so, for Jérôme's well-being might depend upon it.

'Come now, citizeness, we've waited long enough! You are first cousin to Henri Antoine de la Pérouse and François his brother?' Command sounded impatient, and she realised he must have been asking the question for some time.

'Yes.' Her eyes moved at last to the other faces ranged alongside Command, and saw one or two that were familiar, kinder faces on the whole, those of men she liked, whose children she had taught, whose wives were friends of hers. 'You know that,' she added, remembering that it was he who had denounced her. Why bring up this old matter now, when she had thought it done with?

'But not all my comrades here know it. I think they should. Tell us now, you had several meetings with your cousin, the spy and returned émigré, François de la Pérouse, before he was justly arrested and condemned?'

'I denounced him myself.' She picked out one face. 'You, Citizen Benoît, you took my statement that day.' Benoît's face remained so impassive, cold even, that she wondered if she had mistaken his identity; yet if it was not Benoît, it was his double. Unnerved, she turned back to Command. 'I explained the whole matter to the Committee of General Security, in full. They were satisfied.'

'Who was satisfied? The suspect David? The traitor Le Bas, who shot himself rather than face his just punishment?' She stared at him, remembering that David and Le Bas were known to be close to Robespierre; and Le Bas was said to have been under arrest, along with Robespierre, two days ago. 'The veil has been torn down, citizeness. Your protectors are gone. We seek the truth.'

'I told the truth. And it wasn't David I spoke to, or Le Bas. Citizen Voulland, I think it was, most of the time, and Citizen Vadier, once.'

'I wouldn't know about that. I've only your word for it, and we know how much that's worth. There was something they didn't know, citizeness, and we know it now. There was only one reason you denounced your cousin to the Section. Your husband had told you that the Committee of General Security had got wind of things, and you wanted to make it look as though you were the good citizen you pretended to be.'

'That's a lie! I didn't know about your denunciation until after I made my statement here.'

'So you want my friends here to believe an ex-nun, cousin of an émigré, a woman who lied about her name to get a pension – you expect them to believe you sooner than a known good citizen like myself?'

'I'm telling the truth,' Isabelle retorted stubbornly, and then she grew suddenly weary of the whole business. 'Where's Jérôme?' she asked. She looked at Benoît as she spoke, but it was Commard who answered, with unmistakable malice.

'Duvernoy, like all members of the General Council of the Commune present at the session of the ninth Thermidor, went to the guillotine yesterday.'

Please let him just be playing with her, like a cat with a mouse! Surely that must be it . . .? It could not possibly be true. Two days ago Jérôme had kissed her goodbye before returning to work, in the most ordinary way. Even in these terrible times, men did not go to their deaths so suddenly as that. And the whole council . . . Even if not all were present, there were more than a hundred members. What could they have done, to deserve so wholesale a slaughter as Commard's words implied? No, it was impossible! 'Let me go back to my children, please,' she heard herself saying. She longed to be with them, to hold them, to reassure herself they were safe, that her whole world had not suddenly been blown to pieces.

'When you've answered our questions,' said Commard, and he began once more, putting to her the questions she had answered time and again before the Committee of General Security. Wearily, wanting him to be done, she answered each question, but now she scarcely bothered to put him right when he twisted her answers to his own ends. If he was lying about Jérôme, then Command had no power to hurt her. If he was not ... what did it matter then?

At last they let her go, releasing her to the custody of one of the men who had brought her, who took her back to the cell. The children were there still, crouched together on the bed, Aurore holding Aristide in her arms. The boy had fallen asleep, but Aurore, her face smudged with tears, looked white and frightened, with something of the rigidity that Isabelle remembered from their first days together. When Isabelle came to put her arms about her, she clung to her mother, sobbing wildly with relief.

Finding strength and courage from somewhere, Isabelle reassured the child, distracted her somehow from thinking of why they were here, deflected that repeated question about 'Papa', as much because it seemed to stop her breath as because she did not know how to answer it. Time enough to find an answer when she knew the truth herself. Finding occupations for Aurore helped to keep her own mind occupied, so that it could not return to the horrible thing that lurked in its darkest corner.

But when at night Aurore slept at last and Isabelle lay on the bed with the two small bodies warm against her own, then there was no keeping it out.

They said Jérôme was dead. The 'Widow Duvernoy', they had called her ... If it was true, she did not feel it, not really; her mind had not grasped it, still less her emotions. Nothing seemed quite real. Part of her felt instinctively that at any moment she would wake and find herself lying beside Jérôme, and he would turn over and make love to her, and drive the nightmare away as he had before, with that other nightmare. Yet that nightmare had been real enough.

She felt numb, full of a sense of dreary resignation, which was not acceptance, because she did not understand that she had anything to accept. Even the interview with Command seemed unreal, here in the cell. Yet that had most certainly happened. And she knew her danger was real. Whatever had become of Jérôme, Command wanted her death, that much was clear. And if what he said was true, if Jérôme was indeed dead, then she did not care what became of her.

Except for the sake of the children. If the worst had happened and they were fatherless, then they needed her more than ever. Their very survival depended upon her.

A dreadful anxiety began to tear at her mind. Round and round her thoughts went, seeking some way out, for herself, or failing that for the children. She thought of Marianne at last. She would care for them, surely. Through all the differences that had divided them, her friendship had remained staunch. She had no children of her own – from choice, Isabelle supposed, remembering Marianne's long-ago hints that she knew of some way of preventing pregnancy. But for all that she clearly loved Aurore and Aristide. If they should be left motherless, then their mother's friend would comfort them and see that they did not starve.

Could she get word to Marianne? Would they let her send word? Now in the middle of the night it was impossible, certainly – but when day came . . .

The next morning the jailer clearly heard what she said, but would not allow himself to be moved. His orders were that no messages could be sent out or received. In despair, all she could do was to beg him, with tears in her eyes, keeping her voice low so that Aurore should not hear and be troubled, that if anything happened to her he would send word to Marianne Colin at the print shop of Pierre Maurichon, off the rue St Martin. 'Maybe,' was all he would say, but she thought she saw some softening of his expression.

Later that day they came for her again, for more questioning, she supposed; but this time she was taken out to a carriage and driven away, in spite of her protests at leaving the children.

They took her to the Hôtel de Brionne, to the only too familiar offices of the Committee of General Security. This time it was not so much fear that was uppermost in her mind, as a desperate anxiety. She could think only of the children, while the same questions were fired at her across the table, those endless questions she had answered so many times before. It was clear that the Committee of General Security had been told what Command had said yesterday – very likely by Command himself – that her own denunciation had come only after she had herself been denounced. But these men were meticulous, checking on dates and times in a way that taxed her memory but gave her hope. At least they had no personal malice against her, and Command had no power to hurt her unless they allowed it.

At the end, she had no idea whether they were satisfied or not, for their faces gave nothing away. There was much scratching of pens on paper and then she was led outside again. To her amazement – and relief – she found the children waiting for her in the carriage, silent and frightened beside a soldier.

They were driven just a short distance, to a fine mansion, built for a noble family but now used as a prison, where they were taken up to a small room under the roof, with straw on the floor and yet another tiny high window. Someone brought them a meal of soup, fish and vegetables, of which Isabelle ate little, and then they were locked in for the night.

She had expected that the questioning would resume again the next morning, but no one came for her, except to take them all down to the cobbled courtyard of the mansion for exercise with their fellow prisoners. There were a number of other children there, and a few prisoners who, like Isabelle, had been locked up only since the events of the ninth Thermidor, but Isabelle shrank from the company of anyone apart from her own children, who were still too bewildered by all that had happened to venture away from her side. More distressing than anything else, her milk dried up and she found herself forced abruptly to wean Aristide, who was miserable without the comfort of her breasts. She too felt bereft by that sudden loss, as if even in smaller things she was being torn from all that had made life bearable.

She tried asking the jailer for paper and pen to write to Marianne, but he demanded money first, and she had none. She tried pleading with him on two or three other occasions, but when that had no result she gave up.

The days settled into some kind of dreary routine, of meals and exercise; and sleep, for the children if not for Isabelle. Her only concern for the long hours that were left was to occupy the children, amuse and educate them and keep them from thinking of what had happened to them or, more to the point, why it had happened. She fended off Aurore's questions as best she could. 'Why can't we go home, Maman?' 'Why doesn't Papa come?' 'Where is Papa?'

Her answers were evasive. 'We must stay here a little longer.' 'Papa can't come just now,' and so forth. She was not consciously or deliberately lying. She herself still did not quite believe that Jérôme would not suddenly appear at the door of their cell, that she would not wake and find it had all been a nightmare. Meanwhile, she simply allowed life to carry her along, so that she drifted on its surface, battening down all her feelings and thoughts as if the better to weather this storm, however long it might last, however fierce and destructive it might prove to be.

She had no idea how many days passed, for they merged into one another, featureless and indistinguishable. After a time, she struck up a tentative acquaintance with others in the prison and one woman, wealthier than she was, paid for her to be supplied with writing materials. She was now able to continue Aurore's lessons in reading and writing; and to write to Marianne. But though the jailer took the letter and she waited hopefully for a visit or some other response, none came. Had Marianne never received the letter? Or – a thought that swept her with a sudden sense of loneliness – had she thrown it away, not wanting anything to connect her with a former friend suspected of treason?

Sometimes fellow prisoners were released or moved to other prisons, less often new faces appeared in the courtyard for exercise, but when Isabelle talked to her fellow prisoners it was about their children, their health, their appearance, safe and unemotional topics. Having no change of clothes for herself or the children, keeping clean was a problem, though she did her best at the well used by the prisoners for washing. Aurore began to make friends with another little girl and join in her play; after a time Aristide plucked up the courage to join them. He had learned to stand and then to walk, and his need for activity made the restrictions of their cell harder to bear. His first birthday passed without anything to mark it. Isabelle was glad he was too young to know what day it was, and that Aurore did not appear to have remembered. To celebrate the occasion would have brought thoughts of Jérôme too close to bear.

One morning, several weeks after their arrest, they were disturbed by a deep reverberating roar, like cannon fire magnified a hundredfold, which seemed to set the whole prison shuddering to its foundations. One of the jailers told them there had been an explosion at the Grenelle gunpowder factory, south of the river. Several hundred people had been hurt, and many killed. 'A Jacobin plot,' said the jailer, and Isabelle felt a sense of shock at hearing the word 'Jacobin', for so long synonymous with revolutionary purity, used as a term of condemnation. She realised then that the world beyond the prison walls had changed for many others beside herself. She was reminded of those early years of the Revolution, when from her convent cell she had heard only distant sounds of the vast changes that were taking place. Would she ever emerge from this different captivity to whatever kind of world waited out there?

The release happened with the suddenness of the arrest. One morning the jailer flung the door open earlier than usual with the brusque instruction, 'Get your things together. Come with me.' There were few 'things' to get together, but Isabelle gathered up the papers they had accumulated and one or two other items, picked up Aristide, took Aurore's hand in hers and followed the jailer, fear and hope contending within her.

Then they were at the door, and there was no carriage

waiting outside, no soldiers, nothing but a street, two passing women glancing curiously her way, someone emptying a chamber pot from a window in the house opposite, a cart lumbering by. 'Go on then,' said the jailer, pushing a paper into her hand. She glanced at it, but her eyes would not focus on the words. Then she looked at the jailer, and saw nothing on his face but impatience. She took a deep breath and stepped out into the street.

# Chapter Twenty-Five

Isabelle and her children had been arrested on the tenth Thermidor, year Two of the Republic, July 28th by the old calendar. They were set free on the fifth Frimaire, year Three, once November 25th. It had been on a November day four years ago that Isabelle had left the convent, emerging as she did now into the cold rain-drenched streets of Paris.

They had taken only a few steps when Aurore's excited voice broke into Isabelle's dazed consciousness. 'Can we go home?' She gave a little skip from excitement.

'Let's see, shall we?' Isabelle replied cautiously. What would she discover, at the house where she had known her greatest happiness? She had to find out, but her spirit shrank at the prospect. The time was fast approaching when she could no longer keep her feelings submerged. She was free. She would have choices to make. And she would have to face both the past and the future. There was no longer any shutting them out.

They walked through streets busy with people. Passing the Palais Égalité – once the Palais Royal – they saw throngs of young people in extravagant and expensive clothes, the young men with earrings and long hair, curled and braided, and neckcloths so high it was a wonder they could turn their heads, and coats that looked as if they were designed to make the wearer appear deformed; the few young women wearing inappropriately scanty muslins that were almost transparent and clung to their bodies in a way that left little to the imagination. Aurore giggled and pointed at them, until Isabelle rebuked her. The young men had sticks in their hands. They looked harmless enough – even ineffectual – but one never knew. All she was certain of was that things had changed since she had last walked this way. In the months before her arrest no one would have dressed like that, or not openly at least.

There were still queues at the bakers, if rather shorter than she remembered; but then this year's harvest should be available by now. The tricolour was displayed as conspicuously as ever. There were sans culottes in red bonnets, though fewer than there used to be, and only in the poorer streets. The words *Unité, indivisibilité de la République. Liberté, égalité, fraternité ou la mort* were still triumphantly painted over doorways on public buildings, though in one place Isabelle saw that the last three words had been spattered with mud. For the most part she was in no state of mind to notice what was around her.

The house looked exactly as it always had, the shop on the ground floor bright with a lavish display of flowers. She felt her heart thud. She imagined herself mounting the stairs, opening the door, seeing Jérôme turn from his fireside chair to face her and then come running to fold her in his arms.

'Will Papa be there?' Aurore was tugging at her mother's hand. Isabelle forced herself to be calm, suppressed the urge to run with her daughter up to the apartment. She saw a woman emerge from the doorway, a basket on her arm. It was Citizeness Didier, coming her way. The woman saw her and halted, her face blank with surprise. Then she coloured and turned and walked away in the opposite direction. Isabelle felt sick.

'Come on!' Aurore urged.

'Papa won't be there,' Isabelle said, but the child showed no sign that she had heard her mother. She broke free and ran ahead, disappearing through the doorway.

By the time Isabelle reached the door herself Aurore was coming slowly back down the stairs. 'There's a man. He says I can't go in.' She sounded angry rather than dejected.

'Let's go and see,' said Isabelle, wishing there were some alternative to this.

But there was not, and she mounted the stairs. Aurore was right. There was a man, sitting by the fire where she and Jérôme had sat so often, playing with the children, talking over the day. He looked thoroughly at home, an empty plate near him indicating a recent meal, his shoes discarded on the hearth, the bed unmade since he had last slept in it. Her bed, and Jérôme's . . .

'My flowers! You've let them all die!' Aurore ran indignantly to the windowsill, where the pots now contained only shrivelled brown remains of what had once been healthy plants.

'Hey there!' cried the man, and Isabelle called the child back to her side. Then she told the man who she was, showing him her papers as requested. She knew without asking what he was doing there. His job was to keep watch on the property of suspected or condemned persons, until such time as their papers had been examined thoroughly and the goods could be auctioned off for the benefit of the state.

'They've let you go, have they?' the man said, without great interest. 'You can't come back here.'

'Why not?' Aurore burst out. 'Maman, where's Papa?'

Isabelle silenced her and spoke quickly, before the man could think of answering her daughter's question. 'Can I take my own things?'

'Clothes, for you and the children, yes; that kind of thing. But I'll have to get authority, and someone to check what you take.'

It was done, and under the watchful eyes of the guard and a representative of the Section justice department, she gathered into a bag all she could in the way of clothes, toys, books, her few items of jewellery, anything that was obviously not Jérôme's. She agreed with the men that she would make arrangements later to collect any larger items that were unequivocally hers. She felt a horrible choking sensation in her throat as she opened drawers and cupboards and saw Jérôme's coats and shirts and neckcloths, all the things lying there as if he might at any moment come to put them on. But she knew she must not let herself think of that, not yet, not here, not in front of these men.

She did what had to be done and then she set out down the stairs again with the children, Aristide walking now, because there was the bag to carry, and it was heavy. Once out in the street, she silenced Aurore's inevitable questions. 'No, we can't stay, Aurore. I'll tell you why, but not now.' And then she walked to the end of the street, out of sight of the house, and put down the bag and wondered what to do. She felt suddenly more weary than she had ever felt in her life before, as if to take one more step was beyond her.

She looked at the children, and at the bag that contained all their worldly goods: a woman, two children and a bag, all that was left of Citizeness Duvernoy, happy wife and mother, and her home and family.

But then in a way she felt as if Citizeness Duvernoy had gone for ever, along with Isabella Milburn and Sister Sainte-Marie-Madeleine and Isabelle Moulin. She no longer seemed to have anything to do with the woman she had known so intimately all her life, in all her different manifestations. Twice before she had experienced something like this, a period of intense dislocation, a change so great and so sudden that it cut her off from everything that had gone before. But this time it was different, for now she had two small children utterly dependent on her for everything. Somehow she had to find food and shelter for them, to begin again from the state of utter destitution in which they found themselves.

She tried to look at the possibilities before her. Was she still eligible for her pension? She had no reason to suppose otherwise, and in that case there would be a whole quarter's money due to her. But without papers she could not claim it, and she had no papers except the one releasing her from prison, and the marriage and birth certificates she had collected from the apartment, along with Aurore's adoption documents. She could not acquire the necessary declaration of residence without a fixed address; if that was still required, of course.

She decided then that she had to take a chance and seek out

Marianne, the one person she had once thought she could depend upon. Marianne had not answered her appeal from prison, but until she knew precisely why that was she would not give up hope that this one thing still remained to her.

The print shop was exactly as she remembered it. Pierre was there among the men, clattering round on his wooden leg, the red bonnet still stuck at a jaunty angle on his fair head. It might have been only yesterday that she was here last. As soon as she stepped into the shop he grinned and gave a shout to Marianne to come down and see who had called.

Aurore threw herself on Marianne as if with relief and joy that something at least had not changed in this puzzling world that had so suddenly descended upon her. Marianne hugged her, and then Pierre, coming over, swung her up in the air in the way she loved, which made her squeal with delight. Aristide clamoured for similar attention and while Pierre was occupied with the children Marianne came and folded Isabelle into a long and silent embrace, as if she understood everything that she had been through during the past months.

Afterwards, she said, 'I tried to find you, but they wouldn't tell me anything, or let me see you.'

'Did you get my letter?'

Marianne shook her head. 'Nothing.' She grinned, though her lips trembled a little. 'I thought they'd have your head too. Am I glad to see you! Mind, if they had I'd have scoured Paris till I found the children. I promise you that.'

For the first time Isabelle felt the tears spring to her eyes, and they embraced again.

There seemed to be no question but that they would stay with Pierre and Marianne. The attic above their rooms was already occupied by Hubert, Pierre's journeyman, and his wife, so they moved their own bed into the living room, leaving the other room to be made ready for Isabelle and the children, with a makeshift mattress on the floor, until such time as Isabelle could have some at least of her furniture released from sequestration. Marianne set about preparing a meal, ordering Pierre to keep the children amused downstairs. When he had gone, she turned to Isabelle. 'Did they let you out today?'

Isabelle nodded. She wanted to ask so much, but she did not know where to begin. She should have been helping, but she sat dazed and exhausted, watching Marianne busy at the fire.

'They had Pierre in for questioning, but then they let him go.' There was a little silence. Then, her back to Isabelle, Marianne said suddenly, 'I saw him, you know – on the eleventh Thermidor, in the Place de la Révolution.'

She could only mean one thing. 'You were there?' Isabelle felt as if her heart had stopped.

'Yes. He was calm, your Jérôme. Pale maybe, but courageous, not like some.'

'I don't know what happened, not really.' Her voice came like a ghost, whispering into the everyday sounds of the room.

'They arrested Robespierre in the Convention, and those who stood up for him, and sent them off to the prisons. The Commune gave orders they were to be released, and that was done. They went to the Hôtel de Ville. Then the Commune called out the Sections. But the Convention sent word they weren't to rise. They declared outlawed all those who disobeyed them. That meant everyone in the Hôtel de Ville that night. All they had to do then was send in the soldiers, gather up the lot of them, send them one by one to the tribunal to be identified, and then . . .' She made a gesture like a falling blade. 'They guillotined twenty-two that first day, ninety-six more the next two days. The biggest batch of the Revolution. But the end of the Terror, though that's not what they meant to happen.'

'Who's "they"?' Still her voice came only in a whisper, with no force behind it, for she was scarcely conscious of speaking.

Marianne shrugged. 'Tallien, Fouché, Barras, Fréron. There were a good few others, waited to see which way the wind blew before they took sides.'

All names that had been connected with cruel repression in distant parts of France; no, the end of the Terror would not have been uppermost in their minds – fear for their own safety perhaps, but no greater principle.

'Of course,' said Marianne, 'now they heap all the blame on

302

Robespierre, for anything anyone could accuse them of. If you believe them, he was on his way to making himself dictator, with the help of his friends and the Commune – and the émigrés, of course. But the only conspiracy I know of is the one they made, to overthrow him and his friends. You'd think none of them had ever harmed a fly, to hear them now.'

There was a little silence, then Isabelle asked quietly, 'Where is he buried, do you know?'

'They don't mark the graves of the guillotined. There'll be a mass grave somewhere, I suppose.'

So there was nothing to mark his passing, nor could there be; no burial rites, no headstone, not even a mound of earth on which she could lay flowers. He had eaten his dinner and kissed her goodbye and that was it: he had vanished from her life in a moment, leaving no trace behind, except her memories and his son's wide grey eyes.

'I don't know why,' said Isabelle. 'I don't feel anything.' It was not strictly true. Somewhere, deep down, a dreadful wound slowly and steadily bled away inside her, though no one could see it or guess at its existence. One day, inevitably, it would force itself onto her consciousness, and then the pain would be beyond bearing. But today, she could still pretend it was not there.

Marianne held her hands. 'Better that way, I'd guess.'

Suddenly Isabelle stood up. 'I have to tell Aurore. She doesn't know, you see.'

She could see that Marianne looked troubled, almost as if she were uncertain of Isabelle's sanity, but she said nothing when her friend went to call Aurore to her.

Isabelle took the child into the other room and sat her down beside her on the edge of the bed. 'Aurore, I have something to tell you.' It was harder because the child looked excited, as if expecting good news. Somehow the gravity of her mother's expression, the sombreness of her voice, did not seem to have reached her.

'My love, Papa is not going to come back to us.'

The child stared at her open mouthed. Then she said, 'But he didn't say goodbye. Where's he gone?'

'He's dead, my love.' Once it would have been so natural to say, 'He's gone to heaven,' but somehow she could not say it. *The French people acknowledge the immortality of the soul*: that had been in accordance with Jérôme's optimistic faith. But she did not know now what it meant. She felt only emptiness.

Aurore was silent. Isabelle wished she would say something, weep or scream or shriek her anger at her mother. When she did speak it was to put a question, in a tone that was disturbingly matter-of-fact. 'Why's he dead?'

That was the hardest of all. She could not say, 'Because bad men sent him to his death.' It might be what she felt, but it was no good encouraging the child to believe things that, if repeated, could only get her into trouble. In the end, searching her mind, she found some sort of fitting explanation: 'He died for the sake of his friends. He believed he had to help them, though he didn't want to leave us. And because he helped them he was killed with them.' It was enough, more than enough. She had no words left.

Aurore's face crumpled. 'I want him to come back!' Then she began to weep. Isabelle held her and wished she too could weep. The truth of what had happened was beginning to reach her now. She knew Jérôme had gone and would not ever return. But she could not yet feel it.

With the resilience of a child, Aurore finished her weeping and then went to eat the meal Marianne had prepared. Isabelle, exhausted and even hungry as she was, still could not eat, nor that night was she able to sleep, for more than a brief while.

Next day she applied herself to the question of her pension, leaving the children in Marianne's care.

'Watch out for the Muscadins!' Marianne warned her as she reached the door. Pierre, sitting over the dregs of his coffee, stood up and took his coat from the back of his chair. 'I'll go with her.'

'You fool, you'd only make things worse!' Marianne pressed him back into the chair and grinned at Isabelle. 'He's so obstinate. I tell him it's not safe to be seen with that bonnet on his head, but will he listen? It's like a red rag to a bull. You remember—'

'I don't know what you're talking about. Who are these Muscadins?'

Marianne performed an exaggeratedly mincing walk about the room, reminding Isabelle with sudden force of the group of young men seen at the Palais Égalité.

'Idle louts,' said Pierre harshly. 'Rich young layabouts who should be fighting with the armies, but have somehow managed to buy their way out.'

'Yes, I think I saw them yesterday.'

'Take care then,' said Marianne. 'They don't look much, but those clubs they carry – they're weighted with lead. Not funny, if you get hit with one. You remember poor Griffard? They split his head open last week, just for wearing a red bonnet. That's why I tell Pierre —'

'But does no one stop them? The National Guard say?'

'Not them, or not often. Maybe if they slip up and find they're taking on more than one poor bugger all by himself – if it looks as if they might get the worst of it. Not otherwise. They know Fréron's behind them. They smashed up the Jacobin Club a few weeks back – it's closed down now. But we all know they were put up to it. No, you cross the street if you see them. Just in case someone knows you. I don't suppose they'd hurt a woman, but they could be nasty.'

Isabelle was wary, but she saw no Muscadins on the way to the Section office, where she went first to apply for the certificate of residence that was necessary if she was to receive her pension. More than the thought of Muscadins, she was afraid of meeting Commard, but he did not seem to be anywhere about. In the end, her chief impression of that day was not of fear but of boredom and irritation, for the whole process took hours, while suspicious officials checked every detail. By the time she had her certificate it was too late to go in search of her pension.

Next day was much worse. She found that the Commune of Paris no longer existed, abolished wholesale by order of the

Convention after the mass executions of its members. The capital, once so powerful, now found itself without even the elected mayor common to every other village and town in France. It took her a very long time to find the building which housed the new body responsible for the pensions of former religious. Even when she found the offices, there was the inevitable wait before she was called in to make her application for arrears of pension. It was then that things took an alarming and unexpected turn. Her interviewer meticulously noted all the details she gave him and then disappeared from the room. He was absent for some time, and when he returned at last he had a puzzled look. 'I regret, citizeness, that we have no details of the pension you seek. The papers are missing. I understand they were sent to the Committee of General Security some months ago, and have not been returned. But our records indicate that Citizeness Duvernoy, formerly Isabelle Moulin, is deceased.'

Isabelle did not know whether to laugh or shudder. 'What am I supposed to have died of?' she asked, when she had got her breath back.

'There is no record.'

'But I'm sitting here speaking to you!'

'You say you are Isabelle Duvernoy. That is not proof that you are she.'

She began to push her papers across the table towards him. 'Here – my marriage certificate. And my certificate of residence. And this, my release document.'

He scarcely glanced at the papers. 'I have no proof these belong to you, now have I?'

'Isabelle Duvernoy would hardly be in residence anywhere on the sixth Frimaire Year Three if she was dead, now would she?'

'Citizeness, I have already told you – these papers prove nothing.'

She felt at once helpless and exasperated and afraid. It suddenly struck her that perhaps they had released her in error, having intended her to go before the revolutionary tribunal;

that her declared death had merely been noted prematurely, there being no intention that she should survive to return and claim her pension.

The man stood looking at her in obvious perplexity for some time, then he said, 'You brought me no civic certificate, citizeness. When you bring me one, then I will consider looking further into the matter.'

'But how do I eat, and feed my children? I have nothing.'

'Apply to your Section welfare committee. That's the best I can suggest.'

On her way out of the building, Isabelle wondered with a sharp burst of panic if by bringing the matter to the attention of the authorities she might even have put herself in danger. Would they now discover their mistake and arrest her again? She hurried back to the print shop as if fearful that at any moment a hand would be clapped upon her shoulder and the words she dreaded would strike her ear.

Back at the house she told Marianne what had happened, without mentioning her fear. Marianne laughed, but shared her exasperation.

'Never mind,' she concluded, when she stopped laughing at last. 'You know you can stay here until they sort things out. And if they don't – well, there's always a welcome for the late Citizeness Duvernoy, and soup in the pot.'

Isabelle regretted that once, long ago, she had resented sharing with her friend what Marianne gave so generously now.

# Chapter Twenty-Six

It was the coldest winter for more than a hundred years, that winter of Year Three of the Republic.

On what would, in the old days, have been Christmas Eve 1794, two things happened: the deputies in the Convention, making yet another break with the recent past, abolished the Maximum, the law that put an upper limit on the price of basic foods; and the first frost of the winter warned of what was to come. After that, it froze steadily, day after day, without the merest hint of a thaw, until rivers turned to ice and wolves prowled right up to the fringes of the towns. The Rhine froze so hard that the armies of the Republic simply marched across it into Holland, to yet more victories; in Paris the Seine froze; even the Rhône, flowing south into the Mediterranean, was clogged with blocks of ice.

What could be salvaged of the recent harvest, battered by autumn rains, had gone largely to feed the armies. As the temperature fell, lower and lower, so prices rose. Suddenly, it seemed, money went nowhere, even for those who had it, of whom Isabelle, still seeking her elusive pension, was not one. For the very poor, food became an impossible luxury. In Paris, where at least rationing ensured that most households were supplied with a basic portion of low-priced bread, people still died in the streets, of cold and hunger.

Meanwhile, the luxury pastrycooks were doing well, supplying the rich. Tallien, Barras and other leaders of the government gave lavish parties in their houses. Candles burned in their hundreds, music played, scantily clad women hurried from carriages into fire-warmed rooms, delicate food tempted palates weary of the 'bread of equality' so recently common to almost every table – or, more likely, prison fare, for many of the guests at these gatherings were former victims of the Terror. There were even exclusive balls, open only to those who had lost a relative to the guillotine, at which dancers had to wear a symbolic red thread about their throats. Many of the hungry observers of this lavishness remembered the winter before the Bastille fell, when the Court danced while people starved, and asked what good five years of Revolution had brought, if they were back to this again? But this was worse than that earlier time, the winter more severe, prices higher, food scarcer; and France was now at war.

'We should never have got rid of the King,' a woman muttered one day in the queue behind Isabelle, as she waited (as she had been doing since before dawn), ration card in hand, for the household's supply of subsidised bread. 'Things were better in those days.'

'You're wrong,' said another woman. 'We went hungry under the King too. But I'll tell you when we had enough – while the guillotine went on merrily, there was bread for all. It's Robespierre we could do with now.'

That was Marianne's view too, trenchantly expressed. 'It was the worst day's work you ever did, Pierre, to stay at home the night of the ninth Thermidor. If the Sections had risen then, we'd not be where we are now.'

'Do you think I don't know that?' Pierre retorted. 'If I'd known we'd get this lot in the place of Robespierre, I'd not have had a second thought about it.'

He and Marianne between them, advised sometimes by Isabelle, set to work to compose a series of inflammatory posters, cursing the Muscadins and the government and demanding the implementation of the still-shelved Constitution of 1793. Marianne and Isabelle between them saw to sticking the posters up in conspicuous places, choosing their times with care, but helped by the fact that they looked like simple housewives out shopping.

A few nights later, after they had all gone to bed, the occupants of the house were abruptly wakened by a loud banging downstairs, followed swiftly by the clash of breaking glass. Isabelle ran to the window, peering through the crack in the shutters. She felt Aurore creep up beside her. 'What is it, Maman?' Isabelle whispered to her to be quiet, in case they should be heard.

There was not much danger of that; the group in the street below were making an appalling din. Two of them carried lanterns, whose bobbing light glanced on braided hair, coats of exaggerated cut, high neckcloths; and clubs raised in rhythmic accompaniment to their singing. Isabelle had not heard the song before and the snatches that reached her were largely unintelligible; but she knew what it was all the same – the *Reveil du Peuple*; the 'People's Awakening', the anthem of the Muscadins.

The next moment there was more breaking of glass, and the smash of clubs on wooden window frames and what was left of the shutters; and then they were inside, and the clubs clashed on metal. Isabelle glimpsed a shimmering cascade of objects flying out from the shop into the street, and realised they were books and leaflets, being tossed out of the windows, to cheers from inside. The few youths watching in the street piled them up and set light to them, and then danced jubilantly round the bonfire.

A tremendous roar rang out from the room next door, and a cry from Marianne, though whether in warning or support Isabelle could not tell. That Pierre would not stay quietly in bed while his livelihood was destroyed, Isabelle was certain. She heard the thud of feet on the floor above, and knew Hubert was awake too. She commanded Aurore to stay where she was and watch Aristide (who had not stirred) and went through to the next room. Pierre still had his pike, propped up by the hearth, and a battered musket left from his army days. Marianne

311

grasped the musket, reversing it for use as a club, since there was no time to load it, Pierre shouldered the pike. Hubert came downstairs with a savage-looking kitchen knife in his hand. Without a second thought, Isabelle took the poker from the hearth and followed her friends.

Pierre's roar of rage had clearly not made itself heard above the din below, and once at the head of the stairs he was as quiet as his wooden leg would allow, Marianne tiptoeing close behind him, Hubert on her heels. They were half-way down the steps before they were seen; and then one of the Muscadins looked up and gave a warning shout and Pierre roared again and levelled his pike and charged, Marianne shrieking behind him, the musket butt high above her head. As Hubert plunged forward, the dim light struck a sudden gleam from the knife in his hand. Ablaze with a sudden unthinking exhilarating rage, Isabelle raised her poker and ran after them.

The pike's blade met the blond head of one of the youths, and he gave a shriek of rage and pain. His companions closed on Pierre, dodging the blade, battering the pike with their clubs. Dimly lit shapes converged and coagulated into a black tangled mass of fighting bodies. Pierre and Marianne and Hubert knew every inch of that print shop, even in the dark, where the machines were, where the posts ran up to support the ceiling; the Muscadins had only swaying lanterns to guide them, and no weapons but their clubs, but there were more of them, a dozen at least.

Isabelle found herself right in the middle of the throng, hitting with the poker to right and left, until someone knocked it from her hand, and then tearing and scratching like a wild animal at the perfumed silken bodies of her opponents. Feet came running along the street, more lights, a voice shouted. 'Hey, Pierre! Vive les sans culottes!' and a group of their neighbours pushed through the open door and flung themselves into the fray.

It was too much for the Muscadins. A moment more, and then they turned and fled, but only so far as the corner of the next street, where they halted and danced up and down in the middle of the road, jeering and shouting. Pierre's neighbours roared after them, and chased them – as they said later – halfway across the city.

When they had gone, Hubert's pregnant wife came downstairs to give what help she could. Marianne unearthed the last of her scanty store of brandy – brandy was beyond her means now – while the men tried to restore order to the printing presses. In places dark stains on the floor showed that the attackers had suffered injury, though Pierre too, who had jarred his damaged stump, was white with pain. When he had drawn breath enough, he looked around him.

'Bastards! Is this what we've come to, that a man who's given his life to the Revolution has to submit to a rich and idle rabble who haven't the brain to know what they're doing? Me, I shall not submit.'

Marianne, coming down with the brandy, pulled up a stool for him. 'Sit down now, or you'll not be fit to fight Muscadins or anyone else.'

'Who said anything about fighting them? If I have to, yes. But they're not worth the effort. They're just a tool. It's their masters who must be destroyed. The men who've betrayed the Revolution.' He grinned at Marianne, whose eyes were bright. 'Only we take our time, wait for the right moment. Without that we're finished, we play into their hands.'

Warmth came back with the spring, but food grew scarcer, prices ever higher. By Germinal – late March – the bread ration was down to less than half a pound per person, and sometimes the ration failed altogether, leaving no alternative but the bread for sale on the open market, which now cost sixty-five sous a pound, five times what it had just eight months ago. One moonless night, a young widow living a few doors from the print shop took her three children down to the river and drowned them, throwing herself in afterwards. She was not the only mother driven to despair that spring because she could not feed her family.

Pierre and Hubert had made some kind of makeshift repair

to the presses, but they were not working as they should and Pierre could not afford to do a proper job. In any case, there was little demand for his everyday products now. What he printed had no appeal for the rich, and no one else had money to spare for books or leaflets. Isabelle sold nearly all the furniture she had managed to retrieve from her former lodgings (on the grounds that it had been bought with her money and not Jérôme's), but no one was paying much for furniture these days. She and Marianne took in washing for a time, but few people in their part of the city had money to spare for laundry, and soap cost so much it was scarcely worth the effort. Besides, queuing for food took so long it left little time for earning a living.

Apart from the dwindling ration of bread and meat, Pierre's household could scarcely afford any food at all. They made the meat into a thin soup with left-over vegetables begged or filched from market stalls at the end of the day, stretching it out as far as possible and drenching the bread with it to make it seem more substantial. When they ran out of fuel – which happened increasingly often as it grew more scarce and expensive – they ate the remains of the soup cold, which was not very palatable, but better than nothing. Aurore and Aristide, ill with feverish colds during the winter, had been left with troublesome coughs, which nothing seemed to ease. Isabelle, increasingly anxious, saw how thin they were growing. She took them out as much as possible, hoping fresh air and sunlight would somehow make up for the deficiencies in their diet, but the coughs lingered. She was constantly hungry herself, but she could have borne that, if only the children had been fed.

As things grew more desperate, so her anger grew. Taking her children to play in the parks or beside the river she would see what she had never thought to see again in France: the rich and well-fed, laughing and carefree as they brushed heedlessly past the pleading hands of starving beggars. She saw restaurants full of people eating unimaginably delicate and expensive foods, course after course, while her own children pressed their

314

faces to the windows in hungry disbelief. There was plenty in Paris, for those with money.

*I swear to maintain Liberty and Equality, or to die defending them.* So she had promised once. Well, Liberty was being well looked after, the kind of liberty Jérôme had despised, which allowed the strong to climb to power and riches on the backs of the weak, who were left powerless to help themselves. As for Equality – no, no one seemed to care about equality any more. It was a sans culotte virtue, and sans culottes were out of fashion.

In the bread queues women as angry as herself argued and complained and then lost patience. On the day that the Section's bread ration failed altogether, they decided to go and lay their grievances before the Convention. Isabelle went too, with the children and Marianne, marching between mocking gangs of Muscadins, who shouted foul-mouthed abuse and unsavoury jokes. The deputies received them more courteously and promised better bread supplies, though there was little to show for it afterwards . . . Except that companies of Muscadins were seen being drilled in the gardens of the Palais Égalité, as if for some definite purpose. Pierre printed leaflets headed, *People, wake up!*

'If we don't wake up,' he said, 'they'll take our votes off us, along with everything else. We have to have the Constitution brought in, before they change their minds about it.'

The murmurings grew, and the sense of wrong. On the twelfth Germinal – April 1st old style – men and women from all the poorer Sections assembled at the call of the drums and marched together to the Convention. Many wore in their hats inscriptions reading 'Bread and the Constitution of 1793!'. They sang and shouted as they went. Isabelle watched them go, aching to march with them, but she dared not leave the children, and to take them into possible danger was out of the question. Marianne must carry her anger for her.

She heard that they were received politely, but kept talking only until word had been sent to the National Guard units from the richer Sections, who marched in to disperse them, backed

315

up by jeering if inactive Muscadins. After that, the inadequate bread rations were supplemented with rice, which would have been acceptable, had not supplies of affordable fuel dried up altogether, so that no one could cook anything. Having burned all but the most essential furniture, Marianne and Isabelle and the children scoured the gardens and parks for fallen twigs, but others had been there before them and there were none to be found. Without bread, one went hungry: it was as simple as that.

A few days later the Convention ordered the disarming of all 'Terrorists'. A neighbour came to warn Pierre. 'You're on the list – I know, I heard Commard say. They've picked up Fournier and Griffard and Benoît. Lie low for a bit, if you're wise.' Pierre found refuge with a friend some streets away, and though the guardsmen turned the house upside down and took away the pike and the musket, they found no trace of their owner. 'I don't know where the bugger is,' Marianne told them, in the manner of a deeply wronged woman. 'And I don't care. If he wants that slut, he can go to her, that's what I told him. No, I don't know where she lives.'

Whether they believed her or not, there was nothing they could do about it, and they went away again. After a week Pierre returned. He was furious at the disarming. 'What do we do if the Muscadins come again, I'd like to know?' Worse than that, though, was the humiliation. 'I've carried arms since the Bastille fell. I put those bastards where they are. And now they do this to me!'

Defying the authorities, the Sections called the old assemblies together, to meet illegally in permanent session, as they had after August 10th. Pierre was enthusiastic, Marianne less so. 'All they do is talk, that's their trouble,' she said. 'We need action, not committee meetings.'

The sun was warm, there were flowers in gardens and on waste ground, birds sang in trees newly green; but there was no sense of spring among the hungry. From other parts of France came news of massacres of former Jacobins by Royalist murder gangs. In Paris the Muscadins grew bolder, baiting sans

culottes, picking fights with ever greater frequency. The bread
ration fell again, to a quarter of a pound and then to two ounces.
On the open market the price of bread rose to a staggering
sixteen livres a pound, more than a skilled man earned in a day.
Pierre no longer earned that in a week, and Isabelle's pension
was as elusive as ever. They depended now on the meagre
portion of free bread supplied by the Section welfare committee, augmented by occasional handouts from soup kitchens set
up in the wealthier districts. Sometimes that meant Isabelle
spent whole days queueing, simply to make sure the children
ate at all.

At night, in the kitchen with Marianne, she would weep with
rage and despair. 'How can they let this happen, how dare
they?' When one day a small group of Muscadins gathered to
jeer at the men and women queueing at the soup kitchen,
Isabelle's anger caught fire. She put the children aside and ran
with the other women to beat and pummel the mocking young
men, cut their hair, force red bonnets upon their heads.
Astonished afterwards at the savagery of her feelings, she knew
that if it had come to killing, she would have done that too,
without hesitation.

On the first day of Prairial it was the women who beat the
drums and rang the bells, the women who went to the
workshops and drove the men to their Section assemblies; the
women who, impatient as the men argued and drew up
petitions, marched behind drums towards the Convention,
cajoling and threatening their sisters in bread queues and
passing carriages, urging any woman they saw to drop
whatever she was doing and come with them. This time
Isabelle left the children with Hubert's wife and joined them,
for she could take no more. No longer could she simply stand
aside and watch.

So it was that at last she found herself a part of one of those
great angry crowds she had witnessed so often since the
Revolution began, pouring in a relentless raging torrent, like a
river after snows, through the city streets. Now she was at one

with them, merged into the mass of hungry women shouting for justice and bread; their rage was her rage, their despair was hers, and their hope; their hate burned in her as fiercely as it did in all those whose starved bodies jostled her and swept her on. Yet at the same time her own small individual anger and pain, her grief at Jérôme's loss, her fury at her children's hunger, her sense of injustice, all found their voice as a tiny fraction of the great cry of rage that went up from that vast swelling mass of people of which she was a part.

The wave of women swept through the streets and broke in the courtyards of the Tuileries, pouring on into the Assembly. There was no pretence this time that the Convention welcomed them. They were met by men with whips who beat them out again into the streets. 'Like dogs!' said Marianne in disgust, rubbing a bruised temple. Then, 'Where are the men? Never there when they're needed!' She went with others to go in search of them and hurry them up, while the rest – Isabelle among them – hung about in groups, sat on walls, talking, watching, waiting.

They could hear the bells ringing still in the eastern Sections and at last the men began to arrive, their own wave swelling the flood in the streets around the Convention. Pierre was with them, and he had a gun in his hand. 'We got into the armoury,' he explained with a grin. He looked relaxed and happy, like a man who has found himself again.

They surged on, and in the struggle to keep them out a deputy was killed. Isabelle saw a bloodied head waving on the blade of a pike, moving inexorably towards the Convention's president on his raised seat; the president, white faced, bowed his head to the grisly trophy and tried to call for order. After that, there was no more resistance. The people poured into the hall, filling the galleries, crowding onto the benches alongside the frightened deputies, shouting for 'Bread and the Constitution of 1793!', urging the president to sign the petition the men had brought.

All afternoon, far into the night, the arguing went on. For the first time in many months, it seemed, the people were being heard, and not only heard but heeded. Isabelle felt the excitement and hope of those around her, joined her voice to the passionate debates, cheered as votes were taken, decisions made and recorded.

Then at midnight soldiers with levelled bayonets appeared at the doors; the soldiers the deputies had been waiting for, as they endlessly spun out the talking. Within a short time the place was cleared of people.

'Nothing for it now. It has to be armed force,' said Marianne.

That meant the National Guard units of the Sections, and above all the Cannoneers. The bells rang again from first light, and drums called the men to their assemblies. By early afternoon they were ready. Marianne kissed Pierre goodbye. 'Don't come home until you've got everything we ask for,' she said. 'Not just promises – action!'

All afternoon they listened for the sound of cannon fire, for the noise of shouting, or marching feet returning home in triumph. When it was scarcely dark, the men came back. 'Half their own forces came over to us,' Pierre told them jubilantly. 'They gave us all the honours of the Assembly, without a shot being fired. We've got it all – the Constitution, a new Commune, prisoners released, bread we can afford.'

But when they questioned him, they learned that all they had been given was promises. 'You shouldn't have left until it was done, even if it took days,' Marianne protested. 'Words aren't enough.'

'They'll keep their word, you'll see,' said Pierre. 'They know now, we still have the power to make them if they go back on their promises.'

'I hope you're right,' said Isabelle.

They soon knew how wrong he was. Early next morning the Convention called up all loyal forces and quickly surrounded the rebellious Sections. The women went with Pierre to help with the hasty building of barricades; beyond them, they could see the loyal troops lining up, reinforced by well-drilled groups of Muscadins.

319

'There aren't many there,' said Pierre. 'Most of the National Guard's kept out of it.' But by the next morning the ring of troops surrounding the district was complete and impregnable. The men on the barricades, threatened with outlawry, fearful of the suffering that would be inflicted on their families by muskets and clubs and cannon fire, recognised defeat and gave themselves up.

After that the soldiers marched in, with the Muscadins on their heels. Pierre was arrested, and Marianne too. Hubert went into hiding, but his wife, anxious and breathless, brought the news to Isabelle, who was at the house of a neighbour whose husband had died last winter. 'They're looking for you too. I've brought what I could carry of your things.' She thrust a large untidy parcel into Isabelle's hands. 'Stay away till things are quiet. They'll be watching the house. And take care – I don't think I was followed, but you never know.' Then she left as quickly as she had come.

Isabelle summoned the children, who were playing in the courtyard, and went to take refuge with Thérèse, who had long since foresworn politics and was acting again, in one of the many thriving theatres. Once there, she examined the contents of the parcel: there were clothes, and some toys and books, the few items of jewellery she possessed, a print of the Declaration of the Rights of Man, and the pewter cutlery she had brought from the convent, together with one or two additional items of tableware that she had acquired before her marriage. It was an odd assortment, but Hubert's wife had done well, on the whole. Fortunately all her papers, and those of the children, were already in her possession.

The moment the streets were quiet, she left the children and went straight to the municipal treasury, taking with her every one of those precious papers, and in particular her residence certificate and the civic certificate, recently acquired. They could not yet know that she had moved, nor, she hoped, would they have learned so soon that she had played any part in the disturbances of the past days. When they did find out, then her civic certificate would certainly be withdrawn, and all hope of

her pension with it. Better to try one last time to lay her hands
on that elusive money, before she lost all means of doing so.

For once everything went without a hitch. At long last they
had found her records and were able to confirm that Isabelle
Duvernoy was not after all deceased. They did not apologise
for the error, but she did not waste her breath demanding an
apology. It was enough that she had money in her pocket at last,
even if she received none of the arrears due to her, only the
pension for the most recent quarter. She reflected as she walked
home afterwards that one hundred and fifty livres in assignats,
once such a substantial sum, now went hardly anywhere. Eight
loaves of bread at the current market price (which would
doubtless be higher tomorrow), and she would be destitute
again. But it was – just – better than nothing.

Next day, covering her tracks – for the arrests were
continuing – she rented a tiny furnished garret room in a seedy
lodging house, with one damp and bug-ridden bed, a stool and
a rickety table. By a recent law, occupants of furnished rooms
were ineligible for ration cards, but it was all she could afford;
or, rather, more than she could afford, but she had to live
somewhere. In any case, at present she had no wish to draw
attention to her whereabouts by applying for a ration card. She
gave a false name to the landlord, obliged by law to list all the
occupants of his house; he was drunk and did not even glance
at her papers. The house was in a narrow, little-used alley, and
she hoped no one would think to look for her there. She left
word with Thérèse where she could be found, and settled down
to a life of haunting soup kitchens and the back doors of shops,
of begging, and scavenging from rubbish heaps. She had no
money to spare for fuel, but then there was no hearth in her
room, so that cooking was out of the question. More than once
some doubtful meal resulted in severe stomach upsets for them
all, which made her more careful afterwards, for a time. What
flesh remained on their bodies soon fell away, leaving little
more than skin and bone. It took all Isabelle's energy to keep
up the daily search for food. Where, at first, the children had
cried a good deal and complained of hunger, they began instead

to sink into a silent apathy broken only by occasional dreary whimpering. Their coughs grew worse.

Very early one morning in what would once have been mid June – it was towards the end of Prairial – Isabelle woke to a sense of utter hopelessness. She stood in the middle of her tiny room, beneath the small grimy rooflight that let in water when it rained, and looked at the two skeletal children crouched listlessly in a corner, watching her from shadowed eyes, and understood at that moment what it was that had driven Marianne's neighbour to kill herself and her children. What future was there for them, except day after day of worsening hunger, until the time came for them to die in painful indignity?

She still had money left, a few assignats, daily growing more worthless. She could struggle on as she had been doing until now, stretching the money as best she could; every moment of her time, every ounce of her energy, taken up by the struggle to survive yet one day more, in the certain knowledge that she was only staving off the inevitable . . . And she was so tired, so desperately tired.

What if she were to give up the fight? She had enough money left to feed them well for one day and buy a good quantity of landanum or some other drug. They could have a few last hours of enjoyment, and then she could put them all to sleep, never to wake again. If there was another life and a kindly God, then they would find peace and happiness at last. They might even see Jérôme again.

She knelt down and held the children in her arms, and they huddled close, silent, as they were for most of the time these days. Poor frail little creatures, she thought; all small bones, like two birds. It was not for this that they had been brought into the world.

She wanted to weep, but instead she smiled. 'Let's go out and have a picnic by the river,' she suggested brightly. They said nothing, simply rose with mute obedience to their feet, waiting until she was ready.

She opened the door. Someone was coming up the narrow

stinking stairs, up and up towards them. Once she would have been afraid, now she did not greatly care. She stayed where she was, so that when Marianne reached the top stair she was waiting there to greet her.

Marianne looked plump and pink as she had never seemed before, and full of a vitality that lit up the tiny room. 'Prison food,' was how she explained it. 'At least that's one way not to starve.'

But when the first greetings were over, it was clear that her mood was at odds with her appearance. She told Isabelle that a special military commission had been set up to judge the ringleaders of the Prairial days, and Pierre was to appear before it. 'They're fools. They seem to think I had nothing much to do with it,' she said. Her tone had all its old careless vigour, but Isabelle knew she was afraid.

Yet her coming brought hope back to Isabelle. Marianne had the energy her friend had lost, and the knowledge to seek for food in the likeliest places, and they began to eat better again. Isabelle looked back at that moment of despair and was amazed that she should have allowed herself to sink so low. She had not even considered selling her body, as most women in her situation would have done, however reluctantly – though who would have been willing to pay to lie with a scrawny, dirty creature like herself she was not quite sure. Alternatively, she could have gone to the Section welfare committee, risking arrest, if there was still any danger of that. Better a prison cell than what she had condemned her children to. She was furious at her own ineptitude.

'As soon as Pierre's out we'll decide what's to be done,' she told Marianne.

But Pierre never came back to them. Having appeared before the military commission, he left his prison cell only once more, for the last jolting tumbril ride to the guillotine.

Marianne threw herself into a rage of grief, shouting and screaming and sobbing as Isabelle had never done. Something in her noisy agony broke whatever it was that had kept Isabelle calm for so long, and she began to weep too, and once started

323

found she could not stop. They fell into one another's arms and clung together, hugging one another and weeping, for a long time.

It was an end; but it was also a beginning. That night Isabelle slept with a depth and a tranquillity that she had not known since Jérôme's death, and her sleep was full of dreams. She dreamt she was riding again over the border fells, with Jamie laughing at her side; she was wandering by the river, while curlews called overhead; she was walking into a room where her grandmother turned from the fire to greet her with open arms; and it was Aurore and Aristide, grown plump and healthy again, who ran to be folded into that generous embrace.

She woke next morning to a hunger and sense of loss so desperate that it swept aside all thoughts of friendship and compassion and left her with a determination that had formed, if not in sleep, then at the very moment of waking.

'I'm going back to England,' she told Marianne. 'As soon as I can, before the money runs out.'

Her friend stared at her. 'What on earth for? What can there possibly be for you there?'

What indeed? Her family had long ago rejected her. She had no reason to suppose they would welcome her back. On the contrary, if they were ever to discover what kind of life she had led since she left the convent, they would cast her out more firmly than ever. More to the point, almost everything she had come to love and value was here in France, and in every way at odds with the values of her family. Going back to them would not change that. And if they were to cast her out again, she would be as destitute and helpless as she was in Paris – more so, probably, for she would have no possible call on any of the charitable resources available to the English poor. *Whatever cause has driven a man from his native soil, his heart clings to it as a tree clings to the earth* ... Was that true after all, even of a wife and a mother?

'I don't know,' said Isabelle. 'I only know I'm tired of Paris. I'm tired of struggling all the time. I want to see the hills again. I want quiet, for the children as well as myself. Most of all, I want to see my grandmother before she dies, if she's still alive. And I want her to see the children.' She studied Marianne's face, sensing her friend's dismay, and her struggle to comprehend what she was being told. 'I know it makes no sense really. We're at war with England. There's no hope of a passport, so I'll have to find some other way. It's risky too, for the children. They're not strong any more. And I suppose if they find we're gone, we'll count as émigrés and might never be able to return.'

'They'll not know you've gone,' Marianne put in dully. 'I don't suppose anyone knows where you are now.'

'It's a risk though. Because I shall want to come back again, maybe very soon. For one thing, you'll be here.'

'Will I?'

Isabelle was dismayed by her tone, and the sad little half-smile that twisted her thin mouth. She had a sudden pang of guilt and regret, conscious that she was letting down this friend who had done so much for her. 'Marianne, I'm sorry. Don't do anything foolish, please—'

'What's more foolish than going to England?'

'I know it must seem like that to you, but . . .'

'You don't understand me. I meant, I shall come with you – if you'll have me.'

There was a long and astonished silence, into which Marianne laughed at last. 'Is it such a crazy idea as that?'

Isabelle shook her head. 'No – no!' Then she laughed too and flung her arms about her friend. 'What on earth should you want to come for?'

'Because you're the best friend I've ever had and there's nothing for me here any more. I don't want to stay and watch them break up the last pieces of the Republic Pierre built, and all the others. I'll come and see a bit more of the world with you, then maybe we'll find things have got better here. Only we can't do anything to change them any more.' She grinned. 'Besides, I've nothing else to do. It's something different.'

# Chapter Twenty-Seven

It took them two décades – about twenty days – to make ready for their journey.

Their first precaution was to move to other lodgings, even more disreputable than the last, in quite another part of the city, telling none of their friends – not even Thérèse – where they were. They hoped in that way to make sure that they did not appear on any later list of émigrés. If no one knew where they were, then no one would know either that they had gone.

After that, Marianne saw to the disposal of those few belongings they would not need on the journey, exchanging them as far as possible for food or even for the rare and sought-after coins of the old régime that would be much more use to them than assignats. In fact she brought home considerably more money than the goods could have been worth, but Isabelle did not ask how she had come by it. This was not the moment for scruples. It was enough that their purse grew comfortably fat. They kept a necessary change of clothes, a few books (at Isabelle's insistence), and the most valuable items, a gold chain and a small silver watch, both gifts from Jérôme to his wife. Isabelle also took the print of the Declaration of the Rights of Man out of its frame and rolled it inside her bundle of clothes, she did not quite know why. It would soon be obsolete anyway, for the Convention was working on a new one, which would certainly be a great deal less egalitarian.

Meanwhile she did her best to see that they all ate well for their remaining days in the city, trying to restore the health and strength they had lost through months of hunger. No great improvement could be expected in twenty days, but by the time they were ready to set out the children were already beginning to look a little plumper, with more colour to their cheeks, though they still coughed too much. Best of all, they brightened, finding the energy for mischief and laughter.

'We're going on a picnic,' Isabelle told Aurore on the morning of their departure. She did not say any more, for fear that the child might inadvertently let something slip. Once well away from Paris, she would tell her that they faced not a picnic but a journey.

They set out on the second Décadi in Messidor, only six days before the anniversary of July 14th ... Last year they had joined the fraternal banquet in the street outside their house, celebrating together as no one would dare to do this year, away from the official festivities. No longer were the tumbrils rattling in daily convoys to the guillotine, but fear of another kind, the fear of hunger, gripped the poor streets, and a dull sense of despair, while the deputies worked on a Constitution that would take from the poor the last remnants of the power they had bought so dearly ... No longer did Jérôme come home at the end of a hard day to his wife and children, or Marianne lie at night beside Pierre ... Aurore was nearly seven now, tall and too thin, her brother almost a month from his second birthday, with his father's dark hair and grey eyes. They walked beside the two women, chattering and excited.

As it was an official rest day there were families making their way to the suburbs to eat and dance in the sun, though fewer than in the old days, partly because many people still persisted in keeping Sunday instead, so ensuring a break every seven days, in spite of official disapproval. No one gave a second glance at two poorly dressed women taking their children out for the day, baskets on their arms. The guards were not particularly vigilant, so they were not asked for their papers as they passed the barrière. They had no firmer plans than that they must make their way, as unobtrusively as they could, to the coast and there seek a boat to take them to England. It was like the journey Isabelle had made years ago in search of her child: simple in purpose, unplanned, its difficulties left to unfold as the days passed.

In fact, once out on the nearly empty roads beyond the city suburbs, Isabelle was reminded more and more of that long-ago journey, when she had set out with such overwhelming hope and anxiety to find her daughter, the more because they went at first by the same roads and there were things that tugged at her memory, a deserted monastery, a wooded valley, the curve of a river. Since then, how unbelievably crowded had her life been, making the years before, the long years of childhood, seem by contrast slow and empty and uneventful; how much had happened, how greatly had she changed! Then, she had been a frightened girl haunted by past horrors; now, at just twenty-four, she was a widow, turning her feet towards England after years of the greatest joys and the greatest sorrows that perhaps she would ever know. Yet, looking back, there was, she thought, little that she would now have chosen to do differently, little that she regretted. Except of course the one thing she had never had power to change, Jérôme's death.

They travelled as quickly as the children's strength allowed, sleeping sometimes in empty buildings (there were more of these than there used to be), sometimes at inns, where they always paid in assignats, because to use anything else would have drawn attention to themselves. Besides, they wanted to keep their greatest valuables for later. Most of the time they had to depend for food on what they could beg or steal, since the assignats quickly disappeared. If they saw soldiers or National Guardsmen they hid until they had gone by, in case anyone should ask for their papers. For the same reason they avoided towns, even if it meant taking a long way round. After the first day they did not ask for food or shelter at isolated farms, because there they were met with such fear and suspicion, so many threats to set the dogs on them, that it was obvious they were only making things more difficult for themselves. Even at inns they were often received at first with caution, though the presence of the children generally ensured a warm welcome in the end.

They were fortunate, on the whole. The weather held, and it was not too hot, they found just enough to eat and were never without a roof at night, and they met no official unpleasantness. The children even began to show signs of improving health, rather than the exhaustion that Isabelle had feared for them.

Their most frightening moment came on the fourth day as they walked along a straight white road over a high exposed plain, with ripening corn rippled by a light wind to either side of them. Isabelle was carrying Aristide, who slept against her shoulder, a burdensome weight that made every step an effort. They came at last, after what seemed hours, within sight of a wood, running down into a small hollow just on the horizon. And then Marianne halted. 'There's someone there.' Isabelle too had seen three or perhaps four people disappearing into the darkness of the wood just as it came into sight, but she had not thought it important.

'So what?' she asked. Aurore, sensing adult fear, moved closer to her. Aristide, waking up, struggled to be put down.

Marianne shook her head. 'I don't like it, that's all. They could be brigands. I heard they were bad, out in the country, worse than they ever used to be. Remember how frightened they were at that farm near Chantilly? And the one the night before. Sometimes those robber bands send women ahead, just to look over the place. Or to open the door to them at night. Maybe they thought that's what we were.'

Isabelle felt a shiver run up her spine and her mouth went dry, but she said with apparent calm, 'We don't look as if we've anything worth stealing.'

'I don't suppose they'd even turn up their noses at the chance of a few assignats. Besides, they don't stop at robbery from what I hear.'

Instinctively, Isabelle put an arm about Aurore. 'What do we do then? There's no other road.'

'Unless we go back to the crossroads – you know, with the broken statue.'

It was at least two leagues since they had passed the crossroads, with its headless and battered statue of saint or virgin (unrecognisable now) beside which someone had left a small bunch of primroses, already brown and decayed. Passing it the first time, Aurore had asked inconvenient questions, but this time she was too infected by their own anxieties even to look at it.

They took a road that led in a roughly westerly direction, walking as fast as the presence of the children allowed. Sometimes Marianne took a turn carrying Aristide; sometimes Isabelle gave in to his squirming demands to walk and put him down, but he was so slow, so wandering in his course – running to look at this or that, stopping suddenly, enjoying his freedom, full of questions and chatter – that it delayed them unbearably. What if brigands should come upon them at such a time? Distracted by the child, they might not even have seen their attackers until they were on them. As it was, they crossed woods in a state of hurrying terror, watching always for anyone behind or in front of them, and hid from every passer-by, even a lone woman gathering firewood or a man driving a cart.

The westerly route was more wooded, but also rather more populated, so that they had to make more detours. Yet in the end it brought them more quickly to the coast than they had expected. They came to the summit of a hill, pausing there to get their breath, and, looking up, glimpsed a distant blue line beyond the rounded slopes of further hills. 'The sea!' cried Isabelle, with a sudden leap of the heart.

'I've never seen it before!' Marianne exclaimed, as excited as Aurore, who was jumping up and down.

'Is that where we're going, Maman? Are we there?'

Isabelle, trying to repress an urge to break into a run, now that they were at last within sight of their destination, or the first part of it, said cautiously, 'They'll be watching the coast, I'm sure of that. We'll have to be very careful.' She spoke gravely to Aurore. 'We must be very quiet, my love. Do you think you can keep silent all the way to the sea over there? Not a word, not one!' The child nodded, excited rather than

331

alarmed. She seemed to think it was some kind of game.

Isabelle was glad that Aristide was tired now and content to be carried, for that left her better able to watch for trouble. They went by narrow lanes, avoiding any cluster of houses, however small, until at last they came late in the afternoon within sight of the green sweep of a down beyond which, presumably, cliffs dropped to the Channel. A stream cut a gentle wooded path through the downland, emerging in the distance close to a settlement of some kind, huddled on the shore. 'That's where we want to be,' said Isabelle. 'Someone there is sure to have a boat.'

They walked on, following a path beside the stream, always watchful; and then Marianne caught Isabelle's arm. 'Soldiers!'

There were perhaps half a dozen of them, three standing by the edge of the stream, talking together beside a little hut; the rest patrolling various points overlooking the valley. Acting on a mutual instinct, Isabelle and Marianne gathered the children with them into the partial concealment of a nearby tangle of gorse and hawthorn. 'Now what do we do?' asked Isabelle, crouching down. 'If we go on, we'll be seen.'

'We could go back a bit and then see if we can get over the cliff up at the top,' said Marianne, but her tone implied more than doubt at her suggestion and she was not surprised when Isabelle rejected it. Climbing down a precipitous cliff face in the company of a six year old and a toddler was not a practical proposition.

'Maybe we should just walk past them, as if we had every right to be there, and hope for the best,' Isabelle suggested.

'With that many men there, they're not taking any chances. Besides, they all know their comrades are watching them, so they'll be on their best behaviour, I'd say. That means we'll have to show our papers. And then we'll be finished.'

Their papers showed clearly enough that all their links were with Paris. They had no residence certificates for this part of France, and no passports, one or other of which would certainly be required; Marianne was quite right. Isabelle shut her eyes, the better to think what to do. She had no intention of being defeated when they had come so far.

Marianne peered over the bushes, studying the scene for some time. Then she sat down again. 'There's one thing we could try. We walk that way, as you said, just as if we have every right to be there. Then just as we get near the soldiers, Aurore runs off past them, down to the houses. You give a shout and run after her, like any frightened mother. You carry Aristide, of course. And I come after you. The chances are the soldiers will think Aurore's in danger and let us by. They might even give us a hand. I'd like to bet anything they won't think to bother about our papers.' She waited triumphantly for Isabelle's approval, and was clearly surprised when her friend shook her head in dismay.

'They might shoot. Aurore might be hurt!'

'Of course they won't. She's only a child.'

Still Isabelle shook her head, watched with round troubled eyes by the subject of their discussion. 'I wouldn't think of it, not for a moment. I don't know how you can even suggest it. You can tell you've never had children, or you'd never have thought of such a thing.'

At that, Marianne went very quiet, and looked away. Isabelle scrutinised her face, suddenly sensing an unexpected hurt, but she said nothing. It was no time to try and heal hurt feelings, when far greater difficulties faced them. Besides, they ought not to talk any more than was absolutely necessary. She closed her eyes again, picturing the path they had somehow to take. They could try running past the soldiers, knowing that a quickly aimed shot from a distance might well miss them. But then they would be pursued and that would end any hope they might have of negotiating peacefully for a boat to take them to England. They could try talking to the soldiers, making up some story that might persuade them to let them pass. But it would have to be very convincing, and even then it was chancy. Beside, it would be better if they could pass the guards unseen.

'We'll have to wait till dark,' Isabelle said at last. 'Then we can follow the stream down. There are plenty of bushes there, and there's not much moon. If we're very quiet we should do it.'

Marianne's expression suggested that she did not care any longer what was decided. 'If you say so,' she said.

They made their way back to a small wood out of sight of the soldiers, where they could spend the rest of the day in reasonable comfort. Once there, Isabelle said, 'I didn't mean to hurt your feelings just then. I didn't think you'd ever wanted children.'

'I didn't, not until—' Marianne broke off. 'The first time I've ever wished I had, that was when Pierre died. When it was too late.' She shrugged. 'I can't anyway. I realised that long ago. So there it is.' And then she changed the subject.

At dusk they ate some of the food they had with them, and then, as soon as it grew fully dark, Isabelle led them back towards the shore.

The men near the stream now sat in a pool of lantern light about a folding table, on which they were playing cards. A number of bottles stood at their elbows, to Isabelle's satisfaction. With luck, they would not be as vigilant as they ought to be. The men up on the slope of the valley evidently had no lights, but they would certainly be there still, and watching. Isabelle took Aristide in her arms, praying that he would make no noise, and held Aurore's hand tightly, and led the way to the stream at its nearest point, Marianne following.

They crept along the bank, bending to take as much advantage as possible of the scrubby gorse and broom that bordered it. Now and then, where there was no shelter, they crawled on the ground, or as near to it as they could, with Aristide to be carried. Fortunately he was sleepy and not inclined to talk, though once, when his clothes caught on a gorse bush, he gave a squawk of indignation. They all lay still then, holding their breath, listening. An owl hooted somewhere, and the sound of the soldiers' laughter came in a sudden gust over the stream. Then the men began to sing. Isabelle breathed deeply with relief and they moved on again.

They were almost there. Close to where the soldiers sat the stream was well concealed, and Isabelle had passed that point safely, with the children. A little further on, the gorse came to

an end, and the land was more open, so she halted, waiting for
Marianne to catch up with her.

There was a shout, clear into the night; a series of commands
sharply called. The black shapes of the soldiers rose against the
light, then the lantern moved, on towards the stream. Isabelle
saw Marianne begin to run; and then they were on her, and
there was the sound of a struggle. Then the lantern shone full
on her thin angry figure, right in the midst of the group of
soldiers . . . They had come so far, for this!

Isabelle held the children close, watching in helpless dismay.

She heard the men fire questions at Marianne, and then
Marianne's voice carried clearly, full of a manufactured alarm,
though she must indeed be frightened enough. 'Let me go,
citizens. If my husband finds out, I'm for it! But you know how
it is – who wants a stupid fisherman, when there's a fine brave
young soldier far from home and needing comfort? I'm a good
patriot, citizens. I'll always do my bit to serve my country and
keep her soldiers happy.'

It was a dangerous game, as the ribald comments of the men
showed, and their rough moves to kiss her, claiming their share
of the comfort she was offering. Isabelle shivered. Then
suddenly, after a little more talk, they let Marianne go, shouting
a few encouraging words after her. She walked boldly on,
along the path in the faint moonlight, towards the houses on the
shore. The guards resumed their game.

Isabelle was trembling too much to move for some time after
that. Then at last, when the singing began again about the table,
she rose and took the children's hands and hurried quickly
forward, bending low, praying only that they would not be
seen.

They did it. They reached a small belt of windblown trees
that sheltered a garden, and Marianne was there, reaching out
in the dark to take their hands. Isabelle heard her friend's voice
whispering in her ear. 'If we get round the far side of this place,
right under the cliff, then we shan't be seen when day comes.
Or not by the soldiers anyway.'

There was a faint gleam from a tiny moon reflected on the surface of the sea, enough to help them find their way past other gardens, and evil-smelling cottages and outbuildings, to the far end of what was evidently a tiny fishing hamlet. A dog barked once, rattling its chain, but otherwise they met no obstacle. They settled down at last in the shelter of a ramshackle wooden shed beside a pebbly beach and waited for daylight.

It was clear, when day came, that many of the houses in the hamlet were deserted. Perhaps the war had made fishing so difficult that few of its occupants could make a living any more, though it had clearly never been anything but a poor place. There were, however, a couple of boats drawn up on the shore, and a few distant sounds as the remaining inhabitants of the place stirred into life.

'What now?' asked Marianne. 'If we go marching out there asking for a boat, someone will denounce us to the soldiers.'

'Not necessarily,' said Isabelle. 'That depends how we go about it. This is where we need our livres.' She closed her hand about the purse in her pocket that contained their most valuable asset. 'Let's just wait and watch, till the right moment comes.'

It came a little later, when they saw a man scrunch his way along the pebbles to one of the grounded boats, and settle down near it to mend a fishing net. 'You stay here with Aurore,' Isabelle said to Marianne. 'If the soldiers are watching they might just recognise you. But I'll look like just any mother with a child.' There was also the point that Aurore, who could talk clearly as her brother could not, might make some innocent but revealing remark that would betray them.

Isabelle carried Aristide some way onto the beach and then put him down. He ran towards the sea, laughing and shouting at the waves. Keeping a watchful eye on the child, Isabelle made her way steadily but without apparent intent towards the fisherman.

'Do you expect a good catch, citizen?'

He looked at her suspiciously from under thick brows. 'If the good God wills, citizeness.' She was startled at the religious expression – in Paris it would, at the least, have been the

Supreme Being, except that even that phrase was discredited now, since Thermidor; but then they were a long way from Paris.

Aristide was in danger of getting his feet wet, and Isabelle had no change of shoes for him. She carried him back towards the fisherman, ignoring his squeals of protest. 'See how the citizen fisherman mends his net, with such care.' She was relieved when Aristide ceased his noise and looked at what the man was doing, with a momentary concentration.

'You're a fine little lad,' the fisherman said, suddenly softening. He became almost talkative, chatting easily to the child, who responded happily enough for Isabelle to risk setting him down again. When there was a suitable break in the talk, she said, as casually as she could, 'You go out fishing today, citizen?'

'Maybe tonight.'

'Do you go far?'

'I go where the fish are, citizeness – if I can.'

'What's to stop you?'

He nodded out to sea, where the massed sails of a large ship were visible on the horizon. 'Enemy ships. Our own ships sometimes, if they think there's danger. Or they send soldiers along to stop us setting out. There used to be a good few of us fished from here. Now most have sold up. It's hard to make a living these days.'

Isabelle tried not to feel discouraged. 'But you do sometimes fish far out to sea?'

He gave her a speculative look, as if he thought the question rather strange. 'Sometimes, citizeness.'

'Have you ever been right to England?'

He made a contemptuous blowing sound. 'Not me, citizeness! What would I want with France's enemy? Besides, I can't speak their barbaric language. I like to know what I'm hearing, I can tell you.' Then he gave a sudden sly grin and said in an undertone, 'Mind, in the old days, there was money to be made that way – brandy and the like. You could get a good price for it.'

Isabelle knew he was talking about smuggling. Perhaps that was how the men of the hamlet used to make a living. If so, it meant that he might after all be more familiar with the English coast than he had admitted. She was silent for a moment, thinking hard, choosing her words. The fisherman began to show Aristide in great detail how he mended the net, while the child pointed and chattered, apparently greatly interested. At last Isabelle said, 'If it was for the good of France, would you go to England – just to the shore, in your boat?'

He frowned, looking sharply up at her. 'Now why would you ask that?'

'I have a secret mission, myself and my companion. A mission for France.'

'Do you expect me to believe that? You, a woman with a child!'

'Two women and two children, in fact. What better disguise could there be, citizen? Who will ever suspect us of spying? Who would watch his words before a helpless woman? They'll think we're émigrés, I'm sure of it.'

'But how will you understand them?'

'I speak English.'

'Say some!' he commanded, sceptically.

She had spoken no word of English for seven years. Now, suddenly faced with the need to do so, her mind seemed wholly blank. She had learned even to think in French. Had she forgotten all the English she ever knew?

She could see that the man was about to crow triumphantly over the manifest falsity of her claim, when a phrase – meaningless enough – came to her. 'The sea is blue today.'

'What's that mean?' She told him. 'Well, it sounds like English, I suppose . . .' She waited, willing him to relent. 'Why aren't there soldiers seeing you off? Or someone official, to arrange for a boat?'

'It's a secret mission – most secret. The guards up there were tipped off to let us past, of course. But if we fail, they will deny all knowledge of us. If we succeed, everyone who helps us will be rewarded.'

338

He shook his head. 'Too chancy for me. I want something more certain than that.'

She pulled a handful of coins from the heavy store in her pocket. 'Fifty livres, and not in assignats either. Real money.'

To her relief, his eyes shone. 'Give it me, and I might agree.'

'When we step on English soil, then it's yours, I swear.'

For what seemed hours she thought he would refuse; and then at last he nodded. 'Very well then. Tonight, here, at ten. There's not much moon, though it's calm enough. But it's a fair way from here. And the Channel's full of enemy ships.'

Triumphant yet afraid, Isabelle went back to the others and told them what had been arranged.

# Chapter Twenty-Eight

Out on the black heaving surface of the Channel beneath a thin fitful moon, the fugitives sat huddled together in the boat, silent because the slightest murmur might carry to the ears of watchers on the shore or out at sea. The fisherman, anxious not to draw any unnecessary attention to himself, had chosen not to raise the sail until they were well clear of land, and the only sounds were the dip and splash and creak of the oars, the lapping of the waves. Marianne's face looked grey-green and frozen, her expression mingling terror and nausea; the children's eyes gleamed with excitement, as if they still thought the whole thing an adventurous game. If they could have chattered, they might have kept their excitement alive. As it was, the rocking of the boat, the gentle rhythmic sounds, soon lulled them to sleep. Heedless of the drenching spray and the danger, they drooped against their mother, their small bodies warm and relaxed beneath her sheltering arms.

After a time, Isabelle glanced behind her. They had come further than she had thought. The coast of France was now no more than a pale line against the dark sheen of the sea, topped by a dense blackness in which gleamed two or three tiny saffron points of light, where perhaps someone sat late with a sick child or soldiers kept watch. Suddenly, for no good reason that she could grasp, Isabelle began to weep, silent anguished tears that ran unchecked down her cheeks and were quickly dried by the wind. Partly perhaps it was from relief, that in spite of everything they had come safely so far; but more than that, she was filled with a wrenching sense of loss, as if this journey was cutting her adrift more surely than ever from Jérôme and all he had meant to her, from the last precious memories of their life together. It was his land she was leaving; his, and hers too, for it was the land that had sheltered her and given her children life; and she might never see it again. She had told herself that she would come back, but she knew that this journey might be as irreversible as the one she had made when she left the convent. Only, she had shed no tears on leaving the convent, for she had known no happiness there. Now she wept in silence, unheeded and unconsoled. The children slept on; Marianne was too tormented by fear and seasickness to notice.

Then the fisherman drew in his oars and gestured to the women to help him raise the sail, and there was no more leisure for tears. By the time all was quiet again, the boat slipping smoothly and swiftly on its course, there was no sign of land in either direction.

Hours passed, and the passengers on the boat grew chilled and cramped. Marianne's face still had a greenish tinge, though she seemed calmer. Perhaps she was simply too cold and miserable to be afraid of anything any more. Isabelle, conscious that it was her fault that Marianne was here at all, felt a mixture of pity and guilt at the enormity of what she had done. True, it had been Marianne's choice to come with her, but she had been too confused by grief to have considered clearly what she might be letting herself in for. After all, she had only once in her life been outside Paris, and until yesterday she had never even seen the sea. Now this city girl, skilled in surviving in an urban underworld, was about to land in a strange country whose language she did not speak, to travel (if all went well) to a wild and bleak region where all her skills would be useless. She would be wholly dependent on Isabelle, as dependent as the children. As the sky began to lighten, Isabelle found herself for the first time considering the implications of her impulsive, dream-driven decision to return to England.

Seven years she had been away, seven years that had changed her as much as they had changed the country of her adoption. It had never occurred to her until now that England too might have changed; and so indeed might her family. Worst of all, her grandmother might no longer be alive, which would mean that the whole journey would have been in vain. In any case, they had a vast distance to travel before they reached Tynedale, and many unknown dangers and obstacles to face. Indeed, from the moment they set foot on English soil their reception must be in doubt.

It had seemed obvious enough to Isabelle that they would be able to pass themselves off as émigrés, in a country which must have become accustomed to receiving fugitives from the Revolution. But now it occurred to her that the flood of émigrés would probably have ceased after Thermidor, perhaps even well before then, on the brink of war. How far would people in England know what the fall of Robespierre meant, how many would regard their arrival so long afterwards without suspicion? More than that, she had no idea how ordinary people who had no connection with France regarded French émigrés. Many of the revolutionaries had believed that it was only the ruthlessness of the British government that was preventing a revolution in Britain too. If they were right, then nobles and priests seeking refuge there might be looked at askance by many ordinary people. Isabelle also remembered only too well the narrow insularity of most English men and women, to whom someone from the next valley was a stranger, to be looked on with suspicion and treated with hostility. Courtesy to foreigners – even those fleeing persecution – did not come easily.

But she had made her choice and it was too late now to retreat – too late indeed, unless she were simply to ask the fisherman to turn his boat round, for at last they had their first glimpse of the English coast, a grey line rimming the horizon, devoid of salient points, gradually nearing and becoming more distinct, so that very soon they could make out a low shoreline backed by rounded green downland. The fisherman was, by now, clearly very nervous, for his own safety rather than theirs, Isabelle suspected – and with reason. She was sure that the English coast, like that of France, would be watched, and here the man was not so familiar with the hidden landing places, the dangerous currents and channels, the ports to be avoided. She herself felt how exposed they were, making straight for a coast which had no obvious shelter for a boat to make an unobserved landing.

And then, just as she was on the point of yielding to her impulse to demand a return to France, the boat reached shallow water and grounded on the fringe of a deserted pebbly beach.

'Well, that's it,' said the fisherman, his eyes anxiously scouring the landscape in all directions.

Isabelle stood up, setting the boat tilting. Her limbs were cramped, numb and cold and without strength. *What have I done?* she thought; and then she found herself stepping out onto the shore, shoes in her hand.

Marianne passed the children to her, first Aurore, then Aristide. She carried them out of reach of the waves, where they stood, shivering and drowsy, on the wet pebbles, utterly bewildered. Marianne stepped out too, unsteady on her feet and still looking far from well, while the fisherman's expression became increasingly alarmed. He was clearly anxious to leave. But first . . .

'Here, citizen.' Isabelle pulled the heavy purse from her pocket and splashed her way back to the boat. 'Fifty livres, as I promised. And thank you. We wish you a safe journey back.'

Then she and Marianne together pushed the boat out until it was free of the shingle. The man scarcely waited long enough to mutter his thanks before setting his oars in motion and rowing swiftly away.

He was only just in time, for suddenly there were shouts from the head of the shore and three men, one with a gun, came running down the beach towards them. Aurore shrank against her mother. Isabelle picked Aristide up. 'Stand still,' she advised Marianne, as if they were fierce dogs whose fury might be calmed by a quiet reception. 'Let them come to us.'

They waited, watching the men come nearer; large, burly men, roughly dressed, unshaven and unkempt. Isabelle glanced round: the boat was some way off now, too far, she hoped, for a hastily fired shot to threaten its safety.

No one fired, and the men reached them, looking a little less threatening on closer view. They merely had the appearance of having been up all night, on watch perhaps. They smelt a little of beer, but did not seem drunk. But they were throwing questions at them so rapidly, so much all at once, that Isabelle's cold and weary brain could not disentangle their meaning. From somewhere she dragged words to the surface, formed them into a sentence. 'We have escaped from France. Will you help us?' Her voice sounded, to her ears, strange and clipped and precise, as if she were speaking a foreign language.

One of the men pulled off his hat, the other two following suit. The gesture startled her. It was a long time since anyone had shown these conventional marks of respect, to her or anyone else in her sight.

'To be sure we will. Come along with us. My missus will give you food and drink, then we'll see what to do. Will the little lad come to me?'

But Aristide buried his face in her neck, and she had to carry him as best she could. She explained quickly to Marianne what the man had said, filled with strangeness to be hearing English again, to be speaking it, to be in this strange indeterminate place between England and France – for this was not her England, the land of wide sky and windswept moor and rushing burn, but a placid tame countryside of neat hedges, and cottages of flint and thatch with trim gardens.

'Can they be trusted?' Marianne asked warily, as she trudged beside Isabelle, Aurore's hand in hers.

'I think so,' said Isabelle. But she did not feel confident, simply strange.

When they reached the cottage looking over a small harbour, they had no more doubts. The man went in first, to seek his wife; and soon a plump woman appeared, wiping her hands on her apron as if just interrupted in some domestic task, and so moved at their plight that her eyes were full of tears. 'Oh, you poor dears – and the little ones too – such a journey, to escape from those bloodthirsty villains over the water! Come in, my dears ... Oh, how wet you are, to be sure! Sit you down by my good fire. Jack, you go and get all those clothes down from the chest upstairs. We'll soon have you warm and dry...'

Isabelle was quite glad that the woman left no interval in which she could translate more than the most basic instructions for Marianne; she was not too sure how her friend would react to being taken for an escaping noblewoman, fleeing the Revolution. Whatever they had fled, it was not that.

She judged, however, that there could only be an advantage to them in encouraging the woman in that idea, so at the earliest opportunity (it did not come until they were changed into a curious assortment of clothes, their wet things hung to dry before the fire, cheese and ham, the remains of a pie and hot tea on the table near them) she gave their names, adding, 'We are both widows. Our husbands perished on the guillotine.'

The woman wiped her eyes with a corner of her apron. 'Oh, you poor dears! To think such things can happen, and only a few miles away too! Well, you're safe now.'

There was one awkward moment. Taking Aurore's bonnet to put it to dry, the woman had pulled the cockade from it as if it were some thoroughly unsavoury object. 'You'll not be needing this any more, I'm glad to say. The back of the fire's the best place for such things—' She had been about to suit action to words when Aurore leapt up and grabbed her arm, crying in French for her to stop. The woman stared at the child with astonishment. 'Why, dearie ...!'

'She has had to learn respect for the cockade, for her own safety,' Isabelle said quickly. 'She doesn't understand. Let her keep it.'

With some reluctance the woman complied. 'She'll soon learn better, now she's here, I'm glad to say.'

Aurore leaned against her mother, watching the woman with grave disapproval, the cockade clutched tight in her hand. Later, Isabelle tried, fumbling for words, to explain to the child that they were not in France any more and that English people did not treat the French national emblem with respect. It was not easy, and it brought home to her as nothing else could have done how her loyalties were likely to be divided; worse, how her children too might be faced with a conflict. She realised then that it would have been much easier had they indeed been Royalist émigrés, with no reason to regard the Republican government of France with any affection at all.

They stayed overnight at the cottage – they were on the coast of west Sussex, they discovered – and the next day their host, having learned what their plans were, as far as they had any, found places for them on the cart of a carrier friend of his, bound for London. There would be no charge, he assured them. Isabelle suspected that he had paid what charges there were, but she made no great effort to find out. She could not pay him back in assignats, which was the only money she had left, and what valuables they had with them would be needed for the rest of the journey.

In two days they were in London. Expecting a tranquil and orderly city, Isabelle was shocked at the atmosphere of anger and tension that hung over it. There were beggars too, and crowds noisy with rage milling in the narrow streets. Marianne, understanding no words, was nevertheless perfectly able to gauge the mood of the place, and even she was frightened. She understood Parisian anger, but this was alien to her. 'You know what my uncle Henry always used to say?' Isabelle observed. 'He said they never had riots in Paris like they do in London, because of the efficient Paris police. That was before the Revolution, of course.' Marianne seemed more worried than amused by the remark.

Isabelle's only real concern was to leave the capital as soon as possible, but for that they needed money. Marianne said, in the tone of one prepared to make every sacrifice, 'Shall I see what I can get my hands on?'

Isabelle shook her head. 'Don't even think of it. People are hanged in England for the least thing. And you don't know the language. You'd never get away with it.'

Instead, she took her watch to a respectable-looking watch-maker's shop in one of the more fashionable streets, away from the menacing crowds. The man greeted her with a lofty disdain, which changed to greater politeness when she gave a hint of her circumstances. It was obvious he was impressed by the delicacy of workmanship of the watch, though she had no idea whether or not the price she received was a fair one. All she knew was that it was enough to pay for their coach journey to Newcastle, with a tiny sum over for food and lodging on the way. When that was gone, they would have to rely once more on their legs.

It was not a comfortable journey. The coach was full, and its interior stuffy and noisy with talk and pipe smoke, and it jolted and swayed unmercifully. Aristide began to cough again, worse than ever, and by the end of the three-day journey he was as wan and listless as he had ever been.

Isabelle had forgotten how appalling English roads were, deeply rutted and overburdened with traffic, so that accidents were commonplace. It was as if the English could never stay in one place for long, but must be always travelling, all at the same time. As the coach jolted and swayed, Marianne made unfavourable comments, which Isabelle was relieved could not be understood by their fellow passengers.

So many things she had forgotten, or perhaps had never known, for her knowledge of England beyond Tynedale had only ever been sketchy. She had once been to York, once to Durham, and had passed through Newcastle on several occasions, and that was it. The rest of England was unknown to her, until now. It all looked so neat and ordered after France, the fields carefully enclosed with hedges, the trim and prosperous houses clustered tidily about village greens, church and manor house at a sedate distance. Sometimes they would glimpse less tranquil corners, a group of dreadful hovels, tucked away out of sight of the gracious park surrounding a grand mansion, or, further north, mills or colliery settlements, where a thin and miserable-looking population could be seen at work.

Another thing struck her too, when they halted at inns on the way, enduring bad food and lumpy damp beds, because they could afford no better. She remembered how, on first going to France, she had thought French manners elaborately formal after what had seemed the ease and informality of the English – all that bowing and curtseying and flourishing of hands and hats and handkerchiefs, all those long rituals of greeting, which must be precisely right for each occasion and show the proper amount of deference. But those manners had been swept away with the old régime. Now, after the effusive warmth of Republican manners, the English seemed cold and formal and distant, and she wondered if she would ever begin to feel at home again in her native land. There were other things she missed too: the tricolour decorations on every public building, on every bonnet and hat, for England looked drab and colourless by contrast; the singing, for though they heard singing sometimes, it was mostly of a beery and tuneless kind. The children too were less sure of a welcome here. Sometimes they met with real kindness, but at other times, Isabelle felt, the very presence of the children was looked on as an intrusion, particularly when they sat down to eat in the parlour of an inn; most of all when Aristide, exhausted beyond bearing, began his weary and persistent crying. In Paris, she had always felt that children were looked upon as the Republic's future, to be cherished.

Yet they met little open hostility. On a couple of occasions Isabelle heard two people, realising that they had been talking in French, exchange disparaging remarks, on the lines of 'Damned frogs!', but for the most part they met with complete indifference.

Only once did she hear any talk of politics. Two middle-aged men got into the coach at Grantham, and almost immediately became immersed in an intense low-voiced conversation. Not paying much attention at first, Isabelle's interest was caught suddenly by hearing the word 'Jacobins', pronounced in so uncompromisingly English a way that she realised it must have become firmly lodged in the language. She began to listen then, and was astonished to realise they were discussing recent trials of 'English Jacobins'. When there was a gap in their talk, she translated something of what she had heard to Marianne. 'Well, they always said it was not the English who were the enemies of liberty, only their rulers,' commented Marianne. Later, Isabelle saw one of the men looking at her intently, in a manner she did not much care for, but when she stared coldly back at him he looked away and soon afterwards resumed his talk, though now he had turned to food prices. It was clear that in England too people were going hungry this year.

The coach halted soon afterwards to change horses and allow the passengers a rest. Isabelle left the children sitting on a bench in the sun with Marianne, and went into the inn to buy food. On her way out again, she found the man from the coach at her side. He glanced quickly about him and then said to her in a low voice, in heavily accented French, 'A word if I may.' She walked a short way off in his company, while he told her he had heard what she said and drawn certain conclusions. 'May I advise you, citizeness, do not assume that no one can understand what you say if you speak in French. There are many who can. Emigrés of course, but also spies.'

'French spies?'

'English spies. They are everywhere, I can assure you. Wherever the friends of the Revolution are assembled.'

'You were talking of trials.'

'Treason trials – yes, last year. The jury acquitted them, thank God, but it was a near thing. These are difficult times. Last year, Habeus Corpus was suspended. Odd, when the government wishes to vaunt the superiority of our freedoms, that it should destroy our proudest and most ancient one, in the name of national defence. But there we are. Have a care, that's all.'

Isabelle thanked him calmly and they parted, but she was shaken by the incident. England might look solid and old and unchanging, complacent even, but it was clear that it too had been touched by events across the Channel.

They reached Newcastle on July 28th – the tenth Thermidor,

Isabelle realised; exactly a year since Jérôme had died. The city was cold, swept by an unseasonably bitter wind, funnelled between the high walls of houses, swirling dust in doorways, penetrating their thin summer clothes.

'Marat lived here once, before the Revolution,' Isabelle said. 'So I heard.' Marianne, awed, looked with renewed interest at the fine houses and wide streets, and the steep narrow alleys that led down to the more disreputable areas beside the Tyne.

They stayed one night at an inn in Newcastle and the next morning early set out on foot on the last stage of their journey, following the military road west along the line of Hadrian's wall. For the first time since landing in England, Isabelle's spirits lightened. Now at last she was within reach of home – for there was still something of home in this northern land, with its clear light and distant view of the Cheviots and its wide bustling river.

It took them nearly two days to reach Chollerford, where at last they struck the North Tyne river and set out along its western bank. And it was then that Isabelle knew precisely why she had come back. It was not simply that she wanted to see her grandmother, though that had seemed reason enough. Now, nearly at the end of her journey, she realised suddenly that there had been some need in her to link this early part of her life to the new life she had made for herself in France. Even if Jérôme had lived she would still have needed to come back one day, bringing him with her, to show him the place that had helped to make her what she was.

She knew too that she had been wrong to feel that in crossing the Channel she had cut herself off from Jérôme. He was still with her, in this place he had never seen; in his son, his image in miniature, in Marianne, who had known him, in Aurore, who had called him 'Papa' and wept when he had gone, in Isabelle, his widow, who bore his name with pride and loved him still. She carried him with her, in her heart and her memory, as she always would.

With every step the landscape became more familiar, until they reached places through which she had ridden as a child, houses she had visited; corners of village streets, the line of a wood or a hill that brought some tiny memory flooding back in all its force and freshness. She scarcely noticed the others, so wrapped up was she in this journey of rediscovery. It was only when Marianne drew her attention to it that she saw how Aristide was struggling and realised they must stop and let him rest. He looked frighteningly pale and wan, and it was clear that he had almost reached the end of his small resources. A pang of anxious guilt swept through her. Jérôme's son was every moment growing more exhausted and all she could do was immerse herself in memories. What if she were to lose him too, after all they had been through – and all because of her own recklessness in bringing so young a child on so long and arduous a journey? That would be more than she could bear, a double loss, like losing Jérôme all over again.

When they had rested for a time she lifted Aristide into her arms and, tired as she was, carried him for the rest of the way. There was no more gazing at their surroundings, remembering or dreaming. All that mattered was to reach Blackheugh and find rest and care for the weary child.

Late in the afternoon they crossed the river by the ford and walked through Bellingham and then took the narrow road along the northern bank of the river, on through that wide, shallow, beloved valley. Even anxious as she was for Aristide, Isabelle felt a tumultuous confusion of emotions. If she had been asked what she felt at this moment, she could not possibly have put it into words, not simply because the words were lacking, but because so many feelings were mingled together that she could not begin to disentangle or analyse them.

On, slowly, wearily, for the last mile. Then they came to the simple stone gateposts on the right of the road that marked the drive leading to Blackheugh. A moment of hesitation – she did not quite know why – and then Isabelle led the way into the drive. At first they had only a distant glimpse of grey roofs, and the top of a square tower. Then the land rose a little and they saw the house before them, exactly as it had always looked, with the hills rising dark and heather-covered behind it, set on a natural mound above the level of the river and screened from the westerly winds by a plantation of scots pines, the old pele tower somehow at odds with the solid Jacobean symmetry of the main house. A rambling growth of outbuildings in the same weathered grey stone as the mansion, a high wall sheltering the garden to the south east of the premises, and that was it. 'Blackheugh,' said Isabelle, quietly, because she could hardly speak at all. 'Where I was born.'

Marianne came to a halt. 'My God! It's a château! I did not know you were such an aristocrat as that!'

Aurore, alarmed by the derogatory expression, looked anxiously from Marianne to her mother and back again. Aristide, stirred from a brief doze by the voices, began to cry, and Isabelle quickened her pace. 'Even quite poor people used to live in towers around here,' she said. 'It was the safest way.'

She was moved as she had not expected to be moved, almost to tears, by this place that she now knew to be more familiar to her, more essential to her than it had ever been in memory. Some part of her, long suppressed, yet still firmly rooted in her native soil, felt suddenly at home as it had not felt for a long time; but another part – the new Isabelle, independent, questioning, rebellious – felt uneasy, afraid, alien even. What would she find, at this, the end of her journey? She knew that it had been necessary for her to make it, but the outcome might be as difficult as anything she had experienced until now.

She walked ahead of the others, who hung back a little nervously, up to the great studded main door of the house, and then she pushed it open – it was never barred in daytime – and stepped into the hall. The chillness of it, the damp, the gloom, closed round her and, momentarily, the numb misery of that last morning. But she shook it away, and reached for Aurore's hand and smiled reassuringly at Marianne; and then she opened the door of the parlour.

Her brother was there, with his wife, the two forming part of an amiably domestic scene, seated either side of a modest fire. He turned his head, saw her, stared, and then rose to his feet and stood quite still, as if turned to stone. His wife sat with open mouth, equally silenced.

Isabelle smiled, not without a certain malice. 'Good evening, John. As you see, I've come home.'

# Chapter Twenty-Nine

'Isabella!' It was almost a whisper, but the words carried clearly across the room, sharp with accusation, dismay, and a disbelief that was giving way reluctantly to the realisation that this was no apparition but his very own sister, whom he had thought never to see again.

'What are you doing here?' John asked, when at last he had recovered himself sufficiently to string words together.

Of all the many reasons, she chose the simplest: 'I wanted to see Grandmother again.' Then Aristide began to cry with a weary misery that drove all other thoughts out of Isabelle's head. She laid him down on a shabby but comfortable chair near where they were standing and covered him with her shawl, and almost immediately he fell asleep. Aurore, seizing an opportunity to rest her tired feet, slid onto the chair beside her brother and sat there, staring with solemn intentness at her uncle's outraged face.

John was beginning to regain his assurance. 'What are you doing here?' he demanded again, more forcefully. 'And these children – and the girl...' He gestured towards Marianne. 'What right have you to walk in here like this?'

'I was born here, and you are my only living kin. What better right is there than that?'

'You surrendered all the rights you might once have had when you abandoned your most sacred vows. You need not think there will be any welcome for you here. I trust you have made suitable arrangements elsewhere, because you will not be staying.' He glanced towards the two long windows, through which the darkening landscape was visible. Francesca went to draw the curtains across them, and Isabelle saw then that she was well advanced in pregnancy.

'I cannot believe you would be so unfeeling as to turn two women and two children out into the night at the end of a very long journey.'

'You chose to come. You were not invited – far from it. Let me be very clear, Isabella. You are not welcome. I must ask you to leave, at once. If you do not go, then I shall ring for assistance to throw you out. It is as simple as that.'

It was rage not despair that made Isabelle answer, 'And what would Father Duncan say to that?'

'Father Duncan is no longer with us. And how you have the nerve to pursue that argument, in the circumstances, I don't know. *My* conscience at least is clear.'

Conscious that Marianne was curious as to what was being said, Isabelle made a hurried translation. Marianne's response was sharp and colourful and its tone made it immediately comprehensible even to John, who spoke little French.

'Then before we leave, I must insist on speaking to our grandmother,' Isabelle said.

'That is impossible.' Then she was dead after all! But John went on, 'She is no longer in full possession of her wits. She does not see anyone. There is no point; she would not know you. I repeat, you must leave at once – and for good.'

'I shall not leave without seeing Grandmother.' But Isabelle felt increasingly helpless. She had not somehow anticipated so unwaveringly hostile a reception – though quite why she did not know, now she thought about it; there had never been any love lost between John and herself – and where could they go now, if her brother did indeed have them thrown out? She did not know. She was searching through her mind for any former neighbours or friends who might be expected to receive them more warmly, when there was a knock on the door and a nurse came in with a small boy. Seeing that there were strangers present she halted doubtfully just inside the room. The child was about four years old, a thin frail-haired boy beside whom Aristide looked positively robust.

Francesca held out her arms and the boy went to her. For the first time that she could remember, Isabelle saw tenderness in her sister-in-law's eyes; and then, glancing at her brother, a softening in his too, though he looked slightly embarrassed at the same time.

'You have a son then,' Isabelle said softly.

'Yes. Cuthbert.' His tone was abrupt and hoarse, as if he rather resented the emotion that was behind it.

'John, I know I have embarrassed you by coming back. I know there has never been much affection between us. I know you think I have sinned greatly. But there are a great many things you might see differently, if they were explained to you—' She saw the impatience and contempt returning to his expression and quickly got to the point. 'If your child was sick and exhausted, would you not do anything to find him food and shelter? For your child's sake, if not for mine, let us stay here – if only for one night.'

Husband and wife glanced at one another and there was, Isabelle thought, a plea in Francesca's eyes. Then John looked at his niece and nephew, as if trying for once to put himself in the shoes of another person. Isabelle guessed that it was a difficult process, but he must have succeeded at last, for he said, 'Very well, for one night then. But tomorrow you leave.' He reached for the bell pull and tugged at it. 'Do you wish the nurse to sleep with the children?'

'The nurse?' Isabelle glanced at the woman standing quietly near the door. 'The children don't know her. I'd rather they were in with me, or in the next room.'

'No, not her!' John looked exasperated, as if he thought it unpardonable that his sister should add slowness of wits to her other offences. 'That girl is their nurse I take it? Or is she your maid?' He waved towards Marianne without really looking at her.

Isabelle felt herself colouring, not with shame but with a resurgence of the anger she had so recently controlled. 'I have no servants,' she said crisply. 'Let me introduce my dear friend, Marianne Colin.'

The demands of conventional politeness came so naturally to her brother that he made a slight bow, though he made no attempt at an apology. 'Madame!'

'*Citoyenne,*' Marianne corrected him, unthinkingly perhaps; at which his wife smothered an exclamation of horror and John looked as if he were ready to explode.

'You are not in France now, more's the pity,' he said to Isabelle. 'I suppose I should have expected that someone so ready to abandon her most sacred undertakings would go to all extremes. But don't think Jacobinism will be tolerated here.'

'Oh, I don't, John. I remember very little was ever tolerated,' she said.

No one had yet answered the bell, and John rang again, impatiently. 'Too many people are already infected with rebellious notions. You cannot conceive how impossible servants are these days.'

This time Ritson appeared, as plump and self satisfied as ever. Francesca said, 'Kindly see that the blue room is made ready for Miss Milburn.'

'Duvernoy,' put in Isabelle. 'My husband's name was Duvernoy.'

Francesca made no correction. 'Have the room made ready, and beds for the children in the dressing room. And see that the one next to it is prepared for our other guest.'

When the butler had gone, and the nurse had been dismissed too, with instructions to return for young Master Cuthbert in half an hour, her brother said, '*Was*, you said. You are a widow then?'

She was amused at his curiosity, which he was obviously trying to fight. 'Yes,' was all she would say, tantalising him to ask more.

He managed, though with evident difficulty, to resist the temptation. 'I suppose you'd better sit down,' he said grudgingly. 'Are those your children? Or Madame er . . .'

'Mine, yes.' She sat down near them, gesturing to Marianne

to do the same. 'Aurore here you must know about. She was born before I went into the convent.' She saw how he coloured at the reference, as if she had said something indecent. It irritated her, but she decided that the time had come to begin on some kind of explanation that might make her brother understand all she had done since they were last together. 'She is the only reason I left the convent. I realised when I had time to reflect that I would never have taken the vows, if I had not been led to believe that I had no alternative. I realised that the real wrong I had done was in allowing my child to be abandoned. So I set out to find her. I know I was right to do so.'

'You always were ready to think you knew better than your elders – than God Himself too, I don't doubt. Or have you turned atheist as well as Jacobin?'

'You were always ready to think your will and the will of God were the same thing,' she retorted. She was pleased to see she had shocked him; but in a sense the accusation was unfair, for, as she recalled, he had never done anything so definite as to have a will of his own. He had always accepted that what his parents or the chaplain told him was right, without question; but she enjoyed irritating him. She went on calmly, 'My husband adopted Aurore as his own; she took his name. This is the child we had together, Aristide.' She saw that Aurore was watching them intently, recognising the names in an otherwise incomprehensible conversation.

'Outlandish unchristian names you gave them, I observe. Though I suppose the girl was already baptised.'

'Aurore is the name she was given at her adoption. They are good Republican names.'

'Then your husband didn't die on the guillotine, like so many brave and noble men?'

'Yes, he did. As you say, like so many brave and noble men. And women...' she added, with a sudden recollection of Louise's pale, serene face. She regretted that something so serious should have become a matter to bait her brother with and fell silent. She felt suddenly desperately tired and wanted only to escape from this irritable conversation and rest.

'There were rogues went to the guillotine too, remember,' said Francesca. 'Robespierre just one of them.'

Ritson returned to say that the rooms were ready. As they were following him from the room, Francesca said, 'We dined some hours ago, of course. But I can ask Cook to serve a light supper if you wish.'

'Thank you,' said Isabelle.

'In the library then, in an hour. I expect you would like something sent up for the children. Bread and milk perhaps?'

Isabelle thanked her again, genuinely grateful for a consideration that she found rather surprising, though no less welcome for that. Perhaps, she thought, she had misjudged her sister-in-law; or perhaps motherhood had sweetened and softened the cold and supercilious nature she remembered.

The children were amazed at the size and grandeur of the room allotted to their mother, the more so when she told them it had been hers in childhood. They did not notice how faded and musty the hangings were, how threadbare the upholstery, how old fashioned the furniture; all exactly as Isabelle remembered them, but older by seven years. Clearly her brother was no more prosperous than her father had been.

A kindly servant brought bread and milk, and lingered to talk to the children. Questioned by Isabelle, she confessed that she had small brothers and sisters at home, whom she missed, not having been very long at Blackheugh. Isabelle felt that she would have proceeded to pour out her whole life history, encouraged by so friendly a reception, except that a bell suddenly clanged in the distance. The girl jumped, clearly frightened, and hurriedly left the room.

Isabelle put the children to bed, once they had eaten the bread and milk; she was relieved that Aristide seemed almost as hungry as his sister. When they were asleep she went in search of Marianne who, like her, had washed and tidied her clothes as best she could, and then they went down together to the dark and rarely used library, where a tray had been set out for them, containing cold meats and fruit and tea. To Isabelle's relief they were clearly expected to eat alone.

'A château and servants – I never thought you came from somewhere like this!' Marianne exclaimed.

'But you know why I left,' Isabelle reminded her.

'Yes, and now I've seen that bastard of a brother of yours, maybe I understand a bit more. But where's this grandmother you came to see?'

Isabelle explained what her brother had told her. She felt unbearably sad at the thought that she had, to all intents and purposes, seen the last of her beloved grandmother on the day she left home; that the Grandmother Milburn she had known no longer existed, except in memory. She might as well have been dead, if this was how it was to be. 'I shall see her tomorrow, just in case she knows me after all.'

'What then?' asked Marianne. Her gaze settled on Isabelle's face and the light of the single candle on the table revealed an expression of gloom and doubt.

'I don't know,' said Isabelle. 'We shall have to see.'

'It seems to me,' said Marianne, 'that there's nothing for you here, nothing at all. We might as well not have come.'

Isabelle did not say, 'I never asked you to,' because Marianne's words so starkly echoed her own present mood.

# Chapter Thirty

Isabelle woke early the next morning, roused by the unfamiliar – yet once so familiar – call of the curlew. There was the sound of water, too, and wind in the pines, and, faintly, the whistling of a lad starting his day's work in the stables – Jamie himself perhaps? She slid from the bed and went to the window and looked out on the heather-patterned slopes running up beyond the grey roofs of the stables towards the uneven line of the horizon, jagged with rock, broken by the sudden vertical of a lone scots pine against the blue morning sky. She pushed open the window and drew in deep breaths of the sweet pure cold air, unlike any she had breathed for seven long years. Then she went to dress.

The children were awake, clearly rested by their night's sleep. Even Aristide was jumping about the dressing room, exclaiming at things he had been too weary to notice the night before. Marianne, when Isabelle put her head round her door, looked as if she would not stir for hours yet, so Isabelle dressed the children, warned them to be quiet and took them down the back stair towards the side door that led into the stable yard.

So many memories came flooding back as she stepped out onto the straw-strewn cobbles; the smells, horses, leather, hay, dung, mingled with the pervasive sweetness of the moorland air; the sounds, horses snorting and stamping in their stalls, the curlew's long whirring call, sheep bleating on the moor, the swish of a broom on stone flags and a boy's whistle – and there the boy was, emerging from a stall, broom in hand, a sturdy brown-haired lad whom she had never seen before. He halted when he saw her and pulled the battered hat off his head. 'Morning, ma'am.' She supposed that rumour, running swiftly through the servants' quarters, had brought news of her return; otherwise there would never have been that deferential gesture for someone as poorly dressed as she was.

'Good morning,' she said. Aurore, having jumped up and down with excitement at the realisation that she was in a stable yard, was tugging at her hand, begging to be allowed to go and talk to the horses, but a little too awed by the grandeur of her surroundings to dare to break free from her mother. 'Is Jamie Telfer about?'

The lad shook his head. 'There's no Jamie Telfer here.' Quite clearly the name meant nothing to him.

She was about to question him further when he stiffened, his eyes on some point just behind her. She glanced round to see her brother stepping into the yard. He looked exasperated when he saw her. 'What are you doing here? I don't want children getting under the feet of my men.' Then he turned to the lad. 'I want Black Prince saddled up for eleven o'clock, if you please, Ned. How's Sultan? Is the leg any better?'

'I think so, sir.' They went off together to examine the horse in question, which gave Isabelle an opportunity to take the children on a tour of the stables. They had reached the furthest stall and she was just raising Aurore a little so she could stroke the nose of a stolid-looking bay (Aristide, a little nervous of the large animals, remained at her side, watching from a safe distance); when she heard a sharp and peremptory whinny from somewhere just beyond the stable gates. She glanced round and saw a pony standing at the fence in the field just outside the gates, which was kept for animals temporarily out to grass; a sturdy shaggy brown pony with a white blaze.

'Bonny!' She dropped Aurore to the ground. 'Look! There he is – my very own dear pony!' She took the children's hands and led them over to the increasingly excited animal. 'I learned to ride on Bonny.' He whinnied again as she came near, pacing backwards and forwards with increasing excitement, and then stretched his head out to greet her as if he had last seen her only yesterday. She put her arms about him and rubbed her cheek against his shaggy coat and he nudged and nuzzled her, blowing softly, and then he allowed Aurore to stroke him too, and was so obviously gentle and friendly that even Aristide ventured a tentative pat.

'Oh, can I ride him, Maman?' Aurore implored.

'I wish you could, my love, but I don't know. I suppose he belongs to your Uncle John now.' She spoke calmly, but there was a fierce surge of rebellion in her heart at the thought. 'We shall have to see.'

At that moment John came striding purposefully towards them from the stable yard.

'Does anyone ride Bonny?' she asked.

'I have him in mind for Cuthbert, when he is strong enough.' There was a certain grimness in his expression that moved Isabelle in spite of herself, because it implied a lack of hope. 'True, he's a little large for a small child, but he's thoroughly trustworthy. Henry used to love him.'

'Henry?'

'Cuthbert's brother. He died last year.' He immediately brushed aside the possibility of any expression of sympathy by saying brusquely, 'I shall expect you to be away the moment you have breakfasted.'

That returned Isabelle's thoughts to her chief purpose in coming back to Blackheugh. 'When I have seen Grandmother, but not before.'

'I told you she sees no one. She is paralysed and wandering in her mind. It is better for us all that she should be left alone.'

'I came here to see her and I shall not leave until I have done so.'

'You will do as I say in my house.'

He did not, she noticed, threaten again to have her thrown out. Last night she had believed that threat. Now, in the clear light of a fine summer's morning, she saw that such behaviour would only scandalise his neighbours in a way he could not have endured. He had always been concerned about what people thought of him; and even if his neighbours shared his view of his disreputable sister, there were limits to what they would regard as seemly behaviour. Summoning your servants to throw out your own kin (and her children) by force was not seemly. If John had made a name for himself as an eccentric he could have got away with it perhaps, but the very idea of eccentricity had always been enough to make him shudder – even in his sister.

'I cannot see what harm it would do for me to see her.'

'You have not had the caring for her these past years. That is my last word on the matter. Why will you never accept that other people sometimes know better than you do?'

'Because the one time I did I nearly destroyed my whole life and the life of my child because of it.'

'Oh?' Clearly he did not understand the allusion.

'When I abandoned her to go into the convent, of course.'

'Oh, that again! I fear I still cannot comprehend what could have made you act as you did. Last night you implied that some kind of compulsion was put upon you to take the veil, but that is not how I recollect it.'

'I was in no state to do anything freely, after all that had happened. I think I was even a little crazed.'

'A proper penitence for one's sins is hardly the sign of an unhinged mind. On the contrary.'

'Penitence for someone else's sins and for a wrong that has been done to you against your will – that's hardly sane, is it?'

'I don't understand.'

'Cousin Henri would understand.'

She saw a shadow cross his face. 'You haven't heard, I suppose. Our cousin died with great courage, fighting for his King. François too, sent to the guillotine by those barbarians in Paris.'

'François was arrested for spying. I imagine they execute spies in England too.' But that was dangerous ground, for she still felt some uneasiness over her own small part in his fate, and she had no wish at all for her brother to find out what that part had been. 'As for Henri, I heard rather a different story about his activities, but we'll let that pass. I had no reason to mourn him, after what he did.'

Her brother studied her face, as if trying to grasp what she was implying. 'Are you saying—' He looked at Aurore, as if he might be able to find some clue in her features.

'As I told you last night, she was legally adopted by Jérôme Duvernoy, whom I married,' said Isabelle. 'He is the only father she has ever known and the only one I wish her to know. But in blood – yes, our cousin was responsible. He made a habit of it – forcing girls, that is. So I realise now. I was more innocent then, more's the pity.'

The look of disgust on her brother's face was reflected in his voice. 'How dare you besmirch the name of a man of his courage and faith, a man who is moreover unable to answer so disgusting a slur on his name! I did not think even you could stoop so low! You may not know that he spent some months here, and I came to know him well, and greatly to respect him, I might add. It is inexpressibly painful to me to admit that my own sister might be no better than a – whore, is the word, I suppose.' Isabelle was used to hearing coarse language, but on John's lips the word sounded profoundly shocking. What he said next was worse. 'I am convinced that a man of his sense of honour would never have allowed such a thing to happen, unless he were somehow lured into the filthy toils of a deeply evil and conniving woman. If you thought to exonerate yourself by what you have just told me, you are greatly mistaken. You have only succeeded in demonstrating how unfit you are to live under the same roof as decent people.'

There was a little silence. Isabelle saw the children watching the two of them, clearly uneasy at the anger that hung in the air. She was glad that they could understand nothing that had been said. 'I suppose that's confirmed one thing I always believed,' she said at last. 'I would have got nowhere by telling the truth. Father Duncan was the only one I ever told, and he wasn't much more understanding than you are.' With a strong sense that she was wasting precious time, she took the children's

367

hands in hers again and turned back towards the house. 'I will see you later, I suppose.'

'To take your leave – yes, and the sooner the better. After what I have just heard, I think I should choke to eat at the same table as you, but Francesca is expecting you at breakfast, and I have no intention of soiling her ears with your sordid lies. Breakfast will be served in the parlour at ten.'

It was almost seven o'clock, which gave her three hours in which to see her grandmother, supposing her brother did nothing active to prevent her from doing so, which she did not think he would. She hurried back upstairs and woke Marianne, quickly telling her what had happened. 'I've got to see Grandmother, then we'll decide what we do next.' She left the children in Marianne's care and made her way to the passage-way near the kitchen, from which an arched entrance led into the tower. As she passed the kitchen door, the cook – the same large woman who had presided there in her girlhood – came to greet her. The woman's obvious pleasure in seeing her was soothing after her brother's harshness. Isabelle explained where she was going.

Cook shook her head. 'A sad business, Miss Isabella. I hope I drop dead before I get to such a state as that. Not to know your own kin.' She shook her head again. 'Not that anyone sees her now, except Warren.' She nodded towards the broad back of a woman just disappearing through the door that led down to the cellar. 'Her maid, that is. Mr John had her brought in, when the old lady was taken so bad. More a nurse than a servant, you could say. But if I was you I'd keep away. Remember her as she was, that's my advice.'

It was advice Isabelle had no intention of following.

She pushed open the heavy studded door beneath the archway. Inside, a low windowless passage led to a second door, as solid as the last, beyond which was a dark vaulted room, from whose further corner a spiral staircase led up inside the thickness of the wall. Memories came flooding back, of old songs and stories, childish fears – redcap, with his long talons and his blood dyed cap ... Then another little picture flitted into her mind, of Pierre with his red bonnet set jauntily on his blond curls, singing as he limped to the barricades . . . just a few short months ago. It seemed a lifetime. She realised then that even if nothing had changed at Blackheugh, she could never have found it exactly as it was when she left, because she brought back to it now all kinds of baggage accumulated over the intervening years, a baggage of emotions and memories and experiences, which her past had illuminated and which now came back with her to colour and illuminate the present.

She mounted the stair to the room above, ceilinged with heavy beams, its two fine windows looking over the garden and the valley respectively. From there another stair led to the two smaller rooms on the next floor, the further one of which had always been Grandmother's room. Her heart thudding, she knocked briefly on the door and then, knowing she could expect no answer, pushed it open.

Memories were bludgeoned out of existence; Grandmother's room had never been like this. The stench was terrible, a mingling of stale urine and excrement and unwashed human flesh and damp and dirt. The grimy windows let in only enough light to show her that the room was in chaos, every surface littered with a jumble of clothes, utensils, mouldering food, all kinds of things it was impossible to make out in the dimness. There was no fire in the hearth, which might have been excusable at this time of year, except that the room was so damp that its walls, plastered long ago, had an appearance of random patterning from the mould that stained them.

At the far side, against what faint light there was, an old woman sat in a battered chair, huddled under a jumble of rugs; so small and frail, so bent, that Isabelle would have not known her, except that she could be no one else.

'Grandmother—'

The old woman turned her head. Even in the dimness, Isabelle was startled to see that the dark eyes looking at her seemed exactly as she remembered them, bright and alert, younger than the motionless aged body in which they were lodged. Some spirit remained then of the woman she had known.

'Bella!' It was a whisper as frail as the old body, yet the mind behind it could not be wandering: recognition had been immediate. A difficult smile twisted the old mouth. 'My hinny! My grandbairn!'

Unable to speak, Isabelle went and knelt beside the old woman, as she had knelt at their last meeting; except that then Grandmother had held out her arms to welcome her. This time it was Isabelle who put her arms about the old woman, who could only feebly return the embrace, though tears filled her eyes and ran unchecked down her face.

'Oh, Grandmother! Oh, Grandmother!' Isabelle rocked her gently, feeling her throat tighten from emotion. She did not care about the stench that rose from the neglected body, or the damp chill of the air, or the icy hardness of the stone floor under her knees. All she knew was that the grandmother she loved, and who loved her, was still there, and knew her.

They clung together for a long while, and then at last Isabelle felt a slight pressure against her chest and realised that her grandmother was trying to push her a little distance away from her. She sat back on her heels, gazing at the old woman, who was studying her face with great earnestness. 'You've grown into a bonny young woman, my lass. Now, I don't doubt you've a deal to tell me, and I've all the time in the world to hear it.'

'First, though, I want to know about you. John said you were . . .' Isabelle faltered into silence.

Her grandmother smiled grimly. 'Wrong in the head? Aye, that's what he tells them all. To make sure they leave me alone. Though Becky used to keep me informed, until he found out what was going on and sent her packing, that is. Now I have to put up with that Warren woman – surly bitch, when she's sober that is, which isn't often. No, Bella my lass, there's nowt wrong with any of me except these stupid legs of mine. I can't get about and I have to be waited on hand and foot, but I know what's going on – oh yes, I know that well enough!' Her eyes were sharp with hurt and anger. 'I'm not wrong in the head, but they'd like me to be, so they keep me shut in here and hope I'll

370

just die nice and quietly one day. I can't see what they're up to here, you know.'

'Does no one come to you? What about the priest – or is there not a priest any more?'

'Oh aye, there's a priest. Father Stone they call him, came when Father Duncan died, a year or so back. Away at the minute, I understand, to Newcastle, to your Uncle Henry. Warren does gossip a bit now and then, when she's had a few. Though not any gossip I really want to hear, of course. Anyway, what they've told Father Stone I don't know, but he's never set foot in here. Not that I've ever cared much for priests – too priest-ridden by half your father was, and your brother's as bad – but then you know that. In any case, even a priest would be better than nothing – except he'd lecture me on the state of my soul, and what chance have I to commit any sins, I'd like to know, shut up in here all day?'

Now that she had begun to talk it was as if she could not stop, as if all the injustices and resentments kept inside her for so long were pouring out of her. Endless tales of small cruelties, and large ones, of neglect and unkindness, followed one another relentlessly, not only against herself, but against others too. 'Racked the rents up, he has. Any number of tenants have been turned out, people who've lived on Blackheugh land as long as any Milburn. Couldn't pay, you see, not in these hard times. Before I got like this, I used to do what I could, but what can I do now? Can't even talk – no one to talk to. Not that he'd listen, even then. He's out to make every penny he can, never mind who gets hurt on the way. Oh, I know things had got in a bad way, but he didn't have to go so far. Don't let the state of the house fool you, mind. He's near, is your brother. But he's got it put by, plenty of it, what he hasn't ploughed back into the land. Good management he calls it – which maybe it is in a way, but it's not any way I'd choose. In any case who's he doing it for, I'd like to know? His bairns sicken and die, one after the other. Four he's lost, and from what I hear the fifth's likely to go the same way. A judgement maybe, for what he's done to other

371

folks. You remember Matty Dodd? A bairn of his died, the night he was turned out. Mind, I always said your father did wrong when he picked Francesca, putting good Catholic blood before owt else. What use is a Cardinal in the family if you can't breed healthy bairns?

'There's been days I've seen no one, not even Warren. When she's off on one of her drinking binges she doesn't give a thought to her duties. Not that she ever gives much thought to them, but at least when she's sober, I get food of a sort. Pap maybe, fit for a babby, but better than nothing, which is what I get when she's drunk. Then she'll come back afterwards with a bad head and a temper to match and I have to watch it. I get blows with my supper often enough. See the bruise here on my arm, and here ... If I could hit back now! But it's a long time since I could do that ...'

Pity and rage swelled in Isabelle, that anyone should dare to do such things to a helpless yet alert old woman. While her grandmother spoke on, she began to restore some order to the room, putting things away, clearing dust with a rag found in a corner (some ancient item of clothing, she suspected), rubbing the window panes to let in more light, even opening a window a little. She would have to come back with soap and water and a scrubbing brush before the room would be fit for human habitation, but she had made a beginning.

'... Now I've talked long enough. I want to hear all about you.' The old woman's voice was fainter now, and Isabelle realised it was only exhaustion that had brought her to an end.

'Another time, Grandmother. I've so much to tell you, but you have a sleep now, and I'll be back.' She tucked her grandmother round more closely with one of the worn blankets and stroked her hand until the old woman dropped suddenly into sleep, and then she went to pour out her indignation to Marianne: somehow it was easier to do so in French, the language in which she had first learned to stand up for herself.

After that, she made her way to the kitchen. It seemed that Warren was at that moment engaged in one of the drinking bouts Grandmother Milburn had mentioned, which at least meant she was not likely to interfere with what Isabelle was doing. 'Drunk more than sober, that one,' Cook said disparagingly; but she was deeply shocked when Isabelle armed herself with a pail and a scrubbing brush and set out back to her grandmother's room.

John was just coming in from the stables as she reached the tower door. He halted, looking her over in disbelief.

'What do you think you're doing?' Amazement and disgust were equally balanced in his voice.

'Have you seen the state of Grandmother's room?'

'I forbade you to visit her!'

'No wonder! You knew I'd find out the truth about the way you were treating her.'

'I don't know what you're talking about. I suppose she's been raving to you, the way she does sometimes. You could have spared yourself all that if you'd only listened to me. I don't know what you're doing with that pail, but I must ask you to return it at once to the kitchen. I employ a servant to do that kind of thing.'

'Oh yes! Do you know where Warren is now? In the cellar, getting drunk. And the way Grandmother's living – you wouldn't keep a pig in such a state!'

'She doesn't know any different.'

'Even if that were true, it's no excuse. But you know it's not true. You've deliberately neglected her!'

He looked around him hastily. 'Don't speak so loud! Do you want the servants to hear us arguing? May I remind you,' he went on in a lowered voice, 'that how I manage my household is my own affair. You are only here under sufferance and not for much longer either. You have no right to interfere, no right whatsoever! As for walking about the place with a pail like any servant girl—!'

'There are a good many things I've learned to do for myself during the past years, John.'

'So much the worse for you! But in my house, so long as you are here, you behave as my sister should, as a lady, not a servant!'

'In that case, give orders now for someone to set Grandmother's room to rights.'

'I will not be given orders by you or anyone else in my own house!'

'Then I shall do it. The choice is simple. It's in your hands.'

Perhaps in the end he thought it was easier and drew less adverse attention on himself (and on his sister's eccentric behaviour) to give in, for after a short but stormy silence he said abruptly, 'You must be out of this house by midday at the latest!' Then he swung round and strode away from her into the hall, slamming the door behind him. Isabelle, aware of a sudden movement in the kitchen doorway, looked round just in time to catch a glimpse of a slim figure closing the door; she thought it might have been Jane, the girl who had brought the children's supper last night.

She was glad to be able to relieve her angry feelings on her grandmother's floor, and scrubbed away with happy vigour until the worst of the dirt was gone. It all took some time, but at last the room was fresher and the old woman dressed in the cleanest clothes Isabelle could find for her (which was not saying a great deal). She talked as she worked, telling her grandmother much of what had happened to her during the past years and promising that very soon she would bring the children to see her. Since it was already past breakfast time, she had no idea how she was going to accomplish that, in the circumstances, but she was quite sure that somehow she would do it. There was no longer any doubt in her mind as to why she had felt she must come home.

# Chapter Thirty-One

'Where will you go, Isabella?' Francesca asked at breakfast as she poured tea from a silver pot.

'Do you really care?' Isabelle retorted, though she was aware that she was infringing her brother's code of polite manners, which insisted that there should be no explosions of anger in company, unless heavily veiled. She buttered a slice of bread for Aristide and cut it into fingers and passed one to him. The children had been grudgingly accepted at a table from which their cousin was excluded, being still upstairs with his nurse. In John Milburn's house children only ate with adults in exceptional circumstances.

'It would be unchristian of me not to be concerned about you at all,' Francesca said, with a slightly offended dignity.

'Then you needn't worry,' Isabelle reassured her. 'I shall stay here until I am sure that Grandmother is being cared for – in a Christian way.' When her brother had repeated his insistence that she leave by midday, she had contented herself with a stubborn repetition of her own intention to stay, and then changed the subject. She did not see that there was any point in continuing an argument in which neither of them was prepared to concede defeat.

Then, after breakfast, she went to take the children to meet their grandmother; and found that the tower door had been firmly barred. When she confronted her brother with it, he merely said he had given orders and that was that: the door was to be kept locked at all times.

Isabelle and Marianne and the children left the house soon afterwards. John saw them on their way. 'I suggest you return to France with all speed. There is nothing for you in England.' Then he stood in the doorway to watch until they were out of sight.

Not far from the end of the drive they heard someone come running up behind them and turned to see that it was Jane, the young maid, glancing anxiously about her as she ran, as if she fully expected someone to try and stop her. They stood still, waiting for her to catch up, and she halted beside them, holding out a package. 'Some food, in case you need it, ma'am,' she said breathlessly. 'If you can't find shelter, go to my people, up at High Middens. Dodd, they're called. Say I sent you. They'll see you take no harm.'

Searching her memory, Isabelle recollected High Middens, from the days when she used to ride far over the moors, towards the border. It was a bastle, like many of the poorer houses in Tynedale, built for defence, with cramped ill-lit living quarters above a byre. Its occupants kept a few beasts on a couple of acres of land, and lived little more comfortably than their cattle. Greatly touched, Isabelle thanked Jane, and then they watched her run swiftly back to the house.

Once on the road, they found a pleasant place near the river and sat down on the grass to consider what to do. Isabelle met Marianne's eyes. 'What John said, about going back to France – that's what you want, isn't it?'

'We can't, can we? We've no money.'

'I've a few pence left. And there's this still.' Isabelle tugged at the chain about her neck.

'You wouldn't want to sell that.'

'Things don't matter. People do. If you want to go back, then I'll come to Newcastle with you and find a ship to take you.'

Marianne's eyes widened. 'Then you're staying?'

'I can't leave my grandmother like that. I must do something. I don't know what yet, but I'm staying here until I do.'

Marianne said nothing. She looked about her, at the swift flowing river, the hay meadows bronzed with a dense mass of flowers, the wide sky, blue and cloud flecked, the hills quiet in the sun, dotted with sheep, scattered with grey farmhouses; a tranquil scene, but Isabelle knew that to her it must be a strange and lonely one after the constant bustle and activity of Paris, very different even from the great cereal plains of northern France, which was the only countryside Marianne had ever known. Isabelle knew too, as Marianne did not, how this tranquillity could, in winter, quickly become a savage and hostile wilderness.

'I should never have let you come with me,' she said gently.

'It was my choice.' Then: 'Where will you live? With those people Jane told you about?'

'I'll go to them if I have to, but they're poor and it wouldn't be fair to ask too much. I'm going to look for Jamie first.'

It was Cook who had told her where to find him. 'He's done well for himself, he has,' she had said. 'Come into his uncle's farm – a fair bit of land, ten acres or so. Then picked a good wife, with land to her name too – quite a prosperous farmer he is, in a small way. Lives across the Tarset burn, just past Lanehead.'

He would no longer be the Jamie she remembered, her childhood friend; he might be as unwilling to help her as her brother had been. But there was a faint chance that he still had a kind thought for Bella Milburn, and she had to find out.

She waited, watching Marianne's face, wondering what choice she was going to make. 'Which is it to be then? East, to Newcastle? Or west, to find Jamie?' She did not want Marianne to go, and her heart ached at the very thought of it, yet she sensed that if she were Marianne she would not want to stay; indeed, she would probably not have come at all.

'What I want . . .' said Marianne slowly. Her voice sounded odd, harsh and scarcely audible, as if she were struggling to speak through some painful constriction of the throat. 'I shan't find it in Paris either. Pierre . . .' She broke off, unable to say any more.

Isabelle saw that her eyes were brimming with tears. With a

great rush of pity she reached out and put her arms about her friend and held her as if she were Aurore, in need of comfort. She felt the tears rise in her own eyes, for that sense of desolation was one that she understood only too well, the sense that there was nowhere on the face of the earth where peace or happiness could ever be hoped for again. It still came upon her too often for comfort, even a year after Jérôme's death; it took hold of her now.

'Maman! Aristide's going to fall in!' Aurore's voice cut through Isabelle's grief. She turned sharply, saw the boy toddling purposefully towards the river bank, and ran.

She reached him just in time. Through his energetic, angry struggles and his howls of protest at being thwarted, Marianne's voice came clearly, 'You're going to need another pair of hands with that one. Let's go and find this Jamie.'

They came on the place quite by chance as they followed the path beside the brown rushing waters of the Tarset burn. The land rose and then fell again, into a sheltered grassy hollow edged with willow and alder. On its eastern slope, just high enough above the water to be out of reach of spring flooding, stood a cottage, full in the sunlight. It was tiny and nearly derelict, standing in a small walled garden so overgrown with weeds that only the upper parts of the windows were visible above them. Marianne and Isabelle looked at the cottage, and then at one another, and Isabelle knew that the same thought had taken shape within each of them at the same moment.

The field in which they stood was clearly down to hay, so Isabelle led them around its edge and then across a faintly marked path through the tall flower-drenched grasses to the broken gate in the tumbled stone wall. Then she and Marianne looked inside the cottage, while the children explored the small wilderness outside, laughing and shrieking and chasing one another.

The door, wood rotting, hung half of its hinges. Inside, there were just two rooms, one very small, though there would perhaps be space under the steeply pitched rafters to floor out a low attic area. There was a fireplace at one end, without an oven, and two windows, one in each room, as well as the front door that gave into the larger room. The heather thatch was green with moss and grass, but the stone walls were solid enough still and more than two feet thick. The floor was of earth, well trodden.

'It needs a lot of work,' said Isabelle. 'And it never was more than a poor place. But—'

'It's a house, and no one's using it.'

'And if we'd somewhere to live, then Grandmother could come and live with us.'

They did a little dance together round the room. Aurore, looking in at the door, flushed and breathless from running, asked, 'Are we going to live here, Maman? Can I have my own garden like the little Capet?'

'Would you like to, my love?'

Aurore nodded, lips pressed together as if to contain her happiness; and then turned sharply, her face full of alarm. Aristide came running into the kitchen and clung to his mother. The sound of a man shouting reached them, unmistakably angry.

'Here – you! Yes, you, the lass by the door there – what do you think you're doing?'

Aurore, understanding nothing except that the man was angry, stood where she was in bewildered fear. Isabelle picked up Aristide and went out; and found herself face to face with a wiry man whose head of flaming hair seemed to blaze the more against the fresh green of the countryside.

He was a man, not a boy, and his face was contorted with righteous anger, but she could not mistake that hair. 'Jamie Telfer?' she said. 'It is Jamie Telfer, isn't it?'

He stood where he was, open mouthed, as if he were seeing a ghost.

'Don't you remember Bella Milburn? Isabelle Duvernoy, now, but the same lass for all that.'

He stared and stared, shaking his head, making murmurs of disbelief. Then he stepped forward, his eyes going from

Isabelle to Aurore and back again.

'So this is the bairn then – the one you went away . . .' He did not finish the sentence, but it dawned on Isabelle that he had always known why she had gone away. Looking back, she wondered that she could ever have thought that the servants did not know the truth. Servants generally knew even more than their masters, in her experience.

'I should have known she was yours. She's Bella Milburn all over again.' He grinned at Aurore, who shrank back a little, remembering the shouting, afraid it might begin again. 'What do they call you, my lass?'

Isabelle explained quickly to Aurore what he had said, and she replied in a timid whisper. 'She only speaks French,' Isabelle explained to him. She ran her hand over the child's hair. 'She'll learn English quickly enough, but there's been no time yet.'

'But what are you doing here? I thought you were shut up in a convent. I'd even thought maybe they'd slaughtered all the nuns, those revolutionaries. We heard such tales.'

'I expect they weren't all true. Anyway, I married one of those revolutionaries.' And then she told him a greatly simplified version of the rest of her story, and explained who Marianne was.

He listened carefully, still shaking his head now and then, as if finding it all hard to take in. When she came to the part where her brother had turned her out he said, 'So that's what you're doing here – you've nowhere to live. You know this is my property?'

If she had still been the child Bella, and he the boy Jamie, she would have hugged him, with simple joy. 'Then – you don't need it?'

'I'd thought to do it up. I could do with help on the farm. My Ann's not as well as she might be, and she wants help too, about the house. We thought a husband and wife maybe. I've a good flock of sheep, a couple of cows, pigs, fowl, ponies, a bit of meadow. Then there's the spinning.' He looked doubtfully at the two women and the children, and Isabelle knew he did not see in them either the strong labourer or the domestic help he hoped for.

'I can clean and cook well enough, and Marianne here as well. She can spin too. And you know I'm good with horses. I'd soon learn about sheep.'

'Oh, I couldn't ask that of you!' He looked utterly horrified at the idea.

'Why not? Because you once worked for my family, because you used to call my father "master"? I'm just a woman like any other. And a mother too, with bairns to feed and raise.'

'You always were a rebel, Bella.' He shook his head again, smiling reflectively. 'But I don't know. It's not what I had in mind. And if I let you come here, well—'

'Then let us have it on trial – six months say – and if it doesn't work out, then you have the right to turn us out.'

He looked even more shocked at that suggestion, and said so. 'Besides, you couldn't live on a labourer's wage. Especially not the way prices are at the minute.'

'I've lived on less this past year. I learned long since to cut my coat to suit my cloth. Besides, there's a garden here – we can grow some of our own food. Try us, and see!'

In the end, though she sensed he was still not convinced, he agreed to discuss the matter with his wife; and took them with him across the burn to the low farmhouse on the western bank where Ann Telfer sat on a stool by the kitchen fire, stirring something in a pot. That she was a near invalid was obvious enough; her fingers were permanently crooked, her back bent, and her face had the harsh lines of someone in constant pain.

Even making allowances for her state of health, she was not the wife Isabelle would have expected Jamie to choose, for she was somewhat older than he was, a thin, strong-featured woman with a brusque manner. They were clearly on equal and comradely terms, but there was no spark between them and little warmth. But then presumably he had married her for practical and sensible reasons, and not for love.

That she had a kind heart beneath the daunting exterior became evident too, for she heard their story with sympathy

381

and agreed at the end that the cottage should be let to them, rent and fuel free, for six months, while they earned what they could about the house and farm; at the end of which time the position was to be reviewed.

'I'll get the place put to rights, as quick as I can,' Jamie promised them. 'Till then, you can stay here.'

'There's one other thing – my grandmother.'

'I heard she was gone in the head, poor old soul.'

'Aye, you would have heard that.'

Isabelle explained the position and he was sympathetic, but said warningly, 'If you've to care for her too, you'll surely need more than I can pay.'

'Then I'll give French lessons, when you can spare me. I'm not leaving her there, that's for sure. There's one thing more: spread it around she's got her wits about her still. So long as that's known, maybe John will use her more kindly. I don't want any harm to come to her before the cottage is ready for her.'

Jamie, studying her face, shook his head wonderingly. 'I'd not be in John Milburn's shoes, now you're back.' He grinned. 'Better have you as friend than foe, any day.'

'You always were a friend,' she returned gently, and she saw him colour, just a little. He turned abruptly to the children.

'Come and see what I've got out here.' He held out his hand to them and Isabelle urged them to follow him. In a corner of one of the byres lay a mother cat with a squabbling litter of kittens. 'There – you can choose one, one each. They're not ready to leave their mother yet, but by the time your new house is ready they'll be old enough to come with you. Every house needs a cat or two.'

Isabelle translated for them, and the children, amazed, awed, rapturous, crouched down to inspect the kittens.

'It'll be good having bairns about the place,' said Jamie. 'It's the one thing that's been missing.' But his eyes, lingering on Isabelle's face, suggested that it was not the only thing that had been missing from his life during the past seven years.

# Chapter Thirty-Two

Jamie was inside the house, covering the earth floor with stone slabs brought from a ruined cottage on his wife's property. He was whistling as he worked. *My love he built a bonny bower* . . .

So many memories . . . On the roof in the cold October wind, Isabelle was laying new thatch on the repaired timbers, struggling to fasten the springy heather in place. It was hard work, but she knew she did it well and found it deeply satisfying. Jamie had begun the thatching, only reluctantly agreeing to show her how to do it, and even more reluctant, afterwards, to allow her to continue unaided. Now any doubts he might have had were long since dispelled. 'You'd have been wasted as a fine lady,' he had observed one day. She knew it was a compliment.

The leaves on the trees by the burn were beginning to turn to bronze and gold, with here and there the fire colours of a rowan, brilliant in the clear sunlight. There was a rowan in the garden too, near the door, planted to keep out witches, she supposed. But they hardly needed such protection in this place. It had a good and happy feeling about it, as if no one living here had ever known a pain that could not be assuaged or had ever wanted for love. And before long, before the winter, it would be ready for them.

Marianne was across at the farmhouse, spinning more of the fleeces from this year's clipping. It had taken her a little time to learn the techniques needed for the spinning of wool, used as she was to flax, but by now she was good enough even to gain approval from the critical eyes of Ann Telfer. Aurore was there with her, carding the wool ready for spinning. She was proud of her new skill and the two of them kept one another company with their singing and chatter, and, Isabelle suspected, entertained their employer too, even if she could understand little of what they said. Aristide was in the cottage garden, playing with his kitten; his clothes were already filthy. It had been Isabelle's first task, to repair the enclosing wall of the garden and fit a sound gate, to keep her son from wandering while she worked.

The days were beginning to take on a pattern of their own. The only trouble was that there were not hours enough for all that had to be done. True to their agreement, Isabelle and Marianne made sure they conscientiously carried out all the tasks that were required of them. Last week, that had meant hours at the farmhouse in an icy wind salving the sheep with a tarry mixture to keep them free of parasites until next year's washing and clipping. Every day, there was milking to be done, cheese and butter to be made, hens and pigs to be fed, eggs to be collected, byres to be cleaned out, animals to be moved from one pasture to another, and, within doors, cleaning and cooking, washing, spinning. Somehow into the corners of the day Isabelle had to fit the children's lessons, for she had no intention of allowing them to grow up in ignorance. Since there was no other spare time, that had to take place in the evenings, so in the afternoons she would insist that they slept, to ensure that they would be sufficiently awake at night to attend to their books. But working by candlelight was tiring on the eyes, especially when she had been physically active all day.

Perhaps, she reflected ruefully, it was as well no one had as yet replied to her advertisement. Placed in the columns of all local newspapers, it had been worded with great care, offering the services of 'a respectable widow' as a teacher of French. She had made it clear she was prepared to go to the home of any potential pupil, that her accent was excellent, her knowledge of the language fluent and extensive, and that she had considerable experience in teaching young children. She had not expected a large response, but that after more than two months there should have been none at all surprised her. The payment she was asking was not high, and she knew that even in these hard times there were many families of modest but adequate means in the Tynedale area, with ambitions to rise a little in the world – or maintain a position – who might have been expected to welcome such an opportunity offering itself on their very doorsteps.

But it had not happened, and it was in the teaching of English not French that much of her ingenuity was taken up. The children were learning fast; Marianne was finding it much harder. 'Stupid language!' she had been liable to exclaim in exasperation, when faced with something she found particularly hard to pronounce. Though lately, Isabelle reflected, she had begun to pay more attention to the English lessons; ever since the evening, two weeks ago, when among the neighbours gathering to tell stories and sing about the fireside, there had been young Geordie Robson, from the next farm. He had come round two or three more times since then, and Marianne had made the discovery that her broken English was a potent weapon in attracting his attention. She might still be mourning Pierre, but old habits died hard, thought Isabelle, a little ruefully.

'Bella! I'm away home for my dinner. Are you coming?'

She looked down into Jamie's upturned face. 'I'll just finish this. You go on.'

'Shall I take the bairn?'

'If you don't mind.' She sounded doubtful, but she had long since realised that Jamie adored the children, a feeling that was very largely returned. Aristide tucked the kitten under one arm and went with him happily, chattering away in an odd mixture of French and English. Isabelle watched them, the man and the child, side by side, the one so attentive to what the other was saying. She felt a pang of loss, that it should not have been Jérôme who walked with Aristide. But better Jamie than no one, much better.

She was about to resume her work when her attention was

caught by some movement from the opposite direction and she paused to watch: someone was coming up beside the burn towards the cottage.

She did not know him. He was an ordinary-looking young man in the sober black dress that one would expect a clergyman to wear. In fact, some stirring of recognition in her mind said: 'A priest.' She wondered if he would simply walk on by, though where he might be going she could not imagine. But he did not pass. Instead, he waved to her and came swiftly towards the cottage.

'Madame Duvernoy?'

'Yes,' she said, wary.

'Father Stone, your brother's chaplain; I should be grateful for the favour of a word.'

She was greatly tempted to tell him she had no possible reason to wish to speak to her brother's chaplain – or any other priest come to that – but she thought better of it, and made her way carefully down the ladder.

'A most impressive descent,' the man observed. 'I had not anticipated that I should find you engaged in so masculine an employment.'

'I need a roof over my head,' she said briskly, dusting her hands on her skirts; those striped skirts so common in Paris, so conspicuous in England. 'I can't think what business you have with me – unless . . .' Fear clutched at her stomach. 'Grandmother – she's not—'

'I understand your grandmother to be as well as can be expected. You knew, I suppose, that the younger Mrs Milburn had been delivered of a stillborn infant? Your nephew is ailing again too.' She had heard that, and felt a wave of pity for her sister-in-law and for frail little Cuthbert. She murmured something to that effect, but the cold gravity of the priest's expression did not change. 'No, my concern is for your welfare, and that of your brother too, I may add.'

'A pity you haven't concerned yourself with my grandmother's welfare. She might have been more kindly used if you had.'

He looked puzzled. 'I don't understand you.'

'When did you last speak to my grandmother?'

'I understand her to be in no condition to speak to anyone. I also understand that she is liable to grow violent if faced with a priest. My predecessor . . .'

'Why did you not make the effort to see her, just once, to be sure that was true? Is my brother the only one who matters?'

'No, no of course not. But it is not for me to question your brother's veracity unless I have good reason to do so.'

He had not then heard what she had tried to spread throughout the neighbourhood. But that did not excuse him.

'Madame Duvernoy, this is wasting time. I came here to ask you to consider what pain you are causing your brother by remaining in the neighbourhood as you have chosen to do. I regret that I have the impression that you remained with a deliberate intent to cause him embarrassment.'

'Is that what he told you?' She paused, studying the anxious and even kindly face before her. 'How long have you been at Blackheugh? Just over a year, didn't my grandmother say?'

'She knew that?' There was unease in his tone.

'I told you my brother was lying. How you could be in his house for all that time and not have found him out I can't imagine. But that's why I'm staying, not to cause him embarrassment, but to find a way of looking after my grandmother. I told him that. As soon as this place is ready, she will move in with us.'

'I cannot countenance the moving of a frail old woman to live with someone of your character. I must have a care for her spiritual well-being, even if she is reluctant for me to exercise it. There is always hope, for as long as she is under your brother's roof. Here – well, your spiritual condition is a most precarious one. And that perhaps is to put it more gently than the case merits.'

Isabelle felt furiously angry. She sensed that if her brother's chaplain should choose to oppose her, then she would have no means of bringing her grandmother here. At present, she suspected that when it came to the point John would be glad to be rid of responsibility for the old woman, but if his chaplain opposed the move she knew that he would never allow it. 'You come to me knowing nothing of my side of the story, full of all the poisonous lies my brother has told you, and then start preaching to me, without making the least effort to learn the truth.'

She paused, glaring at him, and he said awkwardly, 'It was never my intention – I am of course concerned for you too. But I did not suppose there was another side. Your uncle has very largely borne out your brother's version of events. Perhaps if you were to tell me . . .'

She did, fluently, with anger and indignation and directness. She had no expectation at all that he would accept her story, in any respect. He was after all a Catholic priest, and must automatically condemn both her impurity and her apostasy, whatever their cause.

At the end, he said, 'I see. I must acknowledge that this is very different from the account your brother gave me. Allow me a little time. I should like to consider the matter further. If I may, I will call again.'

She watched him go, with a sense of surprise, but she thought he would be unlikely to return, except perhaps to condemn her further.

He came again the very next day. It was pouring with rain and she was busy in the dairy, churning cream for the butter; she did not hear him until he spoke just behind her, making her jump.

'Forgive me if I startled you. I felt it important that I came to see you again with all speed.' He sat down on the bench and she perched on a stool facing him. 'I have spoken to your grandmother.'

She was delighted. 'Then you know the truth now.'

He coloured faintly. 'Yes. And I offer you an apology that I doubted you. It is of course your grandmother who has the most to forgive.'

'I'm surprised John let you see her so easily.'

His colour grew still more. 'Warren – your grandmother's

servant – she is a good Catholic, as it happens.'

Isabelle did not ask if he had in fact sought her brother's permission to speak to their grandmother; probably not, for he must have realised that John would continue to put forward many good reasons why a visit would be unwise. So, instead, he had gone straight to the old woman's keeper. Isabelle imagined the discreet moral pressure that must have been put upon her to admit the priest to the tower, and smiled to herself. Then Father Stone said, 'We talked of you, your grandmother and I. She had not heard the story you told me, but I had the impression that what she did not know she had inferred. I believe her to be a shrewd woman.'

'Then you won't object if I bring her here?'

'No, I shan't do that. I would have preferred it, perhaps, had she been able to reside with someone else, such as your uncle. But his circumstances do not allow, and besides I think the old lady would object to leaving Tynedale. No, I think for her to come here might well be the best move, for all concerned. Make no mistake: I do not say in any way that you have been without sin in all this. None of us is ever so, of course. But it would seem that in many ways your fault was much less than I had been led to believe. I hope, as our knowledge of one another grows, that both you and I may come to a clear view of the whole business. I even dare to hope that in time you may be brought back within the fold of Mother Church.'

Isabelle thought that most unlikely, for the fold looked from her present position more like a prison than a refuge; but she was grateful for his apparent openness of mind, and for that surprising willingness to admit that he had been wrong.

They talked for a little longer, on more general matters, and she realised afterwards that she had enjoyed the discussion. More than that, she liked the man, finding much to respect in his intelligence and readiness to consider another point of view. When they parted, he promised to come again from time to time, and she looked forward to his next visit, unperturbed by the obvious truth that his chief motive in visiting her would be to seek her return to her childhood faith.

*

A few days later Jamie went to Bellingham market with a number of his sheep and returned at night in a particularly good humour, having sold them for rather more than he had expected. There had been a peddlar there, selling assorted trinkets, and Jamie had bought a spinning top for the children, which they proceeded to squabble over, until he demonstrated it to them and awed them with its dazzling performance. They had been hard at work on their lessons when he came home, but Isabelle declared an end to work (apart from the stipulation that they must speak only in English, which was the usual evening rule). She tided the books away, watching the excited children, with a sense of gratitude to Jamie for making up a little for their lack of a father. Later, while Aurore and Aristide were sitting down to their supper of bread and milk, he found time to give a more detailed account of his day.

'I've solved one thing, mind,' he said to Isabelle. 'I reckon I know why you haven't had the pupils lining up for French lessons. I got talking to Harry Robson – you know, he keeps the alehouse near the church – and he told me your brother's letting it be known that his sister's no respectable widow, but a rabid Jacobin. Not only that, would you believe, but the mother of a bastard, come back from France to preach free love and democracy and all manner of unpatriotic things. Goes without saying no one wants to put their children into the hands of someone like that.'

So that, thought Isabelle angrily, put paid to any hope she might have had of raising a little extra money by teaching. She supposed she would have to think of something else. Then Jamie said, 'I reckon you two are doing so well you deserve a bit rise in your wages. In fact, me and Ann, we suggest that from the day you move into the cottage, you, Bella, get ten shillings a week, with the rest of you, Marianne and the children, paid according to what they earn. We'll scrap the six-month trial period, but you'll still get the place rent free, with fuel all found. We reckon you've proved your worth already.'

Isabelle, jubilant, translated what had been said for Marianne's benefit, and found she had already grasped a little of it.

Later, Jamie said, 'There was a stranger in Harry Robson's place, from Coquetdale, Harry thought, though he didn't sound like a Coquetdale man to me. He was hanging round while I was talking to Harry, listening, by the look of it. Then he came and chatted to us a bit. Some wild opinions he had, not what you'd expect from such a man. He was asking if there were any radical societies hereabouts. I suppose he wanted to join one. Harry told him there was Sir John Swinburne and his cronies over at Capheaton, with their Jacobin airs and graces, but nothing in Tynedale that he knew of.' Jamie grinned. 'I nearly told him he should come and see the two lasses working for me, if he wanted real Jacobins, but I thought better of it. I didn't much like the look of him. You never know these days. They say there are government spies everywhere. Seems unlikely they'd bother with Tynedale, but stranger things have happened.'

They sat for a long time at the fireside that night while Jamie told stories and sang the older border ballads Isabelle remembered so well; though it was no clear boy's voice singing now, but a deep bass, rich and powerful, which filled the farmhouse kitchen to the rafters and awed the children into a respectful silence. He ended with the song he had been whistling the other day as he worked at the cottage, *My love he built a bonny bower*. The tune tore at Isabella's heart, and the words, desolate and full of an inconsolable grief, unfolding their tale of sudden death and desperate loneliness. The child Isabella had liked to imagine herself as the widow in that song, carrying her burden alone, a heroic and tragic figure. Now to hear it was almost beyond enduring, for it seemed to put all her feelings into words. She knew now that there was nothing noble or heroic about such a loss, only unbearable pain.

*Ne living man I'll love again,*
*Since that my lovely man is slain.*
*With a lock of his yellow hair*
*I'll chain my heart for evermair.*

391

The words faded into silence, and no one spoke for a long time. At last Isabelle said quietly, 'It's time the bairns were in bed.' They ran ahead of her up the stairs. Jamie followed, reaching her as she had her foot on the first step. 'That hit home, Bella. I'm sorry.'

She looked round at him, the light catching the dampness on her cheeks. 'I've always liked that song. It does no harm to weep sometimes.'

There was a little silence. 'You loved him, didn't you?'

'Yes.'

There was another silence, while he studied her face. She looked back at him, his features strong and deeply shadowed in the light of the candle she carried; a light that illuminated their two grave faces, isolating them in the pool of darkness about them. From above, the children called, made anxious by their mother's delay, and the darkness of the rooms lit only by moonlight, and the silence. From the fireside, Ann called her husband.

'Goodnight,' said Jamie, very softly. Isabelle turned and went on her way.

Later, when they lay together in their bed in the loft room, soft with the sounds of the sleeping children, Marianne said to Isabelle, 'He fancies you, that one.'

Isabelle did not waste her breath asking who Marianne meant; it was obvious enough. She was glad that the darkness hid her heightened colour; and annoyed with herself for having blushed at all, when there was nothing to blush about. 'Of course he doesn't. We're old friends, that's all.'

'You could do worse,' said Marianne. Isabelle could hear from her tone that she was grinning, in the manner of one who knows better. 'I don't doubt he could do with someone in his bed, his wife being as she is. He's no one to leave the place to either, when he's gone. If I were him, I'd be looking for a new wife, one who could give me children.'

'Marianne, I'm not wanting a lover or a husband. Besides, you can't get divorced in England, not unless you're very rich

392

and very powerful. We're not in France now.' At once she was irritated with herself for having even spoken of such things, as if by doing so she had conceded that Marianne might possibly be right. 'And even if we were, it wouldn't arise,' she said quickly. 'We're friends, that's all.'

'You may be. Not him though.'

Isabelle decided there was no point in arguing any further. She turned her back to Marianne, settling herself for sleep. The bed was not very wide and she could feel her friend's angular bones pressing into her; and was overwhelmed with one of the sudden anguished longings for Jérôme, who would have lain with his body curved against hers and his arms about her, who would wake sometimes to make love to her, with all his tender knowledge of every small thing that gave her pleasure ... If Jamie was indeed lacking the consolations of the marriage bed, he was not alone in that.

By the middle of November the cottage was ready. It was soundly roofed, sweetly smelling of new wood, from the timbers that floored the loft and the shutters inside the windows and the box bed that Jamie had built against one wall of the living room, ready for Grandmother Milburn's occupation. The flagged floor was scrubbed clean, the furniture, given or made by Jamie, was simple but adequate – stools, a bench, a table, a chest, beds in bedroom and loft. On the wall hung the brightly coloured print of the Declaration of the Rights of Man that Isabelle had brought from France, with its attendant angels and the eye of vigilance watching over it. There was a shelf for Isabelle's books, a few essential cooking pots, a rag rug on the floor by the hearth. Outside, Aurore, struggling with the adult-sized tools supplied by Jamie, had already begun to dig over the soil, ready for the plants from the farmhouse garden that Jamie had promised.

They had spent last night in the cottage, with the fire lit to warm the place thoroughly; and at dawn Jamie came to say he was ready.

They walked over the fields to where he had left the cart on the road, and then he drove them to Blackheugh. They had sent word two days ago that they would come today, so that John should be expecting them.

They saw nothing of him. Ritson simply admitted them, with cold correctness, and then led the way to the tower door. This time it stood open and Warren, sullenly cooperative, took them up to Grandmother's room. She was dressed and sitting in her chair, her belongings packed into boxes and bundles beside her. Father Stone came to help, unobtrusively, though he did not quite escape Grandmother's attention. 'About time you made yourself useful,' she said, with scant gratitude. They took the luggage downstairs first, and then came back for her, carrying the chair down to the cart, with her on it. The children, delighted at the novelty of it all, skipped alongside, ran up and down the spiral stairs, showed a noisy appreciation of the old woman's breathless comments on her journey. 'Not been out in the air for three years,' she observed as they carried her out through the door into the misty cold of the morning.

'In summer you shall sit in the garden as much as you like,' Isabelle promised her.

They lifted her into the cart, and the children scrambled in beside her; and then she remembered that her favourite shawl had been left behind. Isabelle ran to get it, and on the way downstairs again met her brother, just emerging from his office.

'We are ready to leave,' she said. 'Perhaps you'd like to say goodbye.'

'I have already done all the leavetaking I intend to do,' said John. Then he added, 'You needn't think I'll come running when you've had enough of her. She's your responsibility now. I don't want to hear another word about her. Disgusting, interfering old woman.'

'You needn't worry,' she assured him. 'I wouldn't think of coming to you, even if I was desperate. But you can be sure that Grandmother will be cared for with all the love that she deserves. That's one thing every good sans culotte believed in – that the elderly merited respect and dignity.'

'Oh, so the old never went to the guillotine, I suppose?' he sneered.

Not wanting to begin again on another round of hostilities, which could lead them nowhere, Isabelle drew a deep breath and forced herself to say, 'I see no reason for us to meet again. But let us at least part on civil terms.'

'It is not I who have been uncivil,' John retorted, at which she decided she was wasting her breath. She turned to go, but he called after her, 'Wait, you'd better take this.' He went back into the office and reached up onto a shelf and took down a book, causing a piece of paper, lodged under it, to flutter down to the floor. 'Grandmother's missal. She threw it at me once when I went in to speak to her about something, so I put it here for safety. I suppose miracles might happen and she might want it again. You'd better take it.'

Isabelle took it and then stooped to retrieve the fallen paper; and then stood quite still. It was, unmistakably, an assignat, worth fifteen sous. She picked it up. 'What's this?' Then she remembered that her cousins had stayed here. 'I suppose one of the cousins left it – but no, I don't think there were assignats about when they left France.' She frowned, looking at her brother.

He was smiling rather oddly. 'As you say, it's an assignat. Look it over. Do you see anything wrong with it?'

She turned it round, studying both sides. Apart from its crisp newness – assignats did not retain their crispness for long – it looked perfectly normal. 'No, it's an ordinary assignat.'

'Made in Northumberland,' said her brother with a note of triumph. He smiled still more at the puzzlement on her face. 'I am proud to say I was involved with the scheme. So were our cousins, of course – with assistance from London. A neat little ruse to undermine the finances of those cannibals in France.' When she still did not seem to have grasped what he was saying, he went on, 'We've shipped hundreds – no thousands – of them out to France and the Low Countries during the last two or three years; since the King's murder, that is. The more there are circulating, the less you can buy with them, and the higher prices go. And the more the people murmur against their government, of course. Neat, you must admit. I like to think it's had a modicum of success, if not quite as much as we hoped.'

She stood there looking from her brother's smiling face to the assignat and back again. She thought of the desperate struggle to survive, especially last winter; the hunger, the money that daily bought less and less; the growing anger that sent the people running to the Convention – and brought that same Convention's revenge down on them. She thought of Pierre, who had died because of it. She thought—

'A woman in our street drowned herself, with her children, because the money she had was worthless and they were starving. It was high prices and hunger made people ask for harsh measures against their enemies. If it hadn't been for that, I think the Terror might never have happened. You have a lot to answer for, John, and everyone else who took part in your cruel little scheme.'

She saw to her satisfaction that she had made him uncomfortable, though it was more than she could hope for that he should admit it.

'Can you not see higher than food prices, to the ideals and the faith that inspired your cousins?'

'Oh, come now, it wasn't high ideals that was behind it, was it? At least, not as far as Pitt's government is concerned. France has always been the arch rival, and they'll do anything to bring her down. Besides, nothing can justify causing the kind of suffering I saw.'

'What of the suffering of your cousins?'

'It was deserved. Not that all who died on the guillotine deserved their end, of course not. But the injustices were not all on one side. I don't want to hear any more about the great principles of my cousins. They were as blind as anyone – more so, for they couldn't see how unjust the old régime was. What the Revolution brought about was better than that, in almost every way – or could have been, if you and all those others had given it a chance.' She handed the assignat back to him. 'Keep it. And when you look at it, remember all the innocent people who died because of it. If it gives you one sleepless minute, that will be something.' Then she turned and left the room.

They halted the cart by the road and carried Grandmother in her chair over the fields to the cottage. As they came up to it, Isabelle propped open the gate and Aurore ran ahead as instructed to hold the door while they carried Grandmother through. In the living room they set her down; and then Isabelle heard Aurore say in a strange voice. 'Maman!'

She looked at the child and then, following her alarmed gaze, at the room. The others looked too, standing still in silent dismay. Everything was in chaos. Papers, books, all their possessions, had been turned upside down, as if someone had been frantically looking for something and did not care how he left the place in the urgency of his search.

'By God, you've been burgled!' exclaimed Jamie. Marianne gave a cry of anger and went to investigate the other rooms. They too had been turned over, but since they contained fewer items, apart from furniture, they looked less disarrayed.

'What's going on?' Grandmother demanded from her abandoned position in the middle of the room. Her bed, made ready before they left the house this morning, had been pulled apart, but Isabelle swiftly remade it. 'We've been burgled, I think,' she said. 'But never mind. Let's get you to bed, then we'll put things to rights.'

'What have they taken?' Jamie asked.

'There wasn't anything worth taking,' Marianne said.

'Look in that jar on the mantelpiece,' said Isabelle. 'There was nearly two pounds in there.'

Marianne looked. 'It's still here.' She sounded puzzled.

The bed was ready, and they put the matter of the burglary aside while they got Grandmother into it. 'You make some tea for us, Aurore. I think we'll be needing some after this,' said Isabelle.

Jamie moved towards the door. 'I'll take a look outside, in case the fellow left signs.' Marianne and Isabelle began to put things to rights, all the time trying to see what might be missing.

In the end, they could find nothing, outside or in, to indicate who had broken in or why. Nothing appeared to have been taken. 'They could easily have found the money. If they didn't take that, what could they possibly have wanted?' Isabelle pondered.

'I'll ask Ann if she heard or saw anything,' Jamie said. But she had not, and Jamie was clearly troubled. 'Maybe I'd best find you a good dog to watch the house,' he said. 'But for now, make sure you keep that door barred. Tomorrow I'll see about putting a strong lock on it.' At the door, on the point of leaving, he turned back, his face anxious. 'Shall I stay tonight?'

Isabelle gave him a little push. 'Of course not. We shall be safe enough. Besides, they might come to your place next, and what would Ann do if you weren't there?'

'Aye, well, have a care, that's all.'

It was advice they did not need. They wedged the bar firmly across the door that night and closed the shutters, and even then Isabelle lay awake for a long time, listening to every night sound and wondering who could have broken in and, more to the point, why they had done so.

# Chapter Thirty-Three

It was still dark and not quite time to get up when a loud and insistent sound jolted the occupants of the cottage into sudden wakefulness. Isabelle sat up.

'What was that?' Marianne demanded sleepily.

'At the door – there's someone at the door.' Isabelle spoke with disbelief, for she had been starkly reminded of that morning in Paris, when the Section's revolutionary committee had come to take her to prison.

'Your Jamie is making sure we're up in time,' Marianne suggested. Then she listened.

It was no polite knock, but a hammering, loud and peremptory. A voice called, 'Open up in the name of the law – come on now! We know you're in there.'

Aurore came scuttling down the ladder from above, looking frightened. Grandmother called out, 'Bella, what's going on?' Aristide, as usual, lay in a profound sleep, immobile on his little bed.

Isabelle got up and quickly pulled on whatever garments were to hand, while Marianne lit a rushlight and handed it to her. She carried it with her to the door. 'All right, I'm coming! It must be a mistake,' she said to Marianne.

It was not a mistake. At the door, when she had it open at last, stood two men with a lantern and a paper in their hands. 'You Mrs Duvernoy? We've to take you in for questioning. You and the other Frenchie woman.'

Isabelle stared at them, still not quite believing it. Surely this was some kind of nightmare, born of past experiences? Except that from behind the men came the sound of the Tarset burn rushing peacefully towards the North Tyne, and through the angle of trees that lined it she glimpsed its waters, silvered by a faint moonlight. From the farmhouse on the further bank a dog was barking, alarmed by the sudden unaccustomed clamour in the night.

'I don't understand. Who are you?'

'Constables from Bellingham. You're to go before the magistrate.' The speaker pushed past her, waving the paper in front of her nose. 'A warrant, see. To search the premises too.'

She caught a brief glimpse of the words written upon it, enough to confirm what the man said. Yet still she could not believe it. Such things did not happen in Tynedale.

One of the men went straight to the bookshelf and pulled the books off it, filling a bag he carried. Then he scooped all the papers out of the chest, adding them too to his bag. Bewildered as she was, it struck Isabelle that he behaved as if he knew exactly what to find, and where.

'It was you then – you that broke in yesterday!'

'Don't know what you're talking about,' said the man. 'Constables don't break into houses.'

His companion turned on Isabelle. 'Hurry up now, the pair of you. We've a fair way to go and he gets impatient if he's kept waiting.'

'Who does?'

'Sir John. The magistrate. Said to be sharp about it, he did.'

Isabelle turned to Marianne, who hovered behind her, and explained quickly what had been said. 'Someone's denounced us,' said the other girl. She seemed angry but unsurprised, but then she did not know England. Nor, it seemed, did Isabelle any more.

'I'm not leaving the children,' said Isabelle. 'And what about my grandmother? She's bedfast. Who's to care for her if I'm not here?'

The men looked at one another; evidently this was not a problem they had considered. Eventually, one of them said, rather grudgingly, 'I'll make sure she's cared for, if you're detained, that is. But bring the bairns with you. The magistrate might want to ask them questions too. Out of the mouths of babes and sucklings – isn't that what they say?'

Isabelle had no idea if that was what they said, but she didn't much like the sound of it. There seemed, however, to be no alternative but to do as they were told. She did her best to reassure her grandmother, who was clearly frightened, though her opinion of men who woke innocent women and children in their beds in the middle of the night was forcefully expressed. Marianne helped to dress the sleepy children. Aristide, who did not remember the last time something like this had happened, was curious about it, but not particularly alarmed. Aurore, who remembered only too well, was very frightened indeed. It was only with great difficulty that either of them could be persuaded to leave their kittens behind. Aurore clearly did not believe the reassurance that the animals would take no harm in their absence. Perhaps she remembered the neglected plants on the windowsill in Paris.

They stepped out into the night. Beyond the garden, four ponies were tethered, which momentarily diverted Aurore from her fear. Then Isabelle saw a lantern bobbing its way across the ford, and Jamie's dog came running ahead to greet them, tail wagging. 'Bella! What's going on?' Jamie had a fowling piece on his arm and looked alarmed and aggressive. He calmed a little when he saw the constables, both of whom were known to him. One of them explained what was happening, at least as far as he had explained anything to Isabelle.

'This is an outrage!' Jamie said furiously. 'Waking defence-less women in their beds. Where do you think you are – revolutionary France?'

'I'm a patriotic Englishman who loves his country, Mr Telfer, as you well know. I'm just doing my duty. If there's any revolutionaries here, it's not us.'

In the end, Jamie could do no more than promise to keep an eye on Grandmother – and the kittens, in response to Aurore's insistence. Then he watched as the women and children were mounted on the ponies and led away over the frosty fields.

At the other side of Bellingham a carriage waited, its lamps glowing in the darkness, and they were bundled into it. They had no idea where they were taken after that, or even how far it was, though the jolting uncomfortable journey seemed to go on for some time, as the sky lightened and a dreary fog rose from the river with the dawn. None of them said anything much, kept silent partly by the presence of the constables who sat in the carriage with them, partly by sleepiness and bewilderment. Still it did not seem quite real to Isabelle. But after a time she found herself thinking of the tales she had heard of the persecutions of Catholics in days gone by. Perhaps such things had not been so unknown in Tynedale, long ago. Perhaps other Milburn women had been woken in the night and hauled before magistrates or thrown into jail, because they served an alien faith. That it was not her Catholic faith that was at issue now, she was quite sure.

The carriage turned into a winding drive, densely wooded and dripping with moisture, and then came to a halt at last in a courtyard enclosed on three sides by buildings of austere grandeur, just visible through the mist. The women and children emerged into the bitter cold of the morning and were led to a side door and into a panelled room, furnished with a large table and chair, two stools, and a bench on which the four of them were told to sit and wait. Then they were left alone.

It was some time before a striking-looking man, dressed in a coat of impeccable cut, came into the room, with another official – presumably a clerk – at his elbow. He took his seat at the table, gazing at them down the length of an impressive nose; but what set the children staring at him in open-mouthed awe was the black eye patch that he wore over one eye. Isabelle feared for a moment that Marianne was about to make some comment on it, for she made a sudden movement and drew in her breath, but fortunately seemed to think better of it. Something stirred in Isabelle's memory. She was sure she had seen this man somewhere before, at some family gathering long ago ... He had been spoken of with disapproval, his presence barely tolerated ...

Then she remembered: Sir John Swinburne, apostate heir to a Catholic family as old as the Milburns. If he had not conformed to the Established Church he would never have been made a magistrate, of course ... Then they must be at Capheaton. Something else, something much more recent, came into her head. What was it Jamie had said one day, about '*Sir John Swinburne and his cronies*', and their '*Jacobin airs and graces*'? She looked at the frowning face of the man across the table and decided that Jamie must have been mistaken. Or perhaps Jacobin meant something rather different in England from what she understood by it.

The clerk placed a pile of books on the table – Isabelle's books – and a sheaf of papers, which Sir John spread out and looked over for a moment. Then he raised his head and studied the women and children again at some length; and then he cleared his throat, the sound breaking with suddenness into the long silence. Aurore jumped, sharply, with alarm. 'May I begin by saying that I am thoroughly conversant with the French language, so that anything you say, whether yourselves or the children, will immediately be understood, in whatever language you speak.'

Isabelle translated his words for Marianne, conscious that she was being listened to with great intentness, presumably in case she let fall any revealing remark. It was not a comfortable sensation.

Swinburne reached out a hand and selected two slim volumes from the pile; she saw that they were Paine's *Rights of Man*, in translation. 'These books were taken from your house, Mrs Duvernoy. Presumably you would not deny that they are yours. Are you aware that this work was from the moment of its issue declared to be a seditious libel, and that the purveying of it by any means whatever is a felony?'

'I have not purveyed it. I bought it in France to read, that's all.' It had been an exhilarating read, too, and she had felt proud that its writer was an Englishman. Later she had seen Thomas

Paine himself, seated in the Convention to which an admiring France had elected him. That, of course, was before the war soured everything, and he became suspect as a foreigner and was imprisoned.

'You have been heard to express seditious views, Mrs Duvernoy.' He picked up a piece of paper and read from it. 'I quote, "Why should game be kept for rich men's pleasure, while the poor starve?"'

The way the words were put together did not sound very like her, but she had no quarrel with the sentiments. Looking back, she remembered saying something of the kind about a month ago, on one of the many evenings when Jamie's neighbours had called. The talk had become quite animated, Isabelle arguing fiercely with one of the other men, Jamie looking on in an amused silence. He liked to tease her about her opinions, sympathising sometimes with the feeling behind them, if not always with the conclusions she had reached. Now she realised that one of the men present that evening must have reported the conversation to the authorities; unknowingly perhaps, possibly by means of a casual conversation at an alehouse, but it was an uncomfortable thought all the same. Might it even have been Jamie himself who was responsible? Isabelle shivered. In France almost the worst aspect of the Terror had been that it destroyed all trust between neighbours and friends; now it was happening to her here, in Tynedale.

Then Sir John held up the print of the Declaration of the Rights of Man, his expression colder than ever. 'Strange object, this, to find in the house of one whose cousins died for the Royalist cause. How do you explain the discrepancy?'

'Not all members of the same family have to hold the same views.'

'This is not a simple matter of taste or inclination, Mrs Duvernoy. England is at war with revolutionary France. Such things as this must be regarded as a matter of life and death, of the entire safety of the state.'

'You surely do not believe that two destitute widows living in a remote place like Tynedale threaten the safety of the state?'

'Let me put it to you as some might see it. I understand that your late husband, Jérôme Duvernoy, went to the guillotine because of his involvement in the conspiracy of Robespierre and his associates.'

'There was no conspiracy – at least not on that side.'

For an instant she thought she saw in his expression a hint of an ordinary human interest in what she said; she even thought he was about to ask her to explain why she held that view. Then she decided that she had imagined it, for he simply continued in the same cold and haughty voice, 'You were not invited to comment ... Further, the man with whom your friend there was residing died for his part in a violent revolt against the government. In short, both men held views of the most extreme kind.'

'But, as you say, they are dead.' She shivered, realising how much was known about her life in France. Someone had clearly been investigating both herself and Marianne with great thoroughness.

'Their widows are not. Their widows, masquerading as émigrées, have come to England and settled here. Now, I have to ask myself, what possible purpose could they have in doing so?'

'The answer is simple. I came to see my grandmother. Marianne came with me, because she is my friend. I have stayed here, because my grandmother needs to be cared for.'

'Yet you had these books upon your shelves and this print upon your wall, openly displayed. Presumably that is in accordance with your principles. And, more to the point, it is an indication as to where your loyalties lie. Tell me, if the Royalist landing at Quiberon bay this summer, in which English naval forces played a considerable part – if that expedition had been successful, would you have rejoiced?'

'No,' said Isabelle staunchly. 'I don't want to see the old régime restored in France. What I would like to see is England making peace with France and recognising the Republic. It's not England's business to interfere. It's certainly not England's business,' she went on, with sudden recklessness, 'to try and create hunger and chaos in France with counterfeit banknotes.'

There was a silence, in which she felt Swinburne's astonishment. She saw it too, in the way his one eye widened. Then he glanced at the man next to him. 'Wills, I must ask you to leave us, if you please.' The man left the room. As the door closed behind him, the magistrate leaned forward across the table, his expression intent, but no longer so coldly hostile. 'May I ask you to explain precisely what you meant by that, Mrs Duvernoy?'

She told him, explaining how she had come across a false assignat, without explicitly saying what her brother's part in the matter had been, though she thought it must have been obvious enough. Then she added her opinion of such proceedings, and how her own experience had coloured it, expressing herself even more forcibly perhaps than she had to John. At the end, conscious that she had revealed much more about her views than was probably wise, she braced herself for the magistrate's condemnation.

She was astonished when Swinburne said, 'I share your disgust, Mrs Duvernoy. I already had some knowledge of the business you mention. I recently discovered where the banknotes were manufactured. To find that such proceedings were being carried on not many miles from my own home, and with the clear connivance of the government, was a bitter blow. I find it abhorrent that a nation which prides itself upon its financial probity and its commercial rectitude should stoop to such means, even in time of war. But there, I have been indiscreet. Let us return to the matter in hand. The fact that we are at war with France is what is at issue here. After all, in France, English residents were imprisoned, no matter what their opinions.'

'You are none of you really threatened here, not by the war. It's different when the enemy's at the frontier, or marching on the capital.'

The momentary sympathy in his expression disappeared. 'You speak as a Frenchwoman, not an Englishwoman. You said, "*You* are not threatened."'

She heard an echo then of Jérôme, when she had first disclosed her origins to him. Did she see herself still as wholly French? 'I think,' she said, 'that I cannot help but have sympathy with both sides. I want France to survive as a Republic, even if I have no great liking for the present régime there. But I don't want any harm to come to England, and I would never seek to do any harm to her. I suppose I can never be all French or all English.'

'And your friend?' He turned to Marianne then and began, in fluent if strongly accented French, to ask her for her opinions. She gave them, as freely and forcefully as she always did, and he listened with courtesy, questioning her now and then, but apparently never shocked by anything she said. Surprised at his lack of disapproval, Isabelle found herself drawn into a lengthy three-sided discussion, which demonstrated clearly enough that though Swinburne might not precisely conform to any French definition of a Jacobin, he was very far from sharing her brother's views.

At the end, there was another moment of silence, and then he said, still talking in French, 'Here I think I must reveal myself. In many respects I am in sympathy with the opinions you hold. My position is well known, and there are of course those who condemn me for it. I share with you, Mrs Duvernoy, the wish that our two countries were not at war. Indeed, like you, I wish that the French Republic could be established in tranquillity and good order, without interference from outside. I even hold the conviction that England could learn something from France, to the benefit of her own people. However, our countries are at war, and I am first and foremost a loyal Englishman. If the peace and safety of England are threatened, then I shall do all in my power to protect her, leaving aside the underhand and despicable means used by our present administration. It is not I who have had you investigated, but when I received a report of the suspicions held in certain quarters, it was my duty both as a magistrate and as an Englishman to investigate them and assure myself that you were neither of you a danger to the state. I believe that I have assured myself of that.

'But let me make it quite clear. It is not in my power to prevent agents of the government from watching you, as most surely they will continue to do, nor can I prevent others who may not share my view of this business from taking action, should they feel it to be necessary. Fear of democracy has reached ridiculous proportions in recent years. Anyone suspected of promoting it is looked upon with the deepest suspicion. For your own sakes then, let me warn you to have a care. Watch what you say and do. Hold what opinions you please, but keep them to yourselves. Regard this interview, if you wish, as a friendly warning. If it frightened you, then I apologise. I had to be seen to be taking the matter seriously. Furthermore, I was anxious that you too should understand that it is serious. I hope that is now plain.'

It was, and Isabelle assured him of it. She felt suddenly exhausted, from relief she supposed, after the strain and fear of the past hours, and perhaps too from anxiety for the future. Sir John sent for refreshments, talking kindly to the children while they ate and drank, and obviously amused at being called 'citizen' by Aurore. Then he returned their belongings to them and told them they were free to go; the carriage would take them as far as Bellingham. On the way back, Marianne said, 'For an aristocrat, he's better than most.'

Even without Sir John's warning, Isabelle thought she would have known that they were being watched. Strangers did not often pass the cottage, yet a man she had never seen before began to take regular strolls beside the burn. Sometimes she glimpsed the same man disappearing into the woods beyond the ford, or watching her through a crowd of people at Bellingham market. She pointed him out to Jamie, who confirmed that it was the very same 'Coquetdale' man who had asked questions in Harry Robson's alehouse. He was now said to be looking for property in the neighbourhood, having come into an inheritance, though few people believed that was his purpose. It was none of it very subtle, but it was disturbing all the same. Isabelle was glad when the first snow of winter blocked the narrow roads and curtailed the man's wandering.

Marianne was awed by the savagely transformed landscape, and made miserable by the cold. When there was no work to be done, she was happy enough to keep Grandmother Milburn company by the fireside, while Isabelle took the enchanted children to slide on old sacks down the smoothest slopes, as she had done as a child, and make snowballs, and delight in being the first to stamp their footprints on an untouched field.

The best place for sliding on the snow was at the top of the field adjoining the one where the cottage stood, where a long steep slope ran down from the edge of the road. One crisply sunny afternoon when Jamie had declared that there was nothing much to be done and they should take the rest of the day off, Isabelle led the children up the hill, sacks in hand, and the three of them spent a glorious couple of hours tumbling and shrieking and laughing in the snow. She could almost believe that she too was a child again, her enjoyment unsullied by pain and loss and memory.

Then Aurore, toiling her way back up the slope, came to a sudden halt, and stared into the distance. Then she said, 'Maman!' Isabelle came up to her, dragging Aristide on his sack. 'There's someone coming,' Aurore explained. She was nervous of anyone she did not know well, understandably enough, Isabelle thought, considering her recent experiences.

The woman struggling along the road from the south did not look particularly threatening. She had a shawl pulled close about her and her head was bent as if to battle against a strong and bitter wind, though the day was calm. Isabelle watched her with curiosity; and then, as she came nearer, realised two things: the first was that the girl was known to her – it was Jane Dodd, the kindly servant girl from Blackheugh; the second that she had been crying and was trying hard to conceal further tears.

Isabelle went over to her. 'Jane, what's wrong?'

There was a moment of resistance, and then it all came out, as if the girl had only been waiting for someone to put a sympathetic word to her before pouring out her troubles. As

Jane sobbed and talked, in broken despairing phrases, Isabelle felt as if she were hearing an old story being retold yet again, varying only in detail from all the other versions of this banal and unheroic tale, and very little even in that. Jane was pregnant, by Ritson, the butler at Blackheugh. She had not wanted to yield to him, but he had used his authority over her; and now she was turned from her position because of it. Her family, who depended on her wage, would most likely throw her out in disgrace. She was ruined, like so many girls before her.

Isabelle felt a surge of furious indignation. Ritson, of course, retained his post, as he always had, whenever this had happened before; as most men did, in his position. But the girl he had wronged lost everything. She had not even been given the wages that were due to her. Her employer's only concession had been to allow her to remain at Blackheugh until the snow had stopped falling and the wind had dropped. It had been made very clear that even that was more than she deserved.

'I'm going to see John,' Isabelle said. 'He has no business to treat anyone like this.'

Jane objected, on the well-founded grounds that any protest would be useless, but Isabelle ignored her. She bore Jane with her down to the cottage, leaving her in Marianne's care, told the children to go no further than the garden, and then set out for Blackheugh, rage giving her speed and surefootedness on the icy surface of the snow.

She did not knock or ask to be admitted. It was probably as well that there was no sign of Ritson. She crossed the hall and walked unannounced into the office, where her brother was seated at his desk with his steward, going through various papers. He looked up and saw her and then said something in an undertone to the other man, who left the room quietly, closing the door behind him. Isabelle did not wait for John to speak.

'I have come about Jane Dodd. How dare you use her so unjustly!'

410

John looked at her with cold surprise. 'Unjustly? The girl is mmoral. Or did she not tell you why she was dismissed?'

'Oh, she told me, yes! Ritson got her pregnant. Not that I wouldn't have guessed who was responsible. It's certainly not the first time, as you know full well. I suppose it's too much to hope you've dismissed him too?'

'Of course not. He's the one reliable servant I have.'

'So he can seduce any girl he pleases and get away with it! Do you warn the girls of the risk they run when they come to work here?'

'Any girl engaged as a servant is aware that certain kinds of behaviour will not be tolerated.' He paused, as if abruptly deciding that the conversation was fruitless. 'You of all people have no business to interfere in my affairs. Furthermore, you show a deplorable lack of proper feeling, to come here on such a matter at such a time.'

She saw then, with a chill trickle of horror running down her spine, that her brother was dressed in black. She stammered, 'At such a time . . .?'

With the horror growing every minute she heard him say, 'Cuthbert died two days ago.'

Isabelle tried to imagine the unimaginable, what it would be like to lose Aristide, and her sense of agonising embarrassment was mixed with a terrible pity. If she had known, she would not have dreamed of coming here today. But to have done so, to have confronted her brother with the unwanted pregnancy of a servant girl, however unjustly punished, when he was mourning the loss of his only surviving child – somehow ignorance seemed no excuse at all. Even to try and form an apology seemed inadequate. How could one begin to apologise for intruding on such grief?

'John, I'm sorry – I did not know.' What use were words, even dismayed words dragged from her with the utmost sincerity? To go and put her arms about her brother, to offer the consolation of an embrace that would say more than words ever could, that might have been nearer to what the occasion demanded; but she had never been on terms with John that

would have allowed such an approach, and after what had jus
passed between them – no, the best thing now was to extricate
herself as quickly and discreetly as she could, putting John's
needs before her sense of shame.

'Would it have made any difference if you had?' he retorted
'I doubt it. That you are here at all only indicates what a lack
of proper feeling you have. After all you have done, your own
immorality – and now this latest ... My own sister, suspected
of sedition! I'm told the government has found it necessary to
keep watch on your house. How do you think I feel about that?
And then you have the effrontery to come here and lecture me
about my behaviour! That is the outside—!'

In spite of everything, Isabelle felt a resurgence of indignation. 'Just a moment, John,' she said. 'If I'm suspected of
sedition, then perhaps you should ask yourself how that came
about? I've done nothing to draw attention to myself. It was
you who spread the word around to everyone that I wasn't to
be trusted.'

'Because I could not with honour allow my neighbours to be
misled as to the kind of person you are.'

'You don't know the kind of person I am. How could you,
when we've hardly met for years and years?' Then she broke
off. Her brother had lost his only child – and here she was
seeking to quarrel with him again, so soon after realising the
enormity of what she had done, however unwittingly. 'I'm
sorry, this is neither the time nor the place.'

'For once I must agree with you. Now, I ask only that you
leave – and do not come near this house again as long as I am
master here.'

She went, not waiting for him to ring for Ritson. In the hall
she saw the person she least wanted to meet, in the circumstances. Francesca was descending the stairs. She looked
appallingly thin and frail, her pallor accentuated by the
sombreness of her clothes. There was no escaping her, for
Isabelle had to cross right in front of the stairs. She halted there,
looking up at her, seeking words that would offer a simple and
unaffected expression of sympathy. Then she saw not only that

rancesca had seen her, but that her face had suddenly become
mask of anguished savagery. She looked so unlike the calm
nd well-mannered woman Isabelle knew that she was
tartled.

'Bitch!'

The word shot across the space between them. If Francesca
ad spat in her face, Isabelle would have been no more
urprised, so out of character was the word and the manner. She
ould think of nothing to say. Words of sympathy died, all the
onventional yet deeply felt things that had been in her mind.

'Come to gloat, have you? Go on then, look over the place,
magine your son here one day. That's what you want isn't it?'

Isabelle stared at her, trying to take in what she said. It was
o far from anything that had been in her mind that it was some
ime before it made any sense. Then at last she stammered. 'No
- no, of course not! How could I?' Then, helpless before the
ther woman's anguished accusing eyes, she turned and fled
rom the house.

She was still trembling when she reached the cottage, where
he brushed aside Marianne's anxious enquiries and took
efuge at once in the bedroom. Marianne followed her there,
nade anxious by the look on her face, and then, full of shame
nd distress, Isabelle told her everything.

'You weren't to know,' Marianne said soothingly. Her
nanner suggested that she thought Isabelle's scruples over-
lone. Then she said with a clear note of curiosity, 'Is she right?
Would you inherit if your brother had no heirs?'

Isabelle raised her head and stared at her friend. 'I don't
<now,' she said. 'I've never thought about it. Don't ask! I don't
vant to find myself asking that either.' She shivered again.

Marianne put an arm about her. 'Come now, don't waste
sympathy on your brother. He's never given you any reason to
feel kindly towards him. So what, if his child's died? It happens
every day, to much better people than him. If he wasn't your
brother you wouldn't waste a thought on him.'

Isabelle considered this. Then she said, 'No, you're wrong.
I have children. I know what it is to fear you might lose them.

413

That's some way to understanding the whole of it. I must feel for anyone who suffers so much.'

But there was also that other matter, which she had begun so impulsively, and now must finish, somehow. She pushed her own feelings aside and went in search of Jane, who was seated by the hearth, staring gloomily into the flames.

'I told you it would do no good,' she said, as Isabelle sat down beside her.

'Got a heart of stone, that brother of yours,' Grandmother put in. 'Always did have.'

Then Isabelle told the old woman of John's bereavement. She did not ask Jane why she had not warned her of what she would find at Blackheugh. After all, she had silenced the girl's protests, in her angry wish to right an injustice. She had only herself to blame. Grandmother, however, was not much more sympathetic to John than Marianne had been. 'I told you, that woman can only breed sickly bairns. There was never any chance that one would live.'

By now, it was too late for Jane to continue her journey home, so she stayed at the cottage for the night, setting out early the next morning. Since it seemed the least she could do, Isabelle went with her, to plead with her family for their understanding. She had the satisfaction, at the end of a long walk and several exhausting hours of discussion, that at the very least they did not immediately and unthinkingly turn the girl out; she thought they even showed some signs of seeing her side of the story. It was probably as much as Isabelle could hope for in the circumstances, having been brought sharply down to a realistic estimation of what her own righteous indignation could achieve.

It was dark by the time she set out to walk the five miles home through the snow, but at least there was a moon, whose light gave a sheen to the crisp white landscape and enabled her to see her way. She felt very alone in this vast silver wilderness, full of unfamiliar angles and planes and pinnacles, in which only one or two distant lights could be seen, where nothing stirred, except her own feet crunching with a deafening noise through the frozen surface of the snow.

She began to think over all that had happened today, wondering what she ought to have done differently, if indeed she could have done anything differently. She even found herself murmuring aloud, as if some other person walked at her side, was disputing with her. 'What would you have done, Jérôme?' she asked that unseen presence. He had been so good at persuading people to do what was right. So often she had seen his charm and eloquence work its magic on some truculent individual, like Citizen Picot on the day they first met. He had been sure too of his principles, never doubting what was the right course, firm in his faith, not only in a benevolent Deity, but also in the possibility of human perfection.

Then she thought, 'Was he so sure, in the end?' She recalled now, as she had not done for many months, his mood in those last weeks before Thermidor, the long silences, the restless nights. What had he been thinking and feeling while the Terror swallowed ever more victims, knowing that he must bear some small responsibility for what was done? Had he ever asked himself what had gone wrong? Had he even begun to doubt the rightness of all the principles he had held so passionately since the Revolution began? Isabelle tried to bring to mind some clue that would illuminate his final state of mind, but she could think of none. He had gone so suddenly from her life, and taken all his secret thoughts with him to the grave. She wondered now if she had ever really known him, that man who had brought her such healing and such happiness.

It was no use then to wonder what he would have done, faced with Jane's unjust treatment. Very likely he would have acted precisely as she had, but that was not important. What mattered now was not what Jérôme would have done or thought, but what his widow Isabelle ought to have done, and why. Slowly, as she considered the matter, small things seemed to fall into place, intuitions and feelings and experiences gathered from many parts of her life. Bit by bit, today's painful events began to take on a much larger meaning; a meaning that seemed to illuminate everything that she had been through during the past years.

That evening, when she and Marianne went to bed, she said to her friend, 'I realised something today. I have never thought of my brother as a person before, a human being, like me or you, someone who is important.'

'He's a mean hard-hearted aristocrat – how you can think anything else is beyond me.'

'He's also a human being. So was Louis Capet, and Marie Antoinette. So was Commard. And Robespierre and Tallien both. So even was Henri . . .' There her voice faltered a little, but she went on, 'Every single one of them.'

'That's all very well, but it's clear enough isn't it? You can hardly say they're all worth the same.'

'That's just the point. They are, even if I don't feel that they are. I think I always knew that, in my mind – only I never really felt it. That's what went wrong with the Revolution. Once you start saying that only some human beings are worth caring about, then you're in trouble. It means you can treat the ones who aren't important as harshly as you like, so long as it suits your interests, like Henri did with me, like so many aristocrats did. Or it means you can kill the ones who don't agree with you, or who've done wrong, without letting it trouble your conscience at all.'

'But what you're saying – you'd have everyone treated the same, criminals, aristocrats, everyone. There'd never have been a Revolution at all that way.'

'Oh yes there would, and I suppose people would still have died, because when there's anger and suffering that happens. But all the cold killing, by people like my cousin, or by the Terrorists too – that wouldn't have happened. You can say that something's wrong, that the people who do it must be punished. You can say that justice requires that some people must give up power and privilege and perhaps even money and property for the sake of the poor. But to say that they're so bad that they must be destroyed, because they're beyond redemption – that's what's wrong.'

'Oh, if you're bringing redemption into it, then you've lost me. I thought you'd left all that behind in the convent.'

416

'I don't know. Perhaps to believe with all your heart that we are all brothers and sisters under God is the best way of looking at it. Then if someone's doing wrong, or being cruel to another person, you have to try and make them understand why they are wrong. If you just kill them they'll never understand it.'

'Oh, I can just see that! There we were, enemies on every side, breathing fire and slaughter against the Revolution, and what does the government do? It sends representatives to sit down and talk to the counter-revolutionaries, and the armies of the despots, and the Royalists and the priests. Come on, Isabelle, they'd have been massacred! It always was them or us.'

Isabelle was silent for a moment. 'I know. But then look what happened in the end, even though the Republic's enemies were crushed. So were many of its best friends too. What's left now is nothing like the Republic Pierre wanted, or Jérôme, or you or me. It's a Republic for the rich, not for the people. Something went wrong.'

'The wrong people went to the guillotine, that's all.'

'I don't think so.' But Isabelle knew she had lost the thread of her argument and could not find it again; or not for now, at least. Yet as she drifted into sleep she still had a conviction that she had stumbled, in a painful and discomforting way, upon a profound truth, and one that must have implications for the rest of her life.

# Chapter Thirty-Four

A haze of green had spread over the trees and there were primroses in bloom at the edge of the wood. The curlews had returned two weeks ago, hard on the flapping wings of the peewits, the last snows had thawed to swell the Tarset burn, Aurore's wallflowers were coming out in the little garden and there was a motherless lamb by the cottage fire, to the puzzlement of the kittens, who were nearly full-grown cats by now.

Outside in the spring sunshine, Marianne was talking to someone, with much laughter. Isabelle, hurriedly mending a tear in Aurore's woollen winter skirt, which would soon be too small for her, did not need to look out of the window to know who was causing the laughter. These days Geordie Robson seemed to have a good deal of business to take him past the cottage, though what his mother thought about it (if she knew) Isabelle could imagine only too well. Few women among their neighbours liked Marianne, who was seen as a threat and a rival, the more dangerous for being foreign and of dubious morals. Most of the men, on the other hand, adored her. Where in Paris she had been an ordinary enough young woman, in Tynedale she was exotic in the extreme. Isabelle could hear her now explaining to Geordie that in French wallflowers were called '*giroflées*', and then heard him tease her, with much laughter, for her stumbling pronunciation of their English name.

Then she heard another voice, and the thud of horses'

hooves. Quickly she dressed Aurore in the mended skirt, wound Aristide's muffler about his throat, and hurried to the door. 'You be sure and come back straight after, and tell me all about it!' Grandmother called after them as they went out to where Jamie was waiting.

He had three ponies out there in the breezy sunlight, his own sturdy bay, and two black shaggy beasts, one smaller than the other. 'The first fine day, we shall go riding,' he had promised Aurore, while the snow was still deep in the hollows. This was not quite the first fine day, for the work of the farm had to take priority, but he had kept his promise as soon as he was able. Isabelle thought she was almost as excited as her daughter, though she remembered with a sharp pang of grief another man who had come to take them riding, one sunny September day when the Republic was as young as their love.

They waved goodbye to Marianne and Geordie, who scarcely looked up to watch them pass, and splashed across the ford and then up the further slope past the farm, onto Thorneyburn Common, where the sky stretched blue and immeasurable over their heads and the hills spread in gentle undulations towards the border. Aristide, perched in front of his mother, soon lost his initial fear, and began to shout his appreciation of the ride. Aurore was in ecstasy, her small face glowing, all smiles. Once, they urged the ponies briefly into a sedate trot; otherwise, they took it gently, so that the children should gain in confidence.

'I recall the very first time we rode out together, Bella,' Jamie said. 'Up on Hareshaw Common it was, and just such a day as this. Mind, I had a job to stop you cantering off and leaving me behind. You always were a headstrong lass.'

She only dimly remembered it, and it was overlaid with many other such memories, all of them happy ones, looked at from where she was now. She thought, 'This is what Jérôme wanted for the children, when we talked, that last night. If only he could be here now, to share it with us.' She wondered if he could see them somehow. She was still a long way from any sort of conviction about his ultimate destination, or that of anyone else, though Father Stone continued to call regularly and spend hours in argument and discussion. She enjoyed talking to him and was glad to have someone who took her stumbling thoughts seriously, but she was nowhere near returning to the fold whose gate he held open so assiduously for her.

Jamie began to sing, one of the old songs, and they all joined in as best they could, fitting the rhythm of the words to the rhythm of the ride. Later, as they turned for home, Jamie said, 'She's her mother's daughter, that lass of yours. A born rider.' They both looked at Aurore, riding a little way in front, confident and in control.

Back at the farm, they halted in the small sheltered stable yard. Jamie came to lift Aristide down, quickly silencing his protests. 'You get away home, my lad. Tell Grandmother all about it, before you forget.' Aurore, helped down in her turn, took her brother's hand, and they ran off towards the stepping stones. Isabelle slipped from the saddle and turned to thank Jamie for his kindness, and then found that she could not speak.

Jamie was looking at her very oddly, his expression at once grave and intense. Frozen by his thoughts into immobility, he stood exactly as he had been standing when Aurore reached the ground, with one hand stretched across the saddle, the other crooked at his side, as if still supporting an imaginary child. Then that hand moved, reaching out to close gently about Isabelle's arm, drawing her towards him. She felt his mouth on hers. And then desire flared up in her, such as she had thought she would never feel again, for any man.

She knew then that it had been there for a long time, waiting for something just like this. Her body was not made to lie alone at nights, for a lifetime of abstinence. She was not a nun. And she was young and healthy and it was spring.

She put her arms about his neck and responded to him with all the longing that was in her. He was not Jérôme, but he was a man, and attractive in his way. And she wanted him with all the pent-up need of her body.

421

Behind them the ponies stamped and snorted. Isabelle came, abruptly, to her senses, and cried out and then pulled herself away from Jamie, though it hurt, terribly, for her body protested at the deprivation suddenly forced upon it again. She could see that for him it was worse, for his feelings were deeper and stronger than her own, more than friendship, more than desire. For him there had been no other beloved person, in whom he had once believed he had found half of himself. For him, Isabelle was no second best.

'We mustn't,' she said. 'There's Ann.'

'She won't know,' he objected, through uneven breathing. 'I'm not taking anything from her. We don't – now—'

Isabelle shook her head. 'It wouldn't be right. You know that, as well as I do.' She did not add, as she might more truthfully have done, that she did not intend to risk another pregnancy. Two children by different fathers was quite enough, and the scandal of bearing a child to Jamie Telfer would be enormous, and utterly destructive to them both – to him most of all, because she supposed she would always have the option of escaping to France.

He turned and bent his head on the pony's saddle, hiding his face. 'Oh, Bella, I love you so!' The words were torn from him in an intensity of pain that hurt her, because she was fond of him.

'I know,' she said. 'But it can't be.' She waited a while and when he still did not move she added gently, 'We must behave as if this had never happened. As if we were back where we were before. There must be no more kisses, not ever. I'm your labourer, that's all. A friend too, if you like. But nothing more.'

He looked up, his face strained. 'Curse you for being right!' he retorted with unusual vehemence. Then he led the ponies into the stable, without another word. Isabelle did not offer to help. She turned and followed the children across the burn.

Marianne had gone out – 'For a walk, she said, with that Geordie Robson', was Grandmother's explanation. 'Always was a bit of a lad that one, but then I reckon he's met his match this time. You can see he's lost his heart to her.' It never ceased to amaze Isabelle how up to date her grandmother always was with the latest gossip, though she never stirred further than the garden and had to depend for her information on Isabelle herself, or the visits of neighbours.

Isabelle had thought, in Marianne's absence, of confiding her new anxiety to Grandmother, but the presence of the children made that impossible. They were both now almost as fluent in English as they were in French, and Aurore in particular understood a great deal of what went on around her. Perhaps it was just as well. Once, the old woman had seemed the repository of all wisdom and all consolation. Now, Isabelle realised that though she could certainly be trusted to be sympathetic, she was more than a little indiscreet. She would have to solve this problem alone, as best she could; if there was any solution.

It was not until she was in bed that night that she had leisure to consider it at length. She lay alone, for Marianne had not come home from her lengthy walk, if such it was.

One thing Isabelle saw very clearly. It was not fair for her to remain here, so close to Jamie, knowing that he felt about her as he did. It would be hard enough for her, tempted as she was; for him it would be a constant pain. Yet she could not leave, or not at the moment, simply because she had nowhere else to go and she had her grandmother to care for. Later, when the day came that Grandmother no longer needed her, then she supposed she would have to move on – back to France, perhaps, as she had always supposed she would one day. Or to Blackheugh...? But no, she must not think of that, still less allow herself to hope for it. Hope and regret alike were futile exercises. Enough to take each day as it came, doing the best she could for her small family, learning about herself and about others.

Marianne came home at dawn, with an aura about her that Isabelle recognised only too clearly. Looking up from the hearth, where she was stirring the fire to life, she realised that just at the moment when she had known that there could be no lasting home for her in this place, Marianne had begun to put down roots, of a kind. It was, she thought, another complication. But then, she had never thought life would be easy.